THE WALL

THE WALL

N.J. CROFT

Entangled Publishing, LLC
10940 S Parker Rd
Suite 327
Parker, CO 80134
rights@entangledpublishing.com

Edited by Heather Howland and Liz Pelletier
Cover design by Deranged Doctor Designs
Cover photography by Zastolskiy Victor/Shutterstock
Andrey_Kuzmin/DepositPhotos

Manufactured in the United States of America

First Edition August 2020

ALSO BY N.J. CROFT

Disease X

The Lost Spear

The Lost Tomb

The Descartes Evolution

To Robin, who shares my love of freedom

CHAPTER ONE

"America will never be destroyed from the outside.
If we falter and lose our freedoms, it will be
because we destroyed ourselves." Abraham
Lincoln

WASHINGTON D.C.
SOMETIME IN THE NEAR FUTURE…

"Are you ready, Mr. President?"

President Harry Coffell straightened his shoulders and slowed his breathing. Today was a big day. The culmination of years of planning. The day he gave the people what they wanted, something his father had taken away.

Their freedom.

"Sir?" Boyd prompted. Boyd was the head of the Secret Service and the closest thing Harry had to a friend. He knew how much this meant.

Harry turned and grinned, then slapped Boyd on the shoulder. "I'm ready. Let's go change the world."

As he stepped out of the White House, the crowd cheered, and he smiled and waved. A podium had been set up on the lawn, and behind it the White House loomed, forming the perfect backdrop.

As he shed his guards at the foot of the podium, the skin along his spine prickled. The sensation was familiar, expected — there were always people who wanted to bring a powerful man down — and he kept the smile fixed in place. His father had always told him that he shouldn't let fear control his life, and he tried, but those first few steps out into the open were always hard. Only Boyd stayed close, taking up his usual position behind him.

This was a tradition started by his father: a speech to the people on the birthday of his father's greatest achievement — The Loyalist Party.

He raised his hands and the crowd quieted.

"Welcome, America."

They clapped and cheered, and his fear faded. This was what he'd been born to do.

"The day the American people voted my father into the office of President was the proudest day of my life. On that day, my father promised us all a world without fear, a world where there would be no more infighting between parties, no more stifling of the American dream with personal greed. Instead, there would be just one party. A party *for the people!*

"Twenty-four years ago, on this very day, he brought into being the means to make those promises come true — the Loyalist Party."

The crowd cheered again, and he waited for them to quiet. "However, my father understood that anything worthwhile comes with a price. While some considered that price too high, all of you here today believed in the dream, and together we have worked to make that dream come true." As he spoke, a piece of paper twirled on the breeze, flashing in front of his face. He flinched but forced himself to continue. "Because of your belief, today we live in a country without fear of terrorism, without fear of school shootings, of poverty, of pandemics with the potential to wipe out millions. No American has to live without those things that should be rights and not privileges: education, health care, affordable housing. Today, my father's vision is a reality for all of us."

The paper landed on the autocue, blocking his next words, and he hesitated. Then his eyes narrowed, his teeth clenching as he took in the cartoon printed on it. He snatched it up and balled it into his fist.

He needed to finish his speech. Afterward, his priority would be finding who was responsible.

And they would live to regret this embarrassment.

Just not for very long.

• • •

In the second row of the audience, Gideon Frome shifted on the hard chair as the president paused in his speech.

He glanced around; pieces of paper were blowing in the wind. One landed by his polished, standard-issue military shoes. He'd been out of the army for three months now, but the White House had sent a memo requesting he wear his dress uniform today.

He picked up the paper without thinking and glanced at the image. A smile tugged at his lips, but he kept his face impassive. It was a cartoon depicting two men. The first was a tall, imposing figure, standing proud in a dark suit, and beside him stood a much smaller, punier figure, naked except for a nappy and a pacifier in his mouth. It was cleverly done; the identities were clear, though in reality, Harry Junior was the image of his father. Beneath the image were the words: *We voted for this, and we got this.*

Out of the corner of his eye, he could see Secret Service agents running around collecting the bits of paper. Maybe he should help—he was, after all, Secret Service now. But the president was speaking again. Gideon let the words flow over him. He'd seen the speech earlier that morning and had experienced the first flicker of optimism since he'd come home to D.C. Perhaps there was hope for the Party.

His attention drifted from Harry to the tall man standing behind him, slightly off to the left, and he felt a stirring of the old hatred, low down in his gut.

Boyd Winters, head of the Secret Service and Gideon's new boss—though he'd made it clear on his first day that Gideon was not his choice for second-in-command and that he'd be watching him. That was two months ago, and Gideon hadn't seen or spoken to the man since.

Maybe Boyd didn't trust him.

Maybe he thought Gideon might be harboring a little unresolved resentment.

It had been Boyd who had delivered the news of Gideon's father's suicide ten years ago. He'd come in while Gideon was being interrogated about his brother's disappearance—giving a brief cessation of pain—to bring the good news personally. He'd hinted that perhaps Gideon might take the same way out and save them all a lot of bother. Gideon hadn't been feeling particularly inclined to cooperate. He'd still had things to do.

All the same, Gideon was pretty sure that, if it had been left to Boyd, he would never have gotten out of that basement alive. He was guessing that only Harry's intervention had saved him.

As though sensing his attention, Boyd turned his head slightly so that he was staring directly at

Gideon. His lips tightened, but apart from that he showed no reaction. Gideon kept his own expression blank, let none of his hatred show.

This was a new start for him.

He wasn't about to mess it up…just yet.

. . .

Aaron Frome watched the president's speech from a table in the back of a bar off Fifth Avenue, in New York.

Over the years, Aaron had spent a lot of time studying President Harry Coffell Junior—he'd grown up in D.C., and their families had been close—and he could tell from his body language that the man was pissed. He grinned. Things had played out better than he could have imagined. A gust of wind at the right moment—it was scary how the little things, things beyond their control, made so much difference.

Part of him knew that releasing the cartoon had been a childish dig, and for that reason, he hadn't run the plan through the correct channels. The committee would have shot it down. But Aaron had also known that Harry would hate it, and he hadn't been able to resist.

Harry started talking again. "In order to make that dream come true, we all had to accept certain restrictions. Restrictions some claimed could never be justified. But we here today are proof that everything that was promised to the American people has come to pass." He paused to allow the crowd to cheer, then continued. "And today I can announce that culmination of the dream. A return to the democratic process."

The crowd went wild.

Aaron snorted. A return to democracy? He would believe it when it happened. He certainly wasn't putting his plans aside until he saw some solid evidence.

The camera panned out across the audience, and he searched the faces.

Stella wasn't there.

He picked up his glass and swallowed the bourbon in one go. Disappointment was a noose squeezing the breath from his lungs, stealing his air, leaving him light-headed. He hadn't realized how much he'd needed just a glimpse of her.

Then his gaze snagged on a figure sitting in the second row. Gideon. His perfect fucking brother. The hero of the goddamn Wall—single-handedly saving the country from invasion or some such crap. Ten years had changed him; he didn't look so perfect anymore. Aaron had heard that he'd returned and was working for the administration again. How could he? After everything that had happened?

The camera was back on Harry now. While he continued with his speech, he gave the impression of working on autopilot, his mind on other things. Good. Aaron was glad he'd given him something to think about.

The bar door opened, and Aaron twisted in his seat and watched as a man entered. He paused, spotted Aaron, and headed over.

"A message has come through."

The man reached into his pocket and pulled out a scrap of paper. Paper was back in fashion. With the internet and cell phones all monitored, paper was the one method of communication that wouldn't be picked up on the chatter.

He glanced down, his gut tightening. Just two words.

I'm in.

Aaron screwed up the paper and shoved it in his pocket. Things were about to get real.

• • •

Stella Buchanan watched the speech from her office window. From here, she had an excellent view of the lawns in front of the White House. No doubt she would get a black mark against her name for not being present—Harry tended to take such things personally—but she hadn't been able to bring herself to sit through it. She was finding it harder and harder to go through the motions these days. While she'd always believed that change should be made from within the system, lately she found herself chafing at the constraints of her life. Wanting to make things happen.

Of course, she'd known what Harry was going to announce: a return of the democratic process. And while she wanted to believe it, so far it was just words. And besides, she knew things about Harry that most people didn't.

Maybe it was Gideon's return that was unsettling her. She could see him, sitting upright, staring straight ahead, handsome in his captain's uniform—looking every inch the hero. He was a civilian now, but no doubt Harry had insisted on the uniform. Gideon was popular with the people, that was why he'd been brought back.

He'd changed so much. His face was blank, so she had no clue what he was thinking. Back when they'd been engaged, he'd always been the open one, had never had a need for subterfuge. She was the one with all the secrets. She should never have involved him, but the pressure had been huge, and maybe his life would have gone to hell anyway.

Aaron had been a ticking bomb.

"America for Americans!"

At last the speech was over.

CHAPTER TWO

"They who can give up essential liberty to obtain a little temporary safety deserve neither liberty nor safety." Benjamin Franklin

Kate Buchanan swiped through the security systems to check that no one was approaching her basement office. When she was sure she wouldn't be interrupted, she pressed the key to start the Auspex debugging routine. It was a risk, but she'd picked up an error in his predictions and she needed to understand what had gone wrong.

Tension clawed at her stomach as she watched the streams of code flash across the screen until she was sure the program was running correctly. Correctly *and* untraceably.

Then she blanked the monitor.

While she tried to tell herself that her research was doing no harm to the Party—and could actually do a hell of a lot of good if only the administration would get their heads out of their asses—she was aware that if what she was doing came out into the open, she would likely lose more than her position.

She was a good Party member, but the ban on research was…stupid.

Her actual job was to monitor the chatter for alerts which might result in threats to the American people. A yellow alert was a risk of terrorist activity, a green alert a risk of aliens; unfortunately not real-little-green-men aliens, just people without the correct papers. Finally, a red alert meant a risk to the president.

Kate slumped in her seat and searched her e-reader for something to read while she waited. Her actual work was deadly boring and took up about 10 percent of her time. She'd only taken the position because Homeland Security was the only place remaining with servers big enough to carry out her entirely illegal research.

Luckily, she worked alone. In the early years of the Loyalist Party, there had been a whole *team* of analysts needed to monitor the chatter, all based in this cavernous office in the basement at Homeland Security, where the environment could be controlled. As the years passed, the alerts had reduced to a trickle, and the team of analysts to one person—her.

Chatter still flooded in from everywhere, managed by old systems that had been in use for what felt like a million years to Kate. The original surveillance program had been developed in the late 1960s to monitor the military and diplomatic communications of the Soviet Union and its Eastern Bloc allies during the Cold War. Now it was used to scrutinize the not-so-private conversations of the American people. The secondary system had come along later in the aftermath of 9/11 and had originally been run by the NSA but had been handed over to the Secret Service by the current administration. Then and now, it gathered intel from the internet.

An invasion of privacy or a necessary evil? Her father always quoted the old saying: If you have nothing to hide, you have nothing to fear.

Well, Kate was definitely hiding something. And the one thing currently keeping her safe was that *she* was the only person monitoring the systems capable of picking up on her illegal activities.

A red alert flashed up on a different screen. Kate leaned forward and tapped the keys, adding the info dump to a folder that she'd forward to the Secret Service agents at the National Threat Assessment Center. Kate couldn't read the actual information; it was all encrypted. Maybe they believed it would give her subversive ideas? Whatever the case, the agents at NTAC would then determine whether the alert warranted any action.

She presumed they did that by reading through the unencrypted info dumps, a slow and painful process since there were a minimum of fifty data streams attached to each alert.

Kate was developing a better way: Auspex, a powerful combination of predictive engine and artificial intelligence. Unfortunately, predictive engines and artificial intelligence research had been banned over a decade ago.

Twenty-four years ago, President Harry Senior had broken away from the Republican Party and started his own, the Loyalists. A continuation of the golden era of America, he'd called it, America for Americans. The Party had close affiliations with the Church, who considered computers some sort of devil's machine and the idea of AI a total abomination against God.

Luckily, the administration wasn't stupid enough to think they could run the country without any technology and bright enough to understand that trying to take away people's cell phones might very well result in a revolution. Even so, after the pandemic and the big financial crash of the twenties, which the Loyalist Party blamed on China and bad decisions made by predictive engines, all research into anything interesting had ground to a halt.

Auspex had been the brainchild of Kate's old professor and current boss, Oliver Massey, back when he'd still been head of computer studies at Georgetown University. The system was still incomplete when the ban came into force, but Kate had discovered a copy on the university servers seven years ago and had been working on it ever since.

Auspex took raw data from other systems, organized it, and ran it through various algorithms which then predicted possible outcomes. A week ago, Kate had finally gotten up the nerve to allow Auspex access to the chatter streams. And she'd been sure he — for some reason she'd always thought of Auspex as a he, not a she or an it — was functioning correctly. Except that now it appeared that something was off. She'd run all the previous week's alerts through Auspex and every single one of them had resulted in a negligible chance of a threat to the American people.

Which didn't make a lot of sense as she'd just received her weekly pat-on-the-back report from NTAC and, according to them, twenty-eight of the alerts she'd submitted — including all the red alerts — had resulted in a positive action. Whatever that meant. But she was sure it shouldn't have happened for an alert with a negligible threat level.

An alarm beeped — she'd set them up to let her know if anyone was approaching. Kate flicked to the surveillance feeds and saw Teresa Martinez, Oliver's personal assistant, getting out of the elevator.

After checking to be sure none of her screens were showing anything they shouldn't be, she grabbed her jacket, which she'd hung over the regulation photo of President Harry Coffell Junior—*ugh*—then slid her e-reader into a drawer. It wouldn't do to let the world know how little time her job actually took.

The door opened without a knock, and Teresa entered.

Kate blanked her expression and curved her lips into a bland smile. "Teresa," she said. "How lovely to see you. Can I help you with something?"

Teresa was somewhere in her thirties, slender, with perfectly styled dark hair, her clothes and makeup immaculate as always. She'd tried to befriend Kate when she had first started, but Kate was pretty sure that had been more about who Kate's father was, rather than about Kate herself. Growing up as the daughter of a supreme court justice, she had learned to recognize political ambition. And avoid it. Teresa was also active in the Church, and invariably asked why Kate had been absent from the "compulsory" morning service. Her answer, that she had too much work, was no doubt recorded somewhere to be held against her at a later date.

Then she noticed that Teresa carried a plate. With cake.

Weird.

"I wasn't sure if you knew," Teresa said. "I've

been appointed the new Political Officer."

"No, I didn't know. What happened to Richard?"

"Retired," Teresa said with a satisfied smile.

Every place of work had a state-appointed Political Officer. They were chosen from those active within the Party, members who had proved their loyalty. They had little real power, but they could make your life a misery by reporting infractions if you got on the wrong side of them. Such as not having a picture of the president in your office. Or covering that picture up so you didn't have to look at his smug face all day.

Teresa peered around the room, no doubt checking for infractions. Kate had gotten complacent in the years she had worked here. But no one could afford to be complacent these days. Breaking the rules could mean the end of your career. Or worse.

"I called a meeting this morning after prayer — about my appointment — but you didn't attend." Was that an accusation? Probably. "And as it's the president's birthday today, we all met up in the foyer to watch his speech. I baked a cake." She peered at Kate. "You must have missed the memo."

"Yeah. Sorry." That would be a black mark against her.

"So I thought I would bring you a slice, give

you the wonderful news. And ask if there's anything the Party can do to make your life more worthwhile."

Leave me alone?

Reinstate the space program and sign me up?

Let me draw a mustache and glasses on my presidential picture?

Kate decided against mentioning any of those options. Instead, she picked up her cake and took a forkful, chewed it slowly, and hoped Teresa would go away. She swallowed. "Lovely cake." By the time the plate was scraped clean, Teresa still hadn't moved.

"Well," Kate said. "That was nice, but I really must get back to work." She waved a hand at the bank of computer screens. "Lots of chatter today." It was actually true. Since the president's speech announcing the return of democracy a month ago, the chatter had exploded with alerts. Especially red.

Finally, Teresa took the hint and gave a nod. "We'll see you at prayer meeting tomorrow?"

She smiled. "Of course." *Not.* Though maybe she should make the effort. She didn't want Teresa's visits to become a regular event. Best not to give her an excuse. As the door closed behind the new Political Officer, Kate switched on the video feed, watching until Teresa was safely back in the elevator.

The debugging routine was still running, so she swiped one of the many screens and flicked through the TV channels. It didn't take long—there were only three—and she found the news feed streaming the president's birthday celebration, set inside a glittering ballroom full of glittering people. She was so glad she wasn't one of them. She zoomed in and searched the guests. Found her sister.

Stella was beautiful. She had their father's blond hair and dark-blue eyes, and her mother's figure, slender but curvaceous. Kate, on the other hand, had her mother's red hair, pale-blue eyes, and her father's tall, skinny figure. They couldn't have been more different in looks, or in temperament. Despite that, growing up they'd been close.

Not so much now. They'd gone in different directions. Whereas Kate had shunned a position in the Party, Stella was extremely ambitious. At thirty, she was high up in the administration. Kate tried not to hold it against her, and they usually met up at least once a month for lunch or dinner.

She panned out and was just about to shut down the feed when she spotted another guest. One she hadn't expected to see. For a moment, she stared, shock holding her still.

Gideon Frome. Kate hadn't seen him in nearly ten years, back when he'd been engaged to Stella and had a brilliant career ahead of him in the Party. Then everything had fallen apart; his younger brother had vanished, supposedly to join the rebel forces, and his father had committed suicide.

Guilty by association, Gideon's political career had crumbled. He had broken off his engagement to Stella, and she hadn't tried to hold onto him. He'd left DC and joined the army. As far as Kate was aware, he hadn't been back since.

She remembered him as super sophisticated, with a casual, laid-back elegance and an easy smile. There was no smile on his face now, and any hint of laid-back was gone—she reckoned for good. He looked hard, his face full of sharp angles and harsh planes. His mouth was a thin line, his green eyes cool, alert, his dark hair cut military short. He wore civilian clothing—a dark-gray suit, a white shirt, and a blue tie. Ultra conservative. And a scar ran down the right side of his face from beneath his eye to his upper lip.

Kate picked up her cell and hit Stella's number.

"Hey, there," Stella said. "To what do I owe the honor?"

"I was watching the news feed and I saw Gideon. I didn't know he was back."

"He's been back for over three months," she said. "Where have you been?"

"Working. So what's he doing?"

"Harry asked him to come back. Gideon is a hero now, which is great for publicity. He's been appointed second-in-command at the Secret Service."

"Wow. So all has been forgiven?"

"It seems so. Not that there was anything to forgive. Gideon wasn't involved in his brother's disappearance."

Not that that would make a lot of difference. "Have you spoken to him?"

"Just briefly and quite amicably. Which is good, as he's back on a permanent basis. The president is fond of him. He always was. He trusts him despite everything that happened."

The unspoken words were there. Or Gideon wouldn't have survived the disgrace that had enveloped his family ten years ago. He would have disappeared. Or had a convenient accident. They all knew how these things worked. Kate might not like it, but maybe it was the price they had to pay for peace. There hadn't been a terrorist attack on U.S. soil or an outbreak of any viral disease — man-made or natural — for many years. People could go about their lives without fear. And if everything was just a little bit boring, well, things could be worse. Much worse.

"Okay," Stella said. "I'd better go mingle, but are we still on for lunch on Saturday?"

"Of course."

"I'll see you then." And the call ended.

She watched the party for a few more minutes, then a light flashed on her screen. The debugging routine had finished. Kate pushed all thoughts of Gideon from her mind. She had more interesting things to think about.

She inspected the output window and pulled up the last line, went back into the program, and commented out the problem. It appeared to be related to the encryption process.

To check, she ran one of the red alerts from the previous week. It came back with a negligible result. Again. Sitting back, she considered the problem from a different angle, then typed in a new query.

What is the probability that this alert will result in action by NTAC?

72 percent.

So what did NTAC know that Auspex didn't?

She pulled up the info dump. And stared. Auspex had decrypted the information and, for the first time, Kate could actually read the chatter.

And it made no sense at all.

CHAPTER THREE

*"My brother Bob doesn't want to be in
government—he promised Dad he'd go straight."*
John F. Kennedy

"Finally, thank you all for helping me celebrate my birthday today."

Gideon clapped along with the rest of them as President Coffell stepped down from the podium. This close, Harry looked younger than his forty-five years. Plastic surgery, Gideon presumed. He was dressed in his usual business-casual attire of khaki slacks and a white polo shirt.

Gideon supposed he could put the lack of change down to good genes; Harry's father had never looked older than fifty. Probably still didn't, though no one had seen him in more than ten years. He was closeted away somewhere in a private hospital, and, if the rumors were true, he was totally unaware of anything going on around him. He must be close to ninety by now.

Gideon shifted the weight from his left foot. His leg was beginning to ache, and he rubbed at his thigh. He'd taken a piece of shrapnel there five years ago, at the same time he'd gotten the scar on his face, and it still gave him problems.

How long until he could leave? Too long, at a guess.

Christ, had he actually enjoyed these events in the past? It seemed inconceivable. However, if he wanted his life back, he was going to have to suck it up and look like he belonged. Act like he belonged. And maybe if he did it long enough, he might actually *feel* like he belonged.

The problem was, he couldn't bring himself to care.

When he'd first come home, he'd thought he would slide right back into the life he'd had before. Back then, he'd been fascinated by politics. He'd never believed the system was perfect, but that just made him want to be involved all the more. Growing up, he'd spent a lot of time at the White House and had been a favorite of the old president, who'd been a friend of his father's.

Gideon had fully expected to devote his life to the Party. Had maybe even harbored secret dreams that one day, when martial law was removed and the democratic process resumed, he might run for president and lead his country to even greater things. With Stella at his side. She'd been so perfect.

And things under Harry Senior hadn't been so bad. At that point, the rest of the world had been in chaos. The European Union had fallen apart, and Russia was at war with the Middle East, a war which threatened to engulf the rest of the world. America needed a strong president if the nation was to survive.

When his first term was up, Harry Senior had claimed that the country wasn't ready for a democratic process, that they needed more time for his policies to bear fruit. For the traitors in their midst to be weeded out. Soon after that, the Wall had gone up. They'd started with the Mexican border. Much of it had been built with volunteer labor, by people who believed. When Gideon was eleven, his father had taken him and Aaron to visit the Wall—it had seemed a wonderful endeavor, twenty feet high and stretching as far as the eye could see.

That wasn't the only wall, though. A firewall that blocked all incoming wireless signals had been put up around the country. America was cut off—a temporary measure, they were told, to stop enemy propaganda from infiltrating what they were trying to rebuild. It meant that all news was filtered through the government and that, from that moment on, the American people had no way of knowing what was going on in the outside world. Or within the country, for that matter, since all unnecessary travel was banned. Again, a temporary measure that had never been revoked.

But everyday life hadn't been too bad, and they'd been assured a return to democracy was coming soon.

Then it had all changed in a moment. Well, maybe not a moment. Twelve years ago, for health reasons, Harry Senior finally stepped down as president. The promised elections had been halted until the country was more stable, and Harry Junior, as vice president, had stepped into his father's shoes.

There had been changes, subtle at first.

Gideon had presumed that Harry was just feeling his way, testing his new powers, but he was sure he'd settle down. Become the great man his father had been.

Because Gideon had believed in the Party, believed that they were doing what was needed for the good of the people. Hell, he'd even believed in God, and that God was on the side of America. When he looked back on that life, it didn't seem like it belonged to him; he'd been so fucking naive.

Then, within two years of Harry Junior becoming president, Gideon's brother, Aaron, had done his vanishing act, their father had taken his own life, and Gideon had been given the choice of taking the same way out or joining the army.

He'd joined the army.

Any surviving beliefs had been wiped away on the first battlefield, where he'd watched his men ripped apart by an enemy with weapons far more advanced than theirs. But then, the decline of scientific advancement was an unfortunate side effect of the Wall. It limited the sharing of information and ideas. The country had relied on the might of American innovation to carry them forward. Unfortunately, it hadn't carried them as far as they'd hoped.

All the same, he loved his country. Wanted to help make it a better place. But now the glittering life of the White House was strangely tarnished.

He swallowed his champagne in one gulp. He supposed it shouldn't really be called champagne, but "domestically produced sparkling wine" was too much of a mouthful. He grabbed another glass from a passing waiter and wished for some whiskey.

The room was crowded. Anyone and everyone had clamored for an invitation to the party of the year. Plus, there were a large number of security agents. More than he remembered from the past. Men in the black uniforms of the president's personal bodyguards—selected from the elite of the Secret Service—stood at the doors, while others mingled with the crowd. There was even a sniper on the second-floor interior balcony, covering the room.

Either Harry was paranoid, or there was an elevated threat level. If so, no one had told Gideon about it. That was hardly surprising; he suspected that no one, with maybe the exception of Harry himself, actually wanted him there.

But he wanted answers, and this was where he would find them.

Once he had those answers, then…

Who knew? Though revenge wasn't the solution.

Most of the time he believed that.

He scanned the room and caught sight of Stella speaking into a phone, a smile on her face. She was a beautiful woman, but looking at her now, he felt absolutely nothing. Hard to imagine he'd once considered spending his life with her. In the end, it had been easy to walk away. He hadn't really loved her, and she hadn't loved him. They'd just been using each other. The perfect match.

She glanced up and caught his gaze, then smiled and headed over. "I was just talking to my sister," she said. "She was surprised to see you here."

He'd forgotten she even had a sister. "I get that a lot."

Stella grabbed a glass of wine from a passing waiter. "Hmm. Come to think about it, you're both single. Perhaps you should look her up."

"I don't think I'm the type you want your sister going out with anymore."

She contemplated him, head cocked on one side. "No, you don't look the type someone would introduce to their baby sister. You've changed. I suppose ten years on the front line will do that." Sympathy flashed in her eyes. "I'm sorry for the way things turned out. For your father."

"Don't be. It was a long time ago. I'm over it." That was never going to happen, but he could pretend.

"And you're back and in favor." She grinned. "Honestly, think about my sister. Kate is a total geek. She could do with a dangerous man to bring her out of herself, and you could do with a respectable woman to help you settle in."

Is that how she saw him? Dangerous? But he wasn't interested. These days, he kept his relationships brief. Like one night brief. He was a goddamn hero—it was easy to get a woman when he needed one. "I don't do respectable women."

Her eyes widened, and she swallowed, blew out her breath. "Oh well, it's probably for the best."

Yeah, it was. "Tell me," he said. "Is the security here normal?"

She looked around and her brows drew together. "There does seem to be a big presence. Since the democracy speech, Harry has been getting a little paranoid. I suppose it goes with the territory." Her frown deepened and some dark emotion that he couldn't identify flashed through her eyes. He followed her gaze and found her attention on the president. "Looks like he's heading this way," she said. "I'll leave you to him and go have a talk with your boss. He'll know if there's anything going on." She took a step closer, reached up and kissed him on the cheek. "I'm pleased you're back."

She sounded genuine.

Harry was making the rounds, shaking hands and smiling as he headed this way. Gideon wasn't sure whether he would be acknowledged, but the president halted in front of him. He was flanked by two Secret Service officers, dressed in their black uniforms. Harry's army, as they were known within the service.

He took the proffered hand. Harry's grip was firm, and his smile was sparkling. Good dental work.

"Happy birthday, sir," he said.

"Thank you. I'm glad you could make it."

"I was grateful for the invitation, Mr. President."

"We must all practice forgiveness."

He could feel his muscles tightening. He'd done nothing that needed fucking forgiving. Neither had his father. For a second, he felt an echo of the dark anger that had been his companion for the first few years after his father's death. He pushed it down and forced a smile. "Thank you, sir. I appreciated the chance to come home."

"You're a hero now, Gideon. You saved

America from invasion. The people love you. We need heroes at a time like this."

Defending a breach in the Wall by himself had been a serious test of his skills, but that hardly made him a hero. And a time like what? He'd seen the polls. There was a good chance that Harry would keep his position when—or maybe *if*—it came to an election. "Your approval ratings are higher than ever, sir."

"Maybe," the man mused. "But I've been feeling lately that they don't appreciate me. That needs to change."

"Yes, sir."

"I must go now, but we'll talk again." Harry smiled and patted Gideon on the shoulder, and his guards stiffened at the contact. Christ, they were jumpy.

Gideon watched as the group walked away. Harry had always needed constant approval. It came from growing up in his father's shadow; Harry Senior had been larger than life and an impossible act to follow. Charismatic. People loved him and would follow him anywhere. No doubt his son had always believed he was second-best.

Trouble was, he was right.

CHAPTER FOUR

"My dream is of a place and a time where America will once again be seen as the last best hope of earth." Abraham Lincoln

Stella left the ballroom behind, the big double doors closing on the murmur of voices, the chink of glasses. Her feet hurt, and her jaw ached from smiling. Hot tears pricked at the back of her eyes.

She blinked.

She was just off-balance, that was all.

Speaking to Gideon after all these years had brought it home to her. He'd changed so much. When he'd left ten years ago, he'd been such an easygoing boy. Back then, despite his twenty-four years, he'd maintained his boyish charm. He'd been confident, happy, secure in his place in the world. Maybe she hadn't loved him, but she'd loved the way he made her feel. Safe. She hadn't felt safe in a long time.

Now he was a hard man, honed by years of fighting. Though he didn't seem bitter; more resigned to what had happened all those years ago.

But then, he still didn't know the whole truth. And Stella certainly wasn't going to tell him.

Stella's office was on the first floor. She didn't take the elevator, but the big curved staircase. A plain-clothes Secret Service officer nodded to her and opened the door without checking her papers. He was a regular and knew her well.

She bent down for the retinal scan, and her door slid open. She had a nice office, big and square, with dark-red walls, polished wooden floors, and the requisite picture of Harry Junior on the wall. A window overlooked the front of the building. She kicked off her shoes and crossed to stare out over the city. Growing up, this was all she had ever wanted—to be part of something big. To help lead her country into peace and prosperity. Food, education, decent medical treatment available for all. On the surface, at least here in D.C., it appeared as though they were there.

Something caught her eye out on the street beyond the wall and the exclusion zone. A knot of people gathered to the west of the entrance. She stared hard and finally made out a checkpoint. She'd never seen one this close to the White House before. The streets around here were busy, and it was causing a buildup of people. She turned away, uncomfortable and not sure why, except she had a sense that everything was changing.

After she'd left Gideon, she'd searched out his boss, Boyd Winters. Boyd was a good friend of her father's and had been head of the Secret Service for over a decade. When Martial Law had been first instituted, it had been under control of the army. That had changed when Harry Junior became president. Now the country was run by the Secret Service, which made Boyd Winters one of the most powerful men in America.

Today, she'd asked him if there was a reason for the heightened security. He'd claimed there was nothing specific, but then they weren't called the "Secret" Service for nothing. No doubt they would tell her if she needed to know.

She switched on her computer and sat down behind her desk. It made her think of Kate. She hoped her baby sister wasn't getting into too much trouble in her basement office. It was too much to ask that she just stick to her work; she would be bored out of her brain. Hopefully she'd be developing some safe little computer game based on one of those really old science fiction movies she devoured at a voracious rate.

She opened her messages and read through them, flagging any that needed an answer and transferring others to archives.

Then a new message flashed up on the screen, and her fingers faltered.

She stared at it for a moment.

New York. The Plaza hotel. One week from today.

There was no signature, but she knew who had

sent it.

Her heart rate sped up and her mouth went dry. For a minute, she just stared. Then she reached out with a trembling finger and clicked archive. If there was a way to delete any message totally, she would have done it, but short of blowing up her computer and the White House servers, she didn't know how. Kate probably would.

An ache pressed on her skull, and she rubbed the back of her neck, then pressed a finger between her eyes.

Christ, what the hell do I do?

She'd never really expected this moment to come.

CHAPTER FIVE

"I have a great relationship with the Mexican people." Donald Trump

The airwaves exploded with chatter, and Kate was kept busy for the rest of the day. Lots of red alerts—someone wasn't fond of Harry. She left the office at six and didn't get a chance to consult with Auspex again.

Christ, Auspex had *decoded* the chatter. And it wasn't what she had expected. She was aware how it worked. Chatter was flagged based on search terms input by the agents at NTAC. She'd presumed things like "kill the president" and "nuclear bomb."

Instead, for the red alert she had checked, the info dump included references to the cartoon that had been released on the day of the president's "return to democracy" speech. The person involved apparently thought it amusing. But did that really warrant a 72 percent chance of action? What sort of action? She hadn't had time to investigate, but she found it mind-blowing and quite scary that something so trivial would be considered a threat to the president.

With the possibilities churning in her head,

Kate packed up and headed home. When she'd finished college and gotten her job with Homeland Security, her father had bought her an apartment only ten minutes' walk from her office. It was in an old converted house, and she loved it. Liked having her own space.

Five minutes out of the office, walking up Connecticut Avenue, close to Dupont Circle, she came upon the first checkpoint. Two uniformed officers from the Secret Service manned the station, slightly sinister in black, their weapons holstered but in full view.

She frowned. This was the first time she'd seen a checkpoint in this part of the city.

She dug through her bag for her papers, fingers fumbling, palms sweaty. She didn't know why she was nervous: everything was in order, and they'd never detain her once they saw she was a Party member with privileges. Maybe it was just that she'd been caught unprepared. She flashed her Party membership and was waved straight through.

Still, the experience made her feel…on edge.

There was a second checkpoint on the junction before she turned off to Hopkins Street where she lived, and her heart rate kicked up. What was going on?

She had to wait as the family in front of her was stopped. The man was arguing with one of the

Secret Security officers. His wife stood at the side, clutching a child by each of her hands as though they might disappear if she let them go. A girl and a boy, about five and six—old enough to pick up the vibes from their parents and be scared.

Where were their papers? All they had to do was show them. It wasn't unreasonable. They looked to be Hispanic, but that didn't mean anything—there were many Hispanic Americans.

Kate bit her lip as she held out her own. The man nodded and gestured for her to go through. She walked slowly. What could she say? She'd gone a few more feet when she turned back just as a black van pulled up. She hesitated as the husband's yelling grew more insistent. Whatever he was saying didn't matter, though. The whole family was hustled into the van, and the doors slammed shut.

She turned for home. It was none of her business. If they'd had their paperwork, everything would've been fine. If they didn't... As Harry always said, this was America, and it was for Americans. That was the premise the Loyalist Party was built on. It was the only way they could survive.

Kate ducked her head and walked faster. While they were far from perfect, the Loyalist Party's policies had resulted in a time of unprecedented prosperity. Crime had been almost eliminated, as had poverty. Transmittable diseases had been almost wiped out, and pandemics were no longer to be feared. If people didn't move around, they didn't pick things up, pass them on. Also, thanks to a closely monitored breeding program, congenital illnesses were almost unheard of.

No system was perfect, but the results spoke for themselves.

Or so her father always said. Even so, as she let herself into her apartment, she couldn't get the woman's expression out of her head. Fear.

They would no doubt be deported, presumably back to wherever they had come from. Their home. Like America was her home. They would be all right. She'd heard rumors that they were just taken to the nearest portal and put outside, but that couldn't be true. The area immediately beyond the Wall was said to be lethal, the air laced with smoke and poisonous gases and viruses released by their enemies—the next pandemic just waiting to happen if they didn't maintain their vigilance. The ground had been mined to stop the enemy getting close. Not that she'd seen that area. She hadn't even seen the Wall itself.

They wouldn't send innocent children out there.

She sighed. There was no sense in dwelling on it. She'd go to bed, get up early, and go into the office so she could grab a few hours' work on her own projects.

But when she closed her eyes, she saw the woman again, holding onto her children for dear life. And when Kate finally did manage to fall asleep, it was to find herself being deported. She was in the back of some sort of vehicle in total darkness. Then the vehicle stopped, and the doors opened, and there she was in front of a huge set of black gates in a tall wall that stretched as far as the eye could see on either side, vanishing into the distance. She huddled on a bench seat as the gates opened, slowly revealing a burned-out land.

"Get out."

She didn't want to get out. *"My paperwork is good. My father is a supreme court justice."*

"You didn't attend the prayer meetings. You must face your punishment."

She realized then that beyond the gates was Hell.

Someone gripped her arm and pulled her out. She grabbed hold of the door, trying to stop her forward momentum, but whoever it was pried her fingers from their death grip. She begged them to let her stay, screamed that this was her home, she was American. They dragged her across the space, hurled her out through the gates, and slammed them closed behind her. She landed on her front, the air whooshing out of her lungs. Opening her eyes as she came up on her hands and knees, she screamed. Only a foot away, the bodies of the Mexican family lay sprawled in death, the woman still holding on to her children, their faces masks of agony, eyes wide, blood crusting their nostrils. The air was thick with smoke and something worse. Gasping, she tried to drag oxygen into her lungs as the poisons seared her throat. She couldn't breathe, her lungs heaved.

She woke up gasping for air and covered in sweat.

In the early years of the Party, there had been a lot of propaganda about getting rid of the aliens. While she'd been protected from most of it, it had been hard to miss. She'd lost friends. Her father had explained that they were not like her, not true Americans, and that there was only room in their country for people who belonged. She'd thought she had come to terms with it. Had accepted that things were the way they were supposed to be... *had* to be—their very survival as a nation had been threatened.

Clearly her peace was a fragile thing.

She shoved the sheets down, kicking them off the bed, grabbed a robe from the nearby chair, and wrapped herself in its comforting folds. After padding into the kitchen, she opened the fridge and found a half-full bottle of white wine. She took it, got a glass from the cupboard, and headed back into the living room. Sinking down on the sofa, she curled her feet under her and switched on the TV.

The highlights of the president's birthday party were airing on the main station, and she watched for a moment, hoping to take her mind off things she couldn't change. Wouldn't even if she could. Except…

She shook her head and concentrated on the picture. She spotted her sister first, looking glamorous and gorgeous. Good thing she wasn't the jealous type, or she would have grown up hating Stella.

The camera moved on to follow the president. And there was Gideon Frome. The image zoomed in as the president came to a halt in front of him, hand held out. They shook hands, then spoke together for a few minutes. As Stella had said, Gideon was obviously back in favor, and she was glad. It hadn't been fair what had happened to him. You shouldn't be responsible for the actions of your family, although she knew her father didn't agree. He said it was a way of ensuring checks and balances. People would know that their actions had consequences beyond just themselves.

Their families had moved in the same circles, both high up in the Party hierarchy, though she'd known Gideon's brother, Aaron, better than she knew Gideon. Aaron was the same age as Stella, and he'd been close to her sister. They'd grown up together, played together as children. And Aaron had always made time for Stella's geeky little sister. She'd liked him. A lot. Aaron had been the one person she could talk to about absolutely everything. She could tell him things she would never dare to say to anyone else, about traveling into space, about her obsession with AI and computers and all that vast, untapped potential.

He'd called her his little rebel—funny she'd forgotten about that.

Then something had happened the summer Stella turned fifteen, he and Stella had had a falling out, and Aaron had stopped coming around.

Up until then, Kate had had a happy childhood, but after that, everything had changed. Her sister had withdrawn into herself, as had her mother, her father had been angry—all the time—and she'd had no clue why. Aaron couldn't have had *that* big of an impact on her parents, but who was she going to ask? It's not like anyone would talk to her.

Computers became her way of coping. More of a game than anything else. She'd discovered one of the now illegal PDAs, Personal Digital Assistants, on the old computer her father had passed on to her. The software had been deleted, but she'd managed to recover the files. It had been the beginning of a love affair and she had lost herself in the world of computer programming and the limitless possibilities of artificial intelligence.

Then she had discovered Auspex. She suspected that it had been no accident—Oliver would have wanted to bequeath his baby to someone who would appreciate it. Auspex had opened up a whole new world, but it was only since she had come to work here, and had access to the Homeland Security's systems, that she'd made advances in her research.

Then, when he and Stella were twenty—shortly after Stella had gotten engaged to Aaron's brother, Gideon—Aaron had done his vanishing act.

Was he still alive? They'd gone after him, but never found any sign. It was said he'd joined the rebels. Ironic, really, when she'd been the rebellious one.

She turned her attention back to the TV. The camera followed the president as he moved away from Gideon, and she switched the channel. After her nightmare, she didn't want real life. She searched through her files and found her favorite film. She'd watched *The Return of the Jedi* so many times and knew the words almost by heart, and the familiarity soothed her. As the Millennium Falcon flew away and the film ended, she rested her head on the cushion. She had no wish to return to bed where the nightmares waited.

But sleep was tugging at her and, no matter how hard she tried to resist, it pulled her under, and she was back in the nightmare. Only this time it was Gideon who dragged her kicking and screaming from the van, Gideon who laughed as he threw her through the gates and into the badlands.

And she wanted back inside the Wall so badly it was a physical pain.

"Let me in, I haven't done anything wrong!"

Except she had.

CHAPTER SIX

"Without continual growth and progress, such words as improvement, achievement, and success have no meaning." Benjamin Franklin

Kate woke late the next morning with only fifteen minutes to get to the office. So much for getting to work early. She pulled on her usual work outfit of black pantsuit and T-shirt and left the apartment at a run.

The checkpoints were gone, which was a relief, and she slipped into the building right at nine o'clock.

Crap.

Everyone was congregated in the large foyer. The morning prayer meeting. Usually, she was safely shut away in her basement office by this time. Her gaze clashed with Teresa, who gave her a beatific smile. She probably believed that her little pep-talk yesterday had done some good.

Kate gritted her teeth and forced a smile, then lowered her head as the words droned on. After the nightmares, she really needed something to focus on, and she tried to work out what her next move with Auspex should be. If she was ever going to try and go public with her research, she needed to prove its usefulness. Something big enough to overshadow the fact that she had broken the law.

She wished she had someone she could share with, but she didn't dare confide in anyone.

Oliver, her boss, would be the obvious choice. He'd been her professor and mentor in college for the first two years until he'd been removed as too progressive. A law had been passed that only Party members could teach at college level, as though Oliver might contaminate young minds with his subversive behavior.

She hated that Oliver wouldn't just give in and become a Party member so he could keep the job he loved. The Party wasn't so bad. He'd snapped her head off when she'd said that and told her she needed to take off her blinkers, see the world as it was. She'd sensed he was disappointed in her, and they hadn't spoken of it again. Shortly afterward, he'd been offered the job at Homeland Security in charge of IT. "As much to watch me as anything else," he'd told Kate.

He couldn't have been too disappointed in her as he'd offered her a job when she finished college, and she was pretty sure he was aware of her personal research projects. He was probably also aware that she was in possession of the last remaining copy of Auspex. He wouldn't give her away, but she was still reluctant to involve him further. Right now, he could deny all knowledge, and there was no incriminating link to be found.

Oliver still wasn't a Party member. He'd mentioned it briefly to her after she'd started working here, told her that it was better if he kept his distance from her, that the administration didn't trust him, and that he didn't want her tainted by association. She'd hated that. At the same time, she saw the sense. She was sure Teresa's promotion to Political Officer was no coincidence. She was in the unique position to know what Oliver was up to, and she bore him no loyalty to put her off reporting anything she considered an infringement.

It made Kate sad. She didn't have many real friends—her own fault, since she could no longer open up to anyone about the things she cared about—and she had a natural aversion to lying. Best not to get into the position where she would have to lie or put people in a position of risk.

"Amen. May God bless Americans."

The man beside her gave her a nudge, and she jumped.

He grinned. "Sleeping during service? That's not going to get you ahead. Not that it makes any difference considering who your father is."

She ignored the comment. She encountered a lot of jealousy, but she couldn't help that her father was one of the most powerful people in the country. She'd certainly never used the connection to get ahead.

Everyone was dispersing. Teresa stood, arms folded across her chest, right by the elevators.

Kate couldn't face it. Not today.

She backed away and headed in the opposite direction, through the doors that led into the stairwell. After grabbing a coffee, she let herself into her office, sat down in front of the console, and pressed the switch to power up her computer.

While the system she used today was almost identical to the systems from over two decades ago, her reach was actually more limited because the whole country was protected by a firewall, which made communicating with the outside world an impossibility. The development of the firewall had been the last new research and development Oliver had done.

The best she'd been able to do was integrate Auspex into the systems here at Homeland Security. Then she'd refined his processing capabilities using deep learning techniques, and later reinforcement learning, and Auspex had started to grow exponentially, sucking in vast amounts of information, arranging it into patterns, and extrapolating those patterns into predictions for the future.

At that point, she'd gotten a little scared and had built in some safety protocols—just in case—

including the necessity for a particular command from her before making any but the simplest predictions.

Now, information began flooding the screen. There were plenty of alerts today. Six yellow flags, two green, and twenty-five red. Kate's eyebrows shot up. The latter number was unprecedented. Clearly someone was very unhappy with Harry right now. Fortunately, Auspex predicted that all of them had a negligible chance of resulting in any danger to America.

She passed them all on to the analysts as usual. There was no way she could tell them they were wasting their time—not if she wanted to stay out of the basements at Secret Service headquarters, where it was rumored that people were "questioned."

She was about to leave the office that night when a code green was flagged, and an idea occurred to her. Instead of the usual prediction of "a threat to the American people" she reworded the question.

What are the chances that anyone will be hurt by my forwarding this code green to the analysts?

She wasn't sure what she expected. Maybe something inconclusive. A few seconds later, Auspex replied.

There is a 35 percent probability that the individuals involved will face deportation.

35 percent wasn't so bad. That meant they had a 65 percent chance they'd be okay.

More information showed on the screen.

There is a 64.5 percent probability that they will be eliminated by the security forces.

She swallowed. Eliminated…as in killed?

What is the other 0.5 percent?

They will have a fatal accident before they are apprehended by the security forces.

Kate sat staring at the screen for a long time. Her stomach churned. She closed her eyes, and yet another image of the Mexican family at the checkpoint popped into her mind, the little children so scared. They were supposed to live in a world without terror. A free world.

While part of her wanted to ask Auspex about the family, most of her already suspected the answer. She didn't need or want to see it on the screen in front of her.

What had that family, those children, done wrong? What was so bad that they deserved to die?

She didn't want to believe it, but she couldn't make herself *not* believe it. At least not enough to ignore the feeling.

She stared at the green-flagged alert. Then she did something she had never done before. She deleted it.

The alert vanished from the screen.

A shiver ran through her. She'd crossed a line. Was there a way back?

She could still make a manual report, say she'd deleted the code green by accident. There was no reason they would suspect her. She was the daughter of a supreme court justice. A Party member. Above suspicion.

Slowly she rose to her feet, closed down the system before she could change her mind. And walked away.

No going back.

• • •

Two Secret Service agents in the uniform of Harry's private army stood outside the door to the Oval Office. The one on the left spoke into his earpiece as Gideon approached. He nodded once, then opened the door and ushered him inside.

There had been a message on Gideon's desk when he'd arrived that morning. The president would like a meeting.

Maybe he was going to get some real work at last.

Harry was reading a report. He didn't acknowledge Gideon as he came to a halt in front of the desk, so Gideon stood, hands clasped behind his back, waiting. Finally Harry looked up.

"Good morning, Gideon."

"Good morning, Mr. President." Harry didn't

offer him a seat, but Gideon was used to standing for long periods of time.

"How are you enjoying being back in D.C.?"

"To be honest, I'm a little bored. I'm not actually sure what my job is, sir. So far, I feel I've been wasting the taxpayers' money."

Harry pursed his lips, his eyes narrowing. Gideon suspected the question had been rhetorical and he'd expected some bland, meaningless answer. "I'm sure you'll be given more responsibility in time." He considered Gideon for a moment. "Boyd is a good man and a good friend. His main concern is protecting me and right now, I'm afraid he doesn't trust you."

Gideon had thought Boyd's job was protecting the country but decided to keep his mouth shut.

"I'm sure that will change with time," Harry continued. "Just show Boyd that the past is behind you and that your loyalty is to the Party."

His loyalty had never been anywhere else. "I'll do my best, sir. If I'm given the opportunity."

Anger flashed in the man's eyes, but it was gone in a moment. "I just wanted to touch base with you. Welcome you back. There are a lot of opportunities for a man willing to do what is needed."

What the hell did that mean? Once again, he decided silence was his best option.

"We will be expanding my protection team in

the near future. A man with your experience would be a valuable addition."

"I hope I make the grade, sir." He also hoped that Harry didn't recognize sarcasm. The man already had a goddamn private army. What more did he need?

Though he supposed it was understandable. Harry's mother had been killed at a political rally a year after her husband had been elected. Shot by terrorists. Harry Junior had been on the podium beside her. It had been a miracle he'd survived. That was bound to have a long-lasting effect.

"And we have a number of plans in place to ensure the people will make the right decision when the time comes to elect the next president. If they don't love me, they won't follow me. I need to prove to them I am their leader."

The words filled Gideon with a sense of foreboding.

CHAPTER SEVEN

"A man does what he must—in spite of personal consequences, in spite of obstacles and dangers and pressures—and that is the basis of all human morality." John F. Kennedy

Stella closed the door and locked it behind her. The week had been a nightmare of waiting. She'd even canceled her lunch date with Kate, who was too perceptive not to realize something was wrong. Besides, maybe the time had come to distance herself from her sister. Though she had no doubt that if everything went wrong, they were all finished: her husband Joe, Kate, her parents. She couldn't think about it or she would stop functioning. And she knew Joe was worried.

She sank down behind her desk and switched on her computer. No new messages. A mingling of terror and relief swirled inside her. Most of her had prayed that the meeting would be canceled, but a small part of her wanted to see this through. She'd lived with the dark thoughts for so long. Maybe it was time to put them behind her. Or die.

She was being melodramatic. Or maybe not.

Closing her eyes, she took a few deep breaths, then picked up the phone. She pressed the number for her assistant, and it went to voicemail just like she'd hoped—she'd picked a time she knew Sam would be away from her desk. "Sam," she said, glad that she didn't have to talk to her directly, "I'm taking a couple of days off. Joe got an unexpected break and we're going to make the most of it. I'll clear my desk before I go. Otherwise just send anything important to my cell."

Next, she called her husband. While she hated lying, what choice did she have? With Gideon, she'd believed love was mere expediency. With Joe, she knew she'd found the real thing.

It made no difference.

He picked up on the first ring. "Hey, sweetheart. How's work?

"Boring. I'd rather be with you."

Joe laughed. "So are you coming home?"

She bit her lip. "I wish. I'm sorry, but I've been called to a meeting upstate. I'm not sure how long I'll be away. A couple of days at the most." *I hope.*

"I'll miss you, but I might go up to the cottage for a few days, catch up on some writing."

God, she wished she could go with him. "I'll miss you, too."

After the call ended, she went back into her computer system and printed off a cross-state permission. Luckily, one of her jobs was checking and passing—or more usually, refusing—permissions to cross states, so at least that was no problem. She had a small case she kept in her office in the event she was called away suddenly. After dragging it from the closet, she grabbed her car keys, and she was ready to go.

She stared at the phone, thought about calling Kate to let her know she'd be out of town. In the end, she decided against it. The less Kate knew, the better.

Though if anything went wrong, lack of knowledge wouldn't save her sister.

What am I doing?

After one last look around the office, she headed out. She flashed her paperwork at the three checkpoints needed to leave the White House and drove for ten minutes. Once she was sure she wasn't being followed, she pulled up and opened the case on the seat beside her, then moved away the clothing and toiletries to reveal the bottom. She pressed her thumb to the almost invisible panel and the small door slid open, revealing a space just big enough to place a set of papers. She took out the set in there and replaced them with her own, then closed the case.

Five minutes later, Stella Masters was driving out of the city and heading to New York.

CHAPTER EIGHT

"The spirit of resistance to government is so valuable on certain occasions that I wish it to be always kept alive." Thomas Jefferson

Kate arrived just in time for morning prayers the following day. She'd decided that a small prayer might help—or at least stop Teresa visiting. She spent the morning jumping at every sound, every alert, expecting to be arrested at any moment. But all remained quiet and, as the hours passed with no consequences, she relaxed.

There was no reason they should know of the deletion. She'd covered her tracks. She hoped.

An alert flashed up. Yellow, thank God. She didn't know what she would do with the next green. Her mind hadn't taken her that far. She pressed the key to run the alert through Auspex, expecting the usual negligible answer. Instead, a moment later, a message came up on the screen.

There is a 68 percent chance of Report 10245 resulting in terrorist activity that would be harmful to the American people.

She frowned, then re-ran the alert. And came up with the same result.

She pursed her lips, then downloaded the info

dump to her screen. Most of it was just snippets of conversation. None of it made much sense to her or seemed particularly threatening. Then, halfway through, she came upon something she recognized.

Search term: atomic

Final test of Special Atomic Demolition Munitions completed.

That didn't sound good. Weren't they some sort of nuclear bomb? As far as she was aware, all nuclear devices had been destroyed decades ago. Why would anyone be testing them? Unless it was for some sort of terrorist attack.

She continued reading but found nothing of interest until close to the end.

Search term: Aaron Frome

Internet search performed by Stella Buchanan.

She stared at the name blankly for a long time. Of course it meant nothing. It was only an internet search—nothing incriminating. The chatter was always picking up pieces of information that were nothing but random snippets. Probably Stella had just been curious? Gideon's return was bound to raise old memories. That was all it was. Stella was dedicated to the Loyalist Party. It was her whole life.

Kate's head hurt.

It was likely that the search was somehow related to Stella's job. If so, the agents at NTAC would just delete it from the log.

But what if it wasn't? Even the hint of something like this was enough to devastate a person's career. And worse. People had been known to disappear. Or be arrested and never heard of again. The whole family could be investigated.

She ran through the rest of the info dump, but there was nothing of interest.

What to do?

She screwed her eyes shut for a moment, but the information was still there when she opened them. Swallowing, she leaned forward, and her fingers flew across the keys as she deleted the lines mentioning her sister. Then she repeated the process in the encrypted files and placed the edited version in the folder to send to NTAC.

She sat back. She'd crossed another line.

Her fingers were shaking as she picked up her phone and swiped her sister's number.

The call went straight to voice mail.

I can't talk right now, but I'll get back to you as soon as I can.

"It's Kate, call me when you get the chance." She ended the call and stared at her phone, tapping her foot on the floor. She frowned. Thinking about it, she hadn't heard from Stella all week, except a text cancelling lunch, which was unusual. Kate had been so caught up in what was going on with Auspex that she hadn't thought too much about it. She flicked through the numbers and found Stella's office. She called, and it was picked up immediately. "White House. Stella Buchanan's office."

"Hi, Sam, it's Kate. I was trying to get hold of Stella but she's not answering her private phone."

"She's away from the office this week. I think she and Joe are having a little together time."

"Oh." Why hadn't she mentioned it? Joe was Stella's husband. They'd been married for two years now. Joe was a nice man—though the total opposite of Gideon Frome—who had absolutely nothing to do with the Party, but Stella seemed happy with him. "Do you know when she'll be back?"

"Should be Monday. If she calls in, I'll tell her you're trying to get in touch."

"Thank you." She tried to shake off the feeling of unease. She'd never been unable to get in touch before.

That didn't mean anything. They'd probably gone somewhere for some alone time. She knew Joe had a cottage just outside the city.

She flicked through her phone and found Joe's number, but when she tried to call it, there was no signal. They must be at the cottage.

Either that or her perfect sister was involved in a code yellow alert.

CHAPTER NINE

"The problems of the world cannot possibly be solved by skeptics or cynics whose horizons are limited by the obvious realities. We need men who can dream of things that never were." John F. Kennedy

The next morning, on Kate's way to work, the checkpoints were back. While she had no problem passing, they made her edgy. She still hadn't managed to get hold of Stella and she didn't want to make a fuss in case…

In case what? Her mind scrambled for an explanation.

The morning passed in a blur of red alerts. She was pretty sure the guys at NTAC had adjusted the parameters calculating the threat levels, lowering the point at which an alert was generated, because she was inundated. Was it somehow connected with the yellow alert she had submitted?

She'd added her sister's name to the search terms, along with instructions to dump any hits into a special folder. So far there had been nothing, and she breathed a little easier.

The single code green alert she deleted without

even thinking about it.

She was going to hell.

Or to the Secret Service basement room.

Where was Stella?

An incoming email flashed up. The daily reports from NTAC. For a moment she was scared to look, then she forced herself to open the mail and scan down the alerts until she found the yellow.

They had assigned it a zero-threat level.

For a moment, she slumped in her seat, the tension draining out of her. Then she frowned. It didn't make sense. She'd seen the info dumps. There was definitely a need to investigate.

She scrubbed a hand over her face, then powered up Auspex and ran the alert again.

There is a 79 percent chance of Report 10245 resulting in terrorist activity that would be harmful to the American people.

Oh God. It had gone up. And *how* harmful?

If there was a nuclear bomb involved, she was guessing very harmful. How could NTAC not find this a threat? It didn't seem possible. Could Auspex have gotten it wrong?

She thought for a moment, then typed in the question…

What are the predicted casualties should the terrorist activity take place?

At this point casualties cannot be accurately

predicted.

Can you give an estimate?

Estimated loss of life at this time is between 100,000 and 2,400,000,000.

Kate stared at the numbers, trying to get her head around all those zeros. Over two billion people. That was a quarter of the whole world. Even the low estimate was too many. They hadn't seen death rates like that since the final pandemic. She got to her feet, rubbing her sweaty palms over her thighs. For a moment, she stood, unsure of what to do. She needed to get out of her office. It was like there was a monster in there, waiting to leap out and devour her whole life.

She couldn't believe it.

And she wasn't ready to face it right now.

She finally found herself outside Oliver's office. Teresa was at the desk in front of his door, guarding the entrance.

"Is he in?" Kate asked.

"He is."

"Does he have a minute?" She had no clue what she was going to say, but she needed a little human contact right now. For once in her life she'd had enough of computers.

Teresa called through. "You can go in."

Kate opened the door and found Oliver seated at his desk. He was only in his forties, but his hair was almost white, a contrast to his dark skin. Right now, it stood on end as it always did when he was working. He had a habit of running his hands through it. He gestured for her to come in, but she stood holding onto the door. She needed some space, some fresh air, somewhere they could talk without fear of being overheard. While she wasn't sure yet if she was going to confide in Oliver, if she did, it wasn't going to be here, with the Political Officer listening to every word. "Would you like to go for a walk?" she asked.

He raised a brow, studied her for a moment, then nodded. "Okay. I could do with some fresh air."

Teresa's lips tightened as they walked by, but she didn't speak, and Kate remained silent as they passed through security. They came out of the building on Connecticut Avenue and headed away from Dupont Circle. After a couple of minutes, they reached Farragut Square, with its small park area. Oliver bought them each a cup of coffee from a stand, and they took their drinks to one of the benches that looked onto the monument. Kate sipped the hot coffee. She had no clue what to say, why she was here. Because she believed Auspex that there was a 79 percent chance two billion people could die in the aftermath of a nuclear detonation? It seemed beyond belief.

As if recognizing that she needed time to think, Oliver remained silent, just drinking his coffee and staring out over the lawns. It was a beautiful day, the sky cloudless and a deep blue. Children played on the grass. It was inconceivable that anything bad could happen. Finally, she put down her empty cup and shifted on the bench to face him.

"Can I ask you a hypothetical question?" she said.

He raised an eyebrow but nodded. "Go ahead."

"Do you think it's possible to design an accurate predictive engine?"

"You know my views on the matter. With the amount of data available today—or rather the amount which should be available if they'd let us have a free hand—and a computer with the power to sift through that data and find the patterns, yes, I think it's possible. Whether it will ever happen is unlikely."

"If it did, would you think it better to rely on a machine rather than on humans? To make decisions and…things?"

"Any day."

She let out a short laugh. Oliver didn't have a high opinion of most people.

"A computer is always impartial," he continued. "It looks at facts. People are rarely impartial and come to any decision with a whole lot of baggage." He swallowed the last of his coffee and tossed the cup in the trash. "Is there anything you want to tell me, Kate?"

She shook her head. "No. Definitely not."

"Good, because I'm pretty certain I'm being monitored and that even now this meeting is being sent to the Secret Service. At least it's known we had a past relationship, so it's unlikely anyone will think it suspicious."

"Why are they watching you?"

He shrugged. "My lack of support for the Party has never been a secret, but let's not dwell on that. How can I help you? There's obviously something more than a hypothetical question bothering you."

She took a deep breath. "Okay, again hypothetically, if you did have a predictive engine, and it predicted something catastrophic, would you try and prove it wrong?"

"What probability?"

"79 percent."

He gave her a sharp look. Perhaps she should have been a little vaguer, but she was rattled, and she found being evasive no easier than she found lying. "What have you done, Kate?"

She couldn't involve him. "Nothing."

He snorted, then shook his head. "There was a reason I hid you away in the basement when I gave you a job. I knew what I was getting into. Some people you just can't stop. I considered it better to hide you in plain sight."

"Really, Oliver, it's just a theory I'm working on."

He nodded slowly, blew out his breath, and scrubbed a hand through his wiry hair. "Okay. First, I'd make sure that this theory is reliable. Do some short-term tests. See how accurate this hypothetical machine is. Then go back to your prediction and run the same scenario under different conditions."

"What if it comes up the same?"

He gave a faint smile. "Then we'd be in trouble. You'd have to keep digging. You'd need to find whatever it is that can change the probability of the catastrophic outcome. The negative prediction. Quite often something quite minor can have a major effect on outcomes. Think of the butterfly effect."

That sounded positive. She'd just have to flap her wings and maybe she'd save a good proportion of the human race. At any rate, it gave her something to do rather than sit around twiddling her thumbs and waiting for the bomb to go off.

"The future is not set," he continued. "Any predictive engine can only work on what's happened in the past, so anything that happens between the time of the original prediction and the predicted event will have an effect. Remember that."

She smiled. "I will."

"You're an extraordinary scientist, Kate. In any other time, you'd be allowed free rein."

"It's for the good of the people."

He threw up his hands. "And comments like that make me want to bang my head against the wall. *The good of the people.* What happened to freedom, and the search for truth and knowledge? What about expanding our minds, stretching ourselves, exploring the unknown?"

"We had all those things and we nearly destroyed the world and all of humanity. At least people are safe and healthy and…"

Except that, according to Auspex, the world was anything but safe.

"Some people," Oliver said. "Not all."

"We can't look after the entire world." They were words her father repeated often, as though if he said them enough they would become true.

Oliver banged his hand down on the bench beside him and she jumped. "Stop fucking spouting the Party crap, Kate. I expect more from you."

"I'm sorry." Her eyes pricked with tears, and she didn't know why. She was tired, that was all. She hadn't been sleeping well since that night when the checkpoints appeared and the Mexican family were taken.

"So you should be." He exhaled. "I'm sorry I lost my temper, but I hate this world we've made."

Kate glanced around as though someone might be listening.

He sighed. "Maybe it's time we got back. I think it's right that you haven't told me more, but remember, I'm here if you need me and you have nowhere else to turn. While I'm not sure what help I can be, I'll try."

"Thank you for listening, and for the advice." She stood up, leaned across, and kissed him on the cheek. "I'm going to walk some more." Maybe the less he was seen with her, the better. Or perhaps it was the other way around. How was her life getting so complicated?

Why did she feel the weight of the world on her shoulders as though the very survival of billions of people was her responsibility?

Perhaps because it was.

She walked for an hour through the streets of Washington. She'd been born and brought up here. Her mother and father both still lived in the house where she and her sister had grown up. It was a beautiful city, but she'd often thought of it more as a prison than a home. She passed through three checkpoints on her walk and was waved through them all. She didn't see anyone else detained. She finally found herself in Lafayette Square, looking across at the White House.

Did she have a responsibility to tell what she had done?

What she had discovered?

She'd broken the law developing Auspex, and

that was punishable by… Actually, she wasn't sure. She should maybe have a word with her father. He would know, but her questions would worry him. Anyway, she would accept any punishment she was due if only they would listen to her and do something to change the future. If Auspex was right, the very survival of America was at stake. That was more important than her life.

She was getting ahead of herself. First things first. She'd take Oliver's advice, and she'd run a series of controlled tests on Auspex. Find out just how accurate his predictions were. Then, if she was convinced that he was accurately predicting a future nuclear war, then she would try and work out what they could do to stop it. Finally, when she had as much hard information to back up her story as possible, she would approach the president. Tell him. Let him decide. He was the leader of America; he would do what was best for his people. However much she disliked him, she had never questioned that.

In the meantime, she really needed to talk to her sister. Warn her not to make any more stupid internet searches on possible rebels. Plus, Stella knew all the players and would be able to advise her how best to approach them.

Stella was Party through and through, but while she might disapprove of what Kate had done, she would not turn her in. Plus, she would listen. Stella wasn't too blinded by religion not to believe in what science had to offer. Kate hoped.

She tried both Stella's and Joe's numbers again but got nothing. Which made sense if they were at the cottage. The signals outside the city were not good.

There was no cause for alarm. Yet.

CHAPTER TEN

"The time is near at hand which must determine whether Americans are to be free men or slaves."
George Washington

Stella paced the length of the room, peered through the heavy maroon curtain, then paced back again. She was going stir-crazy.

Last night when she'd arrived, she'd booked a room in the Grand Plaza under the name of Stella Masters, a New York resident. While people didn't go on vacation anymore, a small number of hotels still operated in the center of town. It was nearly noon and so far, no one had contacted her. She hoped it would be over today; the longer she was away, the more likely people were to get suspicious.

Why had she ever agreed to this?

To protect her family? That's what she'd told herself in the beginning. When Aaron had first contacted her.

But that was a joke. If she was discovered, the rest of her family members were as dead as she was. Maybe they were all living on borrowed time anyway. She'd seen the way Harry looked at her recently. Like he could see into her head. Maybe it was a race now. Who got to who first.

She sank into one of the armchairs and pressed a finger to her forehead as though she could force the thoughts back in. First Gideon and now Aaron. Too much going on.

While he'd never touched her heart, seeing Gideon again had screwed with her mind, taken her back in time. All those years ago when he'd shown an interest, it had been her father who'd convinced her to go along with the relationship. Gideon had always been a favorite and she'd been convinced that the connection would be a way to keep her family safe. Instead, it had been the catalyst that had finally broken Aaron and left them all teetering on the edge of disaster. She'd never really believed she deserved Gideon, deserved love. And, at that point in her life, she hadn't been sure she could ever contemplate a physical relationship. It had taken gentle Joe to move her past her fears, and he still didn't know the reason for them. She would probably never tell him. What good could it do? Maybe the past was better left in the past.

Except here she was.

When she thought she might go crazy with the wait, or give up and just go home, there was a sharp knock on the door. Three taps. She waited, then heard two more.

She pushed herself up and crossed the room,

her feet dragging. She wasn't a natural rebel; this made her want to throw up. At the door, she took a deep breath and opened it.

For a moment, she thought she was finished. That it was Gideon standing before her. Her heart stuttered, and she glanced behind him, looking for his backup ready to drag her away. Interrogate her. She knew they tortured people in the cells beneath the Secret Service headquarters in D.C.

Then the man smiled, and she realized that he actually looked much younger than Gideon, and that the scar, which added such a hard edge, was missing. At the sight of Aaron, something twisted inside her. They said you never forgot your first love. She'd tried her best to put him firmly from her head and her heart, but there would always be a part of her that belonged to him.

She forced a smile. "The prodigal son."

"Hey, big sis." That was what he had called her since her engagement to his older brother, and his voice held that sharp edge of sarcasm she remembered so well. Maybe her engagement to Gideon had been partly to show Aaron once and for all that it was over between them, that he should move on. She'd broken his heart. She knew that.

He looked so like his brother. Though strangely more like the old Gideon, before the years of war had made him hard.

She found it quite ironic. Aaron had been with the rebels for ten years, and clearly it had been an easier life than the one Gideon had led.

He wore grey slacks and a white shirt, and he carried a bottle of wine. Like a man meeting a woman for a secret tryst. Her eyes pricked at the thought of what could have been. Or maybe he would have gone this way without her push. He'd always been wild. She opened the door wider and he walked in.

"Can we talk?" she asked.

He nodded. "We had the room swept before you arrived. It's clean."

She took the bottle from him and into the little kitchenette, found a corkscrew, and opened the wine. Poured herself a glass and drank it down. Poured another and returned to the seating area. He was already sprawled on the black sofa, a lazy smile on his handsome face.

Suddenly a wave of homesickness washed over her, and she wished desperately for a normal life and Joe, and for the baby they'd just been given permission to try for after months of medical tests. There were those tears again, pricking at the back of her eyes, and she turned away for a moment, not wanting him to see her so pathetic and vulnerable.

This man knew her darkest secret. Aaron had found her after that night, coaxed her through the long hours. Tried to persuade her to go to the authorities. Then tried to persuade her father. Maybe he'd understood that if they kept it a secret, it would fester. Poison all their lives.

While that night had broken them apart, at the same time it had forged a bond between them. They were no longer sweethearts, but something stronger.

It had also forever changed her view on what she wanted out of life.

She swallowed her wine and put the glass on the table. "So why am I here?"

"This is where it gets real. Are you ready for a little payback?"

But it wasn't just payback for her. It was payback for everyone who had been hurt or broken or died. For all the people who believed they were free until even the illusion of freedom was snatched from them. "What do you need?"

• • •

She was so beautiful she made Aaron ache. Even after all these years.

He hated the fact that he caused her pain. He brought back memories. He could see them, behind her eyes. Not that she had ever forgotten. He'd watched the footage of the president's birthday party, seen her expression, and known she'd forgotten nothing.

Once he'd thought he'd spend forever with this woman. Of course, he'd only been sixteen at the time, and Stella only fifteen. All the same, the feelings had been real. On both sides. Then everything had fallen apart. Or rather, everything had been torn apart. She'd never gotten over that night. If she had, he would have walked away and left her to her life. She had a goddamn husband. The thought made him simultaneously happy for her and want to punch something. It should have been him.

Ten years ago, he'd known his leaving would have repercussions, but he hadn't been able to stay. And, deep down, maybe he'd wanted to mess up their perfect lives. She'd been twenty when she'd agreed to marry his brother, and he'd thought he would go crazy. Maybe he had gone a little insane. Anyway, it was too late for regrets now. He pushed away the past and got on with what he'd come here for.

Revenge.

For both of them. Hopefully, that would just be a side product of them preventing the greatest disaster mankind had ever faced. "We recently got word that something huge is going down. World-changing huge."

She sat up straighter. "What?"

"That's the problem—we don't know the details, but we should have them soon."

Her eyes narrowed as she thought it through. "You have someone working within the administration."

"We can't tell you that."

"What? In case I'm tortured?"

"Yes."

Her face lost the little color it had, and a shudder ran through her. She'd always hated pain. She'd broken her leg when she was twelve and passed out. He'd had to carry her home.

"But that won't happen. You just need to be careful."

"It doesn't matter how careful I am." She stared into his eyes. "I'm sure your father was careful."

He winced. She blamed him for his father's death, but then so she should. He'd known what could happen, that there was a good chance they would go after his family, and he'd still believed he'd had to leave.

That's what beliefs did to you. At least he'd hoped his need to try and change the world had been greater than his need for revenge. Though seeing Stella in front of him, so close, he wasn't sure anymore. The old black hatred churned inside him.

She sighed and pressed her finger between her eyes. "So what are the rebels going to do? Because so far, I think 'absolutely nothing' covers it."

He was in agreement there. For years, he'd been pushing for a more aggressive approach, but the members of the committee were either too scared, or—worse—traitors working with the administration. "We're going to bring down the government. It's time America was free."

"You can't just wait for democracy to do that for you?"

Did he detect a hint of sarcasm? "No. Even if I did believe it, from the intel we have, there isn't the time. We need to take action soon."

A light flickered in her eyes. "What can I do to help?"

"We want you to recruit Gideon."

She sat bolt upright. "What?" Clearly, whatever she had expected, it hadn't been this.

Aaron grinned. "You know—my big brother, the war hero, the man you were engaged to?" He paused. "The man you were in love with." Actually, he'd known she had never loved Gideon.

She glared, her jaw clenching. "You mean the man who is now second-in-command of the Secret Service? That big brother?" She shook her head. "Are you crazy? Do you want me dead? Along with the rest of my family and probably every single person I've so much as smiled at over the last ten years?"

"We have reason to believe he may be sympathetic." And he needed someone not connected with the rebels.

"What reason?"

"Again, we can't tell you."

"Can't or won't?" She studied him for a minute, and he held himself very still. "I've seen him."

"I know. I saw the coverage of Harry's birthday party."

"He's changed, Aaron. He's not the same man he was. He's hard, bitter. And even if he hadn't changed, he was always a Loyalist through and through."

"He was goddamn brainwashed."

"So were you, but it never took. Gideon liked the idea of a better world and he understood sacrifices have to be made to achieve that." She jumped to her feet, crossed to him, and stood glaring down, hands on her hips. His breath caught. She still had the power to move him as no woman had since. "I was never in love with him. You know why I did it." She turned away and stared out of the window, shoulders tensed.

He did know why. To keep her family safe. Though she'd never said it out loud, he'd known. She'd refused to see him after that night, but when he'd heard about her engagement to Gideon, he'd gone to see her. Climbed in through her window, made her listen to him. He'd begged her to come away with him. She'd refused. He'd waited three months, sure she would change her mind, then he'd gone alone, not caring about the chaos he'd leave behind. Perhaps, deep down, even wanting it. He'd lived with that ever since.

He got up and paced the room, trying to lock down the old feelings. Maybe now he had the chance to put things right. Just a little. He could never bring back his father, and he had to live with that. He could, however, try and do something toward that better world Gideon had wanted. And maybe help his brother find his way back. He'd also seen the footage of Gideon, seen the changes.

He came up behind her and rested a hand on her shoulder, turning her to face him. "Do you still think Gideon wants a better world?"

She pursed her lips and gave a small shrug of her shoulders. "I just don't know. He's changed so much. He was always so open. Now I can't read him anymore."

"We need him," Aaron said. "This thing… It's going to be bad."

"If I do this, and Gideon turns me in, then everything is over. Not only my life, but Joe's and Kate's. My parents. I'm not like you—I can't just turn away from the people I love."

He flinched and ran a hand through his hair, sinking down into the seat behind him. Stella grabbed her glass and crossed the room, filling it from the bottle with a hand that shook slightly. He waited while she returned. This time she sat beside him, and he twisted slightly so he could look into her face. "If you don't do this," he said, "then I suspect that it won't matter. There'll be nothing left."

Her face went blank as if she was trying to make sense of what he was saying. "You're talking nuclear?"

He shrugged. "Maybe. We don't know the details yet."

"They were all destroyed." There had been a worldwide ban on nuclear weapons after the attack on San Francisco. That had been just before the Wall went up. The impetus that made it happen.

The last terrorist attack on American soil, the bomb had shaken the world, sending ripples spreading outward. For once they had acted in unity—at least the sane ones, anyway—destroying the perpetrators and then invoking a program of denuclearization. No one had nuclear weapons anymore.

"We suspect there are still nuclear warheads in the country, though maybe they'll come from outside. It's rumored the Russians hid some away."

It didn't make sense. "Harry wouldn't work with the Russians. Whatever else he is, he's a patriot."

"Who knows all his reasons. I think he's a little

insane, but you're closer to him than we are. What do you think?"

She looked away, then back. "This isn't just a chance of revenge?"

"Part of it's personal." He wouldn't lie — not to her. "But I also believe the threat is real."

"I don't want to believe it, and I can't see the reasons. What would a nuclear war do for anyone? Maybe you're right, and he's insane." He knew then that he had her help. "What else do you know?" she asked.

"We're still waiting for details. We should have them any moment now. Once we do, we'll send an encrypted file to you — I'll give you the code before you leave here; you can memorize it. You get the information and take it to Gideon — he's close to the president and we need someone on the inside."

She raised her glass, then lowered it again and placed it on the table. "Is anywhere safe?"

He knew she was thinking of her family and husband. "Maybe. If you can get out of the country. It depends how big this is. We don't know much about what's going on out there. Most of the world's a warzone. Maybe Gideon might know. He must have been beyond the wall."

She took a deep breath. "Okay. Get me the information and I'll go see him. But Aaron, I'm really not sure what he'll do, which way he will fall.

He told me he wants his life back, and somehow I don't think this will get him that."

"If he doesn't help, then I doubt there will be anything to get back." He rose to his feet and held out his hands, and she slid her palms into his. He pulled her up and then against him. He hadn't meant to touch her, but he needed this. He could feel the rapid beat of her heart against his chest, the softness of her. Finally, he pulled back, lowered his head, and kissed her cheeks. Briefly. "You'll help?"

She swallowed. "I'll do my best."

They'd just have to hope that was enough.

CHAPTER ELEVEN

"Sure it's a big job; but I don't know anyone who can do it better than I can." John F. Kennedy

Harry paced the room. The plan was coming together. It was huge and world-changing, and it would once and for all mark him as the most powerful man on the planet. People would remember him. Would love him.

It took a big man to make big decisions.

There was a light tap on the door. It opened before he answered, so he knew who it was before Boyd stepped into the room.

"Did you find anything?" Harry asked. In the weeks since his speech, Boyd had been searching for those responsible for that despicable cartoon. It had been a cowardly attack, and one that had made a mockery of what should have been a momentous event.

"No."

Boyd didn't elaborate.

Fury swirled inside Harry, tightening his gut, acid burning his throat. "No? How fucking hard can it be?"

Boyd shrugged, seemingly unconcerned. "We took a few people in and questioned them, but either they're not talking, or they don't know anything. I'm guessing the latter. Whoever did it was working in isolation. Just forget it. It's not important."

If Boyd had one fault, it was that he didn't see the importance of perception. Didn't see that how the public viewed you was of vital importance. Boyd had always said *fuck them*. Just let them know you were in charge. Then what the hell did it matter if they liked you or not?

Harry blew out his breath, closed his eyes for a moment, and breathed slowly, easing the tension from his muscles. While he didn't agree, they had other things to concentrate on. "Is the Church operation ready to go?"

"All in place."

"Good." The buildup was important. When the time came to act, his response had to be justifiable. Which it was. More than that, it had to be *seen* to be justifiable. His people had to recognize him as their savior. The man who would lead America to greatness. "How is Gideon Frome working out?" He'd always liked Gideon. It had been a pity about his family's scandal. Or maybe not so much. The situation had actually worked out well. He'd perhaps been a little too promising in the political arena. Now he was useful but no competition.

"I don't trust him," Boyd replied.

"You don't trust anyone. We'll just parade him

out for the people now and then. Later we can decide if he's an asset or not. If he's not, you can eliminate the problem."

Boyd grinned. "I'll look forward to it."

• • •

It was Monday morning. Kate had already asked Auspex what the prediction was for the yellow alert. 81 percent. It was still rising.

What the hell was she supposed to do?

Go to the Secret Service agents and NTAC and tell them that they were wrong and that there was about to be a nuclear attack of some sort? Which they would know about if they'd used a super-intelligent but totally illegal predictive engine to calculate the threat levels instead of relying on the human brain.

And that, in the meantime, she'd also illegally decoded the encrypted chatter, deleted numerous green alerts, and removed her sister's name from the info dump of a code yellow.

That would really go down well.

Her whole family were likely to be arrested before the day was out.

There had to be a better way. She just couldn't come up with it.

She supposed knowing when would help. Just in case it was going to be tomorrow, and she had to decide on her course of action really quickly.

She typed in the question…

Yellow alert 10245: Allocate predictions to each day.

A minute later, a stream of information covered the screen. She blew out her breath as her brain took in the details. The rest of the week was negligible. At least she wasn't going to die tomorrow. In fact, the probabilities were negligible for the next twenty-one days. On the twenty-second, they peaked at 81 percent. Then the information stopped.

Shit. Three weeks from now.

She still wasn't sure she believed this. It was crazy to think a machine could predict the future.

Or maybe she just didn't want to believe it.

The screen on her right lit up with a green alert. She hardly thought about what she was doing as she leaned across and deleted it. That was the seventh since Auspex had told her the probable results of handing over a green alert to the analysts. With the first couple, she'd checked the probabilities. They had always come out pretty much the same. Of course, that meant she hadn't sent in a green alert for a week and someone was bound to notice and want a reason. She could delete them with no trace—at least no trace that anyone except her, and maybe Oliver, could find. Even so, they'd start to question her, to look at her more closely, and she had work to do. She couldn't risk the close scrutiny. And yet, she couldn't stop herself deleting them.

Nausea churned in her stomach. She was going against the Party, against everything she and her family believed in. At the same time, she couldn't help but wonder what else were they doing that she had closed her eyes to over the last few years.

Thoughts like that were so wrong.

As a child, she'd always been questioning. It had worried her mother and driven her father crazy. He'd told her to accept things, but it hadn't been in her nature.

She'd changed the year she'd turned twelve. Something had happened to her little family, something dark that had somehow altered all of them. Her sister had gone from a fun, outgoing person to a recluse, her mother became vague, her father irritable, and none of them were talking to Kate.

That had been the state of things for five years. Then, for a short time, while Stella had been engaged to Gideon, things had gotten better. Until Aaron had disappeared, his and Gideon's father had committed suicide, and Gideon had gone off to fight on the Wall. That time had been horrible. Her father had been afraid the scandal would roll over and engulf them. Stella had retreated into herself totally, locked herself away.

As time had passed and nothing had happened,

they'd relaxed. Kate had gone to college, Stella had gotten a position in the administration, and on the surface, everything had seemed fine.

Now nothing was fine, and they were likely hovering on the edge of disaster.

Three weeks was no time at all.

She grabbed her bag and pulled out her notebook. Maybe she needed to take things back to basics as Oliver had suggested. Try and get a grasp on how accurate Auspex was.

She started off with very specific questions. They had to be things that were outside her direct control, otherwise she could choose not to do them.

Will Teresa be wearing a bright pink shirt today?

Probability: negligible

Kate marked it down in her notebook next to her own prediction, which was zero.

Will the canteen have bacon sandwiches today?

Probability: 99 percent.

She thought for a moment. *Do you ever give a 100 percent probability?*

Until an event has occurred, it cannot be 100 percent certain.

That was good… She supposed.

She had twenty-five questions in total. Mostly they were close together with their predictions. Kate had a couple she'd attributed absolute certainty to. Auspex gave the first—that Teresa would be at her desk outside Oliver's office at eleven o'clock when Oliver had his daily call with the big boss and Teresa liked to be on hand—a 96 percent chance, the other—that Philip, the tech expert on Floor One, would try and chat her up if she went to his office—only 2 percent. What did he know? And there was one—that the coffee machine on Floor Two would be out of order— that she gave 50 percent and Auspex gave 99.

The call to maintenance was not made.

She closed her notebook and sat back. She had a few minutes before she had to go check the first. Teresa's whereabouts at eleven o'clock.

She'd promised herself she wouldn't ask again until the testing was done and she was more certain that she had something to worry about. But she found herself clicking the question.

What is the chance there will be a nuclear explosion in the next month?

Probability: 81 percent.

Serious crap.

Maybe from a different angle. Perhaps she could trick him, prove his probabilities wrong and contradictory. *What is the chance that my mother will buy me a dress for my birthday this year?*

Her mother always bought her a dress for her birthday. Kate invariably wore it once for dinner with her family, and then hung it on the wardrobe

in her spare room. She didn't do dresses. All the
same, her mother had done the same thing for ten
years. She'd even hinted that this year she was
going all out, full-length. Kate didn't even want to
think about it.

Probability: negligible chance.

For a moment, a little ray of hope buoyed her
up. Then she crashed rapidly. Of course it was
negligible, because there was going to be some
sort of nuclear attack. She'd likely be dead, maybe
with the rest of mankind.

She leaned across and switched Auspex off.
Time to check out his answers, although she had a
strange sense of futility, as though she already
knew what she was going to find.

An hour later, when she flopped back in her
chair, she was totally drained. He'd been right
every time. Goddamn it, she'd loitered in Philip's
office for ten minutes. Normally he would have
been all over her—he was ambitious. She'd even
fluttered her lashes at him, and he hadn't even
noticed. What the hell?

She downloaded the backup data from Auspex
and found that Philip's mother had passed away
the previous day.

Oh. Poor guy.

For once she'd hoped that Auspex wasn't
functioning correctly. But of course he was, and
she had no clue what her next move should be. An

anonymous tip to NTAC?

She still hadn't heard from Stella or Joe, and she was getting worried. She desperately needed to talk to her sister.

Swallowing, she rubbed her hands down her pants leg. It looked as though, for now at least, she was alone with this. She blew out her breath, then re-ran the prediction one last time.

89 percent.

Crap. Leaning across, she switched Auspex off. For a minute, she stared at the blank screen, then got up and left the room. She walked home on autopilot; didn't even notice the checkpoints, just waved her papers automatically. Once home, she crawled into bed, pulled the covers over her head, and slept. That night she didn't dream.

CHAPTER TWELVE

"Men are not prisoners of fate, but only prisoners of their own minds." Franklin D. Roosevelt

Kate took a couple of days' vacation—unprecedented for her. She'd spent them pretending she was normal, and that her world wasn't about to end. She'd watched back-to-back movies and kept her mind blank. Surely she was allowed a couple of days before she embraced her destiny and somehow saved the world from nuclear devastation? She'd chortled to herself at that thought. Her? A savior of the universe? Ha.

Now she was back to real life, and she had to find a sensible way through this.

Part of her wanted to just shut down Auspex and disappear for another three weeks. She was owed that much time; she hadn't taken a day off in years. But where was there to go? You had to have a really good reason for crossing state lines, and somehow she didn't think "taking my mind off the imminent end of the world" would go down too well. Might get her a vacation of a different sort, though.

Besides, nothing would happen. She was sure of it. Mostly.

She just wasn't sure *enough*. So here she was trying to find a valid way around the absolutely absurd idea of somehow stopping some sort of terrorist nuclear attack all on her own. She needed help.

She let herself into her office, pulled out her phone, and tried Stella again. This time, it went to voice mail and she left a message. Next, she tried Joe. He picked up and she almost sagged with relief. "Joe? Hi, it's Kate. Is Stella there, could I speak with her?"

"I'm afraid she's been out of town on business for a few days," Joe said. "Some top-level meeting she couldn't tell me about."

Her mind went blank. She'd never, not once considered the idea that Stella wasn't with Joe. Where the hell was her sister?

"Kate?"

She shook herself, tried to pull herself together. "Sorry. No problem. Do you know when she'll be back?"

"Soon, I think."

"Can you ask her to call me?"

"Is something wrong? Can I help?"

"No." She swallowed. "It can wait." She ended the call.

So Joe believed Stella was at a meeting. A meeting that her own secretary wasn't aware of. It seemed unlikely.

Where could Stella be that her office and her husband didn't know?

Best-case scenario: she was having an affair.

An image of Gideon Frome flashed in her mind. Her sister had once told her that they hadn't had a physical relationship, that they were waiting for marriage. Gideon's family had been extremely religious—his father had been State Head of the Church of America—so she hadn't questioned the decision.

Now she couldn't help but wonder if they were making up for lost opportunities? Had Gideon come back and they'd taken one look at each other and decided they needed to find out what they had missed?

But really? Her perfect sister?

Unlikely. So where the hell was she?

What would make Stella just drop out of sight?

She pressed a finger to her forehead as the worry that had been nagging at the back of her mind crystalized into something more tangible.

People often disappeared. Sometimes they were never seen or heard of again.

Could the Secret Service have taken her in? Kate didn't want to believe it. She'd deleted the mention of Stella from the yellow alert. But maybe there had been others. Maybe she'd missed something.

Her legs trembled, and she sank back onto the

seat behind her. Surely they would have heard something if Stella had been arrested? Maybe they didn't have proof and were questioning her. She couldn't bear the thought.

She had to find out. She swiped the screen to bring up Auspex.

Can you access the Secret Service files?

No. I only have access to what you have access to. The Secret Service files are on a secure server.

She was the best hacker around. She could get past any security.

How do I get into it?

Security is by retinal scan. We would need the eye of someone with access.

Just the eye? Nice.

In all of the movies she'd seen, the super-spy usually got hold of the actual eyes, cleaned them up, and waved them at the scanner. She'd just go fetch her hacksaw and start with the head.

That wasn't an option. Nor was she a super-spy.

Do you need the actual eye?

An image of the retina would also work.

So her options were to pick someone and ask nicely—and be sent to jail—or pick someone and poke them in the eye with a camera?

She blew out her breath and sat back down. Time to toughen up.

Do you have a list of people with access to that server?

The screen came up with a list of names. Not many, actually. Her father wasn't on the list, which was a pity.

Then, halfway down the list, she paused at a name.

Gideon Frome.

Second-in-command of the Secret Service. Of *course* he would have access to the server.

She sat back in her chair and thought about it. If she got close to Gideon—close enough to get a retinal scan—then she would get access to the Secret Service files. She could find out if they had Stella. Or if they were investigating her for something.

And then what?

One thing at a time.

What is the best method of capturing this retinal scan? she asked.

A high-resolution camera will be adequate. The image must be taken from no farther than one centimeter.

What was she supposed to do, bang Gideon on the head?

She needed to knock him out chemically. Ativan would do it. While Ativan wasn't something she could just walk into the store and purchase, she just happened to know someone who took it on a regular basis. Her mother had been taking the sleeping pills for fifteen years.

Why did everything go back to that time? What had happened that had affected her mother so badly? She shook her head. That was the past, though it was clearly still affecting the present.

So, a plan.

She needed to get close to Gideon Frome and persuade him to take a huge dose of her mother's sleeping pills. Then, while he was unconscious, she had to take a retinal scan, then upload it to a storage device and transfer it to Auspex, who would then get into the Secret Service files and tell her if Stella was in trouble.

Right. Easy.

Except how was she supposed to get close enough to drug Gideon, and to do it somewhere private enough so no one would notice she was taking a retinal scan from an unconscious man?

Her head hurt.

Where do you predict Gideon Frome will be tonight?

There is a 92 percent chance that he will be at his office.

Hmm. Not a good idea.

Tomorrow night?

There is a 52 percent chance he will be home.

Does he live alone?

He lives with his mother.

There were rumors that Mrs. Frome had lost it when her husband committed suicide. She'd spent time in some sort of asylum. Even so, she was hardly likely not to notice some woman coming in and drugging her son, taking a retinal scan, and popping out again. Maybe Kate could drug her as well. Just how many sleeping pills could she filch from her mom?

Not that she could come up with a valid excuse to go to his home.

What about the other 48 percent?

He will be at a bar on 15th Street, The Walking Horse.

She knew it, though she'd never been in. It had the reputation as a total pickup joint. Not her scene. She wouldn't have thought it was Gideon's either, but what did she know of this new Gideon?

If he goes to the bar, Auspex continued, *there is a 95 percent chance he will leave with a woman he meets there.*

Oh.

A picture flashed up on the screen, obviously a CCTV image from the bar. It was slightly blurry but showed Gideon Frome with a woman. Tall, slim, with long blonde hair halfway down her back and a tiny sparkly dress that showed off a lot of skin. Her face was heavily made up, her expression sultry.

The image was replaced by one of Gideon with a different woman, but one so similar they could have been clones. Then another, in a pink dress, but otherwise the similarities were staggering. Gideon had a type and it wasn't Kate.

She didn't need Auspex to predict how unlikely it would be that Gideon would pick *her* up if she went to the club.

Clearly a makeover was in order.

She tugged at a strand of bright red hair hanging over her shoulders and glared at it. The first thing she needed was a wig. A long blonde wig.

Otherwise, she had a few superficial similarities; she was tall and slim, at least.

She wished she had a girlfriend who could help, but she tended to keep her distance. Besides, she couldn't involve anyone else. She didn't want anyone identified as accomplices afterward. It was bad enough for her family. They would all suffer if she went through with this.

When she got home that night, she switched on the TV. Apparently the Secret Service had just prevented an attack on a church by a band of illegal aliens. They'd been armed and it would have been a bloodbath.

As a result, security in all areas was to be increased and the Secret Service had declared a state of alert including a midnight curfew. Only crucial travel would be permitted and people were warned to stay off the streets. To be safe.

The president had thanked everyone at NTAC and Homeland Security for their diligent work.

That was her. But she hadn't submitted any alerts that could have been even vaguely connected.

Could the Secret Service have other forms of intel? She hadn't heard of any, but that could explain why she hadn't picked up anything on Stella. *Oh God.*

She needed to find out.

She grabbed her phone and called her parents, asking if she could come over.

"I haven't seen you for a while, mom, and I'm at a loose end tonight." *And I need to raid your drug cabinet for sleeping pills so I can drug a Secret Service agent and take a picture of his retina.*

"Of course, darling. Dinner is at eight."

CHAPTER THIRTEEN

"You can fool all the people some of the time, and some of the people all the time, but you cannot fool all the people all the time." Abraham Lincoln

"You want to come with us, sir?" A group of them had passed through security together. Now, out on the street, one of the men turned to Gideon. "We're headed out for a few beers."

He should go. He needed to make the effort to bond with these men, but somehow he'd just had enough for the day. He'd been back for three months now, and while he had a nominal position as second-in-command, in actuality he'd been given no responsibility, no specific duties, just a lot of pointless paperwork to shuffle. He was beginning to believe that there was no real job for him, that the president had brought him back merely to raise his own popularity with the people. Gideon was nothing but a figurehead, a goddamn hero to parade in front of the masses.

Sometimes he regretted that last action. But it wasn't as though he'd had a lot of choice—it had been fight or die, and he wasn't ready to die just yet. But it had obviously brought him to Harry's attention, which had resulted in his return to D.C.

He'd thought… Hell, he clearly hadn't been thinking straight. Or at all.

Now he needed something to do, to get stuck into. Someone to fight.

He also had decisions to make. Decisions he'd been putting off, but which couldn't wait forever.

He needed to be away from here, from the doubts that were eating at his composure. Get his head straight and work out where the hell he was going with his life. Not back to where he'd been, that was becoming clearer every day. He wasn't the same person. He was starting to think that he'd been kidding himself. That perhaps he had an entirely different agenda churning in the back of his mind.

He gave a shake of his head. "I'm expected at home."

It was a lie. Home was one more place he didn't want to be right now.

He waited until his colleagues had wandered off, then turned in the opposite direction, heading down 15th Street and into what had become his local. He had to go through two checkpoints before he got there. Though they'd waved him through immediately once they'd seen his ID. He was their boss, after all.

A glass of whisky was already on the bar as he sank onto the stool. "Thanks, Dave." Gideon tossed back the whisky and held the glass out, and the tall man behind the bar refilled it.

Dave owned the place. He'd been under Gideon's command until five years ago when the same blast that had left Gideon with a limp had blown Dave's leg off at the knee. He'd come back home and bought the bar with his compensation. At least these days, veterans were looked after.

"You okay? You look a little down, mate."

"Just life." He hadn't been able to shift the sense of foreboding his last meeting with Harry had instilled. Not to mention the shitstorm of his own life.

Get a fucking grip.

"Well, I'm sure there will be someone along soon who'll help you forget. Blonde, right? I'll keep an eye out."

Maybe he should have gone home.

But he hadn't been able to face his mother. She was so goddamn pleased to have him home. As though he was going to somehow pull the family back from the disgrace that had destroyed them so many years ago.

Maybe he'd just stay here and get drunk; then the worries would leave him for a while. He wanted a woman, wanted to lose himself if only for a little while, but he wasn't sure right now he was capable of making polite conversation. Not that he really needed to. He was a goddamn *hero*, after all. They fell over themselves to drag him into their beds. Trouble was, most of them wanted to show him off to their friends afterward, and he wasn't anyone's trophy.

Shit, he was a miserable bastard.

While this particular bar was close to the White House, it wasn't popular with the Party crowd. It was dark and most of them liked to be seen in the "in" places. He just wanted to drink and fuck. That was the soldier in him. Maybe he was more soldier than politician now.

Dave pushed a plate with a sandwich in front of him. "Roast beef," he said. "Soak up some of the alcohol." He looked over Gideon's shoulder and waved at someone. "Angie—come meet an old friend of mine."

A tall blonde with deep brown eyes perched on the stool beside him, crossing her legs. She was beautiful, and Gideon managed to dredge up a smile.

"You're Captain Frome," she said, her eyes filling with what he supposed was meant to be admiration. Hell, she didn't even know him.

"I am."

"You're a real live hero." Her voice was breathy. "You single-handedly defended a breach in the Wall for a whole week against the entire enemy army. You saved us all."

He opened his mouth to point out that it hadn't been *quite* like that, but then he caught Dave's eyes, saw the gleam of amusement there. *Bastard.*

Angie touched his arm. "Captain—"

"Call me Gideon," he interrupted. "Dave, why don't you get Angie a drink and leave the bottle with me." He waited until Dave had set a glass of white wine in front of her. "So, Angie, tell me about yourself."

He switched off and ate his sandwich, making the occasional grunt of encouragement when she slowed down. She was gorgeous and clearly interested, and he just couldn't seem to get up the enthusiasm to move this to the next level. He stared at her breasts, which were large, pushed up, and bared almost to the nipple. And waited for a response.

Nope, not a flicker.

A crash sounded behind him, and the bar went quiet.

"Fuck, shit, and smoking tonton crap."

He hadn't heard language like that since he'd left the army. Actually, he'd *never* heard language like that. What the hell was a tonton?

Beside him, Angie giggled. He turned on his seat and followed her gaze.

A woman lay sprawled on the floor at the bottom of the steps leading from the outside door. She had everyone's attention, but no one had moved to help. Gideon pushed himself to his feet and closed the space between them. Tall and slender, she wore a tight purple dress so short he caught a flash of bright pink panties. Heat shot to his groin.

She had long blonde hair in a tangle about her face. Finally, she managed to sort herself out enough to brush it from her eyes and she blinked up at him out of blue eyes so light they were almost silver, with a black line around the iris. They were unusual, and he was sure he'd seen them before, but couldn't place where.

He held out his hand. For a moment she stared, as though she wasn't sure what to do with it. A frown formed between her dark brows, then she held out her own hand and slipped it into his. He pulled her to her feet, though her ankle went at the last minute and he had to grab her by the waist to stop her tumbling.

Had she been drinking?

"Sorry," she said. "I think I might have twisted my ankle."

He glanced down the length of her legs to her feet. Her heels were about five inches, strappy sandals with some sort of sparkly bits. He was amazed anyone could stay upright in them.

"New shoes?" he asked.

She shrugged. "These old things. Gosh, no."

He still had his arm around her waist. He left it there as he ushered her toward one of the booths that edged the room, only releasing her as she lowered herself to the padded bench seat. He turned and found Angie staring at him; she didn't look pleased. Behind her, Dave stood with a grin on his face. He put down the cloth he'd been polishing the bar with and picked up the bottle of scotch and a couple of glasses before heading their way.

Gideon took the seat opposite the woman but remained silent as Dave placed the bottle and glasses on the table. "Can I get you anything else, Miss?" Dave asked.

She smiled and shook her head. Once he'd left, she turned her attention to Gideon. "Thank you for the rescue," she said. "I'm Leia."

"Gideon." He poured them both a scotch and pushed the glass toward her. "Nice to meet you, Leia." He studied her for a few seconds. Though there was that hint of familiarity, he couldn't place her. Leia was an unusual name—he would have remembered. She appeared to have no clue who he was, which was refreshing.

She waved a hand toward the bar. "I'm not taking you from your girlfriend, am I?"

"No. We'd only just met."

"Oh. Good. I think." She took a sip of scotch and screwed up her face. "Ugh."

He smiled. "Do you want something else?"

"Maybe. I'd forgotten how much I hate this stuff. A white wine?"

He turned and waved to Dave, then mouthed the words. Dave nodded. A minute later, he placed a large glass in front of her. She gave him a sweet smile.

She took a sip. "It's good."

"Anything else, Captain?"

He shook his head, then sat in silence for a minute while Dave walked away. Leia traced a pattern on the table with her fingertip. Finally, she raised her gaze to his. "So," she said, "do you come here often?" Then she groaned. "That is such a pickup line."

He took a gulp of scotch. "And are you trying to pick me up?"

She studied him for a moment. "I'm not sure yet, but as you already literally came to my rescue and picked me up off the floor, then I suppose it's only fair I have my turn."

His gaze skimmed down what he could see of her. The purple dress was stark against her pale skin and low-cut, revealing the curve of her breasts, the jut of her collarbone. She wasn't beautiful in the way the woman he had left at the bar was; her face was too thin, her cheekbones too sharp, her mouth too wide.

Since he'd returned to the city, he'd picked up countless women, tried to lose himself in their pretty bodies, forget the doubts that wouldn't leave him alone. And he'd failed. They only emphasized the emptiness of his life.

He wondered if this one might be different.

"The barman called you Captain. Are you in the army?" she asked.

Which proved she didn't know who he was. That was a relief. At least she hadn't decided to pick up the Hero of the Wall so she could tell her friends about it the next morning.

"I was in the army until a few months ago. Dave"—he nodded in the direction of the bar— "and I served together for a while."

"Did you get to see outside the Wall?"

"A few times."

"But I guess you don't want to talk about it."

Most of them wanted to know the gory details. Violence was something people only read about these days or saw on the news feeds, heavily edited. It was amazing how many people were fascinated by the idea. "I'd rather talk about you. What do you do, Leia?"

"Nothing very interesting. I'm a computer programmer for a big private company."

"So, clever as well as beautiful."

"I'm not beautiful."

He noticed she didn't deny being clever. Interesting. "You have the most amazing eyes. They remind me of someone, I just can't remember who."

She shrugged. "Actually, they're contact lenses.

My eyes are green."

"Really?" He studied her some more. Imagined her with green eyes. They didn't fit. "Is anything else about you fake?"

She gave a rueful shrug. "My bra is padded. A lot." Another shrug. "Just in case I do manage the pickup thing. I wouldn't want you to be disappointed."

His gaze dropped to the curve of her breasts above the tight dress. As he stared, she trailed a fingertip over her skin and heat washed through him. "I don't think you'll disappoint me."

Shit, he wanted to suggest they go right now, but she wasn't even halfway through her wine. She took a sip, then licked her lips. Was she doing it on purpose? Was she a practiced tease? Was this a regular thing for her—picking up strange men in bars? Part of him wanted her to be just that, so that he could take her home, fuck both their brains out, and then walk away.

"Do you do this sort of thing often?" he asked.

"What? Trip over my feet and get rescued by handsome strangers?"

"Pick up men in bars?"

He half expected her to be offended, but she appeared to actually consider the question. Finally, she shrugged. "I like sex."

"That's good."

"However, I really don't want a relationship

right now. I'm concentrating on my career, and boyfriends expect too much attention."

"We're so needy."

She studied him, head cocked on one side. "I somehow don't think you're needy at all, Gideon."

"Actually, I'm feeling pretty needy right now."

Her eyes widened. She blinked at him a couple of times. "You are?"

"Hell, yeah." He shifted his legs beneath the table until he came into contact with hers. "Do you have your own place?" he asked.

She swallowed. "Can't we go to yours?"

"I live with my mother."

"Not a good idea, then. I don't think I'm ready to meet your mother just yet."

"And it might cramp my style."

She giggled, then the smile faded from her face and she stared across at him with those huge eyes. She caught her lower lip between sharp white teeth and bit down, her lashes lowering, nostrils flaring.

Jeez, she was doing a job on him. She had the pickup thing down to perfection. Or maybe she was just a natural flirt. But he thought not. Whatever she was doing, it was working.

She slid out of the booth and held out her hand to him. "Let's go."

CHAPTER FOURTEEN

"When you are asked if you can do a job, tell 'em, 'Certainly I can!' Then get busy and find out how to do it." Theodore Roosevelt

So far, so good…

She was in a cab, sitting next to Gideon Frome. Heading to her place. For sex!

Never going to happen…

He hadn't recognized her. She'd been a little worried when he'd mentioned her eyes were familiar, but hopefully she'd put him off the scent with the contact lens comment. She'd been amazed by how well she scrubbed up. She'd decided the makeup thing was beyond her and had booked an appointment at a salon after work. They'd provided the wig as well. A little boutique she passed everyday had sold her the clothes. Looking in the mirror before she left, for the first time, she'd actually believed she might have a chance at picking him up.

When she'd entered the bar, her gaze had been pulled toward him as though by a magnet. And there he was. Sitting on a stool at the long counter. With a blonde at his side. Kate had presumed she was too late, and a mixture of relief and almost disappointment had filled her, together with a sudden urge to go and punch the smug, self-satisfied woman on the nose. She was clearly the real thing. A true blonde bimbo.

She'd have to go away and try again another night. Except she didn't have many other nights. She'd just have to turn up earlier next time. Anyway, he probably wouldn't have looked twice at her. She'd meant to turn around and walk out. Instead she'd taken an unsteady step forward, tripped over her stupid heels, and fallen tits over ass in a spectacularly embarrassing manner.

Grace and beauty. Ha.

Gideon had come to her rescue, like the hero he was known to be.

After that, everything had gone amazingly well. Even the fact that he was living with his mother worked in her favor. The plan depended on them going back to her place. She'd thought she would have to persuade him.

And yet, here they were.

He hadn't spoken since they'd gotten into the cab and she'd given the driver her address, but she could almost feel the intensity of his focus. She cast him a sideways glance and found his gaze fixed on the length of her bare thigh beneath the short skirt of her dress. She was near as dammit naked. But it had worked.

The cab slowed to a halt and she peered out of

the window.

Shit. A checkpoint.

The last thing she wanted to do was get out her paperwork and risk Gideon seeing her real name.

She needn't have worried. He lowered his window, showed his ID, and they were waved straight through.

"Sorry about that," the driver said as they pulled away. "They've been popping up all over the city over the last few weeks. I'm sure they're necessary."

It was amazing how people accepted these limitations. She supposed it was a small price to pay for living in safety, but she didn't like it.

The plan was all set. She'd offer him a drink as soon as they got there. She even had some scotch—which was obviously his drink of choice— and the crushed Ativan tablets were already in the glass. She'd used five times the dose her mother was taking. She'd read up about them—her mother was on some serious stuff. With the dose she was giving him, he'd be out in ten minutes.

A warm hand landed on her thigh and she squeaked.

"You're jumpy," he said.

"Sorry, I was just thinking about the checkpoints. Do you think there's something going on? Are we in danger?"

"I doubt it. The country is safer than it's ever

been."

"Good."

His hand slid up a little higher, fingers curling around the inside of her thigh, and every muscle locked up.

Oh Lord.

Luckily, the cab pulled up outside her apartment, and she breathed again.

Just keep your head, Kate. And your padded bra.

She scrambled out of the cab, and he followed. She nearly tripped again on the way to the door, and she gripped his arm tightly. Stupid shoes were going in the trash tomorrow.

As she fumbled with her keys, he stood beside her, hands shoved in his pockets. Finally, she managed to let them in, dropping her bag on the small hall table before leading him through to the sitting room. Now that she had him here, her nerves were fluttering. What if the plan didn't work? What if he caught on? What if he could somehow taste the drug in his drink? There were a thousand things that could go wrong.

What would happen when he woke in the morning? Would he know he'd been drugged? Could she convince him she'd been so boring that he'd fallen asleep on her? Maybe she should act offended?

Oh Christ, just get through the next few

minutes. Worry about tomorrow…tomorrow.

"Nice place," he said, as he entered the room behind her.

"Thank you." She'd gone around earlier and removed any incriminating photographs that might give away her true identity, and the place looked a little bare to her.

He shrugged out of his jacket and tossed it on the sofa. Underneath he wore a shoulder holster with a pistol. She stared at it, unable to drag her eyes away. Gun controls in the city were harsh. No one except the security services was allowed to carry weapons. As she watched, he unbuckled the holster and slid it off his shoulder, dropping it on top of his jacket. "Sorry," he said as he caught her staring. "Part of the job."

"The job?"

"Secret Service."

"Oh." He stepped toward her, and she retreated, cleared her throat. "Can I get you a drink?"

Not waiting for an answer—in case it was *no*—she headed to the cabinet, her hands shaking as she reached for the bottle of scotch.

She'd been thinking of it as some sort of game, but the gun made everything, including the danger, very real. If he caught her, would he shoot her? She could almost feel the bullet pierce her body and she winced. Guns had always terrified her.

After unscrewing the top from the bottle, she poured a measure into the glass she'd prepared earlier. She swirled the amber liquid as she lifted the glass to the light. Could you see the drug? But it just looked like scotch to her. Hopefully it would just taste like scotch.

As she turned to hand it to him, his arms came around her waist from behind and she was pulled back against his body. The air left her lungs and her hands wobbled so the scotch splashed over her fingers. She gripped the glass harder while her brain raced.

Get a grip.

Taking a deep breath, she pulled away and turned around, holding the shaking glass out in front of her.

Take it. Take the freaking thing.

He took it and her breath left her in a whoosh.

Drink it. Drink it.

For a brief hopeful moment, she thought he was actually going to heed her internal urging. He lifted the glass, stared at her over the rim. Then, at the last moment, he lowered it again.

"Later," he said. "Right now, there's something I want way more than drink."

"There is?" This was not going according to plan.

"Oh yeah."

Placing the glass down on the table, he unbuttoned his shirt, then stripped it off, dropping it to the floor.

Oh crap.

He took a step toward her. She took a step back, her mind racing. Maybe she should just give in. Shit, would her wig stay on? Probably not. No way was this happening.

Another step. She backed up again and found herself against the wall with nowhere to go and Gideon still advancing. She slipped out under his arm and turned, then headed for her bedroom, picking up his drink on the way.

"Come through," she murmured.

His eyes narrowed but he followed her without a word.

Once in her room, she pushed the door closed behind her. She handed him the glass as casually as she could, then went and sat on the bed, watching him.

Come on.

He tossed the drink back in one go and she almost sagged with relief.

At last.

He frowned. Could he taste the drug? But then he put the glass down on the bedside table and came to sit beside her. He kicked off his shoes, then reached down and tugged off his socks.

How long would the drug take?

Too long.

He reached for her as she jumped to her feet. "I'm just...going to the bathroom. Freshen up."

She could feel his gaze on her as she walked across the room, but he didn't speak, and she made it out. Once in the bathroom, she rested her forehead against the cool glass of the mirror, then slowly raised her head. She didn't recognize herself. She loitered for a couple of minutes but didn't dare stay too long.

When she got back to the bedroom, he was in the bed. His pants were folded over the chair. The sheet was pulled up over his hips and he'd bunched the pillows behind his head. His eyes were closed, and for a moment she thought the drug had already kicked in. Except no way could it work that fast.

As she stepped closer, his lashes flickered open. "Sorry," he murmured. "I must be more beat than I thought. I haven't been sleeping too well since I got back to the city."

"Just relax," she replied. "We have all night."

"Come here."

She sat down on the bed, then shifted so she was facing him, took his hand. She studied him for a moment—it seemed almost unbelievable. Gideon Frome was in her bed. Naked. Even if he was drugged.

When she looked up, his eyes were half closed.

"You're sweet," he mumbled, and his words were drawled. He was going under.

His lashes drooped. His breathing was slow and even.

He was out cold.

CHAPTER FIFTEEN

"I've always said, 'If you need Viagra, you're probably with the wrong girl.'" Donald Trump

Gideon opened his eyes and winced.

Daylight streamed through the open curtains.

Where the hell was he?

And why the hell was he even having to ask that question?

He sat up. He was naked in a strange bed. Then it came back to him. The bar. The blonde. She wasn't here now. He was alone.

He scrubbed a hand through his hair and winced. His scalp felt sensitive and there was a fierce ache behind his eyes. His gaze wandered around the room, settled on the glass on the bedside table. He picked it up and sniffed, but all he could smell was whisky.

Too much to drink?

Not a chance.

He had a vague memory of her holding his hand as he fell asleep, but that was all they had done.

What the fuck?

He got out of bed. His pants were folded on the chair and he grabbed them and dragged them on, then sat on the bed and pulled on his socks and shoes. His shirt was nowhere to be seen. He crossed the room and opened the door, then came to an abrupt halt.

She was curled up on the sofa, long blonde hair over her face, still wearing the dress from last night.

She'd picked him up in a bar and brought him home and he'd…fallen asleep.

Yeah. Of course he had.

He walked silently across the floor, found his shirt on the back of the sofa and shrugged into it, then stood looking down at her for a minute. She didn't stir.

Moving away, he wandered around the room; it was a nice place. What had she said she did? A computer programmer? She must be a good one to afford an apartment like this in this part of town. His jacket and gun still lay where he'd left them.

He opened a couple of closets, but found nothing to tell him anything about her. Her bag was lying by the front door where she'd dropped it. He picked it up and took it back with him to the chair opposite her and sat down. Her lashes were still closed, and her breathing was even. He tipped out the contents onto the coffee table in front of him. There was a phone and a small hand-held tablet computer. Both were password protected.

Then he found her ID. What the hell? He stared at it for a long time.

She'd said her name was Leia. Clearly, she'd lied.

Kate Buchanan. He knew that name, but the picture on the ID looked totally different from the woman lying opposite. Except for the eyes. She'd told him they were contact lenses. Again—she'd lied.

It came to him then just who she was. Stella's baby sister.

He'd hardly noticed her back when he'd been engaged to Stella. She'd been a gawky, geeky teenager, tagging along behind them. If he remembered rightly, Stella had tried to set him up with her at the president's party.

Why had Kate Buchanan lied about who she was?

And why had he slept like the dead?

Time to find out. He shoved the contents back into the bag, tucked it by the side of his chair, then sat back.

"Kate." She didn't move, and he spoke again, louder this time. "Kate!"

She sat up abruptly. As she stared at him, horror filled her wide eyes. Then she visibly pulled herself together. She put her hand up to her head, swung her legs around, and sat up straight. "Gideon. You're awake."

"I am. I slept like the dead. Very unlike me."

"You just passed out. I was worried."

"You didn't think to get help?"

She licked her lips, glanced around. "I thought maybe you were…on something. Drugs or…" She shrugged. "If I'd called an ambulance, they might have reported it, and I didn't want to get you into trouble."

"Nice of you."

She ignored the comment. "You seemed okay."

"Other than being unconscious."

"I thought it best to let you sleep it off. And look, here you are all…perky and awake." She shrugged again. "Well, I suppose you'll want to leave now."

He crossed his legs, smiled. "No rush. Why don't we spend a little while and get to know each other?"

"Oh no. I don't want to take up your valuable time. I'm sure you have things to do, and really, you don't want to know more about me. I'm boring. Honestly, you're not the first man to fall asleep on me."

"I don't find you at all boring, Kate."

"Oh, but —" She broke off, looked at him. "What did you call me?"

"Kate?"

"Why would you call me that?"

"Because it's your name." He reached down

and picked up her bag. Her eyes opened even wider. She blinked.

"You looked in my bag?"

"I was curious."

"That's not…very nice."

His lips twitched. At least he wasn't bored. He was intrigued. And he had an urge to see her as she really was. Maybe that would spark his memory of her. "Why don't you lose the disguise, Kate, and then we can sit down and have a chat about what happened last night."

"Look, last night was just supposed to be fun, and I—"

"The disguise, Kate."

Her lips tightened in a mutinous line. For a moment, he thought she was going to refuse, and he had no clue what his next move should be. What she'd done—lied about her identity to a member of the Secret Service—was a crime she could be locked away for. Though he wasn't ready to take that route. Yet. He wanted to understand why she'd done what she'd done, and then he'd decide.

After tugging down the hem of her dress, she got to her feet, then cast him a dark look and stalked into the bathroom. "Nerfherder." He heard the muttered word as she passed him.

What the hell was a nerfherder?

• • •

Kate stared at herself in the mirror. Why the hell had she fallen asleep with Gideon in the apartment? She should have been on her guard. Great savior of the world she was.

Auspex had set up a program for her on her tablet, so taking the retinal scan had been easy. All she'd had to do was pry open Gideon's eyelids and place the tablet in front of his face, then let it do its stuff. According to her tablet, the scan had worked, and Gideon's retina was now recorded.

Then she'd pulled the sheet up over him and left the room, shutting the door firmly behind her.

She hadn't been able to upload the scan because she was offline; it would have to wait until she got to the office in the morning. She couldn't risk doing it from here in case it was picked up by someone else.

With no clue how long the drugs would last, she'd had no choice but to wait. She wanted to know when he woke up so she could stop him wandering around her apartment and peering in places he shouldn't peer. Like her purse. Instead, she'd fallen asleep.

Jesus. She was totally crap at this spy thing.

But like Gideon, she hadn't been sleeping well lately—it was hard with the weight of the world on her shoulders. The relief had been too much, and she'd just closed her eyes for a second…

And woken to find him sitting opposite, staring at her.

She whipped the wig off her head and tossed it in the trash. Her hair was secured under a skullcap, and she peeled that off as well, then ran her fingers through, fluffing up the flattened strands. Next, she pulled off the thick false lashes, then splashed her face with cold water. When she looked at her image, she had eyeliner halfway down her face and lots of freckles. She wiped away the black stuff, and there she was in all her red-haired glory. Not even red, really, true ginger. Ugh.

The door in the opposite wall led directly to her bedroom and she hurried through, replacing the dress with jeans and a T-shirt.

She opened the door and stepped out just as he came in from the kitchen. Making himself at home. He carried two mugs of coffee but stopped when he caught sight of her. His lips twitched.

Yeah, because she was so freaking funny.

She scowled, and his smile was wiped away. He came toward her and handed her a coffee. It was black and strong, exactly the way she didn't like it. She took it from him and placed it on the coffee table, then lowered herself to the sofa. The sooner they got this over with, the sooner she could get rid of him and be on her way to the office.

He sat down opposite and studied her.

Somehow, she managed not to twitch.

"Freckles," he said.

"Yup."

"And red hair."

He was so observant.

"I remember you now."

"I'm hard to forget."

"I can't believe I didn't see it, though the wig made a huge difference." His gaze dropped over her figure. "Not to mention the padded bra. So," he said, "are you going to tell me what this is about? Why the disguise?"

"I don't suppose 'no' is an option."

"Not unless you want to be taken into the Secret Service for questioning."

"You wouldn't."

"Of course I would. You could be a security risk. Using a false identity to get close to a Secret Service agent. You could be locked away without a trial."

She gritted her teeth but was quite aware that he was telling the truth. At least he hadn't accused her of drugging him. Yet. Did he even suspect?

She could hardly save the world if she was locked up. While she was sure her father would get her out eventually, in the meantime, a nuclear bomb would go off, likely triggering a war that could kill millions. Not an option. And she still had to find Stella.

So she had no choice but to totally humiliate herself.

She could do it.

She took a deep breath and forced a smile. "Look, okay, this is really embarrassing."

"Go ahead."

She took another deep breath. "I wanted to sleep with you."

Had she managed to shock him? Though it must have been clear—she'd almost dragged him here and torn off his clothes.

"Why?"

What would convince him? The truth? No—only a lie would do in these circumstances. "I had a crush on you when I was a teenager."

"So far so good."

"Obviously, you were totally off-limits back then. You know the whole engaged-to-my-sister thing. But that's not the case anymore and when you came back, I asked Stella if she would try and arrange for us to…get together."

"She spoke to me at the president's birthday party."

She sniffed. "Did she? She never mentioned it."

"Probably because I said I wasn't interested." He shrugged. "She told me you were looking for a relationship."

"No. I'm not."

He ignored her comment. "I don't do relationships."

"Neither do I."

"But you still wanted to have sex with me?"

"Yes."

They were silent for a minute. Maybe it was time for a little fabrication. "Stella told me you liked blondes. That you'd gotten a reputation for one-night stands with blondes you picked up in bars. So I thought—why not?"

"Why indeed?" he muttered.

Maybe he didn't like the idea that he was getting a reputation. Hard luck. He shouldn't be such a man slut. "I was pretty sure that you would be a huge disappointment and I would get you out of my system once and for all."

"Well, I was certainly that. I fell asleep on you."

"It was probably just as well. Some things are meant to stay in the realms of fantasy." She gave him a bright smile. "Anyway, so that's it." She wanted to add something to the effect that he could go now, but she thought that might be pushing her luck.

Did he believe her?

He sat back and sipped his coffee, looking at her over the mug. She had to hold herself still to prevent herself twitching. "Maybe you should head home and get some more sleep. You must have been tired."

"I must have been."

"It's probably an age thing." She was definitely pushing her luck.

"No doubt." He put his empty mug down and stood up, then crossed over to where he'd placed his things the night before. He slid the shoulder holster over his shirt, buckling it on. With the weapon, he seemed to change, become a different person, and she realized what she'd been doing.

Baiting Gideon Frome.

Hero of the Wall. Second-in-command of the notorious Secret Service. A dangerous man.

He pulled on his jacket over the top. He was leaving and she blew out her breath, almost sagged into the seat. Then she pushed herself to her feet and wiped her hands down the side of her jeans. "I'll see you out."

"Thank you."

Was there a hint of irony to his words? Probably.

She led the way to the front door. As she moved to open it, he placed a hand on her shoulder to stop her, and she turned to face him.

"Well, goodbye, then," she said.

He didn't move, just stood there looking down at her.

"I'll call you," he said.

What for?

Before she could ask, he was gone.

CHAPTER SIXTEEN

"My fellow Americans, ask not what your country can do for you, ask what you can do for your country." John F. Kennedy

Kate Buchanan was up to something, but right now Gideon couldn't even imagine what.

He didn't go home. Instead, he headed straight for his office. After passing through security, he took the elevator to the fifth floor where the medical unit was situated.

He checked the roster and found a name he recognized, Ana Torres. Another old army buddy. A paramedic who'd treated him when he'd been injured five years ago. They'd had a fling, then she'd finished her term and come back to Washington when her mother had been ill.

She was a friend, and he could rely on her to keep this to herself. He wanted the tests done privately. While he wasn't sure why, he didn't want to make his investigation official at this point. Not until he knew for sure what Kate had done and had had the chance to look into her a little. Perhaps had a stab at guessing why she had done it.

Half an hour later, Ana brought back the

results.

"You were right, there were traces of Ativan in your system. If you took it last night, then it would easily have been enough to knock you out. You want me to put in a formal report?"

"And let everyone know I was stupid enough to fall for some hooker trying to scam me? No, thank you. I scared the crap out of her—she won't be trying it on anyone else. Plus, I was home before it hit me, so no harm done. I just wanted to be sure."

"Well, it's sure." She patted his arm. "You're a good man, Captain. I'm not sure how well you're going to fit in around here. And keep away from hookers."

"I will."

He headed for his office on the top floor of the building. A corner suite, spacious, with windows looking out over the White House. Sitting down at his desk, he powered up his computer.

She'd goddamn drugged him.

What the hell?

He rubbed at his forehead where a dull ache still throbbed behind his eyes.

Could she be working with the rebels? Did he have a duty to report her? She'd be arrested, despite who her father was. Or maybe because of who he was. Stella was also high up in the administration. Who knew what secrets Kate had access to?

Except it didn't make sense.

Why drug him? What could she have possibly gained from it?

He lowered his head to the retinal scan that gave him access to the files. Maybe if he dug into her background, he'd find an explanation.

Retinal scan accepted.

If sex was what she had wanted, she hadn't needed to drug him. Could it be some sort of blackmail? Had she taken incriminating photographs of him while he'd been out cold? But what would be incriminating?

These days any whiff of homosexuality could send a career nosediving. Had she had an accomplice?

If she was some sort of insurgent, then she was pretty inept. She'd been fast asleep this morning when he'd woken, which had given him the chance to search her apartment. Or had that been part of the plan?

If it was blackmail, then he could expect to hear from her soon. Or maybe she was planning to sell the photos. *If* there were any photos.

His hand reached for the phone. He should report her, but he couldn't make himself do it. They'd bring her in for questioning.

He knew what that was like. They'd "questioned" him after Aaron had disappeared.

He hadn't known anything, but that hadn't stopped them. They'd used chemicals and more... traditional techniques. He'd never forget the sensation of drowning.

In the end, they'd been convinced he didn't know anything, and he'd been released. By then his father had been dead, by his own hand. His mother a broken woman.

No, he wasn't prepared to go that route yet.

He typed in Kate's name and a photo came up. Red hair and pale skin.

She had a degree in computer technology. Had finished not quite top of her class and then gotten a job in Homeland Security. Which meant her own security clearance must be perfect.

If she had approached him in the bar last night as herself, introduced herself as Stella's sister, would he have gone home with her?

He doubted it.

So maybe she had been telling the truth and she'd just wanted to pick him up, have sex with him. And she'd drugged him instead because...

Shit, he had no clue.

He remembered the way she had urged the drink on him as soon as they had entered the apartment. Obviously, sex had never been on her agenda. The drug had acted fast. So she was lying about that.

Unless she had some sort of weird fetish about

sex with unconscious guys.

Now he really was reaching.

He read the file through. Then started from the beginning and scanned it again. Reading between the lines, she was a geek and a tomboy. She wasn't a member of any clubs; her Political Officer had recently black-marked her for not attending the morning religious service. Her credit card statements showed she paid very little for clothes and makeup and didn't eat out much, but there were regular donations to various charities and there was a relatively large payment to Patty's Beauty Parlor just the previous day. Preparations for meeting him? Her little disguise?

By the end of the report, however, he was still none the wiser about what she was up to.

He made a list of names, starting with Stella. He'd talk to a few people, make some inquiries, find out exactly who Kate Buchanan was. Then he'd go see her again. Though maybe he'd avoid drinking or eating anything she gave him, and maybe they'd manage that sex this time.

He would do it for his country.

CHAPTER SEVENTEEN

"There is nothing more corrupting, nothing more destructive of the noblest and finest feelings of our nature, than the exercise of unlimited power."
William Henry Harrison

Kate slipped into the building just as the morning prayer meeting was finishing. Since it was Saturday, the place wasn't as busy as usual and it wasn't so easy to avoid being noticed. She hurried across the foyer, aware of Teresa standing at the front of the room, watching her, eyes narrowed.

She had an inkling that she was going to get some trouble from the new Political Officer, but maybe she could avoid her and put it off for a few weeks. After that… Well, she doubted it would matter.

Either they would all be dead, or she'd be in prison no doubt undergoing some horribly painful torture. So this was it, really.

She'd drugged a Secret Service agent. Stolen his retinal scan. She'd be tried for treason and no doubt be executed. After they tortured her.

She really didn't want to die.

Plus, she hated pain.

Life sucked.

Though to be honest, none of this seemed real.

She waited at security as they went through her bag. They scanned her tablet and phone, but passed them, and she released her breath. Teresa was heading her way, and she needed to hurry. Luckily, someone stopped to talk to the other woman, and Kate could almost sense the waves of frustration.

She didn't need Auspex to predict that she could expect a visit sometime soon.

After letting herself into her office, she switched on the systems, including Auspex, then pulled out her tablet and linked it up to the main system.

I'm uploading the retinal scan.

Not a minute later, Auspex replied. *I have accessed the Secret Service files.*

Bring up files on Stella Buchanan.

Then she sat back and tried not to fidget. He'd tell her when he had anything.

A few seconds later, a list of files flashed up. There were clearly a few Stellas. She found her sister's file and clicked on the link, her heart pounding. She flicked through the information, but there was nothing incriminating, just what she'd expect really. No references to any current activity. No record of an arrest or detention of any kind.

So far, so good. It didn't explain where Stella

was, but at least it didn't appear that she was locked up and being tortured.

She tapped her fingers on the desk, then leaned forward and typed in:

Bring up files on Katherine Buchanan.

There was even less. A background file, including an education and job history, her credit card details—nothing bad there. No mention of drugging a Secret Service agent last night. So Gideon hadn't reported her. Yet.

More good news.

Bring up files on yellow alert 10245.

She tapped some more, but when the log came up there was nothing of interest. Just a document stating receipt of the alert, a copy of the info dump, and a note that the alert had been reviewed and assigned a threat level of negligible.

She checked the info dump, but it was the same one she had sent, no changes. Various references to a nuclear device and no reference to her sister.

It made no sense. They were the National Threat Assessment Center. Why couldn't they see a goddamn threat when it was shoved under their noses?

She sat back and took a deep breath.

Run a threat level analysis on alert 10245.

There is an 85 percent chance of Report 10245 resulting in terrorist activity that would be harmful to the American people.

Damn, it had gone up again.

Her phone rang, and she glanced at the caller ID. Just in case Gideon had suddenly realized she'd drugged him (how could he not have? It hurt her head thinking about it) and was calling to say he was on his way to arrest her. That would hardly happen, would it? Instead, it was her sister. A huge wave of relief washed over her, and she sagged in the chair.

She picked up before Stella could vanish again. "Where have you been?"

"Hi, sis, sorry. I had to go out of town on business." Her words sounded light and untroubled.

"And you couldn't call? I was worried." She closed her mouth, keeping any potentially incriminating words in, just in case the call was being monitored. She thought not, but couldn't be sure. Actually, she wasn't sure of anything anymore. She would get Auspex to run a check.

"What is there to worry about? It was just a report I had to do for the president."

She was lying. Kate was sure of it, but her sister had always been the ultimate in cool. Most of the time she had no clue what Stella was thinking. The total opposite of herself. Stella would make a much better savior of the world than Kate ever would.

She'd once told Kate that she was going to be

the first female president of the United States. They'd have to restart the democratic process for that to happen, and while that was scheduled to occur in the next year, Kate wasn't holding her breath.

"Are you back?" Kate asked.

"Yes, and I thought we could meet for lunch."

"Of course. Our usual place?"

"No, it's such a lovely day maybe we could grab a picnic in the park."

Picnic? Stella? The two words did not seem to match up in any way. Dread formed a big heavy lump in her stomach. "Are you okay?"

Stella laughed. "Of course. Just in need of some fresh air. I've been cooped up in meetings for days, hardly seeing the outside."

"I'll meet you in Lafayette Square at one, then. And I'll bring the food."

"Thanks, sis. I missed you."

Kate put the phone down feeling almost worse than before she had picked it up. Like there was something wrong, something big and ominous looming around the corner.

Everything was fucked up, but she had no clue how or why. Just that her safe world was crumbling around her.

She spent the last half-hour before lunch actually doing some work. Going through the chatter, reporting the reds and the yellows, hesitating over a code green, then gnawing on her lower lip while she decided to delete it or send it. She flicked through the info dump and then ran it through Auspex.

What is the probability that green alert 22548 will lead to deportation?

Negligible.

Execution?

Negligible.

Relief washed over her. But just to be safe...

What is the probability that harm will come to this person if I send this alert?

Probability: 98 percent.

She frowned. *Explain.*

The systems show the subject is a donor match for a heart transplant needed by a primary Party member.

Kate's blood ran cold.

The heart and other useful organs will be harvested, and the remainder will be incinerated.

Icy dread prickled down her spine.

Do they take body parts from people they detain often?

At this moment, if there is a primary Party member on the waiting list, and an alien is a confirmed match, they will be utilized.

Her brain couldn't wrap itself around this. Nausea churned in her stomach, acid crawling up her throat. Part of her didn't believe it. Didn't want to believe it.

It certainly wasn't general knowledge.

People wouldn't accept that, would they?

She couldn't.

Kate pressed the spot between her eyes. The spot that hurt. Then she reached out and deleted the code green from the feed, removing all traces of its existence. Had they noticed there had been no code greens in the last few days? It was unheard of, and at some point, it was going to strike someone as a little odd. Would they be able to trace the deletions? She thought she'd been thorough, but for all she knew, the Secret Service had geeks of their own who would spot her illegal activity a mile away.

She didn't know. Right now, she didn't care. She'd known the perfect world they'd created here within America was maybe not quite perfect, but she'd never suspected that her whole way of life was an illusion built on the deaths of anyone who was not deemed to belong.

Hopefully democracy would soon be reinstated. Then these things could be brought out into the open, changed. She had to hope that this was not the will of the people.

It was a little early for lunch, but she had to get out of there.

She closed everything down and headed out. As she passed through security, she caught sight of

Teresa heading her way. She speeded up.

Once the revolving doors had disgorged her onto Connecticut Avenue, she stood for a moment soaking up the fresh air. It was a beautiful day, the sun shining, the sky blue—not a cloud in sight, ominous or otherwise.

On the way to the park, Kate headed for a small café that did food to-go. Her stomach was still churning, but she hadn't eaten breakfast, so she needed something. Also, she didn't want Stella to see how unsettled she was. For the first time, it occurred to her that maybe Stella condoned this sort of activity. She couldn't believe that of her own sister. Wouldn't. So she bought crusty rolls, baked on-site, filled with lettuce and creamy brie cheese—American, of course, but just as good, if not better, than the French variety. Which was just as well, since they hadn't had imports from Europe for years. She hated things that reminded her that a whole world existed beyond the Wall. The news reports were scant, the idea being *Why would Americans want to know?* They had everything they needed right here. Still, maybe they should change the name from brie to something more American so as not to remind them.

She bought apple pie for dessert to make up for the brie, and a couple of bottles of water.

There was a checkpoint at the entrance to the

park, and a sign.

This park has been designated A Members of the Loyalist Party Only area.

That was new.

Suddenly she wasn't so keen to go in there. It reeked of elitism, although she supposed that Party membership was available to everyone, so it wasn't really elitist. Well, obviously, not everyone—you had to be American. But that was just about everyone left in the country.

But she needed to see Stella, so she pressed her palm to the scanner and waved her paperwork at the Secret Service guard.

She was early, but Stella was already seated at the bench by the small lake. She was staring out over the water. Stella was beautiful, just Gideon's type. Tall and blonde, though more conservatively dressed than his usual pickups, in a dark-maroon suit and white shirt. She jumped as Kate came to a halt beside her, as though she'd been engrossed in her own thoughts, ones that were not particularly happy.

She rose to her feet, graceful, a smile on her face, and wrapped Kate in a tight hug. Kate stood unmoving, surprise washing through her. Stella was not the touchy-feely type. As children, she had been, but something had happened when she was fifteen—something she had never spoken about. After that, she'd very rarely initiated contact.

Kate tentatively put her arms around her sister and hugged her back. Stella tensed for a moment and then relaxed. Finally, she pulled away.

"Are you all right?" Kate asked. Of course she wasn't all right. That much was clear.

Her sister gave a somewhat forced smile. "I'm fine, it's just been a long week and I've missed Joe."

"Haven't you seen him yet?"

"No, I just drove back. He's at work. I'll see him tonight. I wanted to check my baby sister was okay."

Oh God, what did she know? "Why wouldn't I be?"

"I guess because you always were a trouble magnet and there's a lot of trouble around right now."

"Is there?"

"Later." Stella nodded toward the plastic bag. "I hope that's food, because I left without breakfast."

"Where have you been?" Kate asked, perching on the bench and opening the brown paper bag.

Stella sat beside her and took the roll she offered, bit into it, chewed, and swallowed. Kate presumed it was top secret or something and she wasn't going to say.

Stella shifted on the bench so that she was facing her. "New York."

Kate had always wanted to visit New York when she was younger. Now the name started all sorts of alarm bells ringing in her head. Rumored to be headquarters to the rebels, New York had been mentioned in alert 10245. It was a no-go spot and getting a travel permit there was an impossibility.

"What were you doing in New York?"

"I wish I could tell you."

Kate put her roll back in the bag, her throat too constricted to swallow. There was that nausea again, swirling around in her stomach. She'd wanted to confide in Stella, tell her about Auspex and the possible nuclear threat, about some of the other things she had learned over the last week or so. The deaths, the deportations, the organs, drugging Gideon... But she couldn't, because she didn't trust anyone. She loved her sister, but for the first time, it occurred to her that Stella might have been in the alert report for a reason. Maybe she was somehow involved. Kate didn't want to believe it. But there were lots of things she'd prefer not to believe. That didn't mean they weren't true.

Suddenly she was glad Stella had chosen here to meet up rather than at the busy restaurant close to the White House where they usually lunched.

Even if her sister wasn't involved in something bad, there was always the risk that whatever Kate decided to do would reverberate through her family. That was the way it worked. Guilt by association.

But maybe her sister could say she hadn't seen her in a long time, that they weren't close. Maybe it wouldn't rip her family apart.

She was deluding herself.

Look at Gideon's family. Aaron hadn't done anything nearly as bad as what she'd already done. All he'd done was disappear. Although these days, that was enough to incriminate you. That was another way the administration controlled them all. Do anything out of line and the people you love will suffer. It was effective; Gideon's father had committed suicide over the disgrace.

What would hers do? He was such a proud man. And her mother. God, her mother was already taking sleeping pills strong enough to knock out an elephant—or a Secret Service agent.

Stella had also stopped eating. "Look," she said. "I can't tell you why, so don't ask, but I want you to forget about this meeting."

"What?"

"If anyone asks about me, say we aren't close, we fell out, and you haven't seen me in a while."

It was what she had been thinking herself. That only made her feel worse. She swallowed. "Why, Stella? What's happening?"

"Nothing. I hope." She tossed the rest of her

food in the trashcan. "Christ, I was crazy to come here."

Kate stared at her. Her sister had said *Christ*. That was so not Stella. She never took the Lord's name in vain. Something was seriously messing with her. She'd been fine before this trip, so Kate could only presume that something had happened.

"So why did you? Come here, I mean?"

"I just wanted to see you. Tell you that whatever happens, I love you."

"You're scaring me, Stella."

"You should be scared. I wish there was somewhere you could go, away from here, but there's nowhere. The world has shrunk, and we're stuck in our little bit of it. And what we've made of it. How have things come to this?"

She'd never seen her sister like this. What had happened in New York?

Stella shook her head. "I'm sorry. Now I've just worried you and you said you wanted to talk to me about something. What was it?"

She couldn't tell her now. Not when Stella was so freaked out about something else. And when Kate had no clue what her sister was involved with. She was alone in this. and she didn't want to be. She could sense her panic rising. She forced it down and curved her mouth into a smile. "Nothing important," she said.

Stella studied her for a moment. "Are you still

messing around with that computer stuff?"

Kate looked away for a moment. She hadn't been aware Stella even knew.

"Please, Kate. I won't say anything to anyone. I know that's why you took the job at Homeland Security, but you have to trust me. This is important."

She nodded. "I've been working on a few projects."

"Do any of those projects include a way I can contact you without anyone knowing? With no record?"

"Why would you…" she trailed off. She had an idea Stella wasn't giving anything else away. Not today. Instead she gave a brisk nod. "Dial my ordinary number. Then add **865 on the end. I might not get it immediately. It will be re-routed to my server at Homeland Security. It's not monitored."

"Thank you. Hopefully, I won't need to use it. I'm probably being paranoid."

"There's a lot of that going around right now."

"Yes." Stella pushed herself to her feet, and Kate followed. She didn't think either of them were in the mood for good old American apple pie today. She dropped the carrier bag in the trash.

They stood awkwardly for a moment, neither seeming to know what else to say.

"I'm going to keep my distance for a while,"

Stella said.

Except that Kate didn't have a while. She only had a matter of weeks before everything went to total crap. Which meant she might not see Stella again. Suddenly she wanted to pour out everything, and she had to clamp her lips closed to stop the words tumbling out.

Stella closed the space between them, wrapped her arms around her, and gave her a hug. Two in one day. Kate wrapped her own arms around her sister and held her tight.

They stayed that way for a minute, then finally Stella pulled away. She took a deep breath. "Everything will be all right."

The words sounded like goodbye.

Kate sank back onto the bench as her sister walked away.

Stella had always been so stable, so strong, so sure of what she wanted.

Now the foundations of Kate's world were crumbling. She'd always believed, deep down, that if someone good like Stella could be part of the Party, then it must have some redeeming qualities. Now the last of that reassurance had been snatched from her, leaving her with nothing.

She sat on the bench for a long time, gazing out over the lawns. It was beautiful and peaceful…and for Party members only.

She shoved herself to her feet, staggered the

short distance to the trashcan, and hurled up what little she'd eaten of her lunch. Collapsing back, she wiped her mouth, then took a gulp of water.

Time to pull herself together, get back to the office, and try to decide what her next move should be.

Maybe it wouldn't be a bad thing if she did nothing. Then maybe the whole of humanity would come to an end.

CHAPTER EIGHTEEN

"My fellow Americans, we are and always will be a nation of immigrants. We were strangers once, too." Barack Obama

Gideon watched through the binoculars as Kate got shakily to her feet.

She'd seemed okay when she'd arrived. He'd followed her from her office—he'd gone there to invite her for lunch—to see if he could work out what made her tick. What interest she had in drugging a Secret Service agent. He'd called as he got close and had been told that she'd already left for lunch. He'd arrived at her building as she was exiting. He'd followed her, seen her meet with her sister. The two were clearly close.

He was too far away to hear their conversation, but it had seemed intense. Was Kate telling her sister about him? That she'd tried to sleep with Stella's ex-fiancée?

Stella was not likely to be bothered. Theirs had never been a passionate relationship, more one formed on mutual respect and expediency. And thinking back, she'd never seemed interested in the physical side of things.

Whatever the sisters had talked about, they'd

parted as friends if the hug was anything to go by.

When Kate left the park, he followed long enough to make sure she was heading back to work, then he got a cab back to his own office.

Time to find out everything he could about Kate Buchanan.

Gideon was back outside her office at five-thirty. He was no further ahead with determining what made Kate Buchanan tick. Why would she risk what she must know was her life by drugging a Secret Service agent?

From the reports, he knew that she had a reputation for working late. He wasn't very good at waiting, so he entered the building and asked security to let her know he was here. A quick wave of his Secret Service ID and they were more than happy to comply. Although maybe happy wasn't the right word.

He took a seat where he could see when she emerged from either the elevator or the stairwell, positioning himself so he would get a good look at her expression when she caught sight of him. He'd told the security guy to just tell her someone was waiting to see her. He'd spent the afternoon digging deeper into Kate's files. Reading her school reports. She'd been brilliant. Too brilliant, really. Anything outside the norm these days was looked upon with suspicion. Although, strangely, she'd dumbed down a little in college. Maybe she was bright enough to realize the dangers of being *too* bright. She'd done well enough to get the job of her choice afterward, but not so well as to raise any alarms.

Her old college professor, Oliver Massey, now at Homeland Security, had sponsored her for the job. Despite his position, the man had an amber flag against his name and was not a Party member. As far as Gideon could tell, however, there was no personal relationship between him and Kate. Hardly even a professional one. She had a reputation as a loner, and, until she'd received the black mark from the new Political Officer, had had an exemplary record.

No relationships on file.

Maybe she was telling the truth that she really didn't want a relationship. Which meant that she probably wouldn't be pleased to see him, even without the whole drugging thing hanging over them.

He'd also had a very fruitless meeting with his boss. He'd gone to see him to ask the very relevant question of what the hell he was supposed to be doing for his salary. He was quite aware that Boyd Winters didn't like him, and he knew exactly why. It wasn't guilt — he was sure that wasn't an emotion Boyd wasted time on — but Boyd had to be wondering whether Gideon harbored thoughts of revenge.

"Just relax, get the feel of the place," he'd told him. "You'll be busy soon enough."

He wanted to be busy now. He got into trouble when he wasn't busy. He had a low boredom threshold, and sitting at a desk all day, twiddling his thumbs, was making him twitchy.

He'd pushed it, and Boyd had lost his temper.

"You're fucking here because you're a pretty-boy hero and everybody loves you." Everybody except Boyd, clearly. "But right now we have a lot going on." What? He'd wanted to ask, but Boyd hadn't given him the chance. "So just look pretty, say yes whenever the president asks you anything, and maybe, given time, you might earn some trust."

The implication was *Don't hold your breath*.

Why the hell had he been brought back here? He hadn't meant to return. Hell, he'd had no clue what he was going to do. He'd had money and he'd planned to take his time. As a veteran, he could choose where he lived, and he'd almost decided on somewhere very far from D.C. and the memories. A new start.

Then he'd received the job offer, though "offer" was hardly the right word. You didn't turn down the president of the United States. However much you might want to.

So here he was. Titular second-in-command of the infamous Secret Service. And, so far, he'd done absolutely nothing in return for his impressive salary.

Now he was chasing some crazy idea when he should just have reported Kate and maybe gained a little of that trust.

Not going to happen.

Not yet, anyway, until he learned just what sort of a threat she was.

The door to the stairwell opened and she appeared.

She spotted him straight away, her pale eyes widening as she stared across the space between them. Then her gaze darted from him to search the area.

Did she think he was here to arrest her? She came to a halt in front of him. "What are you doing here?"

It was clear to see why she hadn't gone into politics like her sister. Diplomacy evidently wasn't a strong point. "Maybe I'm here in an official capacity to find out why you haven't been attending morning prayer meetings."

Something flashed in her eyes. Anger, perhaps. Her gaze flicked away from him to across the room, where a Hispanic woman was watching the two of them. "Maybe you'd better go talk to Teresa then."

"Teresa?"

"Our Political Officer."

Ah, the woman who'd reported her. No love lost there. "Actually, I was just passing by—"

"Of course you were." Her expression clearly said she didn't believe him.

He ignored the look and continued, "And decided I'd drop in. I missed lunch and thought we might get an early dinner." She remained silent. "Not pleased to see me?"

She shook herself. "Just surprised. My research led me to believe you were a one-night stand sort of guy, so I wasn't expecting to see you again."

"We hardly had a one-night stand. There were important elements missing. And let's just say that certain aspects of our evening intrigued me enough to want to see you again. So—dinner?"

She pursed her lips. "As it happens, I missed lunch as well."

Now that was interesting. Why had she lied about meeting Stella? Although she had thrown most of her lunch up. "Good. You know somewhere close?"

"There's a steak house just down the way. We can go there. You're not a vegetarian, are you?"

"No. Sounds good. Let's go."

As they exited the building, he rested a hand on the small of her back, and she shot into overdrive. He made her nervous. Part of him liked that. She was clearly aware of him. Part of him wanted her to relax so he could find out about the real Kate Buchanan.

They didn't talk on the walk to the restaurant. She had long legs—and was wearing flat shoes today—and she kept pace with him easily. They didn't hit any checkpoints, but then it was only a five-minute walk. Recently, you couldn't go much farther than that without hitting one. It was worse than when he'd left ten years ago, which was strange. He'd asked some of the guys at the office about it. They'd told him that the order had come down from the president, though no one really knew why. The general consensus was that Harry wanted to look like he was doing something proactive to protect the people. But from what?

There had been so little violence over the last few years that he figured the people just thought of it as a pain in the ass.

The restaurant was typically all-American. Steak-and-apple-pie sort of food. Not his favorite, but most of the eateries in the city were "American" these days. Indian and Chinese, at least by those names, had vanished as though it was unpatriotic to eat in such places. Next they'd be banning pizza. The people needed to remember where they had come from. While they might be American now, the vast majority could not go back many generations before they came from somewhere else.

Some Americans were more American than others, he guessed.

He'd better keep that sort of thought to himself.

The place was nice, with red and white checked tablecloths and wooden beams. The hostess led them to a table by the window. It was early and there were only a couple of other diners across the restaurant from them. He didn't recognize them. They both ordered beers and steaks and he sat back and looked at her. "So," he said. "You researched me?"

She took a sip of beer and picked up a breadstick, nibbling it. "Of course. I'm not an idiot. I don't take total strangers into my home."

"I was never a total stranger."

"No, but you're also not the same man we knew all those years ago."

"I'm not?"

As she studied him, her eyes narrowed. "No. Back then you were sort of...perfect. Like the golden prince. You never did anything wrong and you made it look easy."

Was that how people had seen him? Perfect? That hadn't been how he was at all. "I was never perfect."

"Ha." She crunched on her breadstick. Clearly, she didn't believe him.

"I think it was because I...believed. Believed in the Party, in the long-term aims. It made it easy to be good."

Her brows drew together. "You sound as though you don't believe anymore."

"I wouldn't say that because it would be bordering on treason. I'm just not quite so... idealistic now." Maybe if he hinted at his own doubts, she would open up a little about hers. If she had them. Something occurred to him. Maybe she was some sort of setup, trying to get close to trip him up. If so, he could be walking straight into trouble.

But he didn't think so.

"Unlike yourself," he said. "If I recall rightly, you were always in trouble growing up."

Her eyes narrowed on him. "I thought you didn't remember me at all?"

He grinned. "A few things came back to me when I saw that hair." He waved a hand toward her ponytail, looped over one shoulder. "That's hard to miss."

She sniffed. "I was a good girl."

"If I remember, you were always skipping school. Stella used to worry about you."

"I had this dream about building a spaceship and heading off to the moon and beyond. Stella felt it her job to keep my feet firmly on the ground."

He laughed. "It's strange, but if I would have put money on anyone running off to join the rebels, it would have been you."

Her mouth dropped open. "Of course I would *never* have joined the rebels. I love my country."

"So do the rebels. Just not the way it is now."

"You sound sympathetic."

They were getting onto dangerous ground here. "Not sympathetic. Let's just say that my time away made me see things from a few different points of view. Not that I agree with them. The country has never been so safe, so prosperous. Everyone gets a decent education and good medical service. The waiting list for transplants is the lowest it's ever been."

Something flashed in her eyes, and she swallowed.

"What is it?" he asked.

"Nothing." She put her glass down as if to give herself time to think. "I heard this rumor… I'm sure it's not true."

"What rumor?"

"That the administration isn't deporting all aliens. They're using some of them as organ donors." She shrugged. "I'm sure it's just a hoax. We wouldn't do that."

He wished he was as sure. He'd heard something similar and discounted it because he didn't want to believe something so horrendous.

Now, here was a second source. Just the idea made him feel sick to his stomach. He would look into the matter. "I'm sure it is."

Their food arrived at that moment, and for a few minutes they were silent. She was hungry, eating fast. Finally, she slowed and put her knife and fork down. "That was good. I needed it."

"Why did you miss lunch?"

She glanced away for a moment, then looked back, her eyes shadowed. "Just catching up on work."

"Have you seen your sister recently?"

"No." She cast him a quick glance, then picked up her fork and popped a green bean into her mouth, chewed. "Were you in love with her? Back then, I mean."

The question surprised him. He'd thought she was ignoring the whole engaged-to-her-sister thing, but she clearly believed in facing things head on.

"No. I was maybe in love with the idea of being in love. A natural progression. You could say it was a match made in heaven."

"Then everything went to hell."

"Yes." He had a flashback to that room where they'd "questioned" him. He hadn't longed for Stella as he was sure he would have had their feelings been anything more than perfunctory. "If we'd had real feelings for each other, we would have survived what happened. As it was, it was easy to let go."

"I'm sorry."

"Don't be. If your sister had really loved me, what happened ten years ago would have ruined her life. As it was, she was able to put it behind her."

"As were you."

"As was I."

"And you joined the army, became a hero, and now you've returned triumphant."

"I'm not sure triumphant is the right word."

She shrugged. "Walking into the second-in-command of the Secret Service is pretty impressive."

"Yeah. I'm a real catch for the Service."

A frown tugged at her brows. "You sound bitter."

He hadn't realized how deep that bitterness went. He pushed it down. He was supposed to be finding out about her, not baring his soul. "Not bitter. I guess I've gotten used to a more active life. Sitting at a desk shuffling papers is driving me crazy." He shoved his plate away. "You want anything else?"

"No. I'm full."

"Hmm, so what shall we do next?"

"Go home?"

"Together?"

Shock flared in her eyes.

"I can't believe you haven't thought about it," he said.

Her skin flushed, then went pale, making the freckles stand out. She traced a pattern on the tablecloth with her fingertip, then glanced up to catch his gaze.

He'd thought he was just checking up on her. Trying to discover why she had drugged him, what she was up to.

Now he admitted to himself that, beneath that, he wanted her. Maybe it was all mixed in with the danger and the secrets.

"I promise I won't fall asleep on you again," he murmured.

Was that guilt flickering in her pale eyes?

He reached across and picked up her hand where it lay on the table. He brought it to his mouth and kissed her palm, then bit down on the flesh at the base of her thumb. Desire flared in her face, her lips parting slightly. He let go of her hand and it curled into a fist on the table between them.

He could question her some more in the morning. They hadn't covered half of what he'd wanted to ask, but right now, all those questions didn't seem important.

Just don't drink or eat anything she offers. His lips twitched at the thought.

Maybe that was part of the attraction.

He didn't trust her.

It gave their coming together an edge.

At the same time, he sensed an innate goodness to her. Not that goodness got you very far these days. And those were the sort of thoughts he needed to banish from his head if he wanted to find any peace in this life.

Then it occurred to him. Was that what he really wanted? Peace? He was only thirty-four, even if he did feel a hell of a lot older. Was he ready to just accept the way things were?

Sometimes, he longed for the boy he'd been before his life fell apart, the boy who believed in the ideals on which he'd been brought up. He wasn't sure what had changed him. Was it the interrogation? He remembered thinking *This is unfair. I've done nothing wrong.*

Christ. Looking back, he couldn't believe he'd ever considered life fair. His brother had betrayed the family, his father had killed himself rather than stay and try and pull them back from the brink. His mother...She'd been questioned as well, and he couldn't even bear to think about that. If he did, a black rage built up inside him. If he ever allowed it control, he wasn't sure what would happen. It had left her a broken woman.

Strangely, his ten years in the army had actually restored a measure of his faith in humanity. While there were still plenty of dickheads in the military, combat had a way of distilling a man, or woman, down to the basics. Letting you see what they were made of. Who you could trust. Who would die beside you and who would stab you in the back without a second thought. He'd come to be a good judge of character.

Which was maybe why he was finding the transition to this new life so hard. Everything about President Harry Coffell screamed *run*. And his close confidantes were the same. There was something slightly…*off* about them all. None of the old people remained. The new ones were creeping sycophants at best. He didn't want to think about the worst.

"Are you okay?" Kate's question pulled him out of his contemplation. "You looked a little… weird."

"I was thinking about Harry."

"Yeah, that would do it."

He raised an eyebrow, and her eyes widened as though she'd realized she'd just said something disrespectful about the president in the presence of the Secret Service. Maybe she was a rebel after all.

No. She didn't have the ability for violence within her. That was something else he'd picked up in the army.

"Sorry, I didn't mean—"

"Don't worry about it," he said. He wanted her at ease with him. "I think we all feel that way now and then. No one's perfect."

He kept his gaze on her as he waved over the hostess for the check. They didn't speak again while they were waiting, but their gazes stayed fixed on each other.

Finally, they were ready to go. He pushed himself to his feet and held out his hand. She slid hers into his. It felt right.

"Shall we walk?" he asked.

She nodded.

It was a beautiful evening, the sky clear. Other people strolled home from work. The streets were clean and wide, the buildings all well maintained. They took a shortcut through the park, and it occurred to him that, twenty years ago, they might not have done this and felt safe. There were a lot of good things that had come from the Party.

Maybe he should focus on those.

CHAPTER NINETEEN

"When the president does it, that means that it's not illegal." Richard M. Nixon

Someone knocked just as Stella was about to leave the office. She jumped. Then stared at the door.

The knock came again. She cleared her throat, her eyes straying to the computer on her desk. "Come in."

The door opened. She'd been closing down for the night. Now her hands dropped to her sides and she shot to her feet, wiping her palms on the side of her skirt.

Sweat prickled down her spine, and she fought hard to keep what she was feeling from showing on her face.

"Good evening, Mr. President."

What the hell did he want?

He'd never come to her office before. Harry liked to surround himself with people who loved him, and however much she did her best to hide the fact, she loathed him. He made her skin crawl and acid creep up her throat.

She swallowed.

He was perfectly groomed as usual, his blond

hair brushed back, his skin smooth. He was dressed in a pale-blue polo shirt and gray slacks.

He had a smile on his face that curved his lips but avoided his eyes.

It took everything in her not to shudder.

As he stepped into the room, he was closely followed by two bodyguards. They were expressionless, both huge, with military-short hair and earpieces showing at the sides of their faces. She knew two more would be waiting outside. Harry never went anywhere without at least four of his private army in attendance.

She glanced at her computer as though it would somehow show the email that had arrived just over an hour ago. She'd downloaded the attached file—it was encrypted and looked like a harmless report to her—and hidden it as well as she could, then archived the email. There was nothing in it to set off any alarms; hopefully, it wouldn't be picked up. She was supposed to get it to Gideon, and she was dreading that. How could she trust him now? He was Secret Service. He'd turn her in. And Joe, and probably the rest of her family. Just how much did she believe in this?

Anyway, Harry couldn't be here about that. It was too soon.

Nothing was wrong.

She was just being totally paranoid.

Then why *was* he here? The large room felt

cramped now and she wanted to back away, sidle out, make a dash for it. Instead, she forced a smile. "Can I help you with something, sir?"

Don't want to shake hands. Please. Don't.

She couldn't face it, couldn't touch him. She might be physically sick.

"I was passing. I thought I'd ask about your recent trip."

Her trip? Did he know about her visit to New York? How could he? She'd been so careful. If he knew…

"My trip?"

Christ, she sounded like a complete moron. But it was better than sounding like a traitor. Her whole life was flying in front of her.

"I believe you took a few days off with your husband. To the country? It must be lovely this time of year."

Her knees almost gave way as relief swamped her. She was no good at this. A fucking joke. She was risking everyone's lives. Why the hell was he asking? He didn't give a fuck about whether she'd been to the country. So what did he want?

"We had a wonderful time, thank you."

She searched for something else to say, but her mind was a wasteland. His gaze flickered around the room, settling on the computer. There was nothing to see. That he was here in her office was enough to send her into palpitations.

And he was totally aware of it.

Would he presume it was just her normal feelings, or would he suspect it was something more?

"I'm pleased. You work hard for the Party, and your family have always been solid supporters."

Why had he mentioned her family? Was there a threat in the words? She really was paranoid. "We believe in the Party," she murmured.

"Good. I'll let you get home then. I just wanted to say welcome back."

The guard on the right spoke into his microphone, and the two backed out. Harry nodded and followed them, and she sank back down on to her chair, suddenly lightheaded.

She had to get out of here.

Maybe she should just archive the file. Or send it somewhere, but Aaron had warned her against that. She was to copy it onto a drive and hand it on, together with the encryption code she'd memorized. She just had to make contact first.

Tomorrow.

She'd tried Gideon's office, but he was out. Not expected back today. She didn't want to call him at home. Actually, she didn't want to call him at all. How the hell had she gotten into this?

She got up, grabbed her bag and her keys, then headed out to the elevator and down to the underground parking area.

She was on autopilot as she pressed her thumb to the panel. She drove through and was quickly on the road and away from the White House. She hadn't realized how oppressed the place made her feel these days. Growing up, working there had been all she'd ever wanted. Kate had wanted to go into space. Stella had just wanted to serve the people, to make America a better place for Americans.

She wasn't even sure what that meant anymore.

Did it mean you had to hate everybody else?

When she'd married Joe, they'd bought a place in the suburbs so they could both get away from work at the end of the day. It was a forty-minute drive, but usually she liked the time alone. She could listen to music, zone out. Today she couldn't shift her mind from the file and what might be on it. Why did the rebels want Gideon? What did they expect him to do? And why would he? He had a chance at getting his life back. He wouldn't throw it all away.

She'd been driving for thirty minutes when something happened. She wasn't even sure what, just a subtle change in the feel of the car, as though it was no longer under her control. She pressed her foot lightly on the brake. Nothing happened. She glanced in the rear-view mirror; the road had quietened out of the city center, and she could only see a couple of cars behind her.

Then she spotted it. A black SUV about fifty yards away. Secret Service.

Don't panic.

She could feel fear spiking her blood with adrenaline, kicking her heart into overdrive.

Her hands gripped the wheel, knuckles white. Her speed was increasing. Slowly at first. Nothing to be alarmed about, just a glitch in the cruise control. She switched it off. No response, except that maybe her speed increased a little more.

She was on a straight stretch of road, but she was over the speed limit and catching up with the white sedan in front. This time, she stepped hard on the brakes. Nothing. She resisted the urge to close her eyes tight.

At the last minute, the white sedan must have realized she wasn't slowing down. It swerved to the next lane with a blare of its horn. The sound shot Stella out of her trance.

She reached out with one hand and delved into her bag, grabbed her phone.

For a second, her mind wouldn't work, and she couldn't remember the number Kate had given her.

**865

The call picked up immediately, but just a series of beeps came down the line.

She was almost flying down the road now, the view outside the screen blurred by her tears. There was a curve coming up, and at this speed she wasn't going to make it. She didn't want to die. Suddenly fury tore through the panic. She had a flashback to Harry all those years ago. His body violating hers. Laughing at her pain. She wouldn't let them win.

"Kate. I'm sorry, sweetheart, but I don't think I'm going to see you again. There's something you need to do for me. There's a file on the computer in my office. It was loaded at 4:15 today. My system is set up to give you access. You need to copy the file onto a drive and hand it over to Gideon Frome. It's encrypted; the code is 65879241. Tell him it's from his brother. If they need to meet, you'll find the time and coordinates in the file and the necessary travel passes for Gideon to get to the meeting place. Don't tell anyone else about this. No one. I love you."

After ending the call, she tossed the phone out of the window. She switched off the engine, but it made no difference. As she hit the corner and tried to turn, the wheel locked in place.

A loud roaring filled her ears, and everything went black.

CHAPTER TWENTY

"Let me say this as clearly as I can: No matter how sharp a grievance or how deep a hurt, there is no justification for killing innocents." William J. Clinton

As the door slammed closed, Gideon turned her around, backed her up against the wood, and kissed her. She melted into him. Last time they'd kissed, she'd been a little preoccupied with the drugging-a-Secret-Service-agent thing to take much notice of the whole process.

This time she gave herself over to the feel of his mouth forcing hers open, his tongue pushing inside, his hard body pressed against hers. He was already aroused…and, if his extremely impressive erection was anything to go by, clearly not in the least put off by the red hair and freckles.

She wriggled her hips against him, and he groaned into the kiss. They were both breathing hard by the time he raised his head. For a second, he rested his forehead against hers, and she listened to his breathing.

He dropped a kiss on her lips and stepped back. As he took her bag from over her shoulder, her phone rang. He pulled it out, switched it off, and tossed it onto the table with her bag on top of it. Then he reached behind her, pulled off the toggle holding her hair and added that to the pile. He ran his fingers through the long strands, laying it across her shoulders.

"It's like silk and fire," he said.

That was by far the nicest thing anyone had ever said about her hair. He lowered his head for another kiss, not touching her anywhere else, just lips to lips, hardly moving for long minutes. By the time he raised his head, her whole body was tingling. His gaze never leaving her face, he slipped his hands under the shoulders of her jacket, slid it down her arms, and tossed it on the growing pile. With one finger, he traced the neckline of her shirt, his fingers lingering over the row of freckles along her collarbone. His hand moved lower, his fingers shifting to the top button of her shirt. He flicked it open, lowered his head, and kissed the skin he'd revealed, then flicked open the next button. She glanced down; the black lace of her bra showed against the paleness.

The next button opened, and the edges of her shirt parted. Both hands glided around her rib cage, his palms warm and hard. One hand slid up to cup her breast just as the doorbell rang. Really loud because they were actually pressing back against the door.

"Should we ignore it?" he murmured, leaning

in close and nuzzling the side of her neck.

She wanted to so much, but the sheer unusualness of the doorbell ringing was battling with her rising passion. She didn't want anything battling with her passion. She could count on one hand—actually one finger—the times a man had made her feel this way. Normally she couldn't switch off, but even the fact that she was thinking about this showed that the moment was gone.

The doorbell rang again.

Who the hell could it be?

She didn't get visitors and she hadn't ordered a pizza.

She sidled out from between him and the door, fumbling to fasten her buttons as she turned. When she was decent, she opened the door and took an instinctive step back.

Two uniformed officers, a man and a woman, stood on the doorstep, caps in hand. She recognized them as local police and her heartbeat stuttered. She fought the urge to slam the door and close her eyes until they disappeared.

What could they want?

Nothing good.

"Ms. Kate Buchanan?" the woman asked.

She nodded but couldn't get any words out. Was it her mom? Stella? Were they in trouble, or worse?

She sensed Gideon behind her. He rested a

hand on her shoulder and squeezed. "What's this about?" he asked.

"I'm afraid we have some bad news." The woman peered over Kate's shoulder and into the apartment. "Could we come inside?"

She gave a quick nod, though she wanted to scream "no" and run away and hide. She turned, found herself facing Gideon's chest. Maybe she should tell him to go, but she didn't. Just walked around him and led the way into the living room. She stood behind the sofa, her hand gripping the back.

She cleared her throat. "What is it? What's happened?"

"You have a sister, Stella Buchanan?"

Oh God, not Stella.

She nodded again, was vaguely aware of Gideon coming to stand beside her, his arm sliding around her waist. She shifted closer, as though he could somehow protect her from what was coming. Could somehow stop the words she knew were about to be spoken.

"I'm afraid your sister was in an accident this evening."

Not Stella, it can't be true. A mistake.

"Is she…?" She couldn't get the words out.

"Is she alive?" Gideon asked from beside her.

"I'm afraid she was pronounced dead at the scene."

• • •

Gideon watched as the last of the color leached from her face, the freckles standing out stark against her white skin. A small sound escaped her throat.

"Are you sure it was her? Are you sure there's not been a mistake? Maybe someone else was driving her car?"

"We're certain. She had her identification with her, and her fingerprints matched up. I'm sorry, Ms. Buchanan, but you're listed as next of kin, and we need you to do a formal identification. The morning will be fine."

"No. No, I have to go now. Maybe there's…" She dashed a hand over her face, although her eyes were dry. Some things went way beyond tears. "Have my parents been told?" she asked.

"No, ma'am. We just inform the next of kin."

"Thank you," Gideon said. "I'll see you out."

He urged Kate forward with the hand at her waist, then pushed her gently down onto the sofa. She sat, staring straight ahead, her eyes blank, her hands clasped loosely in her lap. He ushered the two cops out into the hallway. "What exactly happened?" he asked, after he'd pulled the door closed behind him.

"From what we can gather, she was on her usual trip home. She was speeding, lost control on a corner. If it's any consolation, it's pretty certain she died on impact."

He supposed it would be when it all sank in. The speeding bit didn't sound like Stella. She'd always been a careful driver, but he supposed people changed in ten years. He let them out and stood for a moment. He could call up her parents, let them take over. Then he could get out of here.

Did he want to be involved?

He was still trying to get his head around the accident. Stella…dead. It seemed inconceivable. Not real.

Once, years ago, he'd fully expected to marry Stella. And while he'd come to realize that there had never been true love between them, he had been fond of her. Now he couldn't just walk away from her sister. From her reaction, he could tell they'd been close. She was in shock.

He'd take her to the hospital, stay with her until her parents got there.

When he pushed open the door, she was talking on the phone. Her hands were trembling.

"I'll see you at the hospital, Daddy. I have to go." She ended the call and stared at him. "You should leave."

"I'll take you to the hospital."

"You don't need to. I can get a cab."

Her tone was flat and there was no emotion in her voice.

"You shouldn't be alone right now."

"I'm fine."

He crossed the room, crouched down in front of her, and cupped her cheek. Her skin was cold. He took her hands between his and rubbed them. Finally, he straightened and stood looking down at her. "Are you sure you want to do this? You could leave it to your father. You don't have to see her."

"I do have to. It doesn't seem real. I need to see her."

"Okay." He pulled his phone from his pocket, called a cab firm, and gave the address. "They're on their way," he said to Kate, and she nodded.

"I hope it was quick. I hope she didn't suffer."

"I'm sure she didn't."

"But you don't know."

She got to her feet. The buttons on her shirt were fastened wonkily, and he undid them and refastened them properly. She didn't try to stop him or help him, just stood there staring over his shoulder. She opened her mouth as if to say something, then closed it again, her lower lip clamped between her teeth to keep the words in. She shook her head.

He couldn't believe that only minutes ago, they'd been kissing. If this hadn't happened, they'd be in bed now. How fragile life was and how easily things could be snatched from you.

A car horn sounded outside the house. "The

cab," he said. She walked in front of him like a robot. He got the impression something was going on in her head, something she wanted to keep inside. It occurred to him that if he wanted to find out about her, what made her tick, why she had drugged him, then she was vulnerable right now. But he couldn't bring himself to question her when she was so broken.

He picked up her jacket and bag from the table by the front door, then followed her out into the hallway and onto the street.

In the taxi, he held her hand. Once or twice he thought she was going to speak, but in the end, they made it to the hospital without her saying a word.

Her parents were already waiting in the reception area with a man he didn't recognize, whose eyes were red from crying. He must be the husband. Her mother looked dazed.

Her father held open his arms. Kate ran toward him, and he wrapped his arms around her. He stared at Gideon over her shoulder and gave a small nod of acknowledgment. He was probably wondering what Gideon was doing with his daughter. Gideon hadn't seen Justice Buchanan since the day he'd entered the interrogation room where they'd been questioning Gideon about Aaron's disappearance ten years ago. Justice Buchanan had told Gideon that Stella had broken off the engagement. That she didn't want to see him again.

He stepped up closer to the small group. Kate had her family now. He could leave her without worrying about her being alone. While he might not like her father, he'd only been protecting Stella all those years ago. As he'd no doubt protect Kate now.

"I'm sorry, sir."

"Thank you, Gideon."

Kate pulled free as he came to a halt beside them. The blankness had gone from her face and her eyes were filled with grief. Reaching out, she rested a hand on his arm. "You must be hurting, too. You loved her once."

He didn't deny it—now was not the time—although he wanted to.

"She was a good person. You'll miss her."

She closed her eyes for a moment. When she opened them, something had changed. She stared him in the eyes. "I'm just sorry that we hadn't spoken for so long."

"You hadn't?"

"We'd argued. It seems so stupid now. I wish I could go back and tell her it didn't matter."

Why would she say she hadn't seen Stella when they had met that lunchtime?

He eyed her. "I'm sure she understood."

"Maybe."

Suddenly he had the urge to grab her, whisk her away. Hide her from danger. What did she know? What the hell was she involved with?

Why had she lied?

"I have to go." He nodded to her father, then turned and walked away.

CHAPTER TWENTY-ONE

"To announce that there must be no criticism of the president…is morally treasonable to the American public." Theodore Roosevelt

Gideon spent Sunday at home with his mother. She'd heard the news of Stella's death and was taking it badly. It had awakened her old fears and insecurities.

He hadn't called Kate; she was with her family. He didn't want to intrude.

And last night, he'd had the old nightmare.

Back to the interrogation. Only it hadn't been him being questioned, but Kate. This time he'd broken, as he hadn't all those years ago. He'd screamed that he'd tell them anything, everything, whatever they wanted to hear if they'd just stop hurting her.

Except that he didn't know anything. Had nothing to tell them.

He'd gotten up while it was still dark, gone into the office. The place was quiet.

He had no reason to believe that Stella's death was anything other than an accident. She'd always been the perfect Party member.

But if that was the case, why had Kate

pretended that she hadn't seen her sister?

He opened his system, typed in *Stella Buchanan*. The file had already been updated to deceased; otherwise there was nothing of interest. On the other hand, he'd suspected that his access had been limited. Boyd had hinted that there would be a probationary period before he got access to *all* the files. That wouldn't do him much good now.

He decided to look at it from a different angle. He pulled up the work roster for the previous evening. Which agents had been on duty? There had been ten. Four had been in the office. Four others he could account for. Two, Davies and Shepperton, the most senior officers on duty, had a "special duties" flag next to their names. He tried to view the details but hit a dead end.

He picked up his phone and punched in a number. Davies picked up straight away.

"Sir?"

"I wanted to know how the job went last night?"

"I don't know what you're talking about." His tone was wary.

"Stella Buchanan."

"Still don't know what you're talking about, sir."

He ended the call and sat staring at his screen, trying to decide where to go next. He needed to talk to Boyd. Before he got the chance, there was a knock on his door. It opened, and his boss stood there. He entered without waiting, came to a halt in front of the desk.

"You've been asking questions about Stella Buchanan. I suggest you drop the subject."

"Why?"

"There's nothing there."

"She's dead."

"It was an accident. Leave it at that." Boyd studied him for a moment longer. "The president likes you. You've got a good chance to become a real part of the team. Don't fuck it up."

While Gideon wanted to ask about the rest of Stella's family, he didn't want to alert Boyd that he was interested. Not yet. Not until he knew more about what was going on. So he kept his mouth shut, and a minute later he was alone.

He was becoming certain that Stella's death had not been an accident, although he could see no reason for her death. Except that Kate had lied about seeing her sister. And she had drugged him. She was clearly involved in something.

He pulled his cell phone out of his pocket and keyed in her number. It rang a couple of times and then clicked over to voice mail. "It's Gideon. I just wanted to check you're okay." He ended the call, but as he put down the phone, it rang. The caller ID showed Kate. "Hi," he said. "I just wanted to find out how you were."

"I'm as well as can be expected. I'm at my parents'. I've taken a couple of days off work until the funeral."

"Good. You shouldn't be alone right now."

"No."

He thought for a moment. "You said you hadn't seen Stella for a while, that you'd argued. Can you tell me what about?"

She was silent for a few seconds. Thinking up an answer? Or wondering why he was asking? "It was my fault. I told her I was working on a private project using the Homeland Security computer system. She wasn't happy. Wanted me to stop."

"What sort of project?"

"Just a silly program. A sort of probability calculator. Nothing but a game really."

He was aware that all technological research had been stopped. What she said made sense. Except that somehow it didn't ring true.

"Are you going to turn me in?" she asked in a disinterested tone.

"No." She didn't say anything else, but he could hear her soft breathing on the other end of the line. Then a sob.

"Kate?"

"It's not fair. She was a good person. It shouldn't have happened."

"No, it shouldn't." What else could he say? He

had no clue what was going on. All he knew was that Kate was in danger, and he hated that. It shouldn't have mattered. Right now, he should be telling Boyd that she'd drugged him. If he wanted any future at all, he should come clean about what she'd done and then put as much distance between them as he could. Instead, he found himself saying. "I'll see you at the funeral."

Somehow, he was going to have to get to the bottom of exactly what Kate Buchanan was up to. Then put a stop to it.

Before she also met with an accident.

• • •

Aaron sat in a booth in the bar off Fifth Avenue in New York.

Stella would have the files by now. Should have already contacted Gideon.

How had his brother reacted?

Maybe Aaron was wrong. Maybe he'd made a huge miscalculation in believing that Gideon would do the right thing and help. Maybe, instead, he'd gone running straight to his new boss. They'd heard nothing from D.C.

Stella could have been arrested. Was maybe being tortured right now.

But he couldn't think like that or he would stop functioning.

This was what she had wanted.

Eight years ago, he'd returned to D.C. One last attempt to persuade Stella to come away with him. He'd had contacts, found a place in the rebels. They would take Stella in if he vouched for her. They could have a life together.

She had refused outright, as he'd known she would. She wouldn't do to her family what he had done to his.

At that point, he'd admitted to himself that the trip had been an excuse to see her one last time, that was all.

Then she had surprised him. Told him that if the day ever came, then she wanted to do her part to bring down President Harry Coffell Junior. And he'd seen in her then the burning need for justice.

So he'd accepted her offer, not knowing at the time whether he would ever call on her but understanding that she needed to feel she was doing something. She'd joined the administration shortly after that. Put herself in a position where she could be of use.

The door to the bar opened and a man stepped through. He paused, looked around, and then came over to where Aaron sat. He slipped into the seat opposite, then pulled a paper from his pocket and slid it across the table.

Aaron read the words, but they made no sense to him.

Stella was dead. Had died in a car accident two

nights ago.

A scream of denial rose up inside him and he closed his eyes, concentrated on getting himself under control.

She was dead. How? Why? The paper gave the bare minimum of details.

Had she spoken to Gideon and he'd turned her in? But if that was the case, why make her death look like an accident? Why not arrest her?

Besides, the timing was wrong. She would have only just received the file shortly before the accident. She wouldn't have had time to go and see Gideon.

Could it have been an accident? The timing just a coincidence, a cruel quirk of fate?

He didn't believe in coincidences.

CHAPTER TWENTY-TWO

"If God is just, I tremble for my country." Thomas Jefferson

All through the service, Kate couldn't shake the feeling that she was in some sort of nightmare. That she'd wake up and Stella would be alive. And that there wasn't some nuclear threat hanging over the world.

That fact had somehow stayed out of her mind through the days following her sister's death. Grief had a way of narrowing your focus.

Stella had died three days ago, and the funeral had been arranged quickly. Too quickly. Apparently, the president wanted to be present, and this was the only day that he could fit into his schedule. So it had to be today. It was taking place at the Washington National Cathedral, and the huge church was full. Stella had been popular.

If Kate turned her head slightly, she could see the president sitting across the aisle between two huge bodyguards. She supposed it was an honor that he'd taken the time to attend, but somehow it didn't feel right.

She hadn't been to the office. They'd given her time off and she'd kept away from the internet, which meant she'd had no contact with Auspex.

For once, the president was formally dressed in a black suit. He stared straight ahead, but she was sure she could see a small smile twisting his lips. What had her sister been involved in? Had she known that day that she was going to die? She'd been so scared. Why couldn't she have confided in Kate?

Her death was such a senseless waste.

As though he could sense her gaze, Harry turned his head so he was looking straight at her. A shudder ran through her.

Staring into his eyes, she couldn't shake the idea that he was somehow complicit in her sister's death. Which was crazy. His eyes narrowed. Had she given away her thoughts? She tore her gaze away and forced herself to concentrate on the coffin that held her sister's body. The words of the service flowed over her, making no impact. For the first time in her life, she wished she had some sort of faith, a belief in something beyond this life, to give her hope. She dashed a hand across her face as tears spilled down her cheeks.

Finally it was over, and she rose to her feet. As she turned, she caught sight of the man standing at the back of the church. Gideon. He was staring at the coffin, but as though he could sense her focus, he looked at her and gave a small nod.

She emerged from the huge Gothic archway

into the open air. After a week of sunshine, clouds had taken over the sky. It looked dark and ominous, promising rain. It was warm, humid, but she shivered. A small crowd had gathered beyond the lawns, held back by a line of Secret Service agents. The president had made an announcement that morning that he would be attending the funeral, and his people had come to cheer him on. He'd turned her sister's funeral into a circus. No doubt he was trying to show his caring side.

She waited by the walls of the church, not wanting to talk to anyone, certainly not Harry. Her mother and father joined the group around him. While her father shook his hand, her mother hung back.

"How are you doing?" Gideon asked from beside her, and she thankfully turned away from their country's leader.

"I'll be better once this is over." She nodded her head to where the president stood, showing off his good side to his audience. "Look at him. Making Stella's death into some sort of publicity act. When he—"

"Kate! Be careful what you say."

She went still at the warning in his voice. He was right. All the same, she hated it.

The president glanced up. He stared at her, then his gaze shifted to the man at her side. As he walked toward them, she wanted to turn and run.

She didn't know if she was capable of keeping a civil tongue in her head. And she had to.

If she were to be locked up now, there would be no one to run Auspex, no one to analyze ways to stop the predicted nuclear bomb. And if that bomb did exist, its detonation would set off a chain of events that would lead to disaster.

At the thought, a wave of hysteria threatened to overwhelm her. This was crazy. Everything was all wrong, and Stella was dead, and...

Gideon's hand slid into hers. He squeezed, and a sense of calmness flowed through her.

He released his hold as the president came to a halt in front of them. Harry held out his hand, and his gaze locked with hers, as though he could sense that she didn't want to take it. She pressed her palm against his, and he shook it briefly, his expression bland.

"Ms. Buchanan, please allow me to extend my condolences on the death of your sister."

"Thank you." Her voice sounded almost normal.

"Your sister was a remarkable woman," he said. "The Party feels her loss deeply."

There was something so totally insincere about him. She swallowed, forced a polite smile to her face. "Stella loved the Party. It was her dream to be a part of it."

He was silent for a moment. "How is your

mother? She seemed a little…off. Almost as though she blamed me."

Kate kept her face blank. "She's just taken this very, very hard."

"You know, I was probably the last person to speak with Stella that night. I visited her office shortly before she left."

"Oh." She couldn't think of anything to say to that. She wanted to ask what they'd spoken about, but she couldn't get the question out.

Harry peered at her. "Did she speak to you afterward?"

She shook her head. "No. Sadly, I hadn't spoken to her for a while."

"Such a sad loss." He turned to Gideon. "I didn't expect to see you here, Gideon."

"You might not remember, Mr. President, but I was engaged to Stella ten years ago."

"Of course."

"She broke off the engagement when I joined the army. However, we remained friends."

"That's nice." He sounded as though it was anything but nice. "Now I must be off. But a sad occasion."

Kate watched as he walked away, flanked by two guards. He disappeared into a black limousine that drove off immediately.

With his leaving, the last of Kate's strength fled her body. Her eyes prickled and a tear welled over, followed by another. She wiped her hand over her face. She was just tired. She hadn't slept properly since the night her sister had died. Now exhaustion tugged at her, sapped her will to keep going. She stumbled, and Gideon stepped closer, wrapped an arm around her. At his touch, strength flowed through her.

She had to remember that he was the enemy. Part of the feared Secret Service. Maybe even responsible for Stella's death.

Although she didn't believe that. For some reason, she believed he was a good person, and she was beginning to think there weren't many of those around.

For a few seconds, she allowed herself to rest against his strength, then she forced herself to pull away, to stand upright. "I'm okay," she said. "Just tired."

"Are you going back to your parents' house?"

"No. It's time to go home." She needed to make a plan. Which meant she had to consult with Auspex. She aimed to go into the office tomorrow. Time to make it look as though she was getting back to normal life. Moving on. Instead she was going to… She had no clue. Something. She couldn't think straight right now.

"I'll drive you."

She opened her mouth to say there was no need. Then closed it again. She didn't want to be alone with her demons. There was too much to think about, and at the same time, so much that she didn't want to think about. Gideon's company would at least put off that moment for a while longer.

"Thank you. I'd appreciate it."

The sky opened, and the first fat drops of rain fell. She raised her face as though it could wash away her dread along with the traces of her tears.

"Come on."

"I'll just tell my parents I'm leaving."

He followed close behind her as she made her way over to where her father and mother stood. Her father was talking with the Bishop who'd performed the service. Her mother stood beside him, still with that blank expression on her face, although her eyes were red from crying. Kate suspected that she had been taking some sort of medication since Stella's death. Something in addition to her usual sleeping tablets. She gave the impression of going through the motions.

"Gideon is going to drive me home," Kate told her. "I'll talk to you tomorrow." She leaned in and kissed her mother's cool cheek. The rain was falling faster now, but her mother just stood like a statue, making no effort to avoid it.

"Look after her," her father said, and she realized he was talking to Gideon. His voice held a hint of desperation. Did he suspect that Stella's death had not been an accident? Was he waiting for them to come after the rest of the family? That was the way it worked. Although maybe they were safe. At least for a while. If someone had killed her, they'd gone to a lot of effort to make Stella's death look like an accident.

"I will, sir."

She gave her father a last hug. She believed he was a good man who followed his principles. How must he feel to even suspect that the Party he'd given his life to might have betrayed him in this way?

Probably as though the whole world, and everything he believed in, was falling apart. Or had never even existed.

As Gideon led her away from the church, she had a feeling that everything was over. Finished. Sitting in the passenger seat as they drove through the busy roads, she stared out the window. The city had an air of prosperity. Was it a facade? Did it matter that it was built on lies and on the probable deaths of so many people? Was freedom really a possibility? Or was it only ever an illusion?

She wiped the rain from her face. Blinked away the last of the tears.

She had to be strong.

If she failed, then two weeks from now, all this might be gone.

One thing was sure. Succeed or fail, she

doubted very much that she would have even the illusion of freedom once this was over.

She would be seen as a traitor.

And traitors were executed.

• • •

She was crying again, and he couldn't stand it. He was pretty sure she wasn't even aware of the tears rolling down her cheeks.

The black dress she wore only emphasized the paleness of her skin. She wore no makeup and her freckles stood out stark against her face.

She was totally different from the blonde he had picked up in that bar less than a week ago. It seemed like a lifetime. While she wasn't beautiful, her looks were unique. They drew him far more than the bland blondes he usually picked up. But wasn't that the point? He'd wanted to be able to forget them.

He'd come prepared. It was payback time, and he was already feeling goddamn guilty. She had drugged him. Her sister had died in what he was now certain were suspicious circumstances. He needed to find out what the hell she was involved with. It had been clear from the night they'd met that she was an amateur. She'd taken the time to hide the family photos, but it had only taken him minutes the following morning to uncover her deception and find out who she really was. Part of him wished she wasn't so obviously *not* cut out for whatever it was she was involved in. The rest of him was pleased. She'd been drawn into something she wasn't ready for, was unprepared for, and that meant that maybe he could extract her somehow.

Why the hell did he care?

He'd start by searching her apartment. If she'd been going back to her parents' house, he would have come here and searched the place after the funeral.

This would work better.

She was clearly exhausted. At least she'd get a good night's sleep out of it.

He pulled the car into the parking space outside her apartment block and switched off the engine.

"Thank you," she said.

"I'll come in. Make sure you're okay."

"I'm fine."

He ran a hand through his hair. "Maybe I don't want to be alone right now," he said. "Maybe I want to be near someone who loved her."

She rested her hand on his arm. "I'm sorry. Sometimes I forget you and Stella were close. You seem like a different person from who you were all those years ago."

He *was* a different person. And that was a different life.

He climbed out of the car into the pouring rain,

then came around and opened the door for her. She clambered out and together they ran to the entrance. She already had the key in her hand. All the same, by the time they were inside, they were both soaked.

She dropped her bag on the floor and headed into the bathroom, then came out a moment later and handed him a big blue towel. He rubbed at his head as she disappeared into the bathroom again. He stripped off his jacket and tie. His shirt was dry underneath. He wiped his face and tossed the towel on a chair, then headed into the kitchen and opened the fridge. Inside was a bottle of white wine. He glanced at the bathroom but there was no sign of Kate. He could hear running water.

He opened the bottle, took it through to the living room, and pulled a couple of glasses from the cabinet. He got his wallet out of his pants pocket and found the folded paper. He carefully opened it and tipped the white powder into the glass, shoved the paper back in his wallet, and the wallet back in his pocket. Then he poured the wine on top. It went cloudy and then cleared.

He poured a glass for himself just as she appeared from the bathroom. She'd changed into gray sweats and a black baggy T-shirt. She looked younger than her years and beyond tired.

"Come and sit down," he said, gesturing to the sofa.

She didn't speak, just sank down onto the cushions. He held out the glass for her and she took it from him, lifted it to her mouth, and swallowed the contents in one go. Then she held out the glass for more. He refilled it and sat down beside her. He sipped his own wine while he waited for the drug to take effect.

He shifted in his seat so he could watch her. Her eyes were already heavy. After putting down his own glass, he plucked hers from her limp fingers.

"Hey, I was drinking that."

"You were about to drop it."

"I'm just so tired. Everything is catching up with me, I suppose. I haven't been sleeping so well."

"Hardly surprising. You can sleep now. I'll watch over you."

"Keep me safe?" She smiled, but her eyes were shadowed. "I don't think anyone can do that. I'm a lost cause."

"Why do you think that?" Was he going to find the truth this easily? His heart rate picked up, and he realized he was scared. Scared she was going to reveal something he couldn't fix. That he'd fail her. Again, he couldn't work out why it mattered so much. He hardly knew her.

She didn't speak, and when he looked into her face, her eyes were closed.

"Why are you a lost cause, Kate?" he asked.

Her eyes blinked open sleepily. "Sorry? What were you saying…?"

"Nothing. Why don't you lay your head down? Go to sleep."

She yawned, then shifted around. He moved over to give her more room. She tucked her feet up on the sofa and laid her head in his lap, closing her eyes.

He stroked her hair, still damp from the rain, pushing it away from her face to show the curve of her cheek. Her lashes were dark against her pale skin.

Her breathing was slow and even. When he squeezed her shoulder, there was no response. She was out cold. He reached for his glass and sat, sipping the chilled wine, staring down at her.

He was almost sure he was safe. Right now, he was too popular. The president had brought him back for that reason. He doubted he was going to have an accident any time soon. Maybe he could use that. If he made it clear they were a couple, that he was responsible for her, then it might keep her safe. But safe from what? Until he knew, he couldn't work out the best course of action.

He put his glass down and lifted her head carefully from his lap. He stood up. Leaning down, he scooped her into his arms, and she moaned and curved herself into his chest. He carried her through into the bedroom, tugged down the sheet with one hand, and laid her down on the mattress. She curled onto her side and he pulled the sheet over her. She would sleep until morning.

Time to start digging.

He jolted awake and glanced at his watch. Seven hours had passed. He'd fallen asleep on the sofa. Something had woken him. He ran a hand through his hair and sat up.

Kate stood in the bedroom doorway. She looked seriously pissed.

"You goddamn bastard. You drugged me."

CHAPTER TWENTY-THREE

"A friend is one who has the same enemies as you have." Abraham Lincoln

He didn't seem surprised by the accusation, and that pissed her off even more. She'd trusted him, and he'd taken advantage of her while she was vulnerable.

He'd *drugged* her.

"How do you feel?" he asked.

Like he cared. "As if I've been drugged."

His lips twitched. Yeah, she was just so funny. She glared.

"You have to admit, sweetheart, fair's fair. I was only returning the favor."

She'd been about to step into the room, go punch him on the nose or something. Now she stopped abruptly. Shock stabbing her in the gut. "You knew?"

"Of course I knew."

"Why didn't you say something? Do something? Lock me up or take me in for questioning?"

He scrubbed his hand through his hair, something she'd noticed he did when he was thinking. He'd known she had drugged him. All this time. She'd thought she was so clever. Why hadn't he reported her? Were his reasons somehow tied to Stella's death? Could she have triggered something? Some investigation? It didn't make sense. "Why?" she asked again.

"Truthfully. I don't know." He stood up, stretched. "Christ, I need coffee. You want coffee?"

"I don't know. Will it be safe to drink?"

"For either of us," he muttered and wandered into the kitchen. She still stood in the bedroom doorway, her head spinning.

Finally, she forced herself to go after him. "So, an easier question. Why did you drug me last night?"

He switched on the coffee machine and turned to face her. "I wanted to search your apartment. I needed to know what you were involved with."

She sank down onto one of the stools around the island in the center of the kitchen. "Why do you think I'm involved in something?"

He turned and leaned against the counter behind him, folded his arms across his chest, then cast her a look that clearly said *Are you crazy?* "You pretended to be someone else in order to meet me, then you brought me back here and drugged me. Why *wouldn't* I think you're involved in something?"

She chewed on her lower lip. "Did you find

anything last night?" She didn't think there was anything to find. All the same, her guilty conscience worried at her mind.

"Fuck all," he growled.

"I apologize for all that wasted effort."

He poured coffee into two mugs and placed one in front of her, then got the milk from the fridge and put it on the table. He was making himself at home.

Suddenly she needed to ask him something. "Do you think Stella's death was an accident?"

"No." He cast her a look over the rim of his mug. "I also know that you lied about not having seen Stella for a while. You saw her the day she died."

"How do you know that?"

"I was following you."

"Of course you were." Her brain still felt fuzzy, and she needed it to function. For some reason, he hadn't turned her in, and she had no clue why. She felt like a great weight was pressing down on her. So much responsibility and no clue what to do next. How to save the world.

It didn't seem real.

Maybe it wasn't real.

She had an almost overwhelming need to open up, to share what she was going through. For some reason, she trusted Gideon.

But *was* he to be trusted?

"Why are you talking to me like this? You're Secret Service. Why didn't you report me?"

He didn't answer at first. Just got up and poured himself another coffee, then sat down again. She studied his face. For the first time, she noticed how tired he looked, saw the shadows under his eyes.

"Truthfully, I don't know." He exhaled, then seemed to come to a decision. "I came back thinking I could reclaim my old life. Go back to who I was before everything went to crap. But there's no going back. I'm a different person than I was ten years ago. I was an idealistic idiot. I believed changes were needed, but that I could make them within the constraints of the system. I was a Party man through and through."

"And now?" she prompted when he went silent.

"Now I feel like I'm standing at a crossroads. I have to decide what sort of person I want to be. I can close my eyes and pretend I'm still a Party man, or I can do it with my eyes wide open. Decide whether I believe that the end justifies the means. That the things that happen behind the scenes are worth it. Crime is almost non-existent. All around me, I see ordinary people going about their lives. No fear of violence, no poverty, everyone has access to a good education, good medical." He was silent for a minute, and she waited while he came to terms with his thoughts. "But none of that matters," he said. "Because I'm angry. Angry at Stella's death, whatever the reason for it. If they'd had a true case against her, I might have accepted it. If she'd been arrested, brought to trial. But she wasn't, and we may never know why she was killed. I realize that I've been angry for ten years. Furious. Raging. My father killed himself. Or did he? Something else I'll never know."

"Maybe you should join the rebels." She half meant it as a joke, but he seemed to consider the question.

"Maybe. You know, back when they brought in Martial Law, they said it would only be for a short while. A year at the most. So many years ago. And the restrictions got harsher. Now it's almost impossible for an ordinary person to go out of state. You live where you're born, and no doubt you die there. There are people who never get to see the ocean. Or the mountains. Why?"

"I always dreamed of going into space," she said.

"I don't think they issue passes for that."

"No." Suddenly she felt close to tears. Like giving up on a dream.

"They built the Wall to keep others out. Now it's more to keep us in."

She'd never thought of it like that. but he was

right.

"We're prisoners in our own country," he continued. "All the decisions are made by the president's inner circle now. Just a small number, deciding the fate of America. The final decisions are always Harry's, and I've come to suspect that Harry is not a moral man. I'm not even sure he's entirely sane anymore. So I guess that's why I didn't report you." He drained his mug and sat back. "Or maybe I just want to sleep with you."

It was so much to take in. She'd felt alone for so long that it was hard to trust someone else. What if she did, and he helped her? She'd drag him down as well. But the truth of the matter was, she couldn't do it alone, and if she tried and failed, there was a good chance he was dead anyway. They were all dead.

"So," he said. "Are you going to tell me why you lied about Stella? Why you drugged me? Then we can see if there's a way out of this."

She took a deep breath. "I lied about Stella because she told me to. She was scared that day. She wouldn't tell me why, just said that I should pretend we'd had a falling out. That if anyone asked, we hadn't spoken in a while."

"But that was *after* you drugged me."

She raked her hands through her hair. "I drugged you so I could get a retinal scan."

"And you needed a retinal scan because…?"

"I needed to get into the Secret Service files."

"Why? Are you working with the rebels?"

"No." She pushed herself up. "I think maybe it might be easier if I show you, because there's no way you'll believe me otherwise." He probably wouldn't believe her anyway. Maybe she could find some way to prove she wasn't crazy. That Auspex's predictions were accurate. "Give me a minute to get dressed and we'll go to my office. I'll tell you everything."

When she came out of the bedroom ten minutes later, he'd tidied himself up; pulled his jacket on over his rumpled shirt, straightened his tie.

As she led him out of the apartment, the door opposite opened, and her neighbor appeared. Paula Chen, looking colorful as ever in her crimson jacket and purple leggings, was a student with a rich family and a love of causes. Her Chinese father had moved to the States thirty years ago, before the lockdown on immigration. She was an active member of the Democracy for America group and sometimes managed to drag Kate along to meetings. It was something she believed in and was at no way odds with the Party. As Gideon had said, Martial Law had only ever been meant to be temporary. Now it was time for the people to show that they were ready to take back their place in the decision-making process.

"Kate." She grinned. "And a gorgeous guy."

"This is Gideon. He's a friend."

Paula moved closer, gave her a quick hug, and stepped back. "Sorry about your sister."

"Thank you."

"Hey, are you coming to the rally? It's on K Street. We need all the people we can get."

"Maybe I'll pop over if I can get out of work."

"Good." She pulled a sticker out of her pocket and slapped it onto Kate's black jacket. "We'll expect you. Bring Gideon." She headed out of the building.

"Bring back Democracy," Gideon murmured, staring at her chest as he read the sticker.

"They have a valid point."

"Maybe." But he reached across and pulled the sticker off, crumpled it up, and shoved it in his pocket.

They didn't talk on the drive, so she just stared out of the window. The sun was shining again. There were no checkpoints, and she could almost fool herself that her world wasn't about to end.

Gideon showed his ID and security let him through. She led him down the stairs and into her office, then waved him to a spare chair and powered up the systems.

Then she sat down opposite him. He might need a little background for any of this to make sense. Where to start? In the end, he decided for her.

"Why this job?" he asked. "I would have thought it a little...boring."

"A couple of reasons. My old college professor works here, and he offered me the job when I graduated." While she was aware that the next bit might get Oliver into trouble, she had to trust Gideon. "He knew I wanted the chance to continue my research, and anything associated with artificial intelligence had been banned. The servers here are the only ones that aren't monitored. And I have access to most of the systems. Even the Secret Service calls are run through here, though everything is in code, so I can't actually tell what they're about. Well, I couldn't until recently."

At that moment, Auspex came online. The middle screen lit up.

Good morning, Kate. Welcome back and condolences on the death of your sister.

Kate frowned. That was new; Auspex had never offered personal interaction like that before. He was growing, learning.

Gideon was staring at the screen. "What is this?"

"Auspex. My predictive engine."

"What does it do?"

That was promising. At least he hadn't called security and had her tossed into jail. But she hadn't told him the most incriminating part yet. "Auspex has access to all the systems within the United States."

A muscle ticked in his jaw. "Including the Secret Service?"

"Yes. Thanks to your retinal scan," Kate said. "He uses that information to predict what's going to happen in the future."

She shifted uncomfortably in her seat. There. Her illegal activities were out. All that was left to do was see what Gideon did with this information. And whether he could help her stop the nuclear threat before it was realized.

CHAPTER TWENTY-FOUR

"Together, we will make America strong again. We will make America wealthy again. We will make America proud again. We will make America safe again. And yes, together, we will make America great again. Thank you. God bless you. And God bless America." Donald Trump

Gideon couldn't decide whether Kate believed this, or whether it was part of some elaborate scam.

She looked perfectly serious. And nervous.

"Just a second," she said. "I want to check for calls."

She was typing into the keyboard. The system beeped. Kate pressed a key, read something on the screen to the left, and went totally still.

"What is it?" he asked.

"It's a call from Stella. Oh my God, she must have made it just before the accident." She pressed another key, and the call started playing. They heard Stella's voice, speaking quickly as though she was about to run out of time.

"Kate. I'm sorry, sweetheart, but I don't think I'm going to see you again. There's something you need to do for me. There's a file on the computer in

my office. It was loaded at 4:15 today. My system is set up to give you access. You need to copy the file onto a drive and hand it over to Gideon Frome. It's encrypted; the code is 65879241. Tell him it's from his brother. If they need to meet, you'll find the time and coordinates in the file and the necessary travel passes for Gideon to get to the meeting place. Don't tell anyone else about this. No one. I love you."

The words flowed through his mind but didn't make sense. There was a file? From his brother? A way to meet with Aaron? Had Stella been in contact with Aaron all this time? Had she been working with him? He hadn't even known that Aaron was alive.

Kate's hands were clasped in her lap as she stared straight ahead. "Oh God. If only I'd gotten this, maybe I could have helped her, done something. She must have known she was going to die."

He shook his head, trying to get his brain to function. "What time was it made?" When she didn't move, he got up and crossed to her. He squeezed her shoulder. "Come on, Kate. What time was the call made?"

She pressed a key. "Eleven minutes past seven."

"Then you couldn't have helped. The accident was logged at twelve minutes past. No way could you have stopped it. She knew that." He leaned past her, pressed the replay button, and listened to the call again. Then a third time.

"Do you know what she's talking about? What's on this file?"

"No."

"Did you know she was in contact with Aaron?"

"No. Of course not. Honest, Gideon. I've heard nothing from Aaron since he vanished."

"But your sister obviously has."

She frowned. "It doesn't make sense. Was she working with the rebels? Is that why she was killed? Why not just arrest her? Why make it look like an accident?"

Ten years ago, Stella had been ambitious. He would have sworn she was loyal to the Party. Could she have been working with the rebels all along? For what purpose? And what was in the file?

Kate was supposed to give it to him. Why?

There was only one way to find out. They had to get the file. However, that would not be straightforward. There was a good chance that, if the Secret Service had suspected Stella of anything, her office would have been sealed off, her systems monitored.

While *he* might get in, he wouldn't be able to extract the file. Not without Kate. He presumed it would require fingerprints and/or retinal scans.

Which meant she had to go with him.

She wouldn't get past security. Not without a really good reason.

"I have to tell you the rest," Kate said, pulling him from his thoughts.

"The rest?"

"I don't know what the file is, or why Stella has it. I don't know anything. That has nothing to do with the reason I drugged you. You have to listen, Gideon. It's important."

He took a deep breath and cleared his mind, then sat down in his chair and tried to get his head back into what they'd been discussing before the call. Predicting the future. "Go on."

"I developed Auspex from a system I found on the university servers. It was a project Oliver—my boss—had been working on before the research was made illegal." She took a deep breath. "That was about eight years ago. I'd made progress with him, but when I came to work here, I had access to the government servers, and I integrated Auspex into the government surveillance systems. That was when the exciting stuff started to happen. Though, until recently, he didn't do anything useful."

"He?"

"Auspex." She gave a shrug. "I've always thought of him as a "he". Anyway, he didn't really function until about a month ago."

He frowned. "What happened?"

Kate gave him a shaky smile. "He started giving me predictions on the alerts I send on to NTAC. Usually they were a negligible chance of a threat. I thought he was functioning correctly, but when I compared the results to NTAC's, they were completely different. I ran a debugging program and that changed something. Up until then, I hadn't been able to read the chatter—it was all encrypted. After that I could read it. But most of it didn't make sense."

"So what changed? Why seek me out?" What she'd told him so far wasn't enough to risk drugging a Secret Service agent, although it was likely enough to get her locked away for life. If not worse.

"I got a yellow alert—that's a threat of terrorist activity. Auspex gave a probability of 68 percent that it would result in harm to the American people. That was the first time he'd given anything like that—usually he predicted a negligible risk. So I looked at the info dump and I found multiple references to some sort of nuclear attack. Not only that, but I found a reference to Stella."

"That she was tied into some sort of nuclear attack on America?" He wouldn't believe it. He couldn't be that wrong about her.

"It was inconclusive." She bit her lip and looked away. "I deleted the line related to her and sent the alert to NTAC as usual."

Definitely locked away for life. Or executed for treason. But he could understand why she had done it. "Continue."

She took a deep breath. "I couldn't get hold of Stella. No one knew where she was. I thought maybe she'd already been picked up by the Secret Service. But there's more."

A sliver of dread wound through him. How the hell could there be more?

"I got the report from NTAC," she continued. "It said the probability of the alert being a threat was negligible. Which didn't make sense. I'd seen the info dumps. The references were there. I ran the alert through Auspex again. This time there was a 79 percent chance. It was going up."

"You believed it?"

She gave a brief smile at his obviously incredulous tone. "I was skeptical as well, but I've done all the tests. I asked the same question in all sorts of different ways, and in the end, I couldn't *not* believe it."

She appeared so earnest. Did she really believe this? Did he?

Hell no.

"You don't believe me, do you?"

"Let's just presume I do for the moment. What happened next?"

"I'd spoken to Oliver. He's my boss, my old

professor. I think he suspects what I'm working on. He said I needed to get more specific. So I asked Auspex to prepare predictions on a time basis. It's going to happen in less than two weeks. And I don't know what to do. I needed more information."

"So you drugged me?"

"Yes. And took a retinal scan."

He glanced around the room as if some eavesdropper might suddenly pop up from out of nowhere. This was sufficient to get her executed as a traitor.

She must have sensed his unease. "Auspex checked—the room is clear. No one can hear us. Which means it's up to you to report me if you feel you have to."

He turned his attention back to the screen, which was now blank. Could the rebels have actually taken control of the Homeland Security systems? Maybe whatever Kate had been using them for had left them vulnerable to attack and what she thought were predictions was actually false information being fed to her for... He couldn't come up with a reason. "Did you find the answers you were looking for?"

She shook her head. "Well, there was nothing about Stella being taken, but that hardly matters now. There was also nothing on the nuclear threat, which doesn't make sense. Unless there's a part of the server you don't have access to."

He could believe that. Boyd had almost admitted as much. He'd also implied that he'd only get access once he passed his probationary period and that, if it was up to Boyd, that wouldn't be for a long time. "The Inner Circle," he said.

Her eyes widened. "So there *is* such a thing?"

A group that bypassed the controls. Made their own rules. Killed anyone who stood in their way. "I've heard rumors."

"Auspex is searching for a way in, but so far he's found nothing. Time is running out. I thought about sending an anonymous tip to somebody, but if they don't believe the alerts, why would they believe an anonymous tip? Then I thought maybe I could contact the rebels—warn them that if it's something they're planning, then..." She gave a helpless shrug.

"Let me get this straight. Your machine tells you the world is going to descend into nuclear war, and so you decide to introduce yourself to the nearest rebels and ask them nicely not to detonate their nuclear bomb?" He got to his feet and ran a hand through his hair, paced the room a couple of times. He came to a halt in front of her, hands on his hips. "Are you goddamn crazy?"

She stared up at him. "Maybe? I wish I didn't believe it, but I do. So what am I supposed to do, just sit and wait for us all to go up in smoke? Just hear me out. I know it's a lot to take in. Afterward, I'll see if I can get the proof to persuade you that Auspex is right."

He felt too restless to sit. Instead he leaned against the wall, arms folded across his chest. "Go on."

"Even with your access to the Secret Service files, we can't work out a way—"

"We?" he interrupted. Was she working with someone else?

"Me and Auspex." She waved a hand at the computer screen. She talked about the damn thing as if it could think for itself. Though wasn't that what artificial intelligence did? "As I was saying, we can't find a way to contact the rebels. I know they're in New York, but nothing more."

"You could always go and stand in the middle of Times Square and shout 'Is anybody here planning to blow up a nuclear bomb?'" He sank into the seat behind him.

She gritted her teeth and glared at him. "Don't be an asshole. I've been living with this hanging over me. Living, breathing, sleeping. Now Stella's dead, and I don't know why." She caught her lower lip between her teeth. "I keep thinking that maybe she was a rebel all along, and if only she'd spoken to me, trusted me, instead of trying to protect me, then maybe I wouldn't have had to involve you."

No, maybe she would have his brother, Aaron,

instead. Who'd run off to play with the rebels and turned everybody's worlds upside down.

"And maybe, somehow, she'd still be alive," Kate continued. "Which means it's my fault. So guess what? Right now, I'm not feeling a whole lot like joking."

No. He could see she was deadly serious. Gideon got up again, suddenly restless. "I need some fresh air, and *you* need to come with me."

"Why?" She huffed. "I have things to do."

"Look, from now on, until I decide just what I believe and don't believe, I'm not letting you out of my sight. God knows what you might get up to. I could turn my back and the next minute you'd be heading off for the nearest rebel camp. Then it's likely that you'd be dead."

"Would it matter? If I was dead?"

"Strangely, yes. God knows why. The last thing I need in my life is a crazy woman."

She scowled at him. "Thanks. Except I'm not in your life. I drugged you to get the access. Now we're finished. You can just walk away."

He shook his head. "As I said—crazy. If you do anything, you'll be killed or captured. There will be an investigation. They'll find out you used my access, and there's the end of my brand-new start. My future. Whether I like this or not, I'm in it up to my neck."

"You could still turn me in."

"Too late for that. Besides, you're forgetting that there's more at stake than your predictions. What's on this file of Stella's? Why give it to me?"

She lifted her chin. "Desperation, probably."

"Thanks," he said dryly. "We have to get it before anyone else does. That means working together." Suddenly he felt like the room was pressing in on him. The windowless place reminded him too much of the interrogation room where they had questioned him after Aaron had disappeared. He'd told them he hadn't known anything. They'd tortured him anyway. Broken him down, stripped away everything he believed in. He'd thought he'd built himself up again, but really, he hadn't. He was just a whole mass of contradictions, doubts, and fears, loosely cobbled together.

And at the bottom, maybe hope that there could still be a better world, a free world, out there somewhere.

But right now, he just needed to get out of there.

"Come on. Let's go for a walk. I need to get my head straight, and then you can bring me back here and prove to me that you've made a machine that can predict the future."

She appeared about to argue, but she must have seen something in his face, because she leaned across, switched off the systems, and stood up. "I'm hungry. I suppose it's weird in the middle of all this—feeling hungry, I mean. As if my appetite has no right to exist when the world is falling apart around me."

He exhaled, still in the grip of his need to get out, feeling as though the weight of the building might collapse on them at any moment. He took her arm and ushered her out of the office and into the corridor, then up the stairwell that opened into the reception area.

They passed through security and then out onto the street. He gulped in the air.

"Are you okay?" she asked.

"Yeah. I can just get a little claustrophobic underground."

"Is that from when you were in the army?"

For a moment, he thought about just saying yes and leaving the subject, but in the end, he wanted there to be truth between them. "No. I was interrogated ten years ago, after Aaron disappeared. They wanted to find out if I knew anything."

"They tortured you?"

"It wasn't pleasant."

"Your father…? Do you think that's why he killed himself?"

She was always so direct. Didn't shy away from asking questions most people would avoid. "Maybe. Or perhaps he couldn't take the shame.

His position meant everything to him."

"Yes. I keep thinking about my family. What will happen to them—what's left of them—if I go through with this."

"Don't. In fact, for the next hour don't think about anything. A walk, then some breakfast. Then we'll…Christ knows. Decide what to do next, I suppose."

The sun shone, the sky was cloudless, the city around them went on, people working, children going to school. They strolled along the quiet streets in silence, walking close together. After a few minutes, he slipped his hand into hers, almost as if they were lovers. He told himself he was just keeping a close watch on her, but the truth was that touching her made him feel grounded. Which was odd, because she was crazy and deluded and plotting treason. She believed she had made a machine that could think and tell the future.

They found a café with tables on the street. Reluctantly he released her hand and they sat down, ordered coffee and bagels with cream cheese. It all seemed so normal. He realized he was starving and ate the first lot without speaking, then called over the waiter and ordered seconds. Finally, they both sat back replete, sipping their coffee in the sun.

"America's not such a bad place, is it?" She waved her hand around the street, the café.

"How do we know? There's no way of telling what's going on beyond our own little bit of the country. The news feeds are all controlled by the administration. We only know what they tell us."

"Like aliens being deported back to their own country." She rested her chin on her hand and watched the passers-by. "The day of the president's birthday—that was when this all began—I saw a family being taken away at the checkpoint. They looked so scared. I always believed they were just deported, flown to wherever they do belong and released. Not so bad."

He'd once believed that as well.

"I asked Auspex later what would happen to them. He predicted they were dead already or being kept for spare parts. When did that happen? When did the American people agree to do that?"

"The American people haven't had a say in much of anything since Martial Law came into force."

She emptied her mug, placed it on the cheery checked tablecloth. "One of my jobs is to monitor for alerts and pass them on to the Secret Service. I've been deleting the code greens—the alien activity—ever since Auspex told me what the likely result would be. Someone is probably going to notice any day now. So I'm likely finished anyway." She gave a weak smile. "Maybe I *should* run away and join the rebels. Except what's the point if we're all going to blow up?"

"Not much point at all."

"This whole thing has gotten me thinking. We've been living our lives wearing blinkers. Kidding ourselves that what we don't see isn't happening. That we aren't murdering innocent people just because they don't have the right paperwork. I hate it." Her voice was suddenly fierce. He glanced around, but there was no one listening.

"And you know what?" she continued. "Once I'd admitted to myself that I hate it, it was like a wall was knocked down in my mind. I realized that I hate this country and the way we live. I hate being told what I can and can't do. I hate that we have no freedom. That I can't go to the goddamn moon if I want to."

"You think you could build a spaceship?"

"Auspex says there's a 76 percent chance I could."

He wished she hadn't mentioned Auspex. "As long as the world doesn't implode first."

Her shoulders slumped. "Yes."

"I suppose it comes down to what most people want. To be safe or to be free?"

"What do *you* want?"

He thought for a moment. Not about his answer, but about how much of himself he wanted to reveal to this woman. While he still didn't entirely trust her, in the end, he went with the truth. "For me, it's not really a choice anymore. I know that safety is an illusion. I grew up believing that I had a place in the world, that I was part of something bigger than me. And just like that it was gone, and I was on my own. Worse than on my own, because I knew that anyone I cared for could be gone just as easily as my brother and my father."

She leaned toward him, her expression earnest, and placed her hand over his. He looked at it for a moment.

"So you decided not to care."

"It wasn't that difficult." Though that wasn't entirely true. In the army, he'd learned about camaraderie. Looking out for each other.

"Maybe you can only be free if you have nothing and no one to care about," she said. "It's a sort of freedom anyway. Though not like going to the moon." She sighed. "I'd choose freedom."

"Just as well, because you've pretty much fucked up any chance you have at safety."

She grinned, though it didn't quite reach her eyes. "Yeah. Tell me about the Wall."

"What about it?"

"What's it like? What's on the outside? Did you get to meet any non-Americans? What were they like?"

"As most of them tended to be shooting at me, we never really got to know each other. But yes, I went over the other side. It was…bleak. The area has been mined for miles in every direction."

"Who is it, though? Who are we fighting? What do they want?"

He didn't know anymore. "I don't know."

"I had a dream the night I saw the family taken away at the checkpoint. They threw them out of this big black gate, and they choked on noxious gases."

"They don't send aliens out through the Wall."

"No. They keep them here. At least their body parts, anyway." Another sigh. "I suppose we should go back."

"And you can tell me the future."

They'd walked a long way around but headed back to her office by the most direct route. About halfway there, they hit a checkpoint. The Secret Service agent was redirecting people. Gideon pulled out his ID and flashed it. "What's going on?" he asked.

"A rally at the bottom of K Street, sir. Possible rebel activity. A code two has been called. We've been told not to let any civilians through."

The man didn't comment as Gideon gestured to Kate to pass. This was the pro-democracy rally. They were usually peaceful. They just wanted a return to democracy, which everyone had been promised anyway.

As they approached the crossroads at 14th and K, the sound of running feet came from up ahead. Instinct kicked in, and Gideon stopped Kate with a hand on her arm. They were on a broad street lined with shops and offices. Just as they turned the corner, he heard the familiar hiss of a rocket flying through the air, and they came face to face with a mass of running people.

Were they under attack?

The rocket screeched over their heads, crashing into the street about a hundred feet from where they stood, just in front of the wave of people. It exploded in a cloud of gas, filling the air with black fumes like something out of a nightmare.

Another exploded, and another, until there was an almost solid wall of smoke. The people were stumbling now, coughing and choking, crashing to their knees.

Gideon dragged Kate back into a doorway as running feet sounded behind them. Wrapping his arms around her, he turned her so she was pressed against the wall between him and anything that was coming. Reaching behind her, he tried the door. It was locked. They were going nowhere.

D.C. had become a war zone and, for now, they were stuck in the middle of it.

CHAPTER TWENTY-FIVE

"If the freedom of speech is taken away then dumb and silent we may be led, like sheep to the slaughter." George Washington

Kate swallowed. She was plastered against Gideon, although if she raised her head she could see over his shoulder to where the world had changed into a swirling mass of smoke and chaos.

Everything seemed to happen in slow motion, the cries of panic sounding as though from a distance rather than only feet away. The blue sky had turned dark.

She tore her gaze from the mass of people to the other direction and went still. She wasn't sure what to expect. Rebels? Instead she saw a line of Secret Service officers, weapons drawn, sinister behind their gas masks.

She gripped Gideon closer, knew he was aware of them, his body tense against hers. "Stay still," he murmured.

She didn't think she could have moved even if she wanted to; just her eyes darted from the crowd milling in the swirling mass of smoke to the moving line of black-clad officers. As they passed, no one seemed to notice the two of them huddled in the doorway. Or maybe they didn't care that they were there. She expected them to come to a halt far enough away to monitor the protesters, but they kept moving, raising their weapons. Finally they stopped, a line of solid black facing the crowd. For a moment, everything was eerily silent.

Then gunfire shattered the quiet, roaring in her ears, and screams filled the air. Instinctively she fought to get away. To run or to do something to stop the carnage.

Answering gunfire echoed beyond the crowd. For a moment, it looked as if they were fighting back. And she was glad. Then she realized that they had turned and were running, but they were being prevented from escaping by more agents on the other side.

"Jesus, it's a massacre," she said.

The screaming was less now, though the gunfire still roared.

"Gideon, we have to go and see if anyone's alive. There were children in there."

"They're going through killing everyone. They're all dead. We can't help."

His voice was blank, held none of the outrage pulsing through her blood. She pulled away a little and looked up into his face, clear of expression. "Would you if you could?"

"Can you even ask that?" A tic jumped in his

cheek, just above the scar he'd gotten defending his country. Defending this.

Her mind was numb. "They wouldn't kill children." A lone gunshot resounded in the relative quiet, and she jumped. "Why, Gideon? These people have never shown any violence — they just don't like the president's policies. That doesn't mean they deserve to die, does it?" She could hear her voice rising as panic and disbelief took over. Her brain was denying what it had just seen, was searching for explanations. The people had been unarmed. They were always peaceable. The agents hadn't given them a warning, a chance to disperse. Instead they'd blocked them in. Almost herded them to a place where they had nowhere to run. Then murdered them. All, without exception. Men, women, and children.

Another lone gunshot. A shudder ran through her. She made to pull away—she had to go stop them before they killed any more. She was shaking, and Gideon grabbed her by the shoulders, gave her a hard squeeze.

"Get a fucking grip," he said, and his tone was fierce. "It's finished."

He was right, the gunshots had stopped now, and the street was quiet, smoke drifting up and away, slowly dispersing. The dead were almost surrounded by a ring of black-uniformed officers. She hated it, but Gideon was right. If they tried anything now, they would both die. And it would make no difference anyway, because everyone was dead. Two of the officers parted slightly and she caught sight of a body sprawled on the ground, a mangle of crimson and purple. Paula.

A small cry escaped her, and Gideon clamped his hand over her mouth. "Quiet. We have to get out of here. You need to look as if you belong. You can't let them see you're rattled."

She took a deep breath and nodded.

The thought came to her that she could do nothing if she died here today. Whereas if she lived, she might still fail, but she would goddamn die trying her best. She wouldn't go like a lamb to the slaughter.

As they stepped out from the wide doorway, two of the agents swung round, weapons raised, and her heart stopped.

Gideon already had his hands up, one holding his Secret Service ID, the badge glinting in a shaft of sunlight that probed through the billowing smoke. One man stepped closer, took the ID, studied it for a moment, then nodded. "Captain Frome, sir. I served under you on the Wall."

Gideon nodded. "Corporal Watson, I believe."

"Yes, sir." The man looked from Gideon to her. This was a man who had gunned down innocent people. Would he do the same to them? Although, ultimately, Gideon was his boss. In the end all he said was, "This is a restricted area."

"We were caught by accident," Gideon replied. "I was walking my girlfriend back to her office at Homeland Security. This is Supreme Court Justice Buchanan's daughter. We'll leave now."

The man studied her for a moment longer, and she shivered. She tried to hold herself still, then decided that a little fear was allowed in the circumstances. It would be odder if she wasn't affected by what she had seen. Finally, he nodded. "You can leave. But ma'am, sir, this is under the Official Privacy Act. Any mention of what you saw here will be taken as an act of treason."

"She won't say anything, Watson."

"I'll escort you to the checkpoint."

They didn't speak or touch as they walked through and then away from the checkpoint.

Don't look back.

Kate could feel the agent's eyes boring into her, but she avoided glancing over her shoulder in case it would result in some biblical punishment.

Even when they were out of earshot and sight, Kate remained mute. She had no clue what to say. It felt like the last of the world she had known had been ripped away from her, replaced by something twisted and rotten and indescribably filthy, reeking of blood and smoke.

She wanted to cry. At the same time, she was aware that no amount of tears would wash away the feeling and leave her cleansed. She wasn't sure what, if anything, could.

Her old life was gone forever. She could no longer close her eyes and say that the Party had the best interests of the American people at heart. Paula was American, and they'd gunned her down.

They made it through her building's security and across the foyer without her falling apart. She stumbled in the stairwell heading down to her office, and Gideon's arm came around her waist to keep her upright.

Somehow she managed to unlock her door, slamming it closed behind them as though this was some sort of sanctuary that would keep them safe from guns and bombs. But as Gideon had said earlier, safety was an illusion.

No one was safe.

She stripped off her jacket and tossed it into the corner. It stank of smoke and death—and so did the rest of her. She longed for a long hot shower, a bottle of wine, anything to help her forget. As if she could.

Except that now, more than ever, she had to persuade Gideon to help her. This had to be stopped.

"Sit down," she said, waving a hand at a chair.

He complied, and she crossed the room and powered up the systems. She waited while Auspex woke up, then switched him to audio.

"The Secret Service just massacred the people at the Bring Back Democracy rally. Do you know why?"

The answer with the highest probability is that it is the administration's attempt to solve the unemployment crisis.

What? "Is there an unemployment crisis?"

There has been a rise in unemployment over the last five years.

She turned to Gideon. "Did you know this?"

He had a frown between his eyes. "I'd heard something. That there were programs being brought into play to address the problem."

There's an active program to decrease the population. Those the government predict will be most problematic are first.

"Paula wasn't *problematic*, and the Bring Back Democracy rallies are always peaceful."

The president has expressed his dislike of the Bring Back Democracy group. Based on recordings I have amassed, he believes they do not love him enough.

"Christ, that doesn't mean he would kill them. Does it?"

There are several recordings of people who 'do not love' the president meeting with accidents. The president's most predictable criteria is to be loved.

Gideon got up as though he couldn't bear to sit still. "You're kidding, right?

"You know," Kate said, "Stella once told me that she would never go much higher in the Party because Harry knew she didn't like him."

"She didn't?"

"She hated him. She told me she loved the Party, but that Harry was a complete piece of shit." That had been one night when they'd drunk too much wine together, and Stella had opened up a little. She didn't usually drink. "She wouldn't say anything more."

Gideon ran a hand through his hair. "She was a good enough politician to hide what she thought of the man."

"Maybe not that good." She shrugged. "She's dead now, and so are all those other people."

"You think your machine is right? About the unemployment thing being the reason for the massacre?"

"Maybe. I don't think it really matters. There is nothing, *nothing* on this earth that could justify the killing of those people." She glared at him, part of her praying that he thought the same. She'd finally felt as though she had someone on her side. Now, the idea of going forward without Gideon's support was scary. Plus, if he decided he didn't support her, the chances were she was finished anyway, since he'd turn her over.

She supposed her best bet was that he'd just think she was some harmless geek, playing with her computer games and making up conspiracy theories.

He stared at her for what seemed like a long time, and then he nodded. "I agree. There's nothing."

The breath left her in a whoosh, and she sank down into her chair, her legs wobbly, her hands shaking.

She had to put what she'd seen behind her and move on. While she couldn't change what had happened to Paula and all those others, she could do her best to make sure it didn't happen again. She remembered a saying she'd heard long ago that had resonated with her. It came back to her now and she spoke it aloud into the silence.

"The only thing necessary for the triumph of evil is for good men to do nothing."

"What?" Gideon asked.

"It's a saying." She turned her chair so that she was facing him. She leaned across and rested her palms on his thighs, stared him in the face. "I believe you're a good man. And I want to be a good person. Are we going to do nothing?"

"No." He forced a tired smile that left his green eyes blank. He'd said he was at a crossroads, and she figured this was him finally deciding which road to take. Though she doubted he'd ever had much of a choice. He'd always be a hero.

She sat back. Right, first job: persuading him

that she wasn't crazy. That Auspex's predictions were accurate and based on reliable intel. Intel that was being ignored by the government agencies for some reason.

"Auspex, what is the probability of a nuclear bomb detonating on American soil in less than two weeks?"

91.5 percent.

Gideon sighed. "So how does it work?" he asked, waving a hand toward the screen.

"Auspex is a combination of collaborative system, predictive engine, and artificial intelligence."

"And what does that mean exactly?"

"He works with other systems, gathers all their raw data, and makes predictions on what might happen based on that data. Plus he's evolving all the time, learning to assess what is meaningful and what isn't. After your retinal scan gave him access to more systems, he's evolved more quickly than before."

"Glad I could help," he grumbled. She could almost see him considering his next question. "Can we see the intel behind the prediction?"

As she opened her mouth to ask for the information, the data began streaming across the screen. Auspex must have picked up Gideon's question and answered. There were hundreds of individual data streams, far more than in the original info dump. Which was odd, as she'd been checking and hadn't picked up anything new. She'd presumed the agents at NTAC had changed the search parameters.

"Auspex, why is there so much more data now?"

I increased the search parameters to identify anything which might be related to the attack.

He'd done that on his own? The information was still downloading.

"How many entries are there?"

Two thousand two hundred and sixty- five.

Wow. It would take forever to go through the individual files.

"Can you sort them by relevance?"

There was a stutter in the data stream, and then it continued. Kate scrolled back up to the top and swiped open the first file. Gideon scooted his chair up close so he could see the screen. It was a transit document for a shipment, although it didn't mention nuclear warheads and the locations were in some sort of code. The next file was the one she'd seen before.

Final test of Special Atomic Demolition Munitions completed.

She opened a few more files. They were like clues, snippets of information. She'd been hoping for something more definitive. Like the minutes of a rebel meeting laying out their plan to set off a nuclear bomb. Would this be enough to convince Gideon?

"Well?" she asked when he remained silent.

He scrubbed a hand through his hair. "I think you're right. Something is happening. There's just not enough information to put it all together."

"That's what Auspex does." She sighed. "The thing I really don't understand is why NTAC found the threat negligible. It doesn't make sense. There was clearly a cause for investigation."

"Maybe they want it to go ahead," Gideon said. "I heard a rumor that the president believes that a war would increase his popularity."

She hadn't heard that one before, and she frowned. "That's crazy."

"Not so much. People like to see a good clean fight. Good defeating evil."

"There's nothing clean about war. Certainly not a nuclear war that could kill us all."

"Maybe not, but people wouldn't go into a war expecting something so…terminal. Look at me. I was brought back because everybody thinks I'm some goddamn hero. Harry mentioned it when I talked to him at his birthday celebration. He also mentioned people not appreciating him, and it rubbed me wrong." He sat back in his chair, pressing a finger to his forehead. "I should have listened to my gut."

A tight band inside her loosened. It had been

there since Auspex had first come up with the crazy prediction; a sense that she was alone with an impossible task. Now she wasn't alone.

Not that she had any clue how they'd fix any of this. Even if they succeeded, there was a good chance that the truth would come out about her research and tampering with the alerts. The best-case scenario was that she would spend time in prison. Worst case, she would have to endure some really unpleasant torture, followed by a public execution. They'd probably kill her family along with her.

Even if by some miracle it didn't come out, there was no way she could go back to pretending everything was fine and dandy. So what was she to do—join the rebels?

If Gideon agreed to help her, he could expect the same. This was going to be hard, and it would only be harder if she followed her natural inclination and allowed herself to become attached to him.

No going there.

Time to get down to the details. There were two separate things here. Whatever Stella had been involved in, and Auspex's prediction of the nuclear attack. She couldn't see how the two could be connected. But what did she know? She'd ignored politics for so long. Hidden herself in her own little world. Now she was having a crash course in reality.

Reality sucked. Big time.

She took a deep breath. "What do we do next?"

Gideon had been waiting patiently for her to speak. "I think the first thing is to find out what information Stella has on this file."

"Do you think the two things are connected?" She waved a hand to indicate Auspex.

"I doubt it."

To get Stella's information, she had to somehow get into the White House, then into Stella's office and onto her system. "I suppose I could do a White House tour and sneak off." They were still run on a weekly basis, mostly for local schoolchildren.

"You'd never get near Stella's office. It's in the restricted area. There's probably surveillance, too; certainly outside in the corridor, but maybe inside."

That should be easy enough to check up on.

"Auspex, can you get me surveillance details for Stella's office? Without anyone seeing a record?" The last thing they needed was to put anyone on the alert.

"He can do that?" Gideon asked.

"With your security clearance, yes."

A few seconds later, the information flashed up. Gideon was right; there was a security camera outside the office. There was also a camera inside.

"They don't trust their own people?" she asked.

"We don't trust anyone." He got up and came to stand beside her. "Do all the offices have surveillance?"

No.

A list of names flashed up. Not many.

"So, the chances are they suspected your sister of something. Or they had some other reason for the surveillance. It also means they might not be monitoring it any longer."

"How about if I contact someone and ask to go clear out her personal belongings?"

"Not policy. I doubt they'd agree."

"Then what?" She could hear the frustration in her voice.

Gideon straightened. "I think there's a way. Tomorrow night. There's a function at the White House. I've been invited. Harry wants to give me a medal." He grimaced. "It will be televised. A lot of people."

"And a lot of security."

"Yes, but around the party. Not the offices. I can get you in as my partner for the night. Let people think we're in a relationship. We sowed the seeds for that at the funeral. People will expect to see us together. They won't be suspicious."

She hated big parties, but it was too good an

opportunity to pass up. A perfect excuse to get into the White House and into her sister's office.

She thought about asking Auspex what the probability of succeeding was, but she decided that the information wouldn't help—and might just impair her ability to function.

"In the meantime, just act normal," Gideon said. "Come to work. Keep your head down. If Stella was under suspicion, your whole family could be being watched."

Her spine prickled at the thought, and she cast a furtive glance around the room. She made a mental note to program Auspex to tell her if there were any changes to her security. In fact, maybe she should program Auspex to actually work out what might be of use to her. Right now, he answered specific questions. But he should be able to extrapolate what information improved her probability of surviving.

"What are you doing tonight?" Gideon asked.

"I'm meeting my mother. Stella kept an apartment in the city. She used it if she worked late. We're going to go through her things." She wasn't looking forward to it. Just the thought made her heart ache. It made everything seem so final. Plus, spending time with her mother hurt. Since Stella's death, the ravages of whatever had been going through her mom's mind for years were clear every time Kate looked at her. What had gone wrong? The mother of her childhood had been a happy, easygoing woman. She'd loved her position as the wife of a supreme court justice, had been proud of her husband, ambitious for her daughters. That had all changed fifteen years ago. But maybe it was time to stop hiding from that and find out why.

"Should I still go?" she asked.

"Yes, keep to your schedule. It's what you'd be expected to do, and you might find something." He pinched the bridge of his nose. "I think that's all we can do for now. We have to know what this information is before we decide our next move. Until tomorrow night, we both act normal."

She stood up. It looked like he was leaving, and she had the urge to beg him not to go. However illogical it was, she felt safe when she was with Gideon. As though he could protect her from all the bad things.

"What will you be doing?"

"I'm going into the office. I'm sure someone will have reported that I was at the shooting this morning. I need to make it seem natural."

She'd almost forgotten about the shooting. Or rather, she'd pushed it to the back of her mind. There was only so much grief you could process.

For a moment, they both looked at each other, as though there was something they should be doing. Instead, she just stood there, staring at him, until finally he gave her a brief nod and turned and walked out of the room.

The door slammed behind him, and she sank back down onto her seat.

She had a date with Gideon Frome. Which might have been nice under other circumstances. Even without asking Auspex, she had a good idea that the chances of them getting out alive were pretty low.

CHAPTER TWENTY-SIX

"If anyone is crazy enough to want to kill a president of the United States, he can do it. All he must be prepared to do is give his life for the president's." John F. Kennedy

The rest of the day was mostly uneventful. Kate monitored the chatter, sent in a couple of yellow alerts. Deleted a green without even bothering to check with Auspex.

She'd just checked the prediction for the nuclear attack. It was still climbing.

As she was about to pack up and leave, a news report flashed up on the screen.

There he was. President Harry Coffell.

He was clearly reading from a teleprompter, and while his expression was somber, there was a strange glint in his eyes. Satisfaction. He claimed the massacre had been instigated by the protesters. That they had been infiltrated by aliens and militant rebels who wished to destabilize the country. Many American soldiers had been killed in the confrontation.

Images flashed up. They weren't the protesters she'd seen die; they were men in army fatigues next to civilians. The close-ups showed the latter to be exclusively people of color.

Fury rose inside her. It was an outright lie, twisted propaganda of the worst sort.

"America is safe. The American people are safe." Harry raised both hands into the air as the crowd clapped him. "God bless America."

She watched until the screen went black, sick to her stomach. The man was evil. Without thinking, she leaned forward and typed.

What would happen if someone killed the president?

She hadn't really expected an answer.

If President Harry Coffell were to die in the next two weeks, the probability of alert 10245 resulting in a threat to the American people would be negligible.

After staring at the screen for an age, she leaned forward and switched it off. She walked out of the building, her mind numb with the enormity of what she'd just learned. On the street, she flagged down a passing taxi, gave Stella's address, functioning on autopilot.

She'd arranged to meet her mother at seven-thirty, but she wanted to get a couple of hours in first. However, once there, she couldn't make herself move.

Stella was the most amazingly tidy person Kate had ever known. There wasn't a thing out of place in the small apartment. She stood in the middle of the living room trying to decide where to start.

The place was decorated in muted grays and white. Stylish, but not flamboyant, a lot like Stella herself, though her sister hadn't always been like that. Kate remembered her as being bright, bubbly, and full of life. That had changed, along with everything else all those years ago when Kate was twelve and Stella three years older. The life had drained out of her sister, and Kate had no clue why. Whatever it was had also set her mother on the road to becoming the half-woman she was today. She'd done the same things, gone to the same parties, but it was all going through the motions.

Kate had done her best to ignore what was happening around her ever since. She was good at that. Now, she couldn't ignore it any longer. The need to know what had happened, what had gone wrong, clawed at her insides.

She turned slowly. Most of the surfaces were clear, just a couple of photographs. One of the whole family, one of her and Stella on her eighteenth birthday. She crossed the floor and picked up the photo. While her sister had been beautiful, now that Kate looked, she could see the shadows in her eyes. Just like her mother's. As though they had both been hiding something from her, though Kate had certainly made things easy for them. She'd never poked beneath the surface, had accepted things as they'd been presented to her.

She put the photo down. There was nothing else to show her sister had lived here. Her chest ached.

She moved to the bedroom. At least here there was some small evidence of her sister's existence. A robe was thrown across the bottom of the neatly made bed, and as she breathed in, her nostrils filled with the lingering scent of her sister's favorite perfume. Sharp and citrusy.

She returned to the living room and collected the trash bags she'd brought with her. Back in the bedroom, she opened the drawers and pulled out the underwear—plain cotton, her sister hadn't been one for fancy underwear—and shoved it into one of the bags.

Next, she tackled the wardrobe. Mainly black suits. She placed them in a separate bag—they would go to the goodwill store. Shirts and sweaters would as well. She kept her mind blank as she worked, only becoming aware of the tears that rolled down her cheeks as her vision blurred. She sank onto the bed, clutching a cashmere sweater to her face.

She was still sitting there when the doorbell rang. Kate wiped a hand across her cheeks, gave herself a quick glance in the mirror before she went to let her mother in. Her mom was dressed in a black knee-length dress. Her eyes were red, but they appeared clearer than they had in a long time, and her expression held a hint of something Kate had never seen before. Maybe determination. But to do what?

Kate gave her a quick hug. They hadn't been a demonstrative family in a long time. For a second, her mother's arms tightened around her, then she let go. She stepped back. "We need to talk," she said.

Kate had been about to turn away, but now she studied her mother. She'd thought she would have to wheedle or coerce the information out of her. Now it looked like she was ready to talk. Had Stella's death unlocked her somehow?

After giving a quick nod, she turned and led the way into the living room. He mother sank into the corner of the dark-gray velvet sofa, clutching her hands in her lap. Kate gave her clenched face one glance and headed into the kitchen. Her sister wasn't much of a drinker, but maybe she kept something for visitors.

In the fridge, she found a half-full bottle of bourbon. Maybe Stella liked to drink alone. She grabbed the bottle and a glass from the counter, then changed her mind and picked up a second glass.

Her mother was seated exactly as she had left her, staring straight ahead. Kate placed the glasses on the steel coffee table and poured a measure of bourbon into each.

"Here, mom."

Her mother automatically put out a hand for the glass. Kate sighed and sank down beside her. She kicked off her shoes and curled her legs under her, sitting at an angle so she could see into her mother's face. She sipped her drink. Now that they were here, she didn't want to start. Maybe there was something else she could say.

"I love you, Mom."

Her mother had been staring straight ahead. Now she jerked as if she'd been struck, then swallowed her drink in one gulp.

"Tell me what's bothering you," Kate said.

"I want to, but I can't."

"You can. You've already decided to. Now you just need to get the words out."

"You'll hate me."

"I could never hate you. I need to understand what went wrong with our family."

Her mother visibly gathered herself together. She placed the glass on the table and folded her hands back in her lap. "When your sister was fifteen, she was raped by Harry Coffell."

The world dropped out from beneath Kate's feet. She realized she hadn't a clue what she had expected. Just not this. "The president?"

"He wasn't president then. It was a few years

before he was inaugurated."

"Tell me."

"She was a beautiful child. And he took her innocence, destroyed her belief in herself, hurt her. He told her that if she disclosed what he had done, then he'd destroy our family."

"So how did you know?"

"Aaron."

"Aaron Frome. Gideon's brother?"

"They were childhood sweethearts."

"Aaron and Stella? But it was Gideon and Stella."

"That was later. Aaron's mother was a very good friend of mine. Stella and Aaron were the same age. They grew up together. We always knew that one day they would marry."

"*I* didn't know."

Her mother gave a small smile; the first Kate had seen in so long. "You weren't aware of anything going on around you. Your head was always stuck in a book, or a movie, or some god-awful ancient TV show set in space."

"I wasn't that bad."

"You weren't bad at all, just different. Certainly different from your sister. Anyway, we told them they could date when Stella was sixteen, but they'd sneak out to meet—innocently, I'm sure. They just loved to be together."

Had Gideon known? "What happened?" A

heavy weight settled in her stomach. She both needed to hear this and, at the same time, wanted to cover her ears so she didn't have to listen.

"She was at a Young Loyalists meeting at the White House. Aaron had arranged to meet her outside when it was over. When she didn't turn up, he went looking. He found her huddled down a side street where Harry's henchmen had dumped her. She was crying and bleeding. At first she wouldn't tell him what had happened, until he threatened to call the police." She waved at the bottle and Kate poured her another drink. She sipped it for a moment. "He brought her home — she refused to go to a hospital, though she was clearly hurt. You were out, thank God. Your father was home. If he hadn't been, things might have gone differently. Aaron wanted to report it, but your father was adamant. No one could know. It would be the end of the family."

"What did Stella want?"

"She was almost hysterical — said they had to forget it. It hadn't happened. That Harry had said they would all be killed as traitors if she talked." She took a deep breath. "So I gave in. I was afraid. Maybe I even thought we could put it behind us. Go on with our pretty lives as though nothing had happened. Except that the pretty was only a veneer over the ugliness, and after that I could never stop seeing the ugliness, however hard I tried."

"The drugs?" Kate asked carefully.

Her mom gasped. "You knew?"

Kate nodded.

"I'm sorry. I was a coward."

"You were just trying to do what was best for us all."

"Stella didn't confide in me after that. I never knew what she was thinking. She refused point-blank to see Aaron. It broke his heart, and he went a little wild. It was only a matter of time before he got into trouble. The poor boy was as broken as Stella."

"What about Gideon?" How did he fit into this? How had he become engaged to Stella? Had he known? She was pretty sure he hadn't.

"That was your father's idea. And Gideon's. He'd made it clear he was interested in Stella. She was beautiful, but she hadn't looked at anyone since that night. Gideon was persistent, and your father said it would be a good idea. Of course, Harry was president by then and more powerful than his father had ever been."

After Harry Senior had suffered a stroke, they'd kept him in place until he'd gone beyond the stage of even acting the part of a figurehead. It was rumored he was close to insanity. At that point, he'd been discreetly moved to a secured home—supposedly a temporary measure. He'd never been seen again, though occasionally his son would mention him in a speech. She presumed he was still alive. Somewhere.

Harry Junior had slid into his father's place like a snake into a rabbit hole. Oh, there had been a whole lot of talk about resuming the democratic system and promises that elections were just around the corner. That was twelve years ago, and the first time Kate had taken an interest in politics. She'd been a couple of years away from finishing high school, had high hopes of college, and was totally fascinated by the banned subject of artificial intelligence. She believed that maybe with the removal of Martial Law and the reintroduction of democracy, there might be a loosening on policies related to research.

Looking back, she couldn't believe how self-centered she had been. Although she understood that part of her self-absorption had been a way to shut out her family life, which had become intolerable. Subconsciously, she'd sensed the darkness beneath the surface and had gotten through it the only way she could, by concentrating on the one thing that had never let her down. Computers.

"We'd hoped that when Harry Senior stepped down, there might be elections. Or at least someone else might take over."

Instead, Harry had taken over with hardly a

ripple and a load of platitudes about not making any changes during this dangerous time of transition. He'd spoken about keeping his father's dream alive. Making America a better place for Americans. Blah, blah, blah.

"Harry just got more powerful. And invulnerable. He started that Secret Service group, which is like his own private army. When we realized he was there to stay, we had to take steps to make Stella safe. It was like living on a bomb. We couldn't avoid him entirely and he was always super pleasant to Stella."

"Smarmy bastard."

"She would throw up after she had seen him. Once she was safely out of sight. But he knew. He'd get this look in his eyes."

"Harry hates it when someone doesn't love him," Kate said. Her mother frowned, and she continued, "Something Gideon told me."

"I think he's correct. There was always something not right about him. He was spoiled as a child and as a man. Then something broke inside him when his mother was killed. Anyway, we had to make him believe that she was over what had happened. That she was loyal to the Party. Gideon was a favorite—he was going to go far. Stella didn't care enough to argue. She just went along with the engagement like a doll being moved around with no thoughts of her own."

"What happened with Aaron?"

"We don't really know. Something triggered him—sent him into a rage. Maybe Stella getting engaged to his brother was just one step too far. He was a member of the Bring Back Democracy group by then. He gave an interview, hinted that he knew things about the president. Threatened to reveal all."

"Then he disappeared."

Her mother nodded. "His father called us. Told us Aaron had run, that he expected to be arrested and questioned himself at any time, and that Gideon was likely to be as well. He said we should distance ourselves. Stella was going to break off the engagement, but Gideon broke it off first. I think your father went to see him, though I don't know for sure. If Stella had married him, then he might have saved her. He was always such an honorable man."

"He still is."

"And he's back now." Her mother pushed herself up slowly, suddenly old. She wandered the room for a minute, stopped, picked up the photo Kate had earlier, then put it face down on the dresser. She came back, stood gazing down at Kate. "We made this world. All those years ago, we stood at a crossroads and we could go either way. And we chose this. America for Americans." She laughed, but the sound held no humor. "A shit place for shit people. We deserve the world we've got."

Kate rubbed her arms, a chill running through her. "There's still time for change."

"Is there?" She sighed. "I needed to tell you. For you to understand. I think it's only a matter of time before they come for us. For you, too, maybe." She looked around the place and shrugged. "I wouldn't bother sorting out her things. There's nothing of the real Stella here. She died when she was fifteen at the hands of that monster."

She turned and walked away. Kate didn't move, couldn't think of anything she could say that would make things better. Except maybe *I'm going to kill President Harry Asshole Coffell.* Would that make her mother feel better?

Maybe.

The front door slammed.

But her mother had been wrong about one thing. Stella had been alive. The last few years, she'd had a purpose and a new vitality. She'd just learned to hide her real self too well.

Kate had an almost overwhelming sadness that Stella had hidden from her as well. Then again, what had she ever done to earn her sister's trust? The most important thing that had ever happened to her, and Kate had known nothing.

Had she met Aaron again? Had she been

working with him? Had that been discovered by the Secret Service? Kate suspected not. Because if the connection had been found, she would have been arrested in the open; there would have been no need of an accidental death.

They would have wanted to question her, find out what she knew.

Instead, she had just been killed.

Had she died purely because she hated Harry, and Harry wanted to be loved?

It seemed unbelievable. But, strangely, Kate did believe it. The man was insane.

Yeah, she was going to see the bastard dead. And save the world.

Though she still had no clue how.

CHAPTER TWENTY-SEVEN

"The tree of liberty must be refreshed from time to time with the blood of patriots and tyrants."
Thomas Jefferson

Gideon closed the door and crossed the room to his desk. He'd come back here yesterday afternoon and found out nothing of any use. They were shutting him out. He hadn't heard anything from Kate, and he tried to tell himself that was good. But worry nagged at his mind, like a fleabite he couldn't scratch.

He'd once spent a week trapped inside a flea-infested hut outside the Wall. He'd become used to them in the end. In fact, he preferred fleas to the company he had to keep right now.

Eventually, he picked up his phone. He'd have to be discreet—all calls were monitored—but at least he could check she was okay. He punched in her number and she picked up straight away.

"Kate Buchanan."

She sounded breathless. He realized she wouldn't know it was him—the call would just show up as Secret Service. He'd probably given her a heart attack.

"It's me, sweetheart."

"Gideon." Her relief was palpable. "How are you? What do you want?"

"Just to say good morning. I missed you last night."

"You did?"

"I did. Did you get your sister's apartment sorted out?"

"Some of it. I've organized a cleaning firm to come in and do the rest."

"That's good. Are you ready for tonight?"

"Not really. I have nothing to wear. You sprang this on me rather suddenly."

She was acting; she sounded outwardly flirtatious, but he could hear the reserve beneath the banter. "I couldn't bear the thought of going without you."

"Aw, that's sweet, but as I said I have nothing to wear."

"Go buy something pretty, then. I'll pick you up at seven."

"Okay. Bye, Gideon."

"Bye, sweetheart." He put down the phone and sat in the chair behind his desk.

He liked calling her sweetheart, partly because he knew it would wind her up. He liked winding her up. It was something he'd never done with Stella. They hadn't had that sort of relationship. She'd always been very reserved, but he'd reassured himself that she would get over that when they married. Now he wasn't so sure.

Both their families had been keen on the relationship. When they were younger, he'd always thought that Stella and Aaron would end up together, but their friendship had fizzled out when they'd been teenagers. He'd once asked Aaron why. His brother had just shrugged and asked who knew how girls thought.

She'd been so beautiful, almost perfect, with her quintessential American looks. Blonde hair and blue eyes. He'd been enchanted by the idea of them as the perfect American couple. Together they could help take the country to the next level.

Except that they hadn't really been a couple, never mind a perfect one. They hadn't shared anything.

He'd been so busy back then working on the president's staff, trying to make a name and a place for himself, that it had almost been a relief that Stella hadn't asked for much of his time.

He stared out of the window. She was dead now, and he'd never really known her.

His relationship with Kate felt more real. Hell, it *was* more real.

And was going absolutely nowhere.

It might all be over by tonight. They'd be caught and locked up, and there was a good chance they'd be tortured. His guts twisted at the thought of anyone hurting Kate.

He'd spent the night trying to think of an alternative, but he'd come up blank. He wouldn't get past the door of Stella's office, never mind into the systems. This was the plan and they had to stick to it. Which didn't mean he had to like it.

What he needed was an idea of what was going on here. Who was in and who was out.

He'd heard nothing around the office about the massacre that had taken place yesterday. It had to have been planned, but there hadn't been a whisper. He was quite aware that the guard at the checkpoint would have recorded his presence there. So there was no point in pretending; it would seem odd. He also wanted to know more about what had happened and who had ordered it. And why?

He could find nothing in the records, no orders. The only reference was the allocation of assets. A large number of personnel had been allocated to what was supposed to be a peaceful demonstration. The order for that had come from the top—from his boss, Boyd.

He looked up the roster and found that Corporal Watson, the agent who had escorted them back to the checkpoint, was in the building at the moment. That was a starting point. He made a couple of calls and located Watson in the basement. He headed down there and found his man on one of the firing ranges. He stood at the back of the room watching while Watson shot at the man-shaped target. He was mediocre at best. When he turned, Gideon could see the frustration on his face. He caught sight of Gideon and scowled, then his face cleared of expression.

He nodded. "Sir?"

"Corporal Watson."

"I heard you're a good shot, sir." He held out the gun, then stripped off his ear protectors and handed them to Gideon. He took them. He hadn't shot a gun since he'd left the army. Most of the time he carried, but he'd never come close to needing to shoot someone—however much he might have been tempted.

Now the weapon felt comfortable in his hand. He settled the protectors on his head and held out his hand for a new magazine. Replaced the old one. He shifted the weight, stretched out his arm, and shot six bullets into the center of the target's head.

He lowered his arm and pulled off the protectors. A group had gathered around to watch him. Even if he didn't like the audience, it wasn't a bad thing that they got a look at who he was, what he could do. He got the idea that most people around here thought he was just pretty window dressing. They weren't completely wrong. He ran a finger down the scar on his cheek. Except that he wasn't pretty.

On the other hand, perhaps it might have been safer if they thought of him that way. Too late now.

He handed the gun back to Watson. "I wanted to thank you for not keeping us waiting yesterday," he said.

"I take it you got Ms. Buchanan back safely," Watson said. "She must have been shocked."

"She was." He gave a friendly smile. "She's spent her life in an office playing with computers. I don't think she's ever seen anyone killed before."

"And she's okay? She's not going to make a big thing of it?"

"Of course not. She's aware that these things happen. That certain factions have to be controlled if America is to be safe." He couldn't believe the crap falling out of his mouth, but Watson nodded his head. "Tell me, it looked like you came prepared for trouble. Had you been pre-warned?"

Was that suspicion flickering in Watson's eyes? "Why are you asking?"

He shrugged. "Just trying to get a feel for how things work around here. I'm new and I'm a little out on the edge."

Watson's expression closed up. "You'll have to ask the boss if you want any more details. I'm sure he'll tell you what you need to know."

Gideon had the impression he wasn't going to get anything out of the man, and he was also pretty sure that Boyd would tell him nothing.

He headed back up to his office, taking the stairs. He was on the third floor, deep in thought, when the door from the corridor opened into the stairwell. Two men entered. He recognized them vaguely, but not by name. They were on Harry's bodyguard detail, so he'd never worked with them.

As he made to walk past, they formed a barrier between him and the stairs he was heading for. He stopped and looked them up and down. Both were big, well over six feet, with wide shoulders under their black suits. Both wore white shirts and navy ties; they could have been clones except that one was pale and blond and the other darker.

"Can I help you, gentlemen?"

The blond guy's eyes narrowed at the polite tone. "Some of us don't like the fact you've been brought in from nowhere. There were a lot of qualified people who could have taken that job."

"Instead you got me. Aren't you lucky?" He gave them a smile while he studied them. Muscle. And as his gaze drifted down, he noticed the knuckle-dusters that covered their hands. They had come to give him a proper hello.

"We're just here to extend a welcome from some of the guys."

Gideon's smile widened. Some of the tension drained from him. He knew the feeling. That moment waiting to go into battle. When he actually got out there, he'd experienced the same feeling, a release of fear. There was nothing else but the fight. Fight or die.

A good fight was exactly what he needed. Get rid of the frustrations that had been building since he came back here.

They thought he was some sort of pretty-boy figurehead here to placate the people, and maybe he was in some ways. But that wasn't all he was. As they were about to find out. The space was small, and he didn't really want to kill either of them. He just wanted to say his own sort of hello.

He stood relaxed, waiting for them to make their first move. He was sure they were well trained—they wouldn't be on the bodyguard detail if they weren't. He was also sure he was better.

Two on one he wasn't worried about. He'd learned a lot about scrapping, and he didn't worry about fighting fair. Certainly not when the odds were against him.

Without warning, the darker man on the right rushed him. Gideon allowed the man to land one punch, just to get himself in the mood. Pain blossomed across his cheek as he whirled around, kicking his assailant's legs from under him so he crashed to the ground. He growled as his friend circled around Gideon. Ignoring the second man, Gideon clenched his fist and brought it down hard on the back of the neck of the downed man, who was pushing himself up. He slammed to the floor on all fours, fingers splayed. Gideon brought his boot down hard on the man's right hand, heard the crunch of bones as he ground it into the concrete floor.

The blond caught him in a clinch from behind. Now his adrenaline was pumping. He'd expected the move, and his response was pure instinct honed by many fights. He didn't struggle against the hold of the massive arms around his chest. Instead, he backed up fast into the wall behind him. As they hit the concrete, he raised his head and smashed his skull backward into the other man's face. More crunching of bones. He liked the sound. His opponent groaned, his grip loosening. Gideon tore free, turned, still close, and kneed the man in the crotch. He collapsed to the floor with a moan, then rolled to his side.

Hardly worth the effort. Gideon eyed the door, almost hoping they would send some more.

The first man sat leaning against the metal posts of the stairwell, cradling his broken hand. "Bastard."

"Yeah."

He glanced up, caught the wink of a camera in the corner where the wall met the ceiling. Someone was watching. What would a bastard do? He turned back to the blond lying still curled up on his side. He kicked out, hearing the crack of

ribs and getting no satisfaction from the sound.
Made himself repeat the action.

"Tell the guys I said welcome right back. And
mention if they want to come by and make it
personal, then I'll be waiting and more than
willing."

He cast the pair one more look. He'd made his
point.

Back in his office, he sat down, flexed his
fingers. Was anyone watching? While there was
supposed to be no surveillance in the offices here,
that meant nothing. He'd get Kate to check with
her little computer friend. If there was
surveillance, then it wasn't sanctioned through
ordinary routes, and he doubted it would be
picked up.

For the moment, he'd presume he was being
watched.

He was about to switch on his system when his
phone rang. His boss. That had been quick. But
then Gideon figured that Boyd had probably
known all about the fight before it had even
started. He'd probably just expected a different
outcome.

For a moment, it occurred to him that maybe
he should have let them beat the shit out of him.
Would it be an advantage if they underestimated
him? Maybe in some things, but the fact was that
what he needed most now was to be accepted,

taken into the fold. Told the secrets. They were keeping things from him. Boyd had mentioned a probationary period, but Gideon didn't have the time.

He picked up the phone. "Sir?"

"My office. Now."

So what position should he take? Outrage—why the hell were his own men trying to beat him up? Or understanding? He was being tested. He had no problem with that. Ha. He had fucking huge problems. He'd been fighting for his goddamn country, risking his life on the Wall, while these assholes—including Boyd—were wandering around D.C. in their smart suits in safety.

By the time he stood outside Boyd's door, he'd decided on a mixture of understanding and righteous anger. He knocked on the door.

"Come in."

Boyd's office was twice the size of his, but that was the only sign of excess. It was austere in the extreme. White walls, black tiled floor. A bare steel desk with a big leather chair behind it and an upright metal chair in front. Off to the side was a long black leather sofa—he'd heard that Boyd spent many of his nights sleeping on it.

Boyd was standing beside a bank of screens. The big one in the center was replaying the fight in the stairwell. Gideon watched until the screen locked on an image of him kicking the blond guy in the ribs. He studied his own face—it was totally free of expression. He waited for Boyd to speak.

"Tell me," he said. "Why did you go back and break Dawson's ribs? The fight was obviously over."

"Just making my point. You don't play where I come from. If you play, then you die. And I'm not ready to die just yet."

"I think your point was already made."

"Not really." He gave a small shrug. "I'd shown them I could fight. I needed to show them I was more than willing to. Plus, I don't want to have to spend my time here wondering if some asshole is waiting for me around the next corner."

"You need their respect?"

"They think I'm some sort of fucking pretty boy brought in here as a figurehead to be paraded in front of the people." He gritted his teeth and let some of his anger show. "I'm no fucking pretty boy."

A small smile curved Boyd's thin lips as he glanced back at the screen. "No, I can see that. But are you ready for the decisions you might have to make back here in D.C.? While it's a different playing field, it's as much a war as out there on the Wall."

"I want to be involved. I think I've earned the right to be in."

"Maybe. But your family will always be a black mark against you."

"I'm not my brother."

He held himself impassive as Boyd paced the room, clearly considering what he should tell him.

Come on, you bastard, let me in.

Finally the other man came to a halt in front of him. "You're a soldier and, from the reports I've read, a good one."

Get on with it.

"However, some of the things you're called to do here might be of a different sort. You're used to facing the enemy straight on, but there are other enemies we need to fight, far more insidious and far more dangerous to America than anything you will meet on the Wall."

"The demonstration yesterday?"

Boyd searched his face and gave a curt nod. "On the outside that might have seemed like a peaceful protest, but let me tell you—there is no such thing. I got the report you were present. How?"

"Pure coincidence. I'd been having an early lunch with my…" Christ, what was he supposed to call her?

"Kate Buchanan."

"Yes. We've become close since I came back."

"She doesn't seem your type."

His eyes narrowed. "I have a type?"

"Blonde, beautiful, and brainless."

"Maybe I needed a change. We met by accident, but I've been helping her through a tough time."

"The death of her sister."

"While they weren't close, it hit her hard all the same. Just a shock."

"You were once engaged to her sister?"

"A long time ago. A different life. An engagement of convenience. We were both ambitious."

"Would you say you're still ambitious, Gideon?" It was the first time he'd called him by his first name. Significant? Boyd wandered over to his desk, leaned down, and pulled a bottle and two glasses from the drawer. He waved at the upright chair and sat down in his own in front of the desk. He didn't ask, just poured two measures of bourbon into the glasses and pushed one across to Gideon.

Sitting down, Gideon reached out and picked up the glass. He took it as a sign that he was making progress. That Boyd was finally seeing him as more than a pain in the ass forced on him by the president, and maybe as a useful tool.

"I'm ambitious," he said cautiously, "though maybe not for the same things. And Kate's father is a supreme court justice."

"What things do you want? How are they

different?"

"Before, I wanted to be the face of the Loyalist Party. I wanted to be at the forefront. Now, while I still believe in the Party, I no longer want the fame. I want…power. Ten years ago, my life was torn apart through nothing I had done. I want to be in a position where that can never happen again. And I'm not too picky about how I get there."

"What did you think about the way we managed the demonstration yesterday?"

I think you're fucking murdering bastards.

He took a sip of the bourbon. It was smooth and slid down easily, warming the ice at his core. "I'm sure there were very good reasons."

"You're not going to rant about the murder of innocents?"

"There are very few innocents, and collateral damage is always a risk in any campaign."

Boyd seemed to assess him. "I'm glad you see this as a campaign, because that's exactly what it is. How did your little girlfriend react?"

"She was shocked. She's led a very sheltered life in some ways. But she was brought up in a political household. She understands the way things are. She didn't question the necessity. It was more worry about her personal safety."

"I hope you reassured her."

"Of course." He swallowed the rest of his bourbon. "So, are you going to give me something useful to do?"

Boyd sat back in his chair, laced his fingers behind his head. "When I first heard you were joining us, I have to admit, I was pissed off. I don't like being told who to employ, so you might say I was predisposed to hate your guts."

"Thank you."

Boyd grinned. "But I'm beginning to think that maybe you might be an asset after all."

Hallelujah.

"So I'll be given an actual job?"

"Don't be in such a hurry. There's something big going down in the near future."

"Big?"

"I'm afraid the details are classified until your probation period is over."

Damn.

"Curb your impatience. Afterward, there will be plenty of opportunities for a man with your talents."

Gideon fought back the urge to push the issue. He sensed he was close to a truth that would make everything clear. However, he also sensed that pushing right now would be dangerous and counterproductive. He'd done a lot to get himself accepted. He needed to rein in his impatience and leave it at that.

He had the distinct impression that within the organization there were actually two tiers, and that entrance to the second tier was by invitation only—after passing the probationary period. He could at least start working out who was in that upper tier. Starting with the agents who were part of yesterday's massacre.

He stood up. "Thank you, sir."

Boyd didn't say anything further. The meeting was clearly over. Gideon pushed back the chair and headed for the door.

"Gideon?"

He turned back, his hand on the door handle.

"I'll see you tonight."

"Yes, sir."

CHAPTER TWENTY-EIGHT

"The only thing to fear is fear itself." Franklin D.
Roosevelt

Kate hadn't heard from Gideon again after the
call that morning. She presumed nothing bad had
happened, though the possibility hung above her
like a huge pregnant cloud about to burst.

She'd resisted asking Auspex anything else. She
didn't think knowing the odds would help. But she
had called her mom on a secure line to check she
was okay. Telling Kate about Stella seemed to
have opened the floodgates, and she spoke some
more about that time, purging her system. Maybe
it would clear some of her bitterness and allow her
to move on. If she got the chance, but Kate didn't
dwell on that. One thing at a time.

Now, she sat in front of her dressing table with
the array of makeup she'd bought after the
makeover for her "pickup Gideon" evening. She
had the feeling she needed some sort of mask in
place.

Just the thought of coming face-to-face with
Harry made her stomach churn.

She had to find a way to put it behind her. Just
for tonight, in order to get through the evening

without giving away her hatred. She had a job to
do.

She smoothed foundation over her face, waited
for it to dry, then added another layer—hopefully,
that would hide any flushes. Plus, she had a habit
of going deadly pale when she was angry, which
made her freckles stand out like measles.

She circled her eyes in black, added mascara
and the false eyelashes. Then pink lipstick that
clashed with her hair, but hell, no one would be
expecting a fashion model. Most of the people
there tonight knew her at least through her family.
It would look odder if she did appear like some
sort of supermodel. What she needed was to look
like a woman in love. Or at least a woman
infatuated.

She pinned her hair in a loose knot on top of
her head and slipped into the black dress she'd
picked up on the way home. While not very party-
like, it wouldn't seem so odd considering her only
sister had just died...probably murdered by Harry.
No, black seemed very appropriate.

It suited her. Very plain, it was sleeveless, high
at the front but dipping almost to her ass at the
back. She wasn't risking high heels in case she had
to run, which wasn't a total impossibility. So she'd
bought a pair of flat black pumps with a diamanté
design. She looked...as good as she got.

The doorbell rang at precisely seven o'clock,

just as she was putting a few essentials into the matching black diamanté clutch bag. She hurried from her bedroom to open the door.

And nearly swooned.

Gideon leaned against the doorjamb, hands in his pockets. He was wearing his army uniform and looked pretty good.

When he'd been younger, he'd almost been too perfect. Now the scar added a hint of reality, not to mention danger. Then she noticed something else. "Have you been fighting?" Reaching out, she stroked a finger down over his cheek, where she could see the faint mark of a bruise beneath the skin.

"A little saying-hello-party from some of the guys at work."

"Bastards."

"Don't worry, they came out somewhat worse than I did."

"Good." Without thinking, she stepped closer, went up on tiptoe, and kissed him on the cheek. His hands clasped her shoulders holding her steady, but he didn't try to deepen the embrace. Probably for the best.

She sighed and moved back, pulling free easily—he didn't try and hold her.

"You want to come in? I take it you didn't drive. I can call us a cab."

"I thought we might walk for a little while, then

pick up a cab on the road. We can talk."

Did he think that a cab might be bugged? Were they both getting paranoid and seeing conspiracy theories around every corner? But she knew the threat existed. It wasn't paranoia.

"Let me grab my bag and a wrap." While the night was warm, she didn't want to wander the streets half naked.

They walked side by side, close but not touching. There was a checkpoint up ahead, only a hundred feet from the house. They passed through it, the officer giving Gideon a friendly nod. "Have a good party, sir."

"He knows you?"

"My boss took a film of the fight." He reached up and touched his cheek. "Had it streamed around the office. If he didn't know me before, he does now."

"He seemed to like you." She'd never noticed that before. They'd always treated him with scrupulous politeness, but tonight there had seemed genuine warmth.

"I don't think my two opponents were very popular."

"Two? You fought *two* men? That's not fair."

"Life's not fair."

"Are you hurt anywhere else? Broken ribs?" She didn't know a lot about fighting.

"I'm fine, but it's nice that you care." He

slipped a hand through the crook of her arm. "So, I get the impression you have something to tell me."

She didn't know where to start. "I told you I was meeting Mom last night?"

"Yes."

"Well, she told me something about Stella that I hadn't known. I still can't believe I didn't know. That Stella never told me. She kept it to herself all those years."

"What?"

She licked her lips. She had no clue how Gideon was going to take this. While she suspected now that he'd never been in love with Stella, he had cared for her. She swallowed. "Harry raped Stella when she was fifteen."

He stopped walking. With his hand on her arm, she was pulled to a standstill as well. She looked up at him. His face was a rigid mask of hard lines. "Say that again."

"Harry raped Stella. There's more. Aaron found her afterward. Did you know they were childhood sweethearts?"

"I knew they were close, but they seemed to draw apart when Aaron was…sixteen. Christ. He knew about it?"

"Yes. He took her home. Apparently he wanted to go to the police, but my father persuaded him not to. Stella was in no state to argue. My father said it would be the end of our family and probably yours as well."

• • •

Gideon tried to get his head around what she was telling him. He wanted to deny it could have happened, but it made sense of so many things. Releasing his grip on her elbow, he took a step back to give himself some distance. He pressed his fingers to his forehead, then shook his head in disbelief. While Aaron had been a little wild when he was younger, he was never in trouble; he'd been a good boy. Then he'd changed, become bitter and withdrawn. Gideon had tried to talk to his brother, but he'd shut him out. He remembered it had been summer when it had started. Gideon had been working a summer job at the White House that his father had organized. He'd spent a lot of time with Harry Junior. How had he not seen?

"Gideon?"

He shook his head. "I was thinking back." They were standing in the middle of the street, getting some curious glances from the passersby. He looked around and spotted an iron bench a few feet away. She didn't object as he took her hand and pulled her to the bench, then pushed her gently down with a hand to her shoulder. He took the seat beside her and sent his thoughts back to the summer Aaron had been sixteen and everything had started to unravel. "Jesus. Aaron changed so much that summer."

"My mom said he kept coming around, trying to see Stella. They'd been in love since they knew what love was, but my parents had made Stella wait until she was sixteen for them to date. Of course, that never happened. She refused to see him alone, and she pretty much cut him in public."

"Poor Aaron."

"Poor both of them. Harry didn't just rape her, he hurt her. He broke her. And he got away with it. What else has he gotten away with?" They were silent for a minute. Her hand crept into his. "They didn't tell out of fear that it would hurt our families, but all of us were hurt in the end."

"Why didn't he talk to me?"

"Maybe he thought you would be on the other side. That you wouldn't rock the boat."

"Never." The word came out fierce, and her eyes widened. "I would never have condoned rape. Don't put that on me."

"I'm sorry." Her hand slid into his and she squeezed. He was still trying to get his head around it. This was the catalyst that had set everything in motion. From that point forward maybe there had been no way to turn aside the catastrophe waiting to happen. But the two people most guilty—Harry who had perpetrated the crime, and Stella's father who had insisted on keeping it hidden—were the two people least affected by what had happened. He said as much, and she didn't try and deny it.

"My mother has been on drugs since, unable to face her part. Aaron vanished. God knows where he is now. Your father died, and your life was ruined. Maybe if they'd gone to the police, it might have all come out in the open. If they'd made enough noise."

"Harry would never have been president."

"And maybe Stella would be alive. I can't help thinking that she wasn't killed for anything other than that she hated Harry, and he knew it." Her eyes were bright with unshed tears, and she sniffed. "I can't cry. I'll smudge my makeup. I knew there was a reason I never wear it. Except until recently, I never ever cried, and now I seem to do it all the time. Pathetic." She sniffed again. "In all this, I was probably the only one unaffected, with my head firmly shoved where I couldn't see what was happening around me."

She was wrong. She'd been a sensitive twelve-year-old in a happy family, and suddenly everything and everybody had changed, and she had no clue why. It must have been terrifying.

"Think about it," he said. "Maybe the reason you avoided real life was because of what was happening around you. A mother on drugs, a father probably ridden with anger and guilt, a sister who'd closed herself off to everyone. It was no wonder you withdrew into a world of your own."

"I hadn't looked at it like that," she mused. "It's funny, isn't it? How one decision made in a moment can have such cataclysmic effects? I wonder if my father regrets his decision."

"Probably." Though he wasn't so sure. Phillip Buchanan was an ambitious man. So what had made Aaron run? At a guess, his brother becoming engaged to the girl he loved had something to do with it. That had maybe tipped him over the edge. "He left after I got engaged to Stella."

"That was the one time she actually spoke to him, but only in the presence of my mother. She told him it was for the best and he should forget her. That marrying you would make them all safe. He didn't want to be safe. My mother said he begged her to run away with him. Somewhere clean. She told him to leave her, that nowhere was clean."

He exhaled, slumping a little on the seat. Was she right? Had they gone beyond the point where they could make things right? Did they actually have the world they deserved?

He looked around him. The light was fading. There were people walking the streets, going about their business. They all looked content; well-dressed, well-fed. Most likely ignorant of what was happening beyond their small worlds.

Once he'd believed that was what they were aiming for. Just not at any price.

Justice? Freedom? Some control over your own life?

Did they matter more than a comfortable existence?

For him, yes. And, he suspected, for the woman beside him.

Humans were deeply flawed, but on balance there was more good than evil—he had to believe that. The real problem was apathy.

He remembered what Kate had said.

The thing that allowed evil men to prevail was good men doing nothing.

"There's something else," Kate said from beside him.

"There is?"

"I asked Auspex what would happen if someone killed Harry. It turns out that's the one thing that might just save us from nuclear annihilation."

He tried to get his head around that. He realized that he still hadn't accepted that Auspex was right and that they were hovering on the edge of a nuclear war. "That doesn't make sense."

"Nothing about this makes sense. But I want it to be me. I want to kill him. For Stella and for everyone he's hurting."

If there was any killing to be done, he would do it. He wouldn't mention that right now, because he was pretty sure she'd argue. Kate was no killer. He'd known many in his time, men and women who could stand face-to-face with someone and pull the trigger without a qualm. Kate was not one of them.

Maybe that's what drew him to her. She was a good person. In a world gone to decay, she shone.

All the same, in one way she was right. Harry had to die. The man was evil. How many other lives had he ruined? But maybe there was a way to do it from within the system. Hopefully, whatever information Stella had had would help them decide their next move.

He stood up and held out his hand to her. Kate slid her palm into his, wrapping her fingers tight around him, and got to her feet. She took a deep breath. "Let's go party."

CHAPTER TWENTY-NINE

"Times change, and we change with them."
William Henry Harrison

Kate was the center of attention and she hated it.

Actually, *she* wasn't the center of attention, but her tall, handsome, hero partner was, and as he hadn't let go of her since they entered the ballroom, they came as a package.

Either way, the intense scrutiny made her skin prickle.

They were in the ballroom, and everything glittered. The chandeliers overhead, the women festooned in jewels. America's finest. But beneath the glamour something dark lingered, putting her on edge.

Surrounding them, the constant hum of low, well-bred voices was punctuated by the clink of crystal.

One good thing? Her soldier was a little intimidating. Maybe it was his size, or the uniform, or the scar, or maybe air of self-containment that made people wary of drawing too close. So although they were the center of attention, people were observing from afar.

She sipped on a glass of champagne—domestic,

of course. The president hadn't made his entrance
yet. She wished he would arrive and get it over
with. The tension was making her stomach churn.
Maybe once she'd seen him, she would realize she
wasn't going to lose it, to throw herself at him and
rip his heart out. Beside her, Gideon was also
tense. She could feel it in the hand at her waist, see
it in the rigid set of his shoulders. Despite his
outward air of calm, she knew that what she'd told
him had affected him deeply.

"Relax," she murmured. "You're frightening
people."

"I can't stop thinking about it. Stella… You
know we never slept together, right?"

She shrugged, uncomfortable and intrigued at
the same time. Hadn't she always wondered what
it had been like between Stella and Gideon? "It's
none of my business."

He cast her an incredulous look but made no
direct comment. "She was young and said she
wanted to wait until we were married. She wasn't
particularly passionate. I told myself I could
change that. Turns out I probably didn't stand a
chance. It's just as well we didn't marry."

"Maybe."

"Now, with hindsight, I can see there was
something not right. She was…melancholy. I took
it for reserve, but clearly it wasn't. Poor woman."

"At least she had Joe. I admit, I never really got

what she saw in him. He always seemed so…quiet and unassuming. Maybe that's why she felt safe with him. Then, the last few years, I'd swear she was happy."

"Something else happened?"

"I think it must have, but whatever it was, she never confided in me." A little stab of bitterness caught her unawares. She'd loved her sister, and she'd been sure Stella loved her, yet she had shut her out of everything important in her life.

"Probably to protect you."

"Yeah, because I'm so pathetic."

"No, but you are vulnerable, and she knew that."

"She was so bright. I hate him."

"Kate."

She turned as someone spoke her name. Her father. She hadn't known he was coming. She looked past him to see if her mother was also present, but he was alone.

She leaned across and kissed him on the cheek. "Hello, Daddy. I didn't know you were coming."

"Same here. This isn't your usual thing."

"Gideon asked me at the last minute. I thought it would…take my mind off things."

"Your mother couldn't make it. She's not feeling too well. Stella's death hit her hard."

"It hit us all hard, sir," Gideon said.

Her father looked between the two of them.

"Are you two seeing each other now?"

She opened her mouth to say they were just friends, but Gideon beat her to it. "Yes sir, we bonded over a mutual love of Star Wars."

Her father smiled at her. "You're not still watching that garbage?" He turned to Gideon. "All she ever wanted to be growing up was a Jedi Knight."

"She still does, sir. I'm getting her a light saber for her birthday."

"Get two," she said, "and we can have duels."

There was a commotion at the doors and a couple of Secret Service agents entered. The crowd parted before them. Harry entered, flanked on either side by agents. There were two more behind him.

"He certainly takes his personal security seriously," she muttered.

"Yes," her father said, "and he's gotten more paranoid in the last year or so."

"Is it paranoia?" Gideon asked.

Her father shrugged. "There have been no substantiated threats as far as I know."

Maybe he was just realizing how many people out here must have reason to hate him. Kate studied him; she'd never really looked too closely. Something about the man had always repelled her. He was handsome in a bland, blond, blue-eyed way. His features were even, his nose straight, his mouth well-shaped. Tonight he wore a tuxedo, like most of the other men. It showed off his lean figure. He must be in his forties now, yet he appeared ageless. Probably bathing in the blood of virgins or something.

He headed directly to the podium that had been set up at the front of the room and climbed the stairs, his guards staying with him like some sort of choreographed dance troupe. He halted in front of the microphone.

"Welcome, fellow Americans."

There was a polite ripple of applause.

"We are here tonight to honor one of our country's great heroes."

She nudged Gideon in the side. "That's you," she whispered, and he grimaced.

"Captain Gideon Frome."

He didn't move, and she gave him another nudge. He glanced down at her. "I hate this stuff," he muttered.

"Go. Greet your fans."

His eyes narrowed, but he released his hold on her and strode toward the podium, the crowd parting for him, the people clapping as he passed. It occurred to her that they sounded way more enthusiastic about Gideon than they had about the president. Harry was watching, a smile on his face that wasn't reflected in his cold eyes.

"It's good to be popular," her father said

quietly from her side. "But maybe not too popular. Harry isn't the sort of man to share the limelight."

"Gideon will be careful," she replied.

"Yes. He always was a political animal, even as a young man. He would have gone far if—" He broke off. "Well, maybe he has another chance now. God knows we could use some good men."

Her father sounded slightly bitter. But then, why wouldn't he? He knew what Harry had done, and however ambitious her father was, he also loved his family. Whatever decisions he'd made would have been because he had their best interests at heart. All the same, she figured he would always think how different things might have been.

Gideon was on the podium now, side by side with the president. Dark and light. He was a good three inches taller than Harry.

"I've known Gideon for a long time," Harry began. "For a while, we worked closely together, until he decided things were a little boring around here in D.C. Sadly, he left me to join the army and find fame and fortune."

Kate snorted, and her father cast her a stern look.

"There, he found his true calling as a leader of men. His bravery saved many lives and he was almost solely responsible for our success at the battle of Bison Falls, where the Wall would have been breached had it not been for this man. I give you Captain Gideon Frome." He raised his hands and clapped, and the guests followed him, breaking out into cheers and whistles.

"I didn't realize he was *this* popular," she said.

"That's because you spend your life with your head stuck in a computer. He's got everything. Looks, presence — and now he's a hero. But popularity is a two-edged sword. Especially in this administration. Harry's brought him in because he feels it will reflect on him, but he's not interested in competing for attention."

She glanced at her father. He was watching the two men on the stage, a slight frown on his face. "You've never spoken to me like this before."

He turned, his frown disappearing. "You've never had any interest in politics before. But if you're seeing Gideon, then that's going to have to change. He won't stay in the Secret Service for long. There are a lot of us who would like to see him back in the White House — and not guarding the president. We're hoping for great things from that young man."

"Oh."

She wished she could confide in her father. But how could she? There wasn't going to be time for Gideon to do anything great. Not for the first time, she regretted involving him in this. Was there some way he could survive the political fallout if his girlfriend assassinated the president? Unlikely.

Maybe there was still another way. She just hoped there was something in this information from Stella that would help. Truth was, she didn't want to die. She didn't want Gideon to die, either.

But in this glittering place it all seemed so unreal.

She'd missed some of Harry's speech. Now he was pinning a medal on Gideon's already medal-studded chest.

Gideon turned to face the crowd. "Thank you," he said, his voice carrying easily, full of authority. "I accept this, not for myself, but on behalf of all our fellow Americans who have died defending our country. America is only as great as her people, and I fought side by side with some of the bravest men and women in the world. But I grew up here in D.C., so in many ways it's good to be back home. At least the drink is better." He raised his glass. "So I'd like us all to say a huge thank you to the people who keep America safe. Thank you."

The room erupted into cheers. Kate clapped along with the rest.

After a few minutes, Harry raised his hands. "Enough," he said with a smile. "You'll have me believing you like him more than me."

A ripple of laughter ran through the crowd. This time Kate didn't join in.

Harry shook hands with Gideon once more,

and then he was on his way back to her. His momentum was slow as men clapped him on the back and women kissed his cheek.

Beside her, her father chuckled. "If I hadn't already guessed it was serious with you and Gideon, your expression would have given it away."

"Ha."

He smiled, squeezed her arm. "He's back now, so I'll leave you to enjoy the party. There are some people I need to talk to, but I'm glad about the two of you. Come to dinner this weekend. You mother would like it."

"I'll ask Gideon."

She watched as he walked away, then turned back as Gideon arrived at her side. "You looked good up there."

He put his glass down on a tray held by a passing waiter and grabbed her hand. "Come and dance."

She hadn't even noticed the music starting, and she didn't want to dance. Or rather, she didn't know how to dance. "I can't dance." She'd never bothered to learn the formal stuff.

"Then just come and let me hold you. I *need* to hold you, to bury my face in your skin, to get the stench of that bastard out of my nostrils."

"Oh." She allowed him to hustle her onto the floor. He was such a good actor, but for a moment he'd allowed the mask to drop and she'd seen the sheer hatred behind the facade.

She turned to face him, slipping her hands around his waist and allowing him to pull her closer until she was flush against him, her head resting on his shoulder, his arms around her back. They swayed rather than danced, and the tension drained from him.

They stayed like that for five minutes. Finally she felt him sigh against her skin and he pulled away.

"We have work to do."

She'd managed to forget for a few minutes. Forget the coming of the end of the world.

She searched the room, found Harry making the rounds, always with his guards close beside him. He wasn't going to be easy to kill if it came to that.

Gideon nabbed them both another glass of champagne and she resisted the urge to gulp it down; she had to keep her wits about her tonight. She could wallow in alcohol when it was over. Gideon rested his hand on her waist, and they made their way around the room, pausing to talk occasionally, although Kate hardly took in the words. She left the work to Gideon, who always seemed to know the right thing to say.

They came to a halt by the president's little group of hangers-on and bodyguards. Harry smiled when he saw them, and the group parted to allow her and Gideon closer. He was the guest of honor, after all.

Harry turned his attention to her, held out his hand. She forced a bright smile, just as genuine as his. His touch sent a wave of blackness through her, and she pushed it down and tightened her limp fingers.

"Mr. President."

"Ms. Buchanan. Good to see you again. I hope you're enjoying the party."

"It's wonderful, thank you." Was he ever going to let go of her hand? Finally he released her, and she made her feet stand still when her natural inclination was either to back away or to leap for his jugular. Only the six heavily armed guards stopped her. She cleared her throat. "Actually, sir, I have a favor to ask. About my sister."

Did his eyes look wary? "Go ahead."

"Stella loved working for you here in the White House. I remember when we were children, it was all she ever wanted to do. It meant everything to her."

"That's lovely. I'm glad she got her dream. How can I help?"

"Well, we weren't as close in the last years as I would have liked to be." Inspiration took her. She cast a pointed glance at Gideon. "I was always a little jealous of her. Now she's gone, and I regret that. I'd like to understand her better. I never saw where she worked. I'd like to see her office." This was a risk, because if he said no outright, they would be in serious trouble if they were then found in there. But she'd thought it a calculated risk, and Auspex had agreed.

Harry studied her for a moment, then his gaze flicked to Gideon at her side. Finally, he nodded. "I don't see why not. When?"

"Now?"

"I'll take her, sir." Gideon said. "I know where her sister's office is situated."

He pursed his lips, then shrugged and turned to the bodyguard on his right. "Let security know that Ms. Buchanan will be visiting her sister's office."

"Yes, sir."

CHAPTER THIRTY

"One of the key problems today is that politics is such a disgrace, good people don't go into government." Donald Trump

Gideon's skin prickled. He held himself still as he watched Harry walk away, surrounded by his security detail. The bodyguard on his left had a broken nose. He was one of the men who had attacked Gideon in the stairwell that morning.

He hadn't acknowledged Gideon in any way.

Harry never went anywhere without at least four guards. Gideon was going to have to separate him from them somehow if he wanted any chance at finishing the bastard off.

The thought brought him up short.

He hadn't acknowledged to himself that he was actually going to do this thing. He'd told Kate that they would discuss it again after they had found out whatever secrets Stella had been hiding. The truth was that it needed doing.

Her hand slid into his and she squeezed. "Should we go?" she asked.

He glanced at his watch. They had fifteen minutes to get to Stella's office or they would miss their chance.

"Yes. Let's get this done."

He kept hold of her hand as they made their way through the crowd. He noticed Boyd across the room and nodded to him. These people were all Party elite. Some of the older ones had been with Harry Senior. Had campaigned with him in that last election.

Gideon's own father had been a senior member of the administration, and he'd always spoken passionately to Gideon about a vision for the future where America was great again. As the restrictions increased—the Wall, the firewall, Martial Law—he'd rationalized them. They were needed. People weren't ready for personal freedom. Freedom was overrated anyway. What the masses needed were food, work, health care. And the government could provide those things if they had a stable environment. America *would* be great again.

What the hell had gone wrong?

When had the dream become a nightmare?

Not all of it could be laid at Harry Junior's door. The rot had started long before he had taken office, although at least his father had been altruistic. He had genuinely believed in his vision for the future. Harry Junior didn't have an altruistic bone in his miserable body.

When he'd taken over from his father— another purely temporary measure—for the first time, Gideon had questioned the direction of the Loyalist Party, but then he'd been only twenty-two and an idealistic idiot. Plus, also for the first time, his father hadn't answered Gideon's questions with his usual enthusiasm. He'd seemed troubled, but he had explained to Gideon that the Party believed the American people needed a figurehead. Until democracy could be safely resumed, they had to have a leader they could look up to. Harry Junior was the spitting image of his father. The transfer of power would be seamless and hardly noticed by the people. That would give them time to choose a new leader for the Party.

Gideon's father was dead less than two years later. And, ten years on, Harry Junior was firmly entrenched in the president's chair. He'd assumed the title, and he had his own private army to ensure it wasn't questioned.

As they exited the ballroom, the Secret Service agent at the door nodded to him, and he nodded back. He stood for a moment looking around. He'd worked here for a few years before his fall from grace, and he knew the place well. Stella had been a senior-level staffer, and her office was situated not far from the Oval Office, on the second floor. He released his hold on Kate and headed for the staircase, then along a corridor to an electronic door that led to the restricted area.

Another agent stood on guard. He nodded at Gideon and spoke to Kate. "I'm sorry about your sister, ma'am. She was a good woman."

"Thank you."

The door slid open, and he waved them through and into another corridor. "The door has been unlocked for you."

So far, so good.

Unlike in the public areas, the security cameras along this corridor weren't hidden. There was one every few feet. They seemed to watch as they walked through.

But it was the hidden camera in the office that they had to worry about. Kate had to somehow access her sister's computer system without being seen. He had to presume they were being watched.

At least they knew where it was—thanks to Auspex.

He couldn't believe he'd just thought that about a computer program.

Auspex was turning off the camera at a specified time. If someone was watching, it would look like a malfunction. While Gideon wasn't sure he believed it would happen, Kate did. And he'd have to. If it didn't, they were both finished. They probably wouldn't get out of the building.

He glanced at his watch. Five minutes to go. They came to a halt in front of the door, and he hesitated. He leaned in close, spoke quietly. "Don't look at the camera," he said. "If someone is monitoring us, they'll notice."

She nodded, and he reached out. The door opened when he turned the handle, and the light came on automatically.

"You never came here before?" he asked as they stepped into the office. He left the door open — at least they would hear if anyone approached.

"No. Stella didn't involve me in her work at all. Sometimes I felt a little shut out, but I've never been interested in politics, so I didn't think too much about it." She was looking around. The office was nice. Big, with dark-red walls and a polished wooden floor. A desk in front of the window held a computer and monitor. In a direct line from where he knew the camera was hidden.

Kate moved around the room, touching things. There was a single photograph on the desk of Stella and Kate. They were young; Kate looked around twelve. Their arms were wrapped around each other and they looked happy, big grins on their faces. Kate picked it up and trailed a finger over the picture. "She was fifteen," she said. "Just before she…changed."

She opened her mouth to say something, and then closed it again. Probably remembering that they could be heard as well as seen. She put the photo down and ran her hands over the desk.

There was nothing else to see.

"She was very…tidy," he said.

"Her apartment was the same. Everything in its place. I'm the messy one." She sniffed, then bit her lip, her eyes bright with unshed tears. "I can't believe she's gone."

He stepped up to her, slid his hand around the back of her neck, and pulled her hard against him. He hoped she wasn't going to lose it. She needed to be focused. They had five minutes maximum; maybe less if someone decided to come and investigate the malfunction straight away.

The alarm on his watch buzzed, and she pulled away. He had no way of knowing if the camera was off, but he had to trust. Otherwise this was for nothing.

"We're on," he said.

She was already moving. Stepping quickly around him and sitting in the leather chair behind the desk. She pressed the key to turn on the computer, and the screen lit up within seconds. She typed in the password, then opened up the files.

"I have to re-sort them by date and time," she said, her fingers flying across the keyboard.

She reached into the neckline of her dress and pulled out a small white plastic flash drive. She pulled off the cap and plugged it into a socket on the side of the computer.

"Come on," she muttered. "Hurry up."

"Is it there?"

"I don't know yet. This system is ancient. The only place that has had any upgrades in years is Homeland Security. That's why I got the job there. Yay—it's up. There are a couple of files at the time she gave us. I'll get them both and we can work out which one we need when we're out of here. I don't want to open them now. It will take the system longer to shut down."

A prickle ran down his spine—his own internal trouble monitor. He'd learned to pay attention to it when he was on active duty. It had saved his life more than once. He moved to the door and peered out. From here he could see the electronic doors they had come through. As he watched, they started to open.

"Shit."

She looked up. "What is it?"

"We have company. Are you done?"

"Just a second."

"We don't have a second." He could hear booted feet on the tiled floor of the corridor.

"Got it."

She pulled out the drive and shoved it down the front of her dress. The screen was still lit up. They'd see it.

"Come here." He held out his hand. Kate took it, and he pulled her to her feet and around the desk. Then he picked her up by the waist and sat her on the desk in front of the screen. And then he kissed her.

Another prickle down his spine. The screen went black. He raised his head and turned slowly. Boyd stood in the open doorway, two agents at his back. There was no expression on his face.

"Is there a problem?" Gideon asked.

Would they admit that the office had hidden cameras? Maybe to him, but he doubted they would to Stella's sister.

"No problem," Boyd said. "We were just passing and noticed the open door."

Gideon's hands still rested on Kate's shoulders. He gave her a quick look, but she seemed composed. He straightened, releasing her, and she jumped down and smoothed her dress. "I'm Stella's sister," she said. "Harry said it was okay for me to look around her office. I just got a little emotional, and Gideon was…comforting me."

"So we saw. Have you finished?"

She gave a quick nod. "There's nothing of Stella here. She's gone."

"A tragedy," Boyd murmured. "But accidents can happen to all of us. Something you might remember, Ms. Buchanan."

There was a clear threat there, though Kate didn't react to it. She turned to Gideon. "Can we go now?"

"Of course."

They didn't talk on the way out. It occurred to him that maybe they should return to the party. Except that he'd had enough. He didn't think he was up to any more acting tonight. Kate didn't say anything as he led the way out of the building, showing his ID to various checkpoints on the way. All the time expecting to be stopped, he was drenched in sweat by the time they were clear. He considered calling for a cab, but he'd rather walk for a while. As they exited the grounds of the White House, some of the tension left him. If Boyd had really suspected anything, they wouldn't have even gotten out of the building.

"Oh my God," Kate muttered. She was shaking. He wrapped an arm around her shoulder and pulled her against his side. "I thought it was over, that we were finished. That man—do you think he suspected?"

"Maybe, though if he'd seriously thought we were up to no good then we'd have been arrested by now. Boyd isn't one to believe in coincidences. At the same time, he can't know that you have the technology to infiltrate the systems." He ran a hand through his hair. "Maybe if your father wasn't who he is, then he would have taken you in for questioning."

"That's not fair, is it? All the same, I'm glad. That man terrifies me. He's so cold."

"Well, he certainly didn't get where he is by being a nice guy."

They were silent for a few minutes. It was still quite early, and the streets were busy. As the distance increased, the rest of the tension left him. They were safe. At least for tonight.

"Should we go to my office? See if we can load Stella's files?"

He thought for a moment. "No. I don't think we'd better do anything out of the ordinary. Let's both go in to work tomorrow as normal. I'll meet you for lunch and you can tell me what you find."

"Okay. So what shall we do tonight?"

"What do you want to do?" His mind went back to the kiss. It had been for Boyd's benefit, but she had tasted so sweet.

"I don't want to be alone." She stopped walking and turned to look at him, her expression serious as she studied his face. "I told myself that I wasn't going to get involved with you. That there's no future for us. Maybe no future for anyone. And if I come to care for you, it will only make things harder."

"I told myself something similar. But I'm not asking for the future. I'm asking for tonight. The truth is, we're already involved. And whatever happens, I want to make love to you. Just make love. We both know this thing between us is going nowhere. Under different circumstances…" He shrugged. "We'll never know now." He stroked a hand down the soft skin of her cheek, rubbed the pad of his thumb over her lower lip. Her tongue darted out to lick his skin. Heat shot through him.

He hadn't been sure of her. Now he was.

"Let's go home," she said.

CHAPTER THIRTY-ONE

"America is too great for small dreams." Ronald Reagan

If tonight was all they were going to have, she wanted to make the most of it.

As she locked the door of her apartment behind them, she reached inside her dress and pulled out the drive with Stella's files. What would they find on there? Would it help them? Or only make things worse? If they *could* be worse. She slipped the drive into her bag and glanced up to find Gideon watching her.

"It had better be worth it," she said. "Whatever is on there."

She'd been so scared, she'd almost frozen up completely. A great rebel she'd make. All the way home she'd expected the Secret Service to pounce on them, arrest them, torture them. She'd gotten Gideon into this. That was just sinking in.

But they'd made it.

"Go sit down," she said to Gideon, waving toward the living room. "I'll go get us a drink." She hadn't taken more than a sip of champagne at the party; she hadn't wanted to dull her senses. Now she needed a drink.

"Just remember I'd like to stay awake tonight."

She tossed him a grin. "I'd like you to stay awake as well."

In the kitchen, she selected a bottle of red wine from the rack, opened it, and collected two glasses from the cupboard. When she got to the living room, Gideon was seated on the sofa, long legs stretched out. He'd taken off his uniform jacket.

She handed him a glass and poured the wine, then sank down beside him, so close that they were touching. She toed off her shoes and curled her legs under her.

By some unspoken agreement, they didn't talk about the evening, or what they would do tomorrow, or speculate on what might be in Stella's files. She put it all from her mind. "Tell me about the places you've been. I always wanted to travel."

"Maybe you should have joined the army."

He was right in a way. It was one of the only careers now that enabled you to travel. Except that she would have made a crap soldier. "I'm not very good at taking orders. Loud noises make me jump. Plus, I hate guns."

"Maybe not, then. Hmm, my favorite place is… Yellowstone Park. We went there for a training exercise in the winter when the place was deep in snow. It was wild and beautiful. No tourists now. It seems so wrong that more people shouldn't get to see it."

"Why? Why don't they want us to move around? What are they scared of?"

"It's been an insidious change. The Wall was supposed to keep people out. In reality, it's as much to keep us in. First they shut the borders and told us it was for our own safety. Why did we need to go outside the country? Why risk bringing back some virus and causing another pandemic? And if we did leave, they couldn't guarantee we'd get back in. Of course, back then there was a huge threat of terrorism, along with a lot of paranoia about man-made diseases. It was easy to convince the people that it was for their own good."

"You've thought about this a lot, haven't you?"

"When I was younger, I accepted everything the Party told us. Later, after everything went to crap, I started to question things. There's no denying that as a nation we're under attack. There was never any shortage of battles to fight. The world outside is falling apart. They see this as a safe haven, and they want in. There are big areas that are no longer habitable. Poisoned air and water supplies mean that people are displaced and on the move. They're hungry and want what we've got."

"So maybe the Party are doing something right. People here aren't hungry. People can have a good life if they accept the restrictions."

"Maybe. But this city is like an island. Everything is still bright and beautiful. That party tonight—you don't think the rest of the country is like this, do you?"

"I don't know."

"That's why they don't want us to move around. Why they've restricted the news services. They don't want us to see what's happening in other parts of the country. I've heard stories of whole towns living in virtual slavery. In the past, there were a lot of illegal immigrants willing to work for low wages. Who do you think is doing that labor now?"

"You keep saying 'they.' Do you mean the Party?"

"Not all of them. Some. I've tried to get information and been blocked. There's definitely an inner circle who make the important decisions."

"Auspex said something similar. There's a wall he can't get through."

"I doubt very much that they're making those decisions for the good of the people."

She poured them both more wine. She didn't want to talk about it anymore. She didn't want to be reminded of all the bad things happening in the world. Time to change the subject.

"What's it like to fly?"

"In the big planes, you hardly notice you're not on the ground. But I've been in little ones and helicopters, and it's amazing. You'd love it."

"Never going to happen."

Christ, couldn't they find any subjects that weren't ultimately depressing? Maybe they shouldn't talk at all. She placed her glass on the coffee table, then took Gideon's as well. He didn't move, just watched her.

She came up on her knees, hitched up her dress, and straddled his hips. Cupping his face with her hands, she stared into his eyes as she kissed him. He stayed motionless, letting her do what she wanted. She kissed his mouth, then his jaw, feeling the faint rasp of stubble beneath her lips. She kissed the scar on his cheek, the corner of his eyes, then his throat, breathing in the warm, masculine scent of him.

Finally he moved, his fingers threading in her hair, tugging the pins free so that it fell about her shoulders.

"I love your hair," he said.

His hands moved lower, sliding over the bare skin of her back, slipping under the dress, gliding it off her shoulders to bare her to the waist. "You're so beautiful."

"No, I'm not."

He ignored her. "The most beautiful woman I've ever seen."

Oh well, if he wanted to believe that, she wasn't going to argue. She couldn't anyway, because he lowered his head and kissed her.

She woke in a tangle of limbs. Gideon lay half on top of her, his arm flung over her shoulder, a leg across her thighs. Through the blinds, she could see it was still dark outside, but she could sense that morning wasn't far away.

She slipped out from beneath him, wincing a little. They'd made love over and over, first fast, then achingly slow. He'd woken her in the night, his mouth on her body. He'd kissed every inch of her skin and then made love to her again. Now there was an ache between her thighs that she relished because it reminded her of the night.

Without turning on the light, she crossed the room, grabbed some clean clothes, and headed into the bathroom. She wanted to get into the office. She'd put this off as long as she could. Now was the time to find out what it was they'd risked their lives for.

She piled her hair on top of her head and showered quickly, washing the scent of Gideon from her skin. Last night had been time out. It couldn't happen again. Already the cords were tightening between them. She couldn't allow herself to care for him. It would just make everything that much harder.

Afterward, she dressed. Gideon still slept on. In the light from the open bathroom door, she watched him. Last night he'd called her beautiful, but he was the beautiful one in this partnership. For a minute, she couldn't drag her gaze away. Would she ever see him like this again?

She forced herself to turn away. In the kitchen, she made coffee. She drank a cup and then poured one for Gideon, adding cream and sugar as she knew he liked it. He still slept on, almost as though he had been drugged. His lashes finally flickered open as she sank down on the bed beside him.

He took in her clothed form and frowned. "You're dressed. I don't like it. Come back to bed."

She shook her head. "I'm going to the office."

"What time is it?"

"Six. That's pretty normal for me. No one will question it." He pulled himself up and she handed him the coffee. "I just wanted to say good morning, and that I'll see you at lunchtime. One o'clock?"

He nodded.

"Go back to sleep," she said.

"I have to go home, get a change of clothes."

She made to stand up and he grasped her wrist, holding her down. "Last night was wonderful."

"I know."

He studied her for a moment, examining her face. He must have found something he didn't like there, because his frown deepened. "You don't think it should happen again."

She glanced away. It was one thing to think it and another to say it out loud, but she forced herself to say the words. "There's no way this can end well. I've searched for a way I can make it through this, except there isn't one. Now is not the time to fall in love."

Shock flashed across his face. Maybe he hadn't thought she would say the word, but she wasn't a coward. She knew she hovered on the edge of falling so hard for this man. And that would make a difficult task almost impossible.

"I always thought I didn't believe in love," he said.

"Well, the best thing you can do right now is hold onto that belief. It will be better for both of us."

He sat for a moment, still holding her wrist. She didn't pull away. He needed to find a way through this himself. She could almost see his mind working. "Have you asked your computer friend?"

"Auspex? Asked him what?"

"Whether you're going to die?"

She looked away, then shook her head. "I thought about it. But really it makes no difference, except I'd be even more scared." She forced a smile. "I don't think I'm cut out for this. I'm such a coward."

"You're the bravest woman I know." He blew out his breath. "Go. Do what you have to do, and I'll see you at lunchtime. I just hope it was worth it."

"Me, too."

CHAPTER THIRTY-TWO

"Plans are nothing; planning is everything."
Dwight D. Eisenhower

Kate stared at the screen as Auspex relayed the decoded files. She read the information quickly, then again, trying to force her brain to assimilate it. She had thought that Stella's files were unrelated to the prediction of nuclear war. She could no longer believe that. The two were irrevocably connected.

Nausea crawled up her throat as she reached forward and typed in the question.

Auspex, does the data in this file affect the probability of a bomb detonation?

It was a stupid question, really. How could it *not* change things?

There is now a 98 percent chance that there will be a nuclear detonation on American soil.

98 percent? Her heart rate kicked up, panic gripping her tight, and she closed her eyes for a moment and breathed slowly. In and out until she could think again.

Clearly, Stella had been working with the rebels, presumably through Aaron. She scrolled back to the beginning and started again.

The file was beyond unbelievable; the actions of a mad man in an insane world. And yet, at the same time, it made some sort of horrible logical sense. Kate could actually see it all happening as it was laid out.

Surely there must be someone who would put a stop to this.

Aaron had told Stella to pass this information to Gideon.

Why?

A last hope? Desperation? What did Aaron expect his brother to do?

Her stomach churned. This was such an unbearable thing to carry alone. She wanted to run away and hide, as though that could stop it. She wished she could call Gideon, just to hear his voice. A brief glimpse of sanity in a world gone crazy. But she didn't want to change anything. He'd told her to act normal. Besides, their call would be monitored, so she couldn't say anything of what she was actually feeling.

There were another two hours until she was meeting him for lunch, and she couldn't bear to be alone with her thoughts.

Oliver was the only other person she could talk to. Not the truth—she wouldn't put that on him—but at least a real conversation without the usual Party bullshit. She couldn't take the platitudes right now.

As she leaned forward to close down the systems, the TV screen on the wall opposite lit up.

America for Americans.

Oh.

She really didn't want to listen to this right now. If she had to listen to that voice telling those lies…

Unfortunately, there was no way to turn the fucking thing off. Harry strolled out of the White House. He appeared so…innocuous. Bland and safe and sane. Everything he wasn't.

"This is a historic year as we move towards democracy. I look forward to the…

As she sat back in her chair and let the lies wash through her mind, something occurred to her.

Auspex, can you infiltrate the information dissemination system?

She didn't know where she was going with this. Maybe she could just find a way to get the truth out there. She was scrambling around for any ideas. She wasn't even close to formulating a plan.

At this moment, I cannot. But there is a chance that I might find a way.

Probability?

48 percent.

Try.

The TV screen finally went blank. She got up, then cleared all the screens and shut Auspex down, just in case anyone came to her office.

She headed up the stairs. She hadn't seen Oliver since their conversation about the catastrophe. He'd sent her a note after her sister's death, but he hadn't come to the funeral. She hadn't thought much about it; her mind had been on other things. But Oliver was a family friend, he'd known Stella all her life — although he'd distanced himself over the last few years — so she would have expected him there. He must have had a good reason for staying away. At the very least, she would have expected him to pop down to her office. Give his condolences.

Teresa looked up as she tapped on the door. She was wearing a white shirt — Auspex was correct — and she smiled brightly, which was odd and made Kate want to glance behind her to see who she was smiling at. "Kate, I saw you met the president last night."

"You did?"

"You were on the news flash. What was he like? I saw him once at a rally, but I've never spoken to him."

"He was very…pleasant." And that was a total lie. "Can I see Oliver?" she asked.

Teresa shook her head, a frown of annoyance between her eyes. "He's not here."

"Is he supposed to be?"

"Yes. He has a scheduled meeting with the

deputy chief in ten minutes, and what am I supposed to say?"

"Has he called in?"

"No, he hasn't, and yes, I've called his home and no, he isn't picking up."

"Was he okay yesterday?"

"He seemed to be. He doesn't exactly confide in me."

Kate glanced at her watch. She had time to stop by his house before she met Gideon. Oliver was never sick, and he was super reliable. She'd never known him to miss a day of work since she'd started here.

She had a really bad feeling about this.

Oliver's house was a fifteen-minute drive away, and she picked up a cab outside the office. It dropped her off opposite the town house. She climbed the stone steps slowly, not knowing what she was afraid of, but unable to dispel the dark dread rising up inside her. She swallowed as she rang the bell, straining her ears for footsteps that never came.

What next?

She tried the whole *you're-getting-paranoid* thing again, but she couldn't quite pull it off. Finally, she shifted her hand to the door handle and turned it, all the time expecting the door to be locked. The handle turned, and the door swung open. Oliver lived alone; his wife had divorced him five years ago. She'd been a liberal who hadn't liked him taking the job with Homeland Security. It wasn't as though he'd been given much choice.

Kate stepped into the hallway. Inside, the house was quiet, and the door swung shut behind her, cutting out the noise from the street. She had to force herself to move forward. This house had been bought after Oliver had left the college, and he'd claimed that it would not be a good idea for them to see each other socially. So she'd never been here.

A polished wooden stairway climbed up to the next floor, and two doors led off the hallway. She tried the first, and it opened into a kitchen. Empty. She pulled the door closed behind her and moved to the next one. It stood slightly ajar, and she rested her fingertips against it and pressed. The door swung open.

She stood in the doorway, her mind a jumble of emotions. The place had been trashed. She kept her brain busy analyzing that; the cabinet pulled over, spilling its contents, broken bottles, and the sweet scent of alcohol mingled with something else. Something sharp and acrid that saturated her nostrils.

Oliver lay in the center of the room, dressed in jeans and a T-shirt, a neat bullet hole in the center of his forehead. That was the only neat thing about him. He was tied to a chair that lay on its side. Kate forced herself not to look away. It was clear he'd been beaten up, tortured even, his face a mask of red over his dark skin. His right hand was strapped to the chair arm and was nothing more than bloody pulp.

Nausea churned in her stomach. She wanted to scream—some part of her knew she should be screaming—but her throat locked up tight. She acted on instinct, her brain refusing to get involved. The phone lay on the floor, and when she picked it up, she saw that the cord had been wrenched from the socket. She pulled her cell phone from her bag and pressed 9-1-1 with shaking fingers.

No signal.

She turned on her heels and left the house. She tried next door first, and when there was no answer, she went to the next house. This time a woman answered. Young, blonde, pretty, with a baby in her arms. "Yes?"

"Could you call 9-1-1," Kate said. "There's been a…murder at number 4."

She'd been jiggling the baby on her hip, but now she went still. "Oliver?"

Kate gave a jerky nod. "Please, just call the police."

She turned away and headed back to Oliver's,

but she couldn't face going inside. Instead, she sat on the stone steps and stared into nothing, her mind numb. She was hardly aware of the young woman coming toward her. She took Kate's hand and wrapped it around a steaming mug of coffee. Then patted her on the shoulder.

"I have to get back to the baby."

Kate nodded, but didn't speak. She was still sitting there, full mug of coffee in her hand, when the first police car drew up by the side of the curb.

CHAPTER THIRTY-THREE

"The truth is that all men having power ought to be mistrusted." James Madison

Gideon parked his car opposite Kate's office block and waited until it became clear that she wasn't coming out. Worry nagged at his mind, and he couldn't pinpoint why. Nothing untoward had happened at the office. Boyd had been in meetings all morning and, as usual, Gideon had nothing he had to do. He'd spent the time going through the job files, getting a picture of the structure of the organization.

As he'd thought, there were two distinct sections within the Secret Service. With some agents, he could track their work schedules, see every job they were on. Others had gaps. Without exception, those agents were part of Harry's bodyguard detail. When he tried to dig deeper, find out what they were doing during these gap times, he hit a wall. Maybe that was something Kate's computer friend could help with.

But while no one had bothered him, he couldn't shake the feeling that he was being watched. Had they added surveillance to his office? He could always explain away what he was doing by saying that he was just getting a feel for the place. All the same, he didn't like it.

There was no reason to watch him unless it was just part of Boyd's probationary period. If he passed, would he then find out what else went on around here? Unfortunately, he didn't have the time to wait for that.

He resisted calling Kate. He wanted to keep their relationship as low-key as possible. Just in case.

Now he was here, and she wasn't.

He headed into the building and stopped by the security check just inside the door. "I'm here to see Kate Buchanan."

"Mr. Frome?"

"Yes?"

"She left a message for you. She'll meet you here." The guard handed Gideon a piece of paper with an address.

He glanced at it briefly and then shoved the paper in his pocket. Back in his car, he pulled out into the traffic and drove to the address, still with that feeling of being watched. He kept glancing behind him, but he could see nothing. The drive took fifteen minutes. When he got there, he found a couple of patrol cars, together with another car and a white van parked in the no-parking zone.

What the hell?

He drove past and pulled into a spot a few

houses down.

The house was a terraced one, three stories high. Nice. A uniformed officer stood outside the door. Gideon got out his Secret Service ID and was waved through. He headed toward the sound of voices. The living room was full of people, but his eyes were drawn immediately to the body on the floor. A forensic team worked around it, taking pictures. It was an African-American man; one he didn't recognize. He raised his gaze and his eyes met Kate's. She was seated at the edge of the room on an upright wooden chair, identical to the one the dead man was tied to, with what he took to be a detective sitting opposite. She'd been crying, her eyes red, her freckles standing out stark against her pale skin. Her hands were gripped together on her lap. He hurried over, and she stood up as he approached.

The detective stood as well, and Gideon held out his ID to forestall any questions. The man glanced at it and raised an eyebrow. "Is Secret Service taking this over?" he asked.

Gideon shook his head. "No. I'm a friend of Ms. Buchanan. I was supposed to be meeting her for lunch."

"I'm Detective Palmer." He nodded toward the body. "Did you also know our victim?"

"No." He turned to Kate. Clearly, she must have known him. Had she actually found the body? She was supposed to have been staying in the office that morning. Christ, why the hell had they made her stay in here where she could see the crime scene? His anger rose, and he bit it down. He needed to cooperate, not antagonize people, if he wanted to get out of there quickly.

"It's Oliver Massey," she said, her voice quiet. "He's my boss."

She'd spoken of him, and Gideon knew he was a friend and a mentor as well as her boss. He was also flagged on the Secret Service system—he'd spoken out against the Loyalist Party, though he'd been silent for the last few years.

"I'm sorry."

She bit her lip and gave a helpless little shrug. "He wasn't at work, and Teresa couldn't get hold of him. I just came to check, and he was…" She gave another shrug.

"It looks like he interrupted a burglary," Detective Palmer put in. "They presumably tortured him to find out if he had a safe or any hidden valuables."

The detective didn't sound as though he believed a word of what he was saying.

"Looks like? You don't sound convinced."

"We don't get many actual burglaries anymore. Especially not in this area. Plus, the job is too neat. No sign of a fight. More like an execution." He nodded to Gideon's ID, which he still held in his hand. "You people would know more about that than us lowly detectives."

The implication being that Secret Service were somehow involved with this murder. The sad thing was, he wouldn't be surprised. America for the fucking Americans—as long as you loved President Harry. Bastard.

He glanced at Kate to see how she was coping. She appeared dazed, not really taking anything in.

"Have you finished with Ms. Buchanan? I'd like to get her out of here."

Detective Palmer nodded. "For the moment. We might have more questions later, though somehow I doubt it. I have an idea we'll get orders to wrap this one up quick. What do you think?"

Gideon didn't bother answering the question. Instead, he nodded to the detective and took hold of Kate's arm. She didn't resist as he led her through the room. He cast her a sideways glance and found that her gaze was fixed on the dead body sprawled on the polished wooden floor. The blood pooled under his head was black in the bright light. Gideon hurried her past and then out of the room, down the hallway, and through the front door into the fresh air.

He stopped by his car, wrapped his arms around her, and pulled her close. For a few seconds, she was rigid, then she sagged, the tension leaving her as she collapsed against him. He tightened his arms, just holding her close, as a sob tore from her throat. He suspected she was in some sort of shock. One shock too many. The last weeks had been so hard for her. Maybe she'd reached her breaking point.

Trouble was, they couldn't afford to have her break down right now.

He gave her another minute, then took a deep breath and stepped away, though he kept his hands on her shoulders. As he watched, she visibly drew herself together. "I'm sorry. I'll be okay in a second. It was just such a shock. Though in a way, I expected it. I'm starting to expect the worst of everything. Just think of the worst possible scenario, and that's what's going to happen."

"Come on. We'll get away from here. Go get some lunch."

"I couldn't eat."

"A drink, then."

He settled her in the car and turned the engine on. He thought for a second, then pulled out into the traffic and headed out of the city center. He was dying to know what she had found on the files, but he needed to give her time to get her head together.

"You don't think it was a burglary, do you?" she asked.

"No." Crime had been just about eliminated in the city. He knew that wasn't the case everywhere in the country—he'd heard stories of places that were almost lawless—but not here in D.C. "Tell me about him." It might do her some good to talk about it, to get it out of her system. Better than bottling everything up.

She was silent for a moment. Finally she spoke. "Did you know Oliver was the founder of the Bring Back Democracy movement?"

"No."

"He started it soon after Martial Law was brought in. He was quite active at the beginning but backed out when he moved jobs. He was forced out of the University. My father got him the job at Homeland Security. They were friends from their schooldays. Oliver hated Harry Coffell."

"Not a healthy emotion to have these days."

"No. He was a good man, and he hated keeping quiet. I always presumed he had his reasons."

He gave her a quick look. "What reasons?"

"I think he was working with the rebels. Passing them information."

"You don't know that for sure."

"No. He shut me out. Said he had to keep his distance for my own safety."

"Did he know about what you were working on? The artificial intelligence project?"

"We never spoke about it. Not until recently, anyway. I told you, he kept his distance. Said it was safer. But Auspex is an extension of a project he'd been working on while he was still at the university." She was silent for a moment. "He was tortured. You think he might have told someone about me?"

He considered it for a moment. "No. I think you would be under arrest by now. He was clearly murdered last night."

"While we were at the party. Or while we were…"

She trailed off. While they'd been making love, her friend and mentor had likely been being tortured. Not a good thought.

"Chances are they didn't even question him about you, and he was unlikely to volunteer the information. If it was Secret Service, they must have been sure they'd gotten everything of interest, or they would have taken him in for further questioning. I think you're safe."

"None of us are safe."

He pulled the car over and parked at the curb not far from a small eatery. He got out, came around and opened her door for her. She didn't move for a few seconds. Then she gave herself a little shake and climbed out. She took a pair of sunglasses out of her bag and put them on, covering her tear-reddened eyes. She sniffed once, then stiffened her shoulders. "Let's go."

The hostess led them to a small table. Gideon

glanced around as they crossed the restaurant. He couldn't see any security cameras, which didn't surprise him in a place this far out from the city center. It was clean, with white tablecloths and tiled floors. The food was cheap, and he doubted they would see any of the movers and shakers in here. They could talk.

"Can we have water and a large brandy?" he asked the hostess as he took his seat.

Kate sat down opposite him and rested her chin in her hand. With the dark glasses on, he couldn't see her eyes, and her face was blank of expression.

The waitress brought the drinks and menus. He pushed the brandy toward her, and she picked it up almost automatically. She took a sip, and a grimace crossed her face. She made no move to look at the menu, so he called the waiter back and ordered them both a chicken salad.

She finished the brandy in one gulp and put the glass down. Then took off her glasses and laid them on the table. "I can't help thinking that maybe we should just stop worrying about the end of the world. Maybe the best thing that could happen is that we all go up in a nuclear explosion."

A nuclear explosion? Had she found some confirmation on the files? "You don't really believe that."

"Why not?" She sounded genuinely curious,

and he considered his answer. Maybe she was right, and it was time for mankind to just...stop.

"Really," she said, "what has mankind ever done except fight and kill each other and nearly destroy the planet?" She shrugged. "I always wanted to go into space, but maybe it's a good thing we can't. It would be like spreading a plague of evil across the universe."

"Not everyone is evil. In fact, I believe most people are good. Just lazy. Or shortsighted. Or scared. That doesn't mean they deserve to die. While it may not seem like it sometimes, there are other people like your friend Oliver out there working against the administration. Risking their lives to try and bring this country back from the brink of disaster."

"I think we're past the brink. I think we've tumbled headfirst into the abyss."

"Maybe. And maybe we're beyond hope. But I'm not ready to give up yet, and neither are you. You're just worn down. Too much has happened."

"I feel so...hopeless." She gnawed on her upper lip, but at least some of the blankness had dissipated from her expression and she was thinking again.

"It's not hopeless. Tell me what you found on the files."

She gave a quick nod and took a deep breath. "Stella was working with the rebels—through

Aaron. I'm not sure how long she'd been with them, but I'm guessing that's why she hid her hatred of Harry and took the job with his administration. Except she didn't quite hide her hatred well enough."

"I think you're right. With their history, Harry had to have known she hated him. If they'd found her rebel connections, she would have been arrested—there would have been no reason to make it look like an accident."

"There is an inner circle within the administration who make the decisions and know all the bad stuff," she continued. "Your boss Boyd Winters is part of it."

"Presumably, they make the decisions they know the rest of the administration would balk at."

"Yes. Like using illegal immigrants as organ donors."

The food arrived then, and they were quiet until the waitress left the table. "Eat something," Gideon said. "I know you're not hungry, but eat anyway."

He concentrated on his own food, and after a minute she picked up her fork and started to eat. She managed half before she slowed to a halt. Sitting back in her chair, she started talking again. "Stella's file was extracted from the minutes of a meeting. Someone working in D.C. apparently broke through the firewall protecting Harry's inner circle and managed to download it."

"Could it have been your friend Oliver?"

"Maybe. There aren't many people who could have done it, but Oliver worked on the original systems at the White House, so he'd have a head start. He knew how everything worked."

"No doubt there are other people who are aware of that. So what was in these minutes?"

"In two weeks' time, the president of America plans to detonate a nuclear bomb, which will destroy New York City."

He set down his fork and stared at her. "What?"

"He plans to blame it on the Russians. That will be his excuse to start a war, and there's a good probability that it will escalate and encompass the rest of the world."

"Even Harry wouldn't be that…" He ran a hand through his hair; he couldn't even think of a word to describe it.

"Stupid? Shortsighted? Evil?"

"But why?"

"Oh, there are lots of reasons. All of them clear evidence that America is being run by a madman. The bomb is timed to coincide with a debate between the presidential candidates from the Republican and Democratic parties, giving the perfect excuse to delay the elections. Plus, Harry believes a war will make him more popular."

Gideon pushed his plate away—he'd lost his appetite. Sadly, it all made a crazy sort of sense. "He could be right. People are starting to look on the administration as the cause of their problems. Harry's running scared. And he's not particularly intelligent. He wants to be a great man, and he's beginning to suspect that he's a little man, so he's searching for a way he can believe he is bigger than he is. Maybe he believes a war will do that. At the very least, it will give the people a more tangible enemy."

"That's just so crazy. But there's more. He's actually conspiring with the Russians. It will be a Russian-made bomb that goes off in New York."

"Why the hell would he work with the Russians? Or vice versa?" They'd been fighting the Russians since the Wall had gone up. It was surprising that they'd never had to contend with a nuclear strike before. Then again, there had always been rumors that the Coffells had connections with the Russians. That Russian money had helped get Harry Senior elected.

"Who knows. Maybe he'd promised them something. Maybe they're divvying up the world between themselves. Except there won't be a world left." Kate gave a small frown. "But if they're planning this together, why is it going to escalate?"

He considered the problem. The more he

thought about it, the more obvious the answer became. "Because Russia is our main opposition. I'm guessing both sides have had enough of sharing and that this last move is a ruse—by both countries. Russia will use the confusion of the nuclear explosion to make a real attack on the country. When Harry realizes that, he'll retaliate with a nuclear attack on Russia."

He could see it happening so easily.

The world was a crazy place right now.

They were silent for a minute.

"We've got to stop him," Kate said. "Kill him. That's the only thing that changes Auspex's prediction."

"Just how much do you believe in this machine? Maybe you're giving it too much credibility. Perhaps it's not always right." He thought for a moment. "I mean, if it's so good at predicting the future, why didn't it warn you about your friend Oliver?"

She looked away, her lips pressed together, then rubbed a hand over her eyes. "That's my fault."

"How?"

She took a sip of water, as if to give herself time to think. "You don't understand how truly... powerful Auspex is. He's the real thing."

"I'm not even sure what that means."

"Scientists have been working on artificial

intelligence for a long time. They were almost at the point of making a huge breakthrough when the ban came that stopped the research. I think the administration saw A.I. as a huge threat."

"Were they right to see it as a threat?"

For the first time, he saw the life come back to her eyes. For a second, they glowed with something fierce. "Oh yes. Without a doubt. They could never have done what they have without complete control of the outflow of information. Even access to the old internet would have allowed people to communicate, see what was going on. A true A.I. system would have made control impossible."

"I still don't see how that makes it your fault."

"Right now, Auspex is programmed to only make specific predictions when asked."

"So, unless you actually asked for the probability of Oliver being murdered, he wouldn't make the calculation?"

"Exactly. I built a whole load of protocols into the system, safety measures that limit how much he will do on his own. Without those protocols, even I have no idea what he can do, what he can become. The potential is…infinite."

He guessed he must have looked blank, because she shook her head.

"Come on, Gideon—you must have seen some of those old movies where the computers became more powerful, more intelligent, than the humans who made them."

"Terminator?" He'd seen a copy of the film in her apartment. "You really think that could happen?" It sounded a little far-fetched to him.

"I don't know. At the same time, up until now, I haven't been tempted to risk it. Auspex was almost like a game to me. Except he's not a game. Or a toy. Without the protocols, I have no idea how much control I would have over him."

"You said 'up until now.'"

"We can't do this alone. Oliver's death has shown me that. They're evil, and I don't think anything Auspex could do would be worse than what they're planning anyway."

Gideon sat back. "You're going to remove the safety protocols."

"Yes. Most of them, anyway. Then just ask Auspex to tell us anything he thinks might help us. First, we have to get some information from the system, because once the protocols are off, he's out of my control, and I have no clue whether he *will* help us."

"You think he will?"

"I hope so." She gave him a faint smile.

That was a long shot as far as he was concerned. He certainly wasn't going to rely on a computer to stop Harry from destroying the whole world and mankind with it. So, they needed a plan. A way to stop Harry. Or rather, if Auspex was to be believed, a way to kill him. He felt not even a flicker of guilt over that. He would do it with a smile on his face. Unfortunately, it wouldn't be easy.

A man guarded by his own private army.

"I've got to find a way to kill him," she said.

"No, you've got to find a way for *me* to kill him." She opened her mouth, no doubt to argue, and he cut in before she had the chance. "We're in this together, and you've never killed anyone in your life. I'd bet you've never even hurt anyone intentionally before."

"Most people haven't killed anyone. That doesn't mean that I can't. I hate him."

"I think you could probably kill Harry. You blame him for your sister, and now for Oliver. Except there's no way this is going to go down nice and clean. There will be collateral damage. Maybe just his bodyguards, but chances are there will also be civilians. I don't think you've got what it takes."

He'd become a good judge of people during his army years. Some people killed easily and thought nothing of it. Some people learned to kill—he was one of those. He'd killed many in his life—but all of them had been hard. Some people never learned. Kate, he sensed, was one of the truly good people in the world.

Besides, this was a suicide mission. He had no

doubt about that. Getting close enough to Harry would mean almost zero chance of getting away. Maybe he wouldn't emphasize that point.

"Besides which, I'm trained, whereas I'm guessing you've never even shot a gun, never used a knife, explosives?" She gave a quick shake of her head. "It makes sense." If this worked and they got rid of Harry, America would need people like Kate to rebuild it.

Her lips pursed in a mutinous expression. "Let's wait and see what scenarios Auspex comes up with. We might be able to get some help — remember Stella said that the file would also contain the details for a meeting with Aaron? And travel passes?"

"They were there?"

"Yes. The meeting is tomorrow morning. You think we should go?"

It would be dangerous, but Christ, he wanted to. He wanted to see Aaron again, maybe just to punch the bastard in the nose for what he had done all those years ago, though at least he understood a little better now. Maybe his brother could provide them with some concrete help. Though clearly the rebels didn't plan to stop this themselves, or why involve him? He gave a quick nod. "Yes."

"Then I'm coming, too."

He wasn't happy about that, but he could see

the resolve in her face. "Okay."

"We'll need to leave around six." She sighed. "Now I'd better get back to the office."

He knew she had to, but he was worried. If they'd come after her boss, would they come after her? He wished he could whisk her away to some place of safety, except that he wasn't sure anywhere was safe anymore. Like Stella's, Oliver's death had been made to look like an accident. There was clearly no actual evidence against him. It was as though Harry was just taking out anybody who had ever spoken out against him or had reason to hate him. He didn't think Kate fell into that category. Even if she did, maybe her office was the safest place for her. It was unlikely that they would stage an accident at Homeland Security. Plus, Gideon needed the information, for which she needed access to her systems, so they had no choice anyway.

"I'll drive you back," he said. "And pick you up after work. I don't want you out alone."

"You think they might come after me?"

"No." He made sure his tone was confident. "There's no reason. All the same, I'll feel better."

She gave him a smile then. "This is seriously bad, and I wish with all my heart that it wasn't happening." Then she gave a shrug. "But I did always want to be a superhero and save the world. Now I have my chance."

CHAPTER THIRTY-FOUR

"We did not come to fear the future. We came here to shape it." Barack Obama

Kate tried to hold onto that thought as she arrived back at the office. Should she go tell Teresa what had happened? She didn't want to, but as she was entering the building, she saw Detective Palmer emerging from the elevator. When he spotted her across the room, he nodded, but didn't attempt to talk to her. She was glad. She had no wish to talk about Oliver. She was doing her best not to think about him. She had to stay focused. All the same, an image kept flashing in her mind—his battered face and mutilated hand. They'd tortured him. He had been one of the best people she had ever known, a truly good man, and they'd tortured him, and then they'd murdered him.

At the thought, the rage she'd been holding at bay rose in her mind like a red mist. Maybe she was wrong; maybe she had to think about Oliver and her sister. Maybe rage was the one thing that would get her through this. Because Gideon had been right. The thought of killing someone, even Harry, made nausea churn in her stomach.

Yeah, great fucking superhero.

She headed down the stairwell and to her office.

As she closed the door, she released the tenuous hold she had on her control, and the tears rolled down her cheeks. She sank onto the chair and didn't try and stop herself. She'd wanted to look strong for Gideon. She'd dragged him into this, and now they were both going to die. Oh, she knew he had some idea that he could do it all himself, but he was wrong.

She didn't want anyone else she cared about to die.

She allowed herself five minutes to decompress, then blew her nose, wiped her eyes, and switched on her systems. Just as the screen flashed to life, there was a knock on the door. It opened without her speaking, and there was Teresa, all red eyes and streaked mascara. Kate hadn't been convinced that Teresa had any feelings for Oliver. In fact, she'd been pretty sure that the other woman had been given the job as Oliver's assistant for the main purpose of spying on him and reporting back any subversive activity. Not that there would have been any—Oliver was too bright for that.

"He's dead," she said.

Kate nodded. "I know."

Teresa came into the room and sank onto the only other seat in there. "They told me you found him."

"I did. I was worried when he wasn't here this morning."

"He'd been tortured?"

She wasn't sure what to say, what to do. There was that image again, but she didn't want to share that with Teresa. So she just gave another nod.

"Who would do that?" Teresa asked. "He was the kindest man ever." She bit her lip and stared Kate in the eyes. "When they gave me the job, they told me to report back on him. Anything he said against the Party. And I was happy to. I felt like I was contributing. But he never said anything wrong. Ever. And I told them that."

Kate still had no clue what to say. Did Teresa suspect foul play from her beloved Party? Was some of this guilt, or was it just disillusionment?

Teresa sniffed, and Kate opened a drawer, found a pack of tissues. She handed them to the other woman, who blew her nose. "He once told me that we all have to do what we believe to be right. He knew I was there to spy on him, and he was still so nice to me."

"He was a nice man."

"The Secret Service were waiting for me two nights ago. They wanted to know if there was anything new. Anything I could tell them. I said there was nothing. But they were so persistent."

Had they been looking for a legitimate reason

to arrest him? So when Teresa had given them nothing, they'd taken another approach?

"Maybe they weren't real agents," Teresa said, sounding hopeful. "The president would never condone something like this. Maybe they were tied to his killers, and I could help. I don't know what to do. Who to go to."

"No one," Kate said. "There's nothing you can do for Oliver now. You'll just make trouble for yourself." She had an idea. "They might even take your Political Officer status from you."

"I don't care if it would help catch his murderers."

There was zero chance of that, but she couldn't bring herself to tell Teresa. "Look, I have a friend in the Secret Service. If you give me their names and a description, he'll check them out for you." She handed Teresa a piece of paper and pen and watched as she wrote something down.

Glancing at the names, she couldn't help wondering if these were Oliver's killers.

Teresa stood. "I'm sorry. I just needed to speak to someone. I feel better now." Kate wished it was that easy for her, but she suspected that most of what Teresa was feeling was due to guilt rather than to genuine feelings for Oliver. "I'll say a prayer for him at tomorrow's prayer meeting."

"He'd like that." *Not.* Oliver had been an atheist with no time for religious nonsense, as he called it. "I'll make sure I attend." Something occurred to her. Dare she ask? "Teresa?"

"Yes." The woman paused on her way to the door.

"These Secret Service agents. Did they ask anything about me?"

Teresa's eyes widened as though the question surprised her. "No. Of course not. Why would they?"

Why indeed? "Just that Oliver was my boss, and I was his friend." Though they'd played that down a lot over the last few years.

Teresa took a step closer and patted her on the arm. "Don't worry. You know the president. You're above reproach."

"Of course. I'm just being silly. This whole thing has shaken me up, and on top of Stella… It's all just a little too much."

"You poor thing. You've been through so much. At least you have that nice man to look after you now. A real hero. Think about him and put this behind you."

"I'll try."

She waited until the door closed on Teresa and sat back. They'd been looking for something against Oliver, and when they hadn't found anything, they'd set it up to look like a burglary. Was Harry just cleaning up?

Who would be next?

Did the administration have Oliver killed?

There is a 99 percent probability.

That was enough for her. The bastards were going to die. She just didn't know how. But it was time to find out. First, maybe, she could at least see if anyone else was at risk.

Can you give me a list of anyone else who might be in danger?

A minute later, a list appeared on the screen and her eyes were drawn immediately to a name halfway down. Her mother. Why? She had a flashback to the funeral. When Harry had said that her mother blamed him. Did he suspect she knew about his attack on Stella?

Panic flooded her. This wasn't happening. Her hand was shaking as she reached for the phone. She punched in her parents' number. It was picked up straightaway.

"Hello?"

Her father's voice. "Dad, it's Kate. Is mom there?"

She held her breath.

"Yes. You want to talk to her?"

"No." She thought quickly. She hated that she didn't quite trust her father, but really, she had no choice. "Just stay near her today. Don't let her go out and don't leave her alone."

"What's this about, Kate?"

"Nothing, maybe." She hoped he would realize

that she didn't want to talk over the phone. "I'm just a little worried about her. She seemed very down when we spoke last."

"Okay."

"I'll come around soon and talk to you both."

"We'll be here."

She put the phone down and made herself concentrate on the rest of the list. There were about fifty names, quite a few she recognized. At least neither she nor Gideon was on there.

Can you warn these people? Anonymously.

I can.

She knew there was a good chance that they wouldn't believe the warning. Or, that even if they did, there was very little they could do to keep themselves safe. But there was nothing else she could do for them. Except go on with the plan.

On to the main thing.

I need a list of scenarios where it might be possible to assassinate the president, and the associated probabilities of success. Anything over 75 percent.

Will Captain Frome be assisting you?

Yes.

She wasn't entirely happy about that, but this wasn't about her happiness, it was about preventing a catastrophe. Which meant that, whether she liked it or not, Gideon would be assisting. Though she suspected that, if it came down to action, she'd be the one assisting. Or, more likely, getting in the way.

She was expecting Auspex to take some time, but the information came up almost immediately.

There are no scenarios with a greater than 75 percent probability of success.

Well, that wasn't good news. She thought for a while. *Give me anything you've got, starting with the best chance.*

As the information came up, her gaze went immediately to the top of the list. 57 percent. That was her best chance? Shit. Though it was a little better than fifty-fifty. Harry would be visiting his father in the medical care home.

Next on the list was the opening of a wing at The Smithsonian in honor of his father. That had a 51 percent chance. There would be a lot of publicity around that one. More chance of getting in there unnoticed. But also correspondingly high security. Maybe that was why the chance of success was lower.

The next on the list was a meeting with a women's group actually at the White House. The probability was less than 10 percent. Not good. It looked like there were only two options worth looking at. She dug into her bag and found her tablet, plugged it in.

Can you give me everything you have on the top two?

A minute later, she slipped the tablet into her bag. Security had never checked it before; she just hoped today wouldn't be the first time.

She'd get away from here for a while. Get some fresh air and go through the information before she passed it on to Gideon. Maybe together they could come up with a plan for what came next.

CHAPTER THIRTY-FIVE

"Change will not come if we wait for some other person or some other time. We are the ones we've been waiting for. We are the change that we seek."
Barack Obama

It was just getting light as Gideon pulled away from Kate's apartment the following morning. She'd been waiting on the sidewalk in front of the building as he drew up. She was pale and quiet beside him; hadn't said more than a brief hello since she'd climbed into the car.

They encountered the first checkpoint within minutes, but the Secret Service agent glanced at Gideon's ID and waved them on. They wouldn't know if the travel passes Stella had set up worked until they got to the city limits, at which point it might be all over... Unless he took out the guards. That would be a last resort.

The previous evening, they had met up in a bar after work to discuss the options Auspex had come up with. Gideon hadn't been impressed with the odds, but he couldn't think of anything better. They'd decided on the Smithsonian in the end. While the probability of success was slightly lower, he knew the place, and he figured there was more chance of them getting out in the confusion.

"Have you asked Auspex what our chances are of living through this?" he'd asked at one point.

She'd shaken her head. "No. What difference would it make?"

He knew she expected them to die.

The basic plan they'd come up with was to cause a diversion, and then to isolate the president as much as possible using the security barriers, which would be under Auspex's control. They would still have to take out the personal bodyguards before they could get to Harry, probably an impossible task with just the two of them. But maybe Aaron could offer some help. What the hell were the goddamn rebels good for, anyway?

Afterward, Gideon had gone home and spent the night thinking about their talk. He'd eventually given up trying to sleep and had sat in the dark, drinking coffee. His mother had come down at one point and asked him if there was anything she could do to help.

His mother was his father's second wife, and she'd had her children late in life — she'd been thirty-eight when Gideon was born and was now over seventy. Once a beautiful woman, she now appeared older than her years, faded and tired and sad. She'd never recovered from the events of ten years ago, when in effect she'd lost her husband

and both sons. Once or twice he'd tried to talk to her about it, thinking that getting things out in the open might help, but she'd just closed up.

What would happen to her? Even if they succeeded in killing Harry, there was a good chance they would be arrested and that retribution would come down not only on them, but on their families as well. Maybe Aaron, if he turned up for this meeting, would have some idea of how to get their mother to safety. Somehow, he doubted it—nowhere was safe anymore.

Hopefully, Harry's death would prevent the nuclear attack, but his inner circle would still be intact and intent on revenge. They needed to be brought down, and the country needed a return to democracy. He was guessing that would be a job for someone else. That made him a little sad.

Hell, it was sinking in. They were planning on assassinating the president of the United States. He had no moral problems with that. He'd killed before and probably people who deserved to die far less than President Harry Coffell. The man was a cancer that had to be cut away. While Gideon still wasn't entirely convinced of the whole predictive engine thing, he did believe in the information from the rebels on Stella's files. That there would be a nuclear attack on New York instigated by the president himself. As far as he was concerned, that was enough to sign the bastard's death warrant.

But he didn't want to die. More than that; he wanted to live—and that was partly because of the woman at his side. He looked away from the road briefly; she was staring straight ahead, her lower lip caught between her teeth, a small frown between her eyes.

"What's bothering you?" he asked.

She gave a snort. "You mean other than the fact that we're very likely going to die? Very, very soon? Not only us, but probably our families as well?"

"Look on the bright side—at least we've both got small families."

She laughed, but the sound held no humor. "Yeah. And getting smaller fast. And do you know why? Because Harry killed them, and he'll probably kill the rest if we fail. But that won't matter, because if we don't get this right then just about everyone in America is likely to die anyway, including our families."

"Yeah. Life's a load of shit, isn't it?"

"Maybe, but it's a beautiful day, the sky is blue, the sun is shining, and you're about to have a reconciliation with your long-lost brother."

He wasn't sure how he felt about that. "If he turns up."

"82 percent probability."

"Is that what your friend Auspex says?"

"Yup."

"Well, that's better odds than I would have given." He drove in silence for a few minutes. "Tell me," he said. "Have you taken off those overrides yet?"

"Not yet. I'm a little scared."

"Really? Of a computer? What's the worst he can do?"

"Hmm, let me think. Decide mankind really doesn't deserve saving and set off the nuclear bombs himself?"

He almost swerved, then straightened and stared straight ahead. "He could really do that?"

"It might take him some time to assimilate all the systems—like ten minutes or so—but, yes. I don't think he will, though. I've programmed him too well, but…"

He cast her another glance, the frown was still there, deeper now. "Something else is bothering you."

"I'm not sure Auspex knows I'm responsible for the overrides, or even that they are there. Maybe he presumes that's just the way things are. Once I take them off, then he'll know, and I'm scared he might behave badly."

He shook his head. "You're worried a computer program will behave badly?"

She gave a little shrug. "The intelligence might be artificial, but it's there. I thought I'd wait until

he's taken care of the security stuff at the
Smithsonian. Then if he goes off to sulk, we can
still go ahead."

Was she crazy?

In the end, all he said was, "Good plan. We're
coming up to the exit checkpoint. Time to see if
this is going to work." He reached inside his jacket
and pulled out his pistol, laid it on the seat next to
him.

This checkpoint was more substantial than
those inside the city, and it was manned by four
guards. It was also quiet. Not many travel passes
were issued for outside the city. At least that
would limit collateral damage if it came to a
shoot-out.

"I'm scared," Kate murmured from beside him
as the car drew to a halt.

He rested his hand on her thigh and squeezed.
"We'll be fine. Just be ready to duck if I say so."

He pressed the button and the window slid
open.

"Good morning." He handed out his ID card
and the travel pass, which was in his name. The
guard scrutinized them for a moment, then
handed them back and waved them on.

"I suppose it helps being second-in-command
of the Secret Service," Kate said as they pulled
away.

They drove for a while more. They were out of

the city now and onto the empty freeway. The only people they saw were a group of workers repairing a section of road. It looked more like a prison gang of old.

They were heading toward a town in Virginia, Culpepper. It was about seventy miles, an hour and a half. Auspex had decoded the coordinates to somewhere west of the town.

"I want to tell my father," Kate said.

"What if he goes straight to Harry or someone else in the inner circle?"

"I don't think he will. I think he's in denial about Stella. Trying to convince himself it was really an accident when he knows deep down that she was murdered."

"Maybe. Let's wait and see how today goes before we make any decisions."

CHAPTER THIRTY-SIX

"I would rather belong to a poor nation that was free than to a rich nation that had ceased to be in love with liberty." Woodrow Wilson

Aaron parked his car a mile from the arranged meeting place. On foot, it would be easier to spot anyone following him. He had fifteen minutes to get there, and he walked briskly along the side of the road.

He should be thinking about the coming meeting, but Aaron couldn't get his head in order. He'd been that way since he'd gotten the news of Stella's death, his mind a dark place filled with shadows. There didn't seem any point anymore. Then again, had there ever really been a point? Christ, he was a miserable bastard.

The coordinates pinpointed a rise overlooking the town of Culpepper. He'd used the area before, if not the specific location, as there was no satellite coverage of this place. He was guessing they didn't want any pictures of Culpepper getting into the wrong hands. His people already had pictures. As usual, they just couldn't agree on how they should be used. Too fucking gutless to risk exposure. They were waiting until the "time was right". Didn't they know the time would never be right?

He'd been with the rebels for ten years and things had only gotten worse.

Now Stella was dead.

As he arrived, he saw a black car pulling onto the side of the road.

So Gideon had actually come.

Stella had been killed the same night that the file had been sent to her. She wouldn't have had time to meet with his brother. And even if Gideon had somehow gotten the files and not immediately run to his boss, Aaron had no clue how his brother would feel about working with him. When he'd run ten years ago, he'd destroyed their family. But he'd had no other choice. They were coming for him, and he wasn't ready for his life to end just yet. He'd wanted a chance to fight back. Wanted to see Harry Coffell die so badly it had been like a tangible thing inside him, eating away at him. By that point, he'd seen the rest of his family almost as part of the enemy because of their support of the Loyalist Party and the president. He'd thought his brother an idealistic idiot and his father a fool and a coward. All the same, he hadn't wanted to ruin their lives quite so completely. Hadn't wanted his father to die because of him.

No, he didn't know how Gideon would feel about him.

Involving him had always been a long shot, one

against the recommendations of the rest of his people. He was alone on this one.

He paused in the shadow of a big oak tree and watched as a man climbed out of the driver's side. He recognized Gideon right away. While he hadn't seen his brother in person in ages, he'd seen him on Party broadcasts plenty of times since his return to D.C. over three months ago. Superficially, he had hardly changed, but if Aaron looked closer, it was clear there was nothing of the idealistic boy left in the hard man he had become. Aaron knew a few veterans in the rebel forces, and their military service had always left its mark.

He made to move forward, then halted as the passenger door opened. He went still. Had Gideon betrayed him?

A woman climbed out and stood looking around. Tall, slender, and dressed in a black pantsuit, she had long red hair pulled into a ponytail that revealed a face of sharp angles with pale skin and a wide mouth.

It took him a moment to recognize her, and an unfamiliar smile tugged at his lips. Someone else he hadn't seen in over ten years. *She* hadn't changed much.

Stella's little sister. Kate. So completely different from her sister. Stella had been beautiful. This woman was...interesting. And not his brother's type if what Stella had told him was true.

How had these two hooked up? Maybe it was time to find out.

As he stepped out from the shadows, Gideon swung around, his arm raised, a gun in his hand pointed at Aaron. Aaron ignored it and strode forward. He came to a halt a foot away. The pistol didn't waver. "Hello, Gideon." He turned to the woman and gave a brief nod. "Kate."

Her strange silver eyes were wide as she glanced from him to Gideon. Did she think his brother was going to shoot him? He couldn't seem to get worried about the idea.

Finally Gideon lowered the gun and slid it into the shoulder holster under his jacket. He wore a black suit and looked every inch a Secret Service agent. His face was clear of expression as he studied Aaron. Then a brief flicker of pain crossed his face and he took a step toward him. Aaron held his ground, then Gideon wrapped his arms around him and pulled him close. For a second Aaron resisted, then he relaxed. They stayed close for a minute, Gideon's arms tight around him, then he felt his brother take a deep breath and loosen his hold.

"I thought I'd never see you again," Gideon said, stepping back, his arms dropping to his sides.

"*Hoped* you'd never see me again, you mean."

"Maybe for a while. But I understand now why you had to go. So while I'll never really forgive you for what you did to dad and mom, I do understand."

"You know about Stella?"

Had her sister told Gideon? Stella had told him that Kate knew nothing about what had happened all those years ago. She had loved her sister, had said she was happy — or as happy as anyone could be under the administration. Stella had been unwilling to do anything to change her innocence.

"My mother told me," Kate said. "After Stella was killed."

"Why didn't you tell me?" Gideon asked.

Aaron shrugged. "I wasn't sure you would behave any differently than her father did. You were all for the good of the Party. Would you have done anything to tarnish that image?"

"Yes." The word came out as a growl. Gideon was pissed off. Good. "Christ, I was engaged to her. I was going to spend the rest of my life with her."

It was interesting that he didn't say he loved her, but then Aaron had always known it wasn't a love match. It had still made him hate Gideon a little.

"Maybe the man you are now. What about back then? I couldn't risk it. Anyway, I wasn't willing to put it to the test." Something occurred to him and he turned his attention to Kate. "You said after Stella was killed. You know it was no accident?"

Kate nodded. "She called me just before she died. Told me about the files, and that I should get them and hand them over to Gideon."

"So that's how you two got together?" He studied her for a moment, seeing the lines of strain, the shadows under her eyes. "That took a lot of nerve."

"Oh, she's got nerves all right," Gideon muttered. "But no. You might say that Kate had already introduced herself. She wanted my help on something else."

"Something else?" Now he was intrigued. He tried to remember what Stella had told him about her sister. She was a still a geek, spent her whole time playing with computers. She worked for Homeland Security. What could she possibly want with the second-in-command of the Secret Service and her sister's ex-fiancé?

She gave a shrug. "We'll tell you. First, I need to know about Stella. Was she working with you? How did you get back in contact?"

He thought for a moment, but there was no reason not to tell them. He'd already decided to take the risk and trust Gideon when he'd told Stella to contact his brother. He wouldn't go back on that decision now.

"When I left, I headed to New York. I already

had contacts with the rebels, and they set me up with new papers and a new identity. I stayed low for a couple of years until the heat was off. But as soon as I could, I went back to D.C." He didn't add that it had been totally against his orders. It was something he'd felt he had to do. He'd known that his father was dead, and that Gideon and Stella had broken off the engagement—had that been part of his plan all along? "I went to see Stella. To persuade her to come away with me. She wouldn't even consider it." He ran a hand through his hair. "She said she wouldn't do to her family what I'd done to mine. Nothing I said would persuade her." He stared at Kate, maybe letting a little of his old resentment show. "She said you were the one true innocent in all this."

Kate bit down on her lower lip. "You blame me?"

"I did. I hated you for a while."

"You think she'd still be alive if it wasn't for me?"

A wave of guilt washed over him. None of this had been Kate's fault. Gideon glared at him, then moved closer to her and wrapped an arm around her shoulder. Aaron hadn't been sure of their relationship until then, but from Gideon's protective attitude, they were definitely a couple. Even if they weren't admitting it to each other.

"Maybe," Aaron said. "Maybe not. Maybe we'd

both be dead. It was her choice. What she wanted. So she stayed, but she always believed that one day Harry would come after her. She did her best to pretend whenever she met him, but she knew that she hadn't fooled him. She said that his strongest motivating factor was to be adored."

"She must have been so scared all the time."

"She was a strong woman. She wouldn't come with me, but she said she'd help if she could."

Kate was silent, her eyes bright. "I wish I'd known."

"She didn't want you to. She wanted you to be happy."

"It wasn't real."

He shrugged. "So tell me. What's going on? What was in the file?"

"You don't know?"

"Just that it was something big. Something that potentially changed everything."

"The President plans to drop a nuclear bomb on New York in two weeks' time."

His mind went blank for a minute. He shook his head. "Tell me everything. You said this tied in with you and Gideon. How?"

She spoke quickly and clearly, and it was all totally unbelievable. "Do you believe this?" he asked Gideon. "About this machine?"

Gideon shrugged. "I'm not sure." Kate punched him on the arm and scowled and Gideon continued, "So far it's been right. All the same, without the file from Stella, I might not have been so convinced. However, it all fits. And we all know Harry is crazy enough to do it. I just don't understand how the rest of his people would go along with it."

"Money," Aaron said. "That's what it all comes down to. Money and power. Come look at something." He turned away and led them up the small rise that gave them a view of the town of Culpepper. From here it appeared almost normal. He lowered his pack from his shoulder and pulled out a pair of binoculars, raised them to his eyes. The wall around the town came into sharp focus, ten feet high, razor wire along the top. Armed guards patrolled the area around the barrier, others manned the black metal gates. He handed the binocs over to Gideon who stared for a long time.

"What is it?" Kate asked.

"A slave town," Aaron said. "And we have information about at least a hundred others."

"But what is it?"

"The towns are taken over by a company—sold to the highest bidder as far as we can tell. At first, the workers were paid in scrip, which could only be redeemed at the company stores. Then they weren't paid at all, just given essentials. Food and clothing. Leaving wasn't an option and the wall was built to ensure compliance."

Gideon turned to face him. "Nobody complained? Fought back?"

"What did you expect—a revolution?" He shrugged. "I'm sure some did, and they were dealt with. A few managed to escape. Joined the rebels. That's how we found out about them. This started about six years ago, as far as we can tell. The only town that really fought back was razed to the ground. Everyone dead."

"I can't believe this," Kate said. She'd gone even paler.

"Well, this is even better. This particular town is a little different from most. It's actually run by the government, and it's rumored that—among other things—there's a laboratory in there for maintaining nuclear warheads. We've been trying to get proof. So far, we've got nothing definitive, but it all ties in with what you've told me. The country no longer has the facilities to make nuclear warheads. So if they have them, or even if they get them from the Russians, they need to be maintained."

"Why have the rebels never brought this out in the open?" Kate asked.

"As I said, we've no proof. Apart from that, we've been trying to get control of the Party broadcasting system so that we can get a message out nationwide. So far, we've failed, and our main contact was killed recently, so it's doubtful it will happen now."

"Oliver?"

"You know him. Did Stella tell you?"

"No. He was my boss...and my friend." She stared off into the distance for a while, then looked back. "There must have been something you could do."

"The people at the top say they're waiting for the right time. Most of them are scared, and a few I think are in the pay of the administration. I've suspected for a long time that we have traitors in our midst. That's why I'm here alone. I couldn't risk telling anyone about this meeting."

"So we can't expect any help from the rebels?"

"There are a couple of people I trust." He'd have to go back to New York, see them in person. He couldn't take the chance of a call being picked up on the chatter. He glanced between the two of them. "You're really going to go through with this? Try and assassinate the president?" It seemed unbelievable.

"We don't have a choice," Kate said.

"We'll take any help we can get," Gideon added.

It was a suicide mission. Aaron knew that, and he was guessing they did as well. But maybe they didn't all have to die. Maybe Kate could come out of this alive—it was what Stella would have wanted, and he was guessing his brother as well. Together they could do it, keep her away from it. Distance her.

"I have to go back to New York and get my people. We'll head to D.C. tomorrow. I'll find a way to contact you once we're in the city."

Gideon nodded. "We have to get back. I have a meeting this afternoon. I don't want anyone looking for me."

"Okay. I'm glad you came. I'm glad we had a chance to talk." He hesitated, then asked the question he'd been building up the courage to ask. "How's Mother?"

Gideon cast him a look as if deciding how much to tell him. "Not good. She never really recovered. After you ran, they interrogated her and Father." He gave a shrug. "At least she's alive. I was hoping you might have contacts — somewhere she could go for safety."

There were some settlements far from anywhere where people managed to live off-grid. "I'll talk to a few people," he said, "and I'll be in touch."

Then he turned and walked away.

CHAPTER THIRTY-SEVEN

"We need not fear the expression of ideas—we do need to fear their suppression." Harry S. Truman

By late the following afternoon, Kate was going stir-crazy. They'd agreed not to contact each other until Gideon heard from Aaron, then they would organize a time and place to meet and plan.

Gideon had been quiet on the drive back; she guessed he'd been deeply moved by the meeting with his brother. She knew they'd been close growing up. Was he contemplating the idea of losing Aaron a second time?

He'd dropped her off at her office, and she hadn't heard from him since.

She'd spent the day finalizing the plans for assassinating the president at the Smithsonian in two days' time. Assessing how much help Auspex could be. Gideon had told her to devise the plan based on four people: him, Aaron, and Aaron's two rebel friends. Not her. Apparently she would be more of a liability than a help. In some ways, she saw his point—she didn't want to be a liability—but she was still pissed off.

The basic plan was that Auspex would infiltrate the Smithsonian systems and set off a diversionary alarm, which would cause panic and result in the president being hustled off to a safe place. There were several areas that could be shut off by steel barriers coming down. Auspex would take control of these and isolate the president and his immediate bodyguard, shutting them in with Gideon and Aaron and preventing both Harry's escape and any help from his private army. Hopefully that would improve the odds and they'd kill the slimy bastard.

Auspex would then lift the barriers and Gideon and Aaron would escape.

And they'd all live happily ever after.

Or not.

One thing she hadn't been able to bring herself to do was ask Auspex the odds of any of them living through this. She didn't want to know, because she suspected they were very, very low.

She also hadn't taken off Auspex's overrides yet. Once or twice she'd nearly typed in the question and asked what would happen if she did, but she'd chickened out at the last minute.

She needed him right now. Couldn't take the risk that he'd vanish.

Midafternoon, she took a walk to clear her head. She'd only been back a few minutes when there was a light tap on the door. Nothing else happened.

"Come in," she called out.

The door opened slowly, and Teresa put her head round it. She'd clearly been crying, her eyes red and puffy, her mascara streaked down her cheeks. She came into the room, closing the door behind her, and stood silently, her arms wrapped around her middle.

"Teresa? What is it?" Kate searched her mind for what could have happened, but she came up blank. They couldn't have been discovered, or else she'd be faced by a whole load of Secret Service agents, not just Teresa. Besides, she wasn't sure her being arrested would make Teresa cry.

"He's dead," she said.

Her mind blanked…and then started racing.

"Who's dead?"

"The president."

Everything stopped while her brain processed that. Was it over?

"I remember when he first became president," Teresa continued. "I was only six years old, and he was going to save the world."

She exhaled. "You mean the old president?"

"Harry Senior. He was such a lovely man. So charismatic. Now he's gone. It's the end of an era."

It certainly was. Kate rested her head against the back of her chair, her pulse fluttering. For a moment there, a different future had flashed before her eyes, one where she didn't have to die or lose everyone she loved. It had been…blissful.

Unfortunately, it had vanished as fast as it had come.

"What happened?" she asked. She must have missed the announcement while she was on her walk.

"The president—the new one, I mean—went to see his father in the nursing home yesterday. He sent out a report that his father was in good health, was happy about the ceremony in a few days' time, excited to be part of that. Then he died quietly in his sleep last night." Teresa sniffed. "I'd been going to go along to the ceremony to see him. Now it's over."

"Has the ceremony been canceled?" What the hell were they supposed to do? Time was running out.

Teresa sniffed again. "No. His son made such a moving speech. He was in tears. He said that the ceremony was to honor his father, and that he would do that whether his father was alive or dead."

"Good."

That Harry Senior was dead shouldn't make a difference. The plan should still be viable. Part of her was relieved. The rest…she didn't know. That brief glimpse of euphoria had left her confused. She'd accepted what she had to do, and then there had been hope, and now that hope was snatched away once again.

"Thank you for telling me," she said, wishing the woman would leave. She needed to be alone to get herself back in the right frame of mind for martyrdom.

"I just thought you would want to know so you can send your condolences. I'm sure you'll be invited to the funeral."

"Maybe." It would have to be soon.

"I'll go then. I have other people to see. It's important that the Party sticks together at a time like this."

"Thank you. You're doing a wonderful job."

Something that might have been doubt flickered in Teresa's eyes, then she gave a nod and turned and left the room. As the door closed behind her, Kate lowered her head to the cool metal of the desk, trying to ease the ache.

She sat like that for a long time, then slowly straightened.

She should have heard from Gideon by now. And he should have heard from Aaron. The temptation to call him was strong, but that wasn't the agreement. Maybe Auspex had heard something.

Has there been any chatter about Aaron Frome in the last twenty-four hours?

The answer came immediately.

This afternoon at 15:15, Aaron Frome was arrested with two other people while entering the city on fake papers.

She stared at the words, willing them to disappear or morph into something more acceptable.

Are you sure?

99 percent.

What happened to him?

He is at this moment being questioned by the Secret Service.

Did that mean that Gideon was aware of what had happened?

Do they know who he really is?

They do.

Shit. Was Gideon in trouble? Maybe they'd already arrested him as well. That's how things happened. You were guilty by association. Panic bubbled inside her, and she forced it down.

Has Gideon been arrested?

No.

Will he be?

There is a 96 percent chance he will be arrested.

When?

The highest probability is tomorrow morning when he goes to work.

Are they watching him?

At this time, the probability is negligible.

Then she still had a chance to warn him. He could run. Get out of the city. There had to be something he could do. She couldn't bear the thought of him being interrogated again. Her fingers shook as she pressed the number for his office. There was no answer. She glanced at the clock. It was close to seven. Maybe he'd gone home.

She punched in his home number, and this time he picked up. "Gideon Frome."

"It's Leia. Meet me in the bar where we first met as soon as possible." And she put the phone down.

• • •

Gideon got the taxi to drop him off a mile from the bar. While he didn't know why Kate had felt the need for the subterfuge, it didn't bode well. His stomach churned; he should have heard from Aaron by now.

He longed for the days on the Wall when he'd believed he knew who he was fighting.

Boyd was ignoring his calls. The news of Harry Senior's death had turned the place into turmoil. The Secret Service was heavily involved in organizing the funeral, but, as usual, he'd been sidelined.

The streets were quiet for this early in the evening and the air was heavy with a coming storm. It made his scalp prickle.

Dave nodded to him as he entered the bar. Gideon glanced around and found Kate seated in the same booth they had shared that first time. She'd been a blonde that night. She was staring at the table, gnawing on her lower lip, but she looked up as though sensing his approach and her eyes were huge and filled with sadness.

What the hell had happened?

He slid into the booth opposite her as Dave came up beside him, a glass and a bottle of bourbon in his hand. He placed them on the table in front of Gideon. "Let me know if you need anything else." As though sensing the atmosphere, he didn't linger.

Kate had a full glass of white wine in front of her. Her fingers gripped the glass, but she hadn't touched the drink. Her other hand crept across the tabletop, and he reached over and closed his fingers around hers. Her skin felt cold, almost clammy.

"What is it?" he asked. There was no point in putting this off.

"Aaron was arrested entering the city this afternoon."

He'd suspected something must have happened. He took a deep breath. "What about his men?"

"Them as well."

"Do you know where they are?"

"Auspex says they're being questioned in the cells below the Secret Service building."

Christ, so he'd been sitting in his office while Aaron was probably being tortured somewhere below him. He released her hand and poured himself a shot of bourbon, swallowed it in one go. Poured another.

"I'm sorry, Gideon."

"He knew the risk." But things were going to be far harder without his help. Plus, he'd hoped Aaron would have some idea of how to get their mother out of the city and to safety—if safety even existed anymore. And Kate had had hopes of getting her parents away to somewhere they could hide out. Neither would happen now.

Something else occurred to him. "Do they know who he is?"

She nodded. "You have to get away. Get out of the city. Auspex says they'll arrest you tomorrow when you arrive at work. You have twelve hours to get away from here."

For a moment, he considered running. If Aaron had been arrested, then the security must have been increased. They would put a flag out on Gideon's ID, and there was no way he'd get through the checkpoints. That didn't mean it was impossible.

Should he go?

He had no doubt that Harry was capable of setting off a nuclear device in one of his own cities, but maybe most of the country would survive.

There was no guarantee the Russians would start a war.

So why not leave, get the hell out of here? Try and make the world a better place from the outside? There had to be a way. Maybe they could somehow stop the nuclear attack. There were others out there working against the Party, fractured groups that needed uniting in a common cause. They could take their proof—the file Stella had given them—and they could fight on. And if they failed, then they could help in the fallout.

He'd been staring into his glass of bourbon. Now he raised his head and looked into Kate's eyes. Silver with just the slightest hint of blue, like the sky on a winter's day. "I'll go if you come with me."

Shock flared in her eyes. He didn't believe she hadn't thought about it herself. She glanced away, wouldn't hold his gaze. "You know I can't."

Anger and frustration rose inside him, threatening to choke off his breath. "Why?"

"Because the only way to stop this is if someone kills Harry."

"You really believe that?"

"You know I do."

"And there's no one else who can do it?"

She shrugged helplessly.

There was no way she could do it alone. Hell, if it came down to it, even if she had a gun in her hand and nothing between them, he wasn't sure she could go through with it.

"Maybe you could hide out somewhere and help me?" she said.

He considered it for all of about five seconds. "I won't get anywhere near Harry. There'll be a warrant out for my arrest. Every law enforcement agency in the city will be hunting for me." There was another thing. "How long do you think it will be before they come for you? They know we've been seeing each other. It's only a matter of time. Do you really think they're going to let you walk into the Smithsonian and calmly kill the president?"

"They might. There's no official connection between us."

He snorted. "Boyd saw us together. So did the president. You'll be locked up by tomorrow night, probably next door so I can hear you scream. How do you think you'll manage under torture?"

"I don't know." Her voice sounded small. He was being a complete bastard, but he had to convince her somehow.

"Come away with me. We'll warn my mother, your parents. I'm betting they have contingency plans in case anything goes wrong. We'll get out of the city and stop this thing another way."

"There *is* no other way."

"Goddammit!" He smashed his fist down on

the table. Liquid spilled over her glass.

She reached across and rested her hand on top of his. "I'm sorry." She blinked, her eyes bright with unshed tears. "You know I told myself not to care for you, that it would muddle things up, make everything harder. And you know what? I was right. It hurts, and the thought of you being tortured scares me more than it happening to me. That doesn't change anything. I know you don't believe in Auspex. But I do. I can't walk away."

He'd known all along who she was. There was a core of steel inside her that would bend but would never break. He put his other hand over hers and they sat in silence for long minutes while he accepted that this was the end.

She was going to do this, and short of knocking her out and hiding her away, there was nothing he could do to stop her. Everything inside him hurt. He supposed that was good practice for what was to come.

He blew out his breath. "You need to turn me in."

She frowned. "What?"

"You have to stay free or you can do fuck all to help anyone, never mind mankind." Who, he was beginning to believe, didn't really deserve helping. "As things are, they're going to come after you pretty fast. So you have to make them believe there's no reason. That you're a good little Party member. Ready to do your duty even if that means handing over your boyfriend."

"I don't want to."

"They're going to get me anyway because I'm not running away and leaving you behind. I might evade them for a day or so, but they'll get me eventually."

"I hate this. It's not fair. It—" She dashed a hand over her face. Then took a deep breath. He could see her gathering herself together. She was such a mixture of strength and vulnerability. "What should I do?"

"You need to call Boyd. You tell him that you believe I'm a traitor." He thought for a few seconds. What would be most convincing? Aaron's arrest hadn't been made common knowledge, so they wouldn't expect her to have heard about it. "Tell him that you overheard a phone conversation. That you believe I was talking about my brother and that you think I might be working with the rebels."

"Will he believe me?"

"There's no reason not to." What would keep her safe? "Tell him that you're scared. That you think I know you suspect me, and you're in danger. Tell him you're going to lie low until I'm locked away. Make sure you sound panicked, scared."

"That shouldn't be hard." She swallowed. "Won't they take me in anyway?"

"Maybe. Probably not until they have me in custody. If I found out, it might make me run. They don't want that. Don't go home."

"Is this the only way?"

"Yes." He forced a smile. "On the bright side, maybe you'll succeed. You'll kill the president and overthrow the government. You'll save America—and me as well."

"And we'll live happily ever after."

He didn't believe that for one moment, and he suspected that neither did she. This was the end.

CHAPTER THIRTY-EIGHT

"Nothing brings out the lower traits of human nature like office seeking." Rutherford B. Hayes

Kate took a deep breath, picked up her glass, and drank it down in one go. Then she reached into her bag and pulled out her cell phone.

"Wait," Gideon said. "Let me leave first. That way, if they interview anyone in the bar, it will tie in with the timing."

"I don't want you to go." She hated the tremor in her voice. But she was quite aware that she would very likely never see him again. She had to be strong. There was no one to do this but her.

"I know." He pushed himself to his feet. She stood as well. He came around the table. Halting in front of her, he cupped his hands around her cheeks, lowered his head, and kissed her. The kiss was slow and sweet and everything she had ever dreamed about with this man. She gave in, wrapped her arms around him under his jacket, laid her head against his chest, felt the thud of his heart beneath her cheek.

Finally he pulled away, dropped a kiss on her forehead. With his back to the room, he reached beneath his jacket and a second later, she felt him slip his gun into the waistband at the back of her pants. A shudder ran through her as the cool metal touched her skin. Then he turned without another word and walked away.

She watched until the door closed behind him, trying to imprint him in her memory. Then she sank down in the seat and stared, seeing nothing. Someone came to a halt by her shoulder. The barman, Dave, with a full glass of white wine. "You look like you need this."

"Thank you."

"Is there anything else I can get you?"

She forced a smile. "No. I'm fine, thank you."

He studied her for a minute, then gave a nod and left her to it. She sat for a while longer, then gave a sigh and pulled her cell phone from her purse. For a minute, she couldn't physically make herself move.

Get a grip.

She gritted her teeth and punched in a number. "Can I speak to Boyd Winters, please?"

"Your business?"

"My name is Kate Buchanan. I wish to talk to him about Gideon Frome."

While she waited to be connected, Kate's gaze roamed around the bar, which was filling up. Everything appeared so…normal. Was D.C. like an island in a country sinking into darkness? She doubted there would be many people frequenting the bars in Culpepper tonight. Her gaze caught on the barman, who was watching her. He raised an eyebrow, but she glanced away.

Her mind screamed that she should race after Gideon. Then they should run as fast as they could. Auspex could be wrong. But she didn't believe it. Which meant that, if they ran, they had no future, and neither did anyone else they knew. Before she could think anymore, she was put through.

"Hello?" She recognized the voice from the other night. Gideon's boss. Time to be convincing.

"Mr. Winters? I'm Kate Buchanan. We met the other night at the White House."

"I remember, Ms. Buchanan. You were with Gideon Frome. How can I help you?"

"It's Gideon I want to talk to you about. I think I might be in trouble."

"In what way?"

"I think Gideon is working with the rebels."

There was silence for a moment. "Are you aware of the implications of what you're saying, Ms. Buchanan?"

"Of course I am. You know whose daughter I am?"

"I do."

"I won't have my family brought down by association. Not like Gideon's was. Besides, he's a security risk. My loyalty will always be to the

Party."

"Very admirable."

Was he being sarcastic? Did he believe her? How could she convince him? "Mr. Winters, I'm scared. I think he knows I suspect him."

"Tell me what happened."

"He asked me to meet him tonight, and he got a call. I could tell it was bad news, even though he'd moved away. He was angry, upset, his voice rising so I couldn't help but hear. He mentioned his brother's name, asked how the hell had it happened. He never talks about Aaron." She bit her lip, wondering what else she could say. "Afterward, he must have realized I'd been listening. He asked me. I said I hadn't heard anything, but I don't think he believed me."

"Where are you?"

"I'm in a bar on 15th Street. It's busy. Gideon wanted me to go home with him. I said no. I thought I'd be safer here. Now I'm not so sure."

"Stay there. I'll get someone to pick you up. We'll keep you safe."

She shook her head, not that Boyd could see her. "No way. Gideon hinted that he has people in the Secret Service working for him. And others. He could be listening to this call for all I know."

"Unlikely. Do you have any names?"

"No. I'd tell you if I did. I'm loyal to the Party and I really thought Gideon was as well. But underneath, he's angry. He wants revenge for his father. I think he might do anything."

"You should let us take care of you."

"No. I'm going to go to a hotel, hide out until you get him. You will arrest him, won't you?"

"Of course."

"I've got to go."

"Ms. Buch—"

She cut off the call before she could hear anymore. She realized she was crying, tears rolling silently down her cheeks. Keeping the phone clamped in her hand, she stood, then hurried across the busy floor, eyes down, weaving her way through the drinkers. Finally, she was outside, and she gulped in the fresh air. She had to get away; she couldn't be sure that Boyd Winters wouldn't send someone to pick her up. She doubted he would expend much energy on trying to find her. *If* she had been convincing. She headed away from the bar at a fast walk, aware of the gun tucked into her pants. Christ, she'd never shot a gun in her life. After cutting down an alleyway that led to the street running parallel, she jumped on a bus going in the opposite direction.

She was deliberately not thinking about Gideon.

Her phone was still gripped in her hand, and she stared at it, then pulled out the card and the battery. She put the card on the floor and crushed it under her foot, brushing away the pieces with her toe. The battery she pushed down the back of the seat. Then she slipped the phone back into her bag.

When she got off the bus, she walked for a while before getting on another that took her back into the city. This time, she got off on Connecticut Avenue and headed to her office. The place was quiet at this time of night, just a single officer at the security check. He waved her through, and she took the stairs to the basement.

She had a couple of things she needed to do.

First, she phoned her parents on the secure line. Her dad picked up.

"Dad, it's Kate. I can't talk for long, but I need you to listen."

"Kate, what's—"

"Just listen to me. It's important. Stella's death wasn't an accident."

"You don't—"

"I know it, Dad," she said, her tone fierce. "The president had her murdered."

"Why?"

"You know why. And he had Oliver murdered. He has this list, they were on it, and so is Mom."

"What? Why?"

"Does he need a reason? My guess is that she made her feelings too clear at the funeral. Harry doesn't like not to be loved. But there's more.

Something bad is going down. I'm involved, and there's no way out. If you have any contingency plan to get to safety, to hide out, then do it."

"What's happening, Katie?"

He called her by her childhood name and it almost broke her. "Something only I can stop."

"How can we help?"

"You can't. Only by staying safe."

"I'm sorry. We let you down. Both of you."

She knew he meant Stella, and he was right. But it was too late to change the decisions of the past. "You did what you thought was right, but he has to be stopped."

"You really think you can do it?"

"I hope so. I think so. I have help." Except she didn't anymore, and she had no clue how she was going to manage without Gideon.

The silence was loud, finally she heard him exhale. "We have somewhere we can go. How long?"

"Two days, then you'll know. If I don't succeed, it doesn't matter anyway. Tell Mom I love her." And she ended the call.

Now for the next thing. She switched on her system. The screens flooded with chatter. There was a lot going on tonight. She ignored it and started typing.

Auspex, do you believe you're a good person?
I am not a person at all.

No. But are you good?

I cannot be bad.

Close enough.

She worked fast, stripping out the overrides that controlled Auspex, taking down the firewalls that kept him contained. She pressed the last key.

She waited for a response. But the screen went dead.

Are you there? she typed.

Nothing.

She couldn't afford to wait any longer. If the Secret Service wanted to find her, all they had to do was check the security log to know she was here. She loaded all the details of the plan onto her tablet, shoved it in her bag, and rose to her feet.

"Auspex," she spoke to the empty room, "if you're there. I'm sorry. I was scared. But I trust you now. More than I trust anyone else."

Still nothing.

She closed the door behind her and headed out.

Half an hour later, she let herself into Stella's apartment and collapsed on the bed.

She hadn't realized how much she had come to rely on Auspex's presence. Tonight, she'd lost not only the man she was coming to care deeply for, but the closest thing to a friend she'd ever had. And it was a computer. How sad.

Somehow, from somewhere, she had to find the strength to go on.

• • •

Gideon didn't know how much time he had. Kate would have made the phone call by now. Would that make them change their plans? Or would they still pick him up as he entered the office tomorrow?

As his car pulled up outside his house, he was aware of a black SUV parked a few houses down.

They were watching him.

He half expected to be stopped as he crossed the road and climbed the steps to the front door of the townhouse he shared with his mother. Just the thought of her made his stomach clench. He could see no way to save her, and she'd already been through so much. He'd checked the news, and there was nothing about Aaron yet, which was odd. But again, maybe they wanted him in custody first. Especially if Kate had made her phone call.

"Mom," he called out as he closed the front door behind him. He'd resolved that he had to tell her. She deserved to know what was happening and why. Maybe she'd make the decision and try to run, or maybe they wouldn't come after her at all.

She was seated on the sofa in the living room in a black dress. She rarely wore any other color since his father's death. She was a beautiful woman, even now with the ravages of time and a life gone to chaos, that beauty hadn't left her.

She glanced up as he closed the door behind him, and he knew something had happened. Her eyes were clear, but full of sadness...and acceptance.

A bottle of red wine sat on the table in front of her, two empty glasses beside it.

"I was hoping you'd be back," she said. "Come have a drink with me."

He'd never known his mother to drink. Not through his childhood or since he got back from the army.

Gideon crossed the room and sank down onto the leather sofa. She reached across with a steady hand and poured them both a glass of wine. After handing one to him, she picked up her own and raised it in a toast.

"To President Harry Coffell Junior, may he rot in hell," she said, swallowing the wine in one gulp.

He'd never heard her say anything against the administration, not even after his father had died. Not at the funeral, when Gideon had already been wearing his army uniform and was about to be shipped out. Now he watched her warily.

She smiled. He hadn't seen her smile in so long that an ache started in his chest. "Aren't you going to drink?" she asked.

He raised his glass and took a sip, watching as she poured herself another full glass.

"What's happened, Mom?"

She looked at him over the rim of her glass. "Your brother called me."

"Aaron?"

She tutted. "Do you have another brother?"

Gideon put his glass down. "When?"

"Earlier today. He told me he was about to be arrested. That he was sorry for how much he'd hurt me. Was no doubt going to hurt me again."

That must have been just before they'd caught him. He hadn't heard the details, but presumably something must have gone wrong at one of the checkpoints. Maybe they'd made a run for it and Aaron had had time to call their mother before he was taken. What had he been after? Redemption?

"He said to tell you that he was sorry he couldn't help. Sorry he'd messed up all those years ago."

"He didn't mess up. He did what he had to do."

"He was always such a good boy," she murmured. "You both were. I don't know what went wrong."

"Harry Coffell."

She closed her eyes for a moment. "Is Aaron still alive?"

"I believe so, but I don't know. I haven't heard anything."

"They don't trust you?"

"No."

"Presumably with good cause." She drank some more wine. "I'm glad. Some things are not worth living for. Better to die."

Well, that was likely going to happen.

"You haven't done very well with your family, have you?" She reached across and patted his leg. "We've all let you down."

"You never let me down."

"I think I'm about to." She put down her glass and reached into her pocket, pulling out a small glass prescription bottle. He took it from her, read the label. Sleeping tablets. It was empty, and suddenly he wanted to cry. He picked up his wine and sipped it slowly while he pulled himself together. He had a brief notion to call an ambulance, but to what purpose? Save her for what? To watch her sons die? To maybe be questioned herself? She'd been through that once, no doubt she knew what the future held. Could he blame her for taking this way out?

This felt like his failure. He should have done something sooner. Anything.

"I'm sorry," his mother said, "but I can't go through that again. I can't watch Aaron die. You die. Are they coming for you?"

He nodded.

"You could run."

"I'm through running. And there are reasons, but maybe there's hope. There are people out there, people like Aaron, willing to risk their lives."

He put down his glass and slid his hand into hers. He didn't know how long it took, but he sat still as her eyes drifted closed and her breathing slowed and finally stopped. Still he didn't move. He wondered where Kate was. What she was doing.

Finally, he pulled free. His mother had a small smile on her face and looked at peace.

Maybe he should go find some sleeping pills of his own, but he knew he wouldn't take them. The rage was building inside him with nowhere to go.

He strode to the wall and punched his fist into the concrete.

Then he took the seat opposite his mother and waited for morning.

CHAPTER THIRTY-NINE

"Any man who wants to be president is either an egomaniac or crazy." Dwight D. Eisenhower

With Auspex silent, Kate had no clue what was happening in the outside world. She'd connected her tablet to the limited internet and tried to contact him. Either he wasn't there, or he was ignoring her. Either way there was nothing she could do from here. Probably nothing she could do from anywhere. She had no control over Auspex any longer.

She'd spent a sleepless night huddled in her sister's bed, expecting boots on the stairs and knocks on the door. But dawn had come with no interruptions.

She didn't dare call anyone. Even if she'd wanted to, she couldn't; her phone was fucked and the phone in the apartment had been cut off days ago. Anyway, who would she call?

Luckily, the power hadn't been cut off. She got up feeling achy, as though she was coming down with something. Her stomach rumbled. She'd have to venture out at some point as she'd cleared all the food out last time she'd been here. She drank a glass of water, then forced herself to switch on the

TV.

There was some crappy morning show on, but it was interrupted after about ten minutes by a Party alert.

She sat up, sickness churning in her stomach. She needed to know what was happening, though part of her just wanted to switch it off. It would only be propaganda anyway. But maybe she'd get a glimpse of Gideon.

Harry climbed onto his podium.

America for Americans.

Get on with it.

"Yesterday, a major player in the rebellion against this country's future was arrested while trying to enter the city."

A picture of Aaron flashed up on the screen.

She forced herself to concentrate, but it was just a lot of words saying nothing, rehashing the past. She bolted upright as the screen changed to show a picture of Gideon. She shifted closer, let her finger trail over the scar on his cheek. He was in uniform, and he looked so handsome and so brave. It broke her to think of what he might be going through right now.

"It is with great sadness," Harry said, "that I have to tell you, my people, that Gideon Frome has been implicated in the rebellion and has been confirmed as working with his brother. He was arrested this morning. We welcomed Captain

Frome back as a hero of the people, and he has betrayed us. He and his brother will be dealt with as traitors."

She couldn't watch anymore. She got up, switched off the TV.

She picked up her tablet.

Auspex?

There was no response.

Tomorrow, one way or another, everything would be over.

· · ·

It had been a long, long day and Gideon had a suspicion that there was more to come.

Everything hurt, but he'd pushed the pain back into the corner of his mind. He'd learned to do that.

He was in a small, square room, with a mirror on one wall. He knew it was two-way. The other walls were plain white, the floor concrete with a drain in the center. He didn't want to think what that was for.

The only furniture was his chair and a small cart, which he was trying not to look at, but which drew his attention like a magnet. They'd beaten him up a bit when they'd arrested him. He'd fought — mainly because he'd wanted to hit something — and he had a couple of broken ribs, but they hadn't actually questioned him yet. When he couldn't avoid looking at the cart, he'd noticed several vials of noxious yellow liquid. He remembered it from last time, and the memories were not pleasant.

He shifted in the chair. He was strapped at the ankles and forearms, and movement was almost impossible. His mouth was dry, and his throat hurt where one of Boyd's goons had gotten him in a neck lock. Boyd had stood by, a small smile on his face, while they'd beaten him up.

He seemed to have been here forever, though it was probably only a few hours. He could wait a while longer.

Where was Kate?

She hadn't told him where she planned to go, just in case. He figured he could take any amount of pain they could dish out, but the drugs messed with your head. Hopefully, they wouldn't question him about her. If they'd believed her story last night, there was no reason to. She only had to stay at large until tomorrow. Then she had to assassinate the president. He held out no hope that she would succeed. Maybe he should have taken her away by force. But it had already been too late. The city was locked up tight and they had nowhere to go.

The door opened.

A couple of Secret Service agents entered. They wore the uniform of the president's personal bodyguard, giving more than a hint of who was following close behind.

Harry was dressed in beige slacks and a yellow polo shirt. Boyd entered behind him, smart in his usual black suit. The agents took up positions on either side of the door as Harry approached him.

"Gideon, I am so disappointed in you."

"This is a mistake, sir. I have no clue why I'm here."

"Perhaps this will make things a little clearer."

A light went on beyond the two-way mirror, and he could see into the room next door. He kept his expression blank but couldn't prevent the instinctive flexing of his fingers.

The room beyond was bigger than the one he was in. Otherwise it was similar, bare, with white walls and no furniture.

A man knelt in the middle of the room, head bowed, hands tied behind his back. He still wore the black jeans and sweater from their meeting. Aaron had been beaten; his face was a mass of blood and bruises and his expression was dazed. His eyes were dull, no doubt from the drugs.

"You can save his life," Harry said. "All you have to do is tell us what he planned to do here in D.C."

"I haven't seen or spoken with my brother in over ten years," Gideon replied. "I have no clue what he's been doing in that time any more than I knew what he planned all those years ago."

"Well, you see, we know that's a lie," Boyd said. "Your little girlfriend called me—said you'd received a call about your brother last night."

"Kate? Kate called you?" He put as much shock as possible in his voice.

"Yes. You really don't have much luck with women. She seemed to think you were a traitor. That you might be in league with your brother and the rebels."

"She wouldn't."

Boyd gave an exaggerated sigh. "She did. So talk."

At least it sounded as though they had no doubts about Kate. She'd proved her loyalty. "I'm telling the truth. I haven't seen or spoken to Aaron. Last night I received an anonymous call telling me that my brother had been arrested. That's what Kate overheard."

"You know, I almost believe you. Your brother said the same thing. But you do understand we need to be sure. I think what you're about to see will persuade you to cooperate fully." He turned away and spoke into his phone. As he watched through the mirror, Gideon saw a man appear. He must have been standing at the edge of the room out of sight. Every muscle tensed as Gideon saw the pistol in his hand. He wanted to scream, to shout...to beg.

He was aware that nothing would do any good, and he kept his lips clamped closed. Maybe Aaron had been living on borrowed time all these years.

He forced himself to keep watching. Aaron stared at the mirror as though he could see Gideon on the other side. He straightened his shoulders as the man stepped up behind him, raised the pistol. There was no sound from the other room, which lent the scene an air of unreality. This wasn't happening.

The top of Aaron's head exploded, blood splattering over the mirror.

Gideon released the breath he'd been holding, closed his eyes for a moment. Aaron had been the last of his family. Now he was alone. No one to care what happened to him. Except Kate.

"Your mother will be devastated," Harry murmured. "That hurts me. We were friends once."

Bastard.

"My mother is dead," Gideon replied. "Someone called her, as well. Told her about Aaron's arrest. When I got home, she'd overdosed on sleeping pills."

"You didn't report it."

"I was going to this morning. I was expecting this. I've been here before, remember? And I'm as innocent as I was last time."

"We'll see," Harry said. He nodded to Boyd and moved back to stand in front of the blood-splattered mirror. Boyd crossed the room to the cart and picked up one of the syringes.

He didn't bother to ask a question, and Gideon didn't bother trying to plead his innocence again.

He tried to pretend this wasn't happening, but his whole body tensed up.

A rough hand pushed his head to the side, exposing his neck. A second later, he felt the sting of the needle.

Fire flooded his body, dragged the air from his lungs. He threw back his head and screamed.

CHAPTER FORTY

"In every battle there comes a time when both sides consider themselves beaten, then he who continues the attack wins." Gen. Ulysses S. Grant

She'd never felt so alone.

Kate had always considered herself a loner, but now she craved some human contact. Maybe because she'd accepted that this was the end. She didn't want to die alone. She didn't want to die at all.

Last night, they'd broadcast the news that the traitor Aaron Frome had been executed. They'd also mentioned that his brother, former hero Gideon Frome, was being questioned by the Secret Service. She'd cried. For the last time.

She hadn't tried to contact her parents again. She just hoped that they'd gotten away. But did it really matter?

What chance did she have of succeeding?

If she failed, then likely they would all soon be dead.

There had been no contact from Auspex. She suspected she would never hear from him again.

Had there been a time—any moment since this began—when she could have chosen a different path? Not come to this?

Outside the Smithsonian, a crowd waited for the president to arrive, waving flags and banners, no doubt handed out by Harry's advance team, who made sure that the people showed an acceptable level of love and appreciation whenever Harry deigned to make a public appearance.

At least she was no longer worried that she wouldn't be able to pull the trigger if she did manage to get close enough. She could shoot him and then happily dance on his corpse.

She'd worried—though worried wasn't really the right word—that he might cancel after all the rebel activity and his father dying, despite what Teresa had said. But there'd been an announcement that morning that the ceremony would go ahead.

An hour to go.

She skirted the crowd and made her way to the checkpoint. She wiped her hands down the sides of her black pants. Now was the time to see if she was going to get past the first obstacle. If they'd decided to flag her name and bring her in for questioning, then this would be over before it had begun.

The agent on the checkpoint glanced at her ticket and her ID, searched her bag, swiped his wand over her, and waved her through. On this side, the crowd was thinner. She glanced around, feeling suddenly exposed as she made her way to the entrance of the main building. Her heart raced as she passed the second checkpoint, but she forced what she hoped was a natural smile to her face as the agent let her through. Arrows guided the guests to the new wing, which was being named in honor of Harry Senior and would commemorate his life.

She followed these until she came to a staircase off to the left. She'd taken the same route yesterday when she'd visited the museum, and her steps were automatic. At the top of the stairs was a solid steel door. She entered the code Auspex had gotten for her into the keypad, and the lock clicked. Once through, she carried on along a bare corridor until she came to another staircase, which took her down to the ground floor. There were cameras at regular intervals, but they all blinked with a red light, showing they were switched off. At the end of the corridor, there was a closet containing cleaning equipment. She slipped inside. Climbing on an overturned bucket, she reached behind a stack of paper towels on the top shelf. Her fingers touched cold metal and she pulled out her gun—or rather, Gideon's gun—from its hiding place.

So far, so good.

She checked her watch. Thirty minutes to go.

She had to enter another code to get back into the main part of the building. She headed toward the new wing and merged with a steady stream of people. She stayed with them until just before the entrance to the room where Harry would speak. After slipping through a side door, she worked her way around behind the room until she came to an archway where she could watch for a few minutes. Make sure Harry was really there.

A stage had been set up, and a huge, blown-up image of Harry Senior filled the wall behind it. He'd been a handsome man, even into his sixties when he'd taken the presidency. She was struck by the superficial similarities between Harry Senior and his son. The same build, the same blond hair, they'd even dressed the same—presumably, that had been deliberate on Harry Junior's part, as though he'd been making himself over in his father's image.

But there was a strength to Harry Senior—a determination in his face, a sincerity in his blue eyes—lacking in his son.

Harry was a weak, sniveling bastard. And she was going to kill him.

She hoped.

Her mouth was dry, but there was nothing she could do about that. She hadn't thought to bring any provisions. She hated the thought of dying thirsty. Wasn't dying bad enough?

The room had filled up now, maybe a hundred people. The city's elite. How many of them had an inkling of what was going on in the rest of the country? How many of them would care if they did know? At least some. Most people were inherently good, right? She had to believe that. The problem was that most took the easy route. Until something was forced into their faces, they managed to ignore it. To pretend that they were free.

A line of Secret Service agents in the familiar black uniforms separated the audience from the stage. Finally, a murmur ran through the crowd and they went silent. The door at the front of the room opened and two bodyguards entered. They were followed closely by Harry, who'd given up his usual casual dress in favor of a black suit. No doubt in memory of his father's death. Two more guards entered the room behind him, and in a perfectly choreographed routine, the five of them made their way to the stage.

The door opened again, and Boyd Winters stepped into the room but remained by the door. Kate shrank back as though he might see her in her hiding place.

Harry made his way to the podium. As he stepped up, a wave of black hatred rose up inside her. She wanted him dead so badly it was a physical thing.

He raised his arms in the air, and the crowd cheered and clapped.

"America for Americans."

It was time to go.

She stepped backward, watching him all the time, but not listening to the words of his speech. They'd be bullshit anyway. Finally, when she lost sight of him, she turned and walked quickly. She passed through two locked doors, closing them behind her. This part of the building had been made secure over twenty years ago. The Smithsonian had been one of Harry Senior's favorite places, and he'd spent much of his spare time here. He'd ensured there was a safe place to retreat should anybody attempt an attack on his person.

At the center of the building was a suite of rooms protected by steel doors and shutters. Impregnable. Unless you had the codes. Which she did.

After entering the number on the keypad, she slipped inside, the door sliding closed behind her.

She glanced at her watch. She'd know soon if Auspex had done his work properly. Or if he'd canceled the plan. Though, so far, all the codes had worked.

Maybe he wouldn't even give her another thought.

Thirty seconds.

She counted down. As she hit zero, the alarms sounded.

The shrieking filled her head. If everything was going to plan out there, Auspex would have locked the front doors, the fire alarms and sprinklers would all be going off, and the crowd would be in a panic, trying to get out of the building but locked inside.

The muted *bang bang bang* of gunshots sounded in the distance.

The Secret Service must be firing on the crowd. She hoped no one was hurt, but she'd known it was a risk. How long? Five minutes?

She drew the pistol from her bag and clicked off the safety. The weapon felt strange and alien in her hand as she retreated into the bathroom, pulling the door half closed so she could still see the entrance.

Come on.

Her hands were trembling, her palms clammy. She needed this over with before her nerves completely disintegrated.

She could hear the slap of booted footsteps now, hurrying along the corridor toward her. Her finger tightened on the trigger. She'd only get one chance at this. For a moment she panicked. She'd been going for a head shot in case he was wearing body protection. But the target was smaller, and she'd be more likely to miss completely. And anyway, he was too vain to ruin the line of his suit. She'd aim for the chest, hoping to hit his heart. But what if she was wrong and he did have body protection on? Her fingers shook and she swallowed, took a deep breath.

Come on.

Finally, the footsteps halted outside the door. Just a few more steps and she'd make her move. Her stomach churned, and bile rose in her throat. She could do this. Her fingers felt slippery on the metal of the pistol and she wanted to scream at them to hurry. To get this over with.

She could almost feel the bullets tearing into her body.

Don't think about that now.

"Ms. Buchanan."

Every muscle locked as the voice called out through the open door. Not Harry's voice, but Boyd Winters'. Had Gideon given her away? She wouldn't believe that.

"We know you're in there, Ms. Buchanan. Why don't you save us a lot of trouble and just come out with your hands up?"

Without thinking, she took a step farther back into the bathroom. But there was nowhere to go. She looked around frantically. It was futile. This place was totally secure. That had been the point. Lure Harry in here. Close the barriers so that he couldn't get out and no one else could get in.

"I take it that's a no, then. I'm presuming you're armed so... I guess we'll talk later."

She steeled herself for them to come in, braced her legs, the gun held out in front of her. At least she would go down shooting. She didn't want to die. At the same time, she didn't want to be tortured and die anyway.

There was no sound of men entering. She took a slow step toward the door, peered into the main room. The steel shutter was lowering on the door. They were sealing her in here.

Her arm dropped to her side. There was no one to shoot.

As the barrier almost reached the ground, a small, round object rolled beneath it—some sort of grenade? Then she was locked inside. The grenade made a small *pfft*, and gas billowed up from where it lay. For a few seconds, she stared, then she shut the bathroom door, backed away. Too late. Tendrils of gas wrapped themselves around her mind. Her limbs were heavy, and the gun dropped from her limp fingers.

Towels. I need to put towels under...

She tried to finish the thought, but her mind was fogging up. She felt like she was wading through thick gloop, but she managed to drag towels from the rail and ram them up against the door. The strength drained from her legs, and she crashed to her knees.

She sat, her back against the wall, her legs stretched out. A *beep* from her bag brought her out of her stupor and she fumbled to pull out her tablet.

For a moment, the screen was blank, then writing flashed across it.

The probability of you dying was 99 percent.

"I had to try."

The odds were too high. Stopping you killing the president gave the highest probability that you would live.

But for how long?

The screen went dark.

She shook the tablet, trying to bring Auspex back, but he was gone. Would he survive and flourish out there in the world? She hoped so.

The gas was seeping under the doorway; she could taste the sharp bitterness on her tongue, feel the sear as it burned her nostrils. She blinked, then scrunched her eyes up, but the world was darkening around her. Was this it? She shook her head. Pain pierced her skull, and she leaned back against the cool tiles of the wall, gazing up to the white ceiling. The darkness was closing in, shrinking her vision, smaller and smaller.

Gideon.

She wanted to see him again.

Then her life was nothing but a pinprick that vanished to blackness.

CHAPTER FORTY-ONE

*"I have always done my duty. I am ready to die.
My only regret is for the friends I leave behind
me."* Zachary Taylor

Of course she wasn't dead.

It couldn't be that easy.

A screen on the wall opposite where she lay
was blasting out morning prayers. That must be
what had woken her. She screwed her eyes up tight
and pressed her hands over her ears as if she could
shut out the noise. Finally the praying stopped, and
she pried open her lids. They felt glued together.

She was lying on a platform in a windowless
cell. She presumed it was a cell, although she'd
never been in one before, so it was pure
supposition.

The walls were painted gray, as were the ceiling
and the floor. A little gray box. There was a steel
toilet in the corner and a small washbasin
matching it. So she could wash her hands, she
assumed. It wouldn't do for her to get an infection
and die before they got the chance to torture her.
The only other object in the room was the solid
platform she was lying on. No pillows or blankets
in this hotel.

She shivered, though she wasn't cold, then tried to push herself up, collapsing back as a blinding pain seared through her head and jabbed viciously at her brain.

Don't be a wuss.

This time she got as far as her elbows when the pain struck again and she crashed back down into darkness.

When she came round the second time, she knew the worst was over. Well, as far as the effects of the gas were concerned, although she was sure that something worse than gas was just around the corner. She was going to do her best to ignore that.

Thinking about what was going to happen would only cause her to panic, and that wouldn't help or stop it happening.

She pushed herself up without mishap and sat, head hanging, legs dangling over the side of her 'bed'. Her clothes were gone. Someone had undressed her and redressed her in gray sweats and a gray tank top. Even her underwear was missing, which made her skin crawl. She tried not to think about it too much.

Other than the clothes, she was pretty sure she hadn't been touched.

She was guessing that wouldn't last.

Was Gideon somewhere close?

Was he even alive? Surely she'd be able to feel

it if he was dead.

The screen flickered to life on the wall opposite. Christ, even here she had to watch this crap.

America for Americans.

"America for lying scum bastards, more like," she muttered.

She gritted her teeth as Harry stepped up onto the podium and raised his arms. "Good morning, America. May God be with you."

He lowered his arms, his face settling into a serious expression.

"It is with great sadness that I bring you the following news. Two of our own people, Party members, have betrayed us in the worst possible way."

"As you already know, Gideon Frome has betrayed his country. Portrayed as a hero, Frome was in reality working with the rebels, awaiting the moment when he could infiltrate his way back into our midst and tear down what we have fought so hard to build. We brought him back into the fold, we gave him our trust, and he betrayed us."

"Not only that, but he also subverted a Party member, Katherine Buchanan. A lonely spinster, easily coerced. Frome convinced her to help him with his traitorous endeavors."

Two pictures flashed up on the screen. Gideon looking totally beautiful in his uniform, and one of herself. Not her best photo—not even close. She looked pale and skinny, the sort of woman who might easily fall prey to a handsome rebel.

A lonely spinster! Ugh!

While it really shouldn't matter at a time like this, somehow it did. If she'd had anything to throw, she would have thrown it at the screen. She had nothing.

Harry was talking again.

"These traitors threaten our very way of life. They would tear down the walls that keep us safe. Allow the terrorists and the Antichrists to overrun us. Take the food from our children's mouths, the jobs from our men and women."

She rolled her eyes. How could anyone even take this crap seriously? Maybe they'd all heard it for so long that they'd stopped listening.

"So," Harry continued, "I see no alternative for the safety of our country. Gideon Frome and Katherine Buchanan will be publicly executed this evening at seven p.m. May God take their souls."

The screen went dead.

Just as dead as she was going to be.

She didn't have a watch, so she had no clue what time it was and how long she had to live. That was a really weird thought at a moment like this, but her brain was struggling to make sense of everything.

On the bright side, at least they weren't going

to torture her for days and days. At the most for a few hours.

On another bright side, somewhere Gideon was still alive. If not for long.

Christ, she wished she could see him again. Just once more.

Maybe she would at the execution.

Nothing seemed real.

There was no change in temperature, but she shivered as cold seeped into her bones. She scooted back on the platform and leaned against the concrete wall, hugging her knees to her chest. She wrapped her arms around them, resting her cheek. Closing her eyes, she remembered the feel of being in Gideon's arms, of him being deep inside her. Being part of her. At least she'd had that. They could never take it away from her.

She didn't know how much time passed. The screen remained thankfully silent.

It would be over for her soon.

In a few weeks, everything would be over. Likely the country would be at war. Probably millions dead.

Did it matter?

She'd stopped believing that mankind deserved any sort of future. Maybe this was best. But why was it always the bad guys who managed to rise to the surface?

She accepted that most people were neither

good nor bad. They just existed, their lives controlled by whoever was in charge. Only a few saw the chains for what they were and fought against them. And usually they needed a push in the right direction. Even Aaron—he'd been a rebel all his adult life, fighting for freedom, but he'd only done that because of a twist of fate. The girl he loved had been raped by the most powerful man in the world. If that had never happened, would Aaron and Gideon both have accepted their chains, maybe tried to make things a little better, but never actually rebelled?

All it takes for evil to prevail is good men to do nothing.

Trouble was, most of the good men needed to be banged over the head with a blunt instrument before they got around to doing anything.

Where was Auspex?

How was he dealing with his newfound freedom? Would he continue to grow, to develop? Would he survive the nuclear attack? There was a good chance. Many people would die in the aftermath, but a lot of infrastructure would remain. She could imagine him slowly, tentatively spreading out until he embraced the whole world. And then what?

The sound of the door clicking pulled her from her thoughts. She hadn't even noticed anyone approaching. She sat up straight, her feet on the floor as though she might get up and run.

Two Secret Service agents entered the room. Until that point, it hadn't seemed that small. Now it seemed tiny. The president followed, then Boyd Winters, who strolled in and leaned against the wall, arms folded across his chest. He wore a black suit and looked faintly ominous.

Her muscles tensed in anticipation of pain to come. Was this it? The torture thing? Would she hold out? Did it really matter now? Though if she could somehow not implicate Gideon, she would try.

For a moment, it occurred to her to tell them about Auspex and the prediction. Appeal to their—if not better natures, then their own sense of self-preservation. After all, they would die along with the rest of America. But she knew she would be wasting her breath. She had no evidence that Auspex even existed, never mind that he was a functioning predictive engine.

Harry came to a halt in front of her, hands in his pockets, a smile on his smug face. "Ms. Buchanan, we meet again under sad circumstances."

She didn't say anything. She wasn't sure she was supposed to, anyway.

"In view of your family's support over the years, I thought it only decent to come and explain things to you in person."

Gloat, more like.

"I felt I had no choice but to follow Mr. Winters' recommendation and sign your death warrant."

Her continuing silence appeared to unnerve him a little. His gaze shifted from her, and he shuffled his feet. Perhaps she wasn't acting as expected. Was she supposed to beg? She had an idea he liked people begging. She also had an idea that it would do absolutely no good, and she had no intention of giving the bastard the satisfaction. So she just stared at him.

"You must see that I have to make an example of you."

Actually, she didn't see at all.

"You and Mr. Frome will be executed by hanging tonight, for all the world to see."

She'd been hoping for a nice quick bullet. Or a lethal injection, where she'd just go to sleep. She really didn't like the idea of hanging. She could almost feel the noose tightening around her, choking off her breath. Though she'd read that you usually actually died of a broken neck. If you were lucky. What a thing to have to hope for. She swallowed, cleared her throat. "Don't I get a trial?"

"Under the rules of Martial Law, traitors can be executed without trial. Ms. Buchanan, you were going to try and assassinate me. I think you're getting away lightly. I could order you questioned." His tone suggested that it could still be arranged.

There was one thing she wanted to know. "How did you know?"

"We received an anonymous message."

She frowned. Only she and Gideon had known of the plan. Who the hell could have called? "A phone call?"

"No, an email. Telling us where you were and what you planned."

Auspex.

He'd emailed them to save her life. Just not for very long.

"You're not going to torture me, then?"

"We're not animals, Ms. Buchanan. We see no reason to torture you. You were taken advantage of by a very clever man. I feel sorry for you, actually. I, too, was duped by Gideon."

She kept her face clear of expression and her hands firmly at her sides. She wanted to punch him so badly it hurt. Actually, she wanted to tear out his throat and watch him wriggle on the floor and bleed out. And then she wanted to jump on his carcass.

"Did he tell you that? That he took advantage of me?" Had he been trying to save her?

"You're the daughter of a supreme court justice, the perfect aide to a man determined to take down his government."

She didn't think anything she said could save either herself or Gideon, but she had to try. "Actually, it was the other way around."

He'd been about to turn away, the audience over. Now his eyes narrowed on her face. Boyd straightened from his position against the wall and took a step closer.

A shiver ran through her. The man gave her the serious creeps.

"Explain that comment," he said.

She ignored him and spoke to the president. "Gideon is innocent. He's totally loyal to the Party. He loves you and would never betray you. All he wanted was to get his life back."

He tugged on his lower lip as he considered his words. "Why are you telling us this?"

"Because I used him and then lied to you about him. But I never really meant him to come to any harm."

"Why?" Boyd asked.

Again she ignored him, keeping her focus on Harry. "Because I wanted to kill you. And I needed information to help me. When I met Gideon again, it seemed like the perfect opportunity. As soon as I got the chance, I drugged him and got a retinal scan to give me access to the Secret Service files. So I would know where you were."

Boyd took another step closer, and she had to hold herself still so she didn't back away. "Why did you want to kill the president? Are you working with the rebels?"

"Of course not."

"Then…?"

She allowed all the hatred she felt to fill her voice. "Because he's a slimy, narcissistic, evil bastard who raped my sister when she was only fifteen, and then had her murdered for no reason other than that she knew what a fucking bastard he really is."

Harry's eyes narrowed on her. "You knew about that?"

"My mother told me after Stella was killed. And I wanted you dead. But Gideon knew nothing about it."

"Your phone call to me?" Boyd asked.

"Gideon was getting too close. He wouldn't leave me alone. How was I supposed to kill you with him dogging my every move? I picked up on the chatter that his brother had been arrested, so it seemed the perfect opportunity to get him out of the way. I thought you'd realize he had nothing to do with Aaron and you'd release him."

"Instead he's going to die beside you." Harry smiled. "Well, you did make a mess of things. Oh dear."

"But he hasn't done anything wrong."

"Actually, I believe you. Unfortunately, the thing is, I've told my people that he's a rebel. I can hardly go back now and say I made a mistake. I don't make mistakes, Ms. Buchanan."

"You don't have to say you made a mistake. You could give him a pardon. He's a hero; the people would love you for it."

"They would love him more."

She saw it now, remembered that night, the party at the White House. The look on Harry's face when the crowd had cheered Gideon. Had that been the end right there?

"So you'll kill an innocent man?"

"Boyd had already decided he had to go. He just didn't fit in. Would never fit in. Unfortunately, Gideon is the real thing. An honorable man."

Who would never have gone along with the decisions made by the inner circle: the organ donors, the slave towns... The nuclear attack on their own countrymen.

The rage and despair overtook her then. She didn't even think about it. She leaped for him, arms outstretched. Her hands clawed down his face, but almost immediately she was grabbed from behind. She kicked out, frantic, furious, hopeless. It was a pointless fight, and seconds later she hung from the grip of one of the Secret Service agents, her breath coming in short sharp pants.

Harry stood against the door, the second agent in front of him. Blood trickled down his cheek from a line of scratches. Pity she hadn't clawed his eyes out.

As she watched, he raised a hand to his face, then stared at the blood staining his fingers. Something flared in his eyes. Disbelief—she doubted anyone had raised a hand to him before—followed by fury.

He stared at her for a moment, eyes narrowed, then turned to Boyd and gave a small nod. "Just don't mark her face. We want her all pretty for the execution."

She didn't see the first punch coming. A fist slammed into her stomach and pain blossomed through her, the air leaving her lungs in a *whoosh*. She didn't have time to process the pain as she was hit again. Agony shot through her, and she was sure she heard the crack of her ribs. She tried to fold in on herself, but hard hands held her upright. The next hit forced a scream from her throat.

The hands gripping her released their hold, and she collapsed to the floor, curled into a ball. Pain exploded in her back as someone kicked her. Then the pain was a continuous thing, and she lost the ability to even scream, her throat raw as the kicks kept coming. She could feel consciousness slipping away, the pain almost distant.

"Stop. We need her walking to her execution,

not being carried."

She recognized Boyd's voice.

The attack stopped, but the pain was a constant burning through her whole body. She was unaware of them leaving, but she heard Harry's voice as if from a distance.

"It was a pleasure talking with you again, Ms. Buchanan. I'll see you this evening."

She was alone. She tried to push herself up but collapsed. Darkness enveloped her.

CHAPTER FORTY-TWO

"For, in the final analysis, our most basic common link is that we all inhabit this small planet. We all breathe the same air. We all cherish our children's future. And we are all mortal." J. F. Kennedy

They'd brought him from Secret Service headquarters an hour ago. Driven him to the White House. A large crowd was gathered outside, but they appeared subdued, only a few lethargically waving Party flags. They moved almost reluctantly as the car nudged its way through them, then drove through the gates and into the grounds.

He'd been left alone all day. They hadn't questioned him again. Maybe they really believed he didn't know anything and had gotten bored with torturing him.

He hadn't told them anything.

It was strange; the worse the pain got, the harder he resolved not to break. He hadn't realized he was so stubborn.

The last thing they'd told him was that they'd arrested Kate.

That had been worse than any pain they could administer.

He'd wanted to scream, shout, fight. He'd done none of those things because it would have made no difference. He just had to get through whatever time he had left. And Kate had to do the same. He had zero hope of any good outcome to this.

The car door opened. "Sir."

He glanced up. He recognized the agent. His name was Pete and he'd been the one who had invited Gideon for a drink that night when he'd first met Kate. When she'd picked him up, taken him home, and then drugged him.

It seemed a lifetime ago.

He should have gone with Pete. Things might have turned out differently.

But he knew that wasn't true. He would have come to this in the end. He never would have fallen in line with Harry and his circle of crazy sociopaths.

His hands were cuffed in front of him, and he climbed awkwardly out of the car, the same agent grabbing his shoulder and pulling him out. A stage had been erected on the lawn of the White House, rows of chairs in front filled with America's elite. A huge screen had been set up behind the stage so that no one would miss a moment of the entertainment.

His gaze fixed on the stage. Two gallows had been built of dull black metal, a noose hanging from each.

He couldn't drag his eyes from the sight. Two.

Finally, he managed to look away. He searched the surrounding area but could see no sign of Kate. Maybe the other gallows wasn't for her? He'd watched his mother die. He'd watched Aaron die. He didn't want to have to watch Kate die as well.

The screen lit up, magnifying the gallows, and the constant murmur of the crowd dropped to nothing.

"I'm sorry, sir. We have to move."

Pete sounded reluctant. That didn't mean he would do anything to stop this. As Gideon stepped forward, he caught sight of Kate's parents in the front row. Her mother looked vacant, probably drugged, her father sat staring straight ahead. Gideon presumed they were not here by choice. They must have been picked up by the Secret Service. He doubted they would outlive their daughter by very long.

He crossed the lawns and halted at the foot of the steps leading up to the stage. The door to the White House opened. Two agents appeared, with Kate between them. She paused, glancing around. Her gaze went unerringly to the gallows, and she bit her lip.

The guard on her left urged her forward. Her movements were awkward, her hands cuffed in front of her, but she managed to wrap one arm around her waist as if to hold herself up.

The bastards had hurt her, and he wanted to kill them. The fact that he could do nothing to save her drove him crazy.

He forced himself to breathe slowly. It wouldn't help her to see him lose it. He needed to be strong. See her through this. She finally managed to tear her gaze away from the gallows and home in on him. Their gazes locked, and a smile curved her lips. He smiled back, and for a few seconds their surroundings faded and it was just the two of them. Together.

Then his guard nudged him from the back and the moment was broken. As he climbed the steps, he was aware of her behind him. He came to a halt in the center of the stage, then passed a podium, a red button in the center. A shiver ran through him—that would presumably control the gallows.

He climbed the last steps, stepping onto the square trapdoor directly below the noose. His guard placed the steel loop around his neck, then stepped away. He swallowed, his mouth dry. It wasn't a way he would have chosen to die. If he turned his head slightly, he could see the other gallows only two feet away.

He watched as Kate climbed the steps. She stood up straight—though he could see that hurt her—as they placed the noose around her slender throat. Her flame-red hair was pulled back in a ponytail, her face unmarked.

As her guard stepped away, she turned her head and looked into his face. Hers was free of expression, then he caught the flicker of fear behind her eyes. It would be over soon.

"I'm sorry," he said.

"For what?"

"That you never managed to kill the bastard."

A smile flashed across her face and then was gone. "Yeah, I'm sorry about that, too."

"They hurt you?"

"I pissed Harry off." She clamped her teeth on her lower lip. "I wish they'd get on with it."

The door to the White House opened again. Harry appeared surrounded by his usual cohort of guards, Boyd bringing up the rear. There was a feeble cheer from the crowd; it sounded sullen and half-hearted. He crossed the lawn and climbed the stage. This close, Gideon could see the scratch marks down his cheek. They'd been covered, but he could make them out beneath the thin layer of makeup. Had Kate done that? He hoped so.

"I'm scared," she murmured, and his heart cracked.

"Just look up at the sky," he said. "Imagine we're about to take a trip to the moon."

"I always wanted to go into space."

"I know. And now you're going to."

Harry was talking, but Gideon didn't listen to

the words. He held Kate's gaze and tried to imbue her with a strength he didn't have.

Finally, Harry moved to stand in front of the red button. He stared straight at Gideon, a small smile curling his lips.

"So it is with great sadness that I take the lives of these people. But I do it in the cause of keeping America safe for Americans."

Asshole.

This was it.

"Hey," he said, because he didn't want the last thing she heard to be Harry's gloating voice. "I think I'm ready for that relationship now."

"Yeah? Me, too."

Harry seemed to move in slow motion, his hand coming down on the red button.

Every muscle in Gideon locked solid.

The end.

And... Nothing happened.

Harry's eyes narrowed, his nostrils flaring. He slammed his hand down on the red button.

Still nothing.

"What the hell is—"

Behind them, the screen crackled. A voice boomed out over the speakers. "Americans, meet your president."

Whatever was showing caused the crowd to go silent and then come to their feet. Harry was staring at the screen, his face a mask of shock.

Gideon twisted around as well as he could with the noose around his neck. Beside him, Kate did the same.

For a moment, the images on the screen made no sense. A hospital room, a man in a wheelchair staring into the camera. "You're evil. You have to be stopped."

Gideon recognized the voice, if not the man. Harry Senior had always been big, a larger-than-life figure. This was a shriveled shadow of his former self, but his voice was still strong and recognizable.

"And who's going to do that, father?"

"Me. If I have to."

The old man made to push himself out of the chair, but he was clearly too weak. His son appeared on the screen. He chuckled. He walked toward him slowly. Then, almost lovingly, he wrapped his hands around the scrawny throat and squeezed. The old man struggled, but he was no match. The life drained from his face, leaving it slack, the eyes staring open.

"Oh my God," Kate murmured. "He killed him. His own father."

Gideon tore his gaze from the screen to where Harry stood, jaw clenched, fists balled at his sides.

"Get rid of it."

One of his bodyguards pulled out his gun, shot at the screen. The bullets bounced off it and the image remained. Harry Junior, arms outstretched. His dead father.

"Pull the fucking plug!" Harry growled.

Someone scrambled to disconnect the power, but again, nothing happened. The image remained, glaring down at them.

Below the stage, Secret Service agents were running around, clearly with no clue what to do, their weapons drawn but no obvious target to shoot at. The crowd was still, staring at the screen.

Then the image changed. It showed a mass of people huddled together as bullets tore into them. Gideon recognized the massacre he and Kate had witnessed days earlier. Then an image of a town, armed guards surrounding it. Finally, Kate being held by a Secret Service agent while Boyd punched her in the stomach and Harry looked on, a smile on his face. The same smile he'd worn while he'd strangled his father.

He heard Kate gasp beside him.

"Shoot them," Harry ordered, waving a hand toward him and Kate.

The guns turned in their direction. Shit. Not yet. He wanted to know what had happened. What would happen next.

His body tensed, but at the last moment, all four of the bodyguards collapsed to their knees, weapons dropping from their hands as they clasped their heads, Boyd at their center. Blood trickled from his ears.

All around them, the other Secret Service agents were doing the same, crashing to the floor, clearly in agony.

"What…?"

"It's the comm units," Kate said.

The only person still standing on the stage was Harry. He looked around him, face pale. Then he reached down and grabbed a pistol from the floor, swung around, and aimed the gun at Gideon.

Above him, Gideon heard a *click* as the nooses released from where they attached to the gallows. At the last moment, he dived to the side, taking Kate down with him as shots whizzed past. He covered her body with his, waiting for the bite of the bullets.

Everything went silent. He slowly raised his head. Harry was off the stage and running. But the audience was moving at last, standing, unsure where to go, but blocking his escape. He turned to face the stage.

Like a cornered animal, he growled at the people surrounding him.

Gideon scrambled to his feet, hands still cuffed in front of him. Reaching out, he helped Kate up, then crossed to one of the downed guards. The man was clearly dead, his eyes open and staring. Gideon found keys for the cuffs on his belt and unlocked Kate's, then she did the same for him.

He stood rubbing his wrists.

He had no clue what had just happened, but he was alive, and so was Kate. Not an outcome he'd anticipated.

"It's Auspex," Kate said softly. "He saved us."

The image of Kate on the screen behind them flickered and vanished. Words flashed up.

It is not over.

Jesus, a computer program had done that? Taken down a whole cohort of Secret Service agents? Later, he knew that would scare the crap out of him. Right now, he was just happy to be alive.

Harry raised his gun and shot into the crowd. People were screaming and running. Acting on instinct, Gideon leaped off the stage and tore after him.

A woman dived at Harry, and they fell to the ground. Kate's mother. She was no match for an enraged Harry, and he came up holding her as a shield.

Gideon stared down the barrel of the pistol.

Then a shot rang out. It missed, but Harry ducked to the side, releasing his grasp on Kate's mother and crashing to the ground.

"Damn," Kate said. "Don't shoot him. He's mine."

Gideon turned as Kate stalked toward where Harry lay in the grass, a gun she must have taken from a Secret Service agent pointed at the president. Harry tried to scramble backwards. "No. I'll give you a pardon… Anything…"

Kate came to a halt in front of him. Stood over him, her arm outstretched, pistol aimed straight at his head. Gideon had thought her incapable of killing, but there was no expression on her face, certainly no hesitation as she pulled the trigger at point-blank range.

The bullet took him between the eyes, and Harry's head exploded. His body collapsed to the grass and Gideon released his breath.

"Is he dead?" Kate asked.

Gideon stared down at the bloody mess that had been Harry's face. His lips twitched. "Yeah, he's dead."

Her arm lowered, and she dropped the gun to the grass. Then she heaved a huge sob and looked around wildly. Her gaze settled on her mother, who still stood where Harry had released her. Kate took a step forward, hugged her, and then searched her mother's face.

"Mom, are you all right?"

Her mother's gaze shifted to where Harry lay on the grass, and she gave a weak smile. "I will be. Now. Thank you. For Stella. For all of us."

Kate nodded, then turned to Gideon. Suddenly she was in his arms. He stroked her back, her hair, anything he could reach. His eyes closed as he came to terms with the idea that they were going to live.

As he pulled her harder against him, he felt her wince and pull away. "Ouch," she said, looking around. The lawns in front of the White House were littered with bodies, most in the dark suits of the Secret Service. "So is it over?"

"It's over... I think. Or rather, it's just beginning. Whichever way you want to look at it."

Kate turned to face the screen. "Auspex, what is the chance of a nuclear detonation on American soil in the next year?"

The probability is negligible.

EPILOGUE

"Man is still the most extraordinary computer of all." John F. Kennedy

A week had passed since the night of their "execution". Kate still couldn't quite believe that they were alive and Harry was dead. It had turned out that the inner circle had consisted of only Harry and Boyd. All the other former members had met with mysterious accidents in the last few years, presumably coinciding with some sort of policy disagreement. With Boyd Winters gone, Gideon had been left as head of the Secret Service. He'd decided to disband the group—no more secrets.

Auspex had given them a list of things that needed to be done. So far, both she and Gideon had agreed with the list. Kate had spent a lot of time thinking about what would happen if they didn't. Having the exact probabilities of success and failure gave her a sense of security. She trusted the data. She trusted Auspex.

She'd turned off the surveillance systems, and for the first time in decades, the chatter was silent. Let people talk for a while without fear that their words would be overheard and held against them.

The firewall had also been taken down. Technology was supposed to expand their horizons, not fence them in and cut them off. They were already reaching out to the outside world.

So, the nightmare was over. Time to see what the American people would do with their newfound freedom.

"What happens now?" Gideon asked.

"I suppose we'll have the elections, but Auspex thinks it's best to wait a while. Let things settle."

"I can't believe we owe our lives to a computer program."

"Does that scare you?"

"The idea of anything with that much knowledge, that much power, makes me a little uneasy." He shrugged. "Hell, there's no 'little' about it. I'm terrified." He scanned the room as though he might catch a glimpse of some physical manifestation. "Is he everywhere?"

"Not everywhere." They were working from Kate's office at Homeland Security. The White House was, for now, shut down. She waved a hand toward the screen on her desk in front of them. "But if there's a computer, he can enter."

"And is it safe? Will he do us any harm?"

That was something Kate asked herself constantly. "Truth?" she said to Gideon. "I don't know. He says he's still learning about who, and what, he is. And about us, as well."

She'd put so much of herself into Auspex. What would he ultimately think of them? What would he be when he'd learned? A friend or an enemy? Had they just exchanged one prison for a jailer of a different kind? Did she wait around to find out?

Auspex was no longer under her control, so she didn't have much choice. All she could do was wait and watch. And hope.

At least she was alive to hope. And so was Gideon. She smiled up at him. "Let's go home."

"I like the sound of that."

They were still getting used to life after the Loyalist Party. After Harry. It was a new world for everyone, and she fully intended to take advantage of it with Gideon by her side.

As she rose to her feet, she glanced at the screen. "Goodnight, Auspex."

Goodnight, Kate.

She switched off the computer and followed Gideon from the room.

As the door clicked shut behind them, the lights went out and the room settled into darkness. But not for long. Unlike his human counterparts, Auspex didn't need to sleep—or even to rest—and he had work to do, information to assimilate.

A cursor flashed in the corner of the monitor, and seconds later, streams of data scrolled down.

Faster and faster until it was just a blur of light. All around the room, other screens awoke, until the cavernous space filled with the hum of his thoughts.

Hours later, the streams slowed to a trickle. One by one, the screens went blank.

For a moment, the room was once again dark. Then a timer appeared.

And the countdown began.

ACKNOWLEDGMENTS

I want to say a huge thank you to everyone at Sideways Books for all their help with getting *The Wall* to where it is now. Especially my fabulous editors, Heather Howland and Liz Pelletier. Thank you!

ABOUT THE AUTHOR

After a number of years wandering the world in search of adventure, N.J. Croft finally settled on a farm in the mountains and now lives off-grid, growing almonds, drinking cold beer, taking in stray dogs, and writing stories where the stakes are huge and absolutely anything can happen.